Jenny Lane (she/they) writes contemporary stories with queer characters ranging from middle grade to adult. Their stories are queer, whimsical, heartwarming…and always end with a happily-ever-something. There is nothing Jenny loves more than a fire pit, an ocean view, and a good book to read—but they will settle for any combination of these three. When she isn't writing or reading something, she works as a librarian and advocate for literacy.

Joss Wood loves books, coffee, wine and traveling—especially to the wild places of Southern Africa and, well, anywhere. Joss is a mum to two young adults, and occasionally attempts to grow things, with very mixed (mostly bad) results. She and her husband are bossed around by two cats and a Great Dane that is the size of a small cow. After a career in sales, local economic development and business advocacy, Joss writes full-time from her home in KwaZulu-Natal, South Africa.

Also by Jenny Lane

Mills & Boon Love Always

Her Fake Wedding Date in Sicily

Also by Joss Wood

For Business…or Pleasure
is Joss Wood's debut title for Love Always.

Mills & Boon Modern

A Nine-Month Deal with Her Husband
Fast-Track Dating Deception

Cape Town Tycoons miniseries

The Nights She Spent with the CEO
The Baby Behind Their Marriage Merger

Discover more at millsandboon.co.uk.

SECRETLY WORTH BILLIONS

JENNY LANE

JOSS WOOD

MILLS & BOON

First published in Great Britain 2026
by Mills & Boon, an imprint of HarperCollins*Publishers* Ltd,
1 London Bridge Street, London, SE1 9GF

www.harpercollins.co.uk

HarperCollins*Publishers*, Macken House, 39/40 Mayor Street Upper,
Dublin 1, D01 C9W8, Ireland

Secretly Worth Billions © 2026 Harlequin Enterprises ULC

How to Resist Your Billionaire Ex © 2026 Jenny Lane

For Business…or Pleasure © 2026 Joss Wood

ISBN: 978-0-263-41936-8

02/26

MIX
Paper | Supporting
responsible forestry
FSC® C013604

Printed and Bound in the UK using 100% Renewable Electricity
at CPI Group (UK) Ltd, Croydon, CR0 4YY

HOW TO RESIST YOUR BILLIONAIRE EX

JENNY LANE

MILLS & BOON

For Meaghan. And our three wildflowers.

CHAPTER ONE

Blake

BLAKE DIDN'T COME all this way to second-guess herself—not when something that looked a lot like a future was waiting just beyond those doors. So, she pushed the car door open before the driver had fully stopped, heart pounding like it already knew how this all would end. Her heel landed against the stone drive—a declaration, a step toward something she might finally be ready for.

She didn't let herself hesitate.

Her eyes followed a path lined with rosemary shadowed by cypress, before lifting to the entrance of Vella West. It looked like something out of a fairy tale: warm wood and stone features dropped in the middle of lush green vineyards and an endless sky. And Blake just knew that beyond those heavy oak doors, the story that was going to change her life was waiting for her.

Ivy trailed up the sun-warmed stone walls, and antique doors that were no doubt imported loomed under an arch of flowering vines. She was sure their weathered wood contained secrets she couldn't wait to uncover. Bees hovered lazily over the bursts of indigo buds in the lavender planters and butterflies danced through the shafts of golden afternoon light.

Blake tightened her grip on her tote and continued toward the entrance. Her week here was meant to be work—an opportunity to prove she belonged at the writer's table—but something about this place made her feel like she'd already crossed a line. It was as if the social media manager version of herself that left San Diego that morning was already slipping away.

When Robby from PR at Vella West reached out to her on her magazine's official social media, she was certain it was spam. But she showed the message to Tara, her boss, anyway, and was shocked to find it was a real invitation. They wanted someone from her magazine to spend a week at their new resort next to the up-and-coming vineyard of the same name. It was a week full of surprise events and activities designed to wow the traveler.

The entire office got swept up in the magic of it. A flurry of whispered gossip and wild speculations. Vella West was the personal project of a young billionaire in the Napa Valley. It was said that half the resort was painstakingly imported from across the sea and the billionaire oversaw the placement of every stone. Blake couldn't help but get swept up in the magic herself. The whole thing sounded entirely romantic.

Everyone wanted a chance to visit the resort—including Blake. She'd known a head writer would get the assignment. But Ginny went and eloped one week before she was supposed to leave and cashed in her paid time off to spend her honeymoon cliff diving. Which left Blake the perfect opportunity to stop relying on what she was simply *good* at and start going after something she *wanted*.

"Let me go," she'd pleaded when she'd marched into her boss's office late that evening. "I can do it. I can leave in the morning."

"Blake, you know I love having you on this team. Your social media presence has transformed this magazine. But writing an article is different." Tara shifted in her leather swivel chair and frowned. "You don't even travel."

"That's not true," Blake countered. She wanted this. No. She *needed* this. This was her chance. "I've traveled before."

"When?"

"I backpacked through Europe before I started working for you." Blake didn't add that she hadn't *wanted* to travel since that glorious and heartbreaking trip ten years ago. Nothing would ever compare to it. And nothing could make her go through the same loss she felt after it. "I can do this."

She spread out her body, making herself big, as if she was facing a mountain lion and not her narrow-eyed, sharp-tongued boss who only came up to Blake's shoulders. She wasn't sure why her heart and her head had synced up over this assignment, but it called to her like a siren song.

"This exclusive review has already brought in tens of thousands of dollars in ads." Tara pressed her fingertips to her temples and spoke the next part softly. "If it doesn't hit, then we're not just looking at a loss for the quarter. I'm looking at a loss of the magazine."

"I have a degree in art history and creative writing. I can do this assignment justice. I *need* to see this place." She splayed her hands across her boss's desk and faked the courage she needed to say, "I can write a great article. And when I do, you'll promote me to travel writer. I've got this, Tara."

Tara sighed. "I'm probably going to regret this." She pushed a file toward Blake with the tip of her pen. "But if I don't send you, I'd have to go myself. And there's too much to do here." Tara glared at the looming stack of papers on her usually organized desk. "You can get the rest of the details from Chloe. And it better be good. Otherwise, not only will you not get a spot on the travel writing team, you might not have a spot at all."

Blake knew this exclusive article was pulling in enough advertisements to meet their third quarter goal and then some. She knew exactly what was at stake. She and Chloe, Tara's assistant, had speculated about it over lunch a few days ago.

"I understand." Blake clutched the folder to her chest. She had wanted Tara to know she was going to take this seriously. Those words had settled like a stone deep in Blake's stomach. She had been churning them around ever since.

But from the moment the town car pulled off the main highway and headed down the rambling country road, Blake couldn't focus on anything except the feeling she was stepping into a memory. A hazy moment that felt like a sun-worn photograph.

Memories of when she was fresh out of college, with nothing to her name but a passport and a backpack, spending days in the Italian sunshine, kiss drunk from the strawberry wine on Sloane's lips. That had been an incredible summer. Just two women, girls really, whispering secrets and dreams as they lay on a blanket in a field next to an abandoned farmhouse, the trees providing latticed sunshine across their bare stomachs.

It had been love—not at first sight—but definitely fast and hard the way you can only fall when you're young and free and have nothing to lose. They were going to upend their entire lives for each other. Blake had quit her job via email—backing out of her internship-turned–assistant editor position at an up-and-coming magazine. She'd done it for the chance at adventure. At love. She could still remember how exhilarating it had been to watch the email whoosh away.

Sloane had seemed so certain about the future, about Blake. But one morning Blake had woken up and Sloane was gone—a scrawled note on the bedside saying she had to leave for a family emergency. Blake's panic and worry compelled her to leave voicemail after voicemail, until the inbox was full. She'd attempted to look Sloane up because maybe something awful had happened, but it was as if she'd disappeared without a trace.

Blake's worry turned to anger and then heartache. She turned it over in her like a jagged rock in a tumbler. It was still there, all these years later, a heavy and uncomfortable reminder of what happened when you let your guard down, even if the edges had smoothed out over the years.

Blake had never done anything so reckless, or so freeing, since. She'd returned from that summer in Italy and began an internship with a different, lesser-known magazine. If Tara hadn't rescued her, she'd still be fetching coffee on the seventeenth floor with no end in sight.

There was something about the yellow hills, the hint of dirt and earth in the air, that brought her back to the moment. Blake took in the main building—whitewashed walls with stone accents and tall windows, as if it was plucked from the hills of Italy. She'd read up on the place, sure, but seeing it in person was something else. Somewhere behind it, she knew, was the wine bar she planned to visit later.

Past the building, rows of vineyard stretched toward the hills, green and full in the early summer light. Her gaze followed the slope upward to where the cottages were tucked discreetly among the trees—private, just as advertised.

She caught the faint scent of lavender and turned. A stone path led to the spa and yoga studio, if she felt ambitious tomorrow morning. To the left, a string of bistro lights hung above long wooden tables in a garden space clearly designed for lingering evenings and curated dinners. All of it was exactly as she'd imagined—maybe better.

She was going to test out every inch of this resort and capture each moment for the write-up. The contract laid out exactly what she was expected to review. She could post sneak peek shots along the way for her magazine's social media if she wanted, and the full review would print after the week ended. So, this week was about soaking it all in. And Blake couldn't wait. She'd already made a spreadsheet of ideas and was looking forward to a meeting with Robby, the PR manager.

Two concierges opened the wide glass doors and smiled at her as she breezed through. The bright Napa sun warmed her back as she stepped into the lobby. The design of this place, with its slate gray–and–cream–checkered tiles lining the main lobby, was exactly like something from her travel Pinterest boards—the closest she'd come to actual travel in years.

She'd chosen a simple black dress for her arrival, hoping to impress the staff and encourage her own confidence. Her wavy brunette locks flowed down past her shoulders and her wide sunglasses hid most of her face. The black dress wrapped tightly around her waist before billowing out around her hips and falling just below her knees, flaring out in just the way she loved.

Blake did a wide slow turn, admiring the high ceilings, the wooden beams and the quiet trickle of a water feature she couldn't see. She took a slow breath to steady herself and scanned the room for the front desk.

From the side of the building, a door swung open and two people walked through. The first she recognized: Robby Berg, the PR manager she'd been in contact with. They had a short black shaggy haircut and the type of slim pants and button-down shirt that looked ordinary, but Blake was certain a designer insignia was stitched on the pocket. They kept glancing from their tablet to the woman they were talking to. The woman next to Robby had a sleek black bob, a sharp chin and an uncanny resemblance to—no—that was just Blake's memory playing a mean trick.

"Ah, Ms. Miller, you're here," Robby called from the other side of the room. They tucked the tablet under their arm and leaned close to whisper something to the woman next to them. Blake pasted on her most charming smile and turned toward Robby. "I want to introduce you to—"

The woman looked up and grinned broadly before freezing in shock.

Blake knew that face. She'd watched that face make promises it didn't intend to keep. Blake had been ready to follow Sloane across all of Europe. In fact, they'd planned to do so. They were going to catch a train and go wherever the wind blew them for as long as it would last, seeking every dilapidated home until they found one to fix up.

But this woman, the one standing twenty feet away from her, was not, in fact, a figment of one of Blake's many dreams. She was here. In Napa. Walking toward her.

Sloane was real in a way Blake couldn't deny. She had the same sharp jawline Blake remembered, the kind that caught the light just right, warm olive skin and a sweep of dark hair that framed her face like a curtain falling perfectly into place. Her eyes—the deep midnight blue Blake had always gotten lost in—locked on her now, wide and unblinking.

Sloane's smile faltered as her eyes roamed over every inch of Blake. Like she wasn't sure what she was seeing. She looked like she'd seen a ghost. One she wasn't ready for.

Her mouth shaped Blake's name without quite saying it—more a whisper, a prayer, like speaking it aloud would cost her something.

Blake's throat went tight. There were a hundred versions of this moment she'd imagined. This wasn't any of them. It was better and a thousand times worse. Because she was mad at Sloane, still, after all this time. And the rock she'd thought she'd honed into a smooth and dull burden in her stomach launched into her throat, jagged edges tearing at her insides, making her feel sick to her stomach. Angry tears pricked at her eyes. She wanted to reach out and touch Sloane to prove she was real, but she balled her hands into fists, determined not to give Sloane the satisfaction of knowing exactly what she could still do to Blake after all this time.

Sloane, for her part, seemed completely unaffected— apparently living hours away this entire time with some kind of job in public relations. That was comical. Sloane, who couldn't pick up a phone, was in charge of relating to people.

Sloane took another step toward her and reached out her hand, but then must have thought better of it, because she immediately snatched it back. Sloane's eyes swept over Blake, taking her all in. Blake worked to hold still and keep the turmoil hidden beneath her surface.

A familiar wave of heartbreak washed over her, and instinctively, she shielded herself, her defenses springing into action. She couldn't trust Sloane. Even if her body ached to be wrapped up in a hug, her brain told her to stand her ground.

But nothing could have prepared her for the way Sloane's mouth dropped open, as if she'd seen a ghost— an unwelcome one at that—when she stammered, "What are you *doing* here?"

CHAPTER TWO

Sloane

SLOANE COULDN'T REMEMBER what she'd eaten for breakfast that morning, but she'd never forget the way Blake Miller looked as she turned and caught sight of Sloane in the lobby of Vella West. Shock and surprise and a flash of crimson creeping up her neck. Blake Miller looked stunning with her chestnut-brown hair down and loose and free. Sloane remembered how she'd knot it on top of her head when she was writing or hiking. And Sloane had loved watching her unspool it at the end of the day.

That was how Sloane always thought of Blake, which was to say more often than she should. When Sloane couldn't sleep, or when she couldn't make it through the last five minutes of a meeting, she'd imagine Blake with her hair falling loose like cinnamon swirls in the air. But it was nothing compared to seeing her now. Ten years older, frazzled from a day of travel.

Real.

Sloane wanted to pull her in for a hug and see if she still smelled like the floral bodywash she'd lugged around Europe like a prized possession. But that would definitely be weird. You don't get to throw your arms open wide for the woman you left in a youth hostel in Italy without saying goodbye.

"I'm here to write a review of this resort," Blake said as she threw her shoulders back. It took Sloane a moment to realize she was answering her question. Blake's nose scrunched when she was frustrated. It was scrunched now. "And I'm supposed to get checked in right now. It was— *nice*—to see you."

"Blake, wait." There were a million things Sloane wanted to say to Blake. But they all soaked into her tongue like dry wine. All she could do was stare. Blake obviously didn't want her apologies, not that she was sure how to apologize. Sloane had done what was necessary. To protect her family, to protect Blake from what Sloane was being asked to do.

She reached out one hand and placed it on Blake's arm. The connection felt warm, like sunshine on her shoulders when she was riding on the trail. "I hope you enjoy your stay. I'm certain Robby will take good care of you. It was good to see you."

Sloane didn't miss the moment that Blake's eyes flashed with heat. Blake was ready to fight—just like they had many times that summer. They were arguments that ended with both of them naked and tangled in bedsheets at three in the morning. It had always left Sloane's lips swollen from kissing and her body sore in the best way the entire next day.

But the heat cooled into something else entirely. A little wistful. Tired. Which was much, much worse. Sloane wanted to brew some tea, curl up on one of the hidden-away rooms of the resort and find out every single detail of Blake's life since they'd last seen each other.

But Sloane didn't do that. She didn't take down time

to catch up with friends. She worked, she took care of Nico and she didn't think about what things were like before. There was too much to do to think about what might have been.

Still, she was dangerously close to offering just that when Robby interrupted. "Ms. Miller, welcome. As I said before, I'm Robby. It's so lovely to meet you." They shot Sloane a confused face of frustration before ushering Blake away.

And thank goodness. Sloane needed to get herself sorted before she could be around Blake. Robby took Blake by the elbow and guided her over to the check-in counter. Blake looked back over her shoulder once and Sloane offered her a head nod, too nervous to open her mouth.

Her phone vibrated in her pocket with a meeting reminder. Sloane took three deep breaths and walked toward the wine bar. She was late for a tasting with her head chef.

It didn't take her long to find Robby later that afternoon. Their office was on the fourth floor, directly opposite Sloane's. And they always left the door open to let in as much light as possible.

She leaned on the door and waited for Robby to look up. They didn't. She was about to clear her throat when Robby sighed.

"I know you're there. Your thoughts are *very* loud." Robby looked up from the stack of papers in front of them and raised a brow. "Want to tell me what that was all about?"

"You know I'm your boss, right?" Sloane pressed her lips together in an attempt to be serious. Robby rolled their eyes and went back to the computer screen clicking around until social media was up.

"Three thousand likes," Robby said as they pointed at a post with the doors to the resort. "Our followers are up and this one photo from her account has three thousand likes." They glanced at the computer and smirked. "Three thousand and seven. I don't know how you know her, but she is going to be good for the resort."

Sloane swallowed thickly and looked at the computer screen. "*Elsewhere?* Is that…this is her social media?" Sloane blinked at the screen. She couldn't see the other photos and thank goodness for that. When she'd left without saying goodbye ten years ago, she vowed she wouldn't look back. She did not know what Blake had been up to. She thought she'd be a writer. Not a social media influencer. But three thousand likes had to mean something. Her heart ached with sadness and pride.

"I trust you, Robby," Sloane said with a huff. "I was just surprised. Is this…she's the person you contracted to promote the hotel?"

"Sort of. She's with *Elsewhere Magazine*. She's going to write a classy review—and *then* post it all over socials. I *hope*." Robby crossed their arms over their chest and frowned. "I am very good at my job. I think her magazine's take on travel will really appeal to a wide audience. So, you need to fix whatever *that* was in the lobby. We need her, Sloane."

Sloane nodded. Sloane's plan for this resort hinged on bringing in a new generation to Napa. Showing them that a weekend at a winery wasn't all about wine. That you didn't need to be a sommelier to enjoy everything Napa offered. They'd crafted custom packages to ensure every experience was unique. And if they did it right, if they created enough buzz, then maybe they'd really make something of this resort.

And Robby was right. It needed to be perfect. Yes, she had her uncle's money, but she wasn't going to sink all of it into a resort that wasn't a solid investment. In four years, she would hand this all over to Nico. His care and legacy were entrusted to her, and this resort was a gamble. She needed this to work.

Sloane needed to smooth things over with Blake if she wanted any hope of a positive review. Any hope that Blake would actually enjoy herself. Hell, what if Blake was half-way home by now, all because Sloane had given her a weird look and then a head nod? She needed to fix this.

"She's still here, right?" Sloane asked, panic already clawing at her chest.

"Something tells me there's a story here." Robby leaned back in their chair and a chunk of black curls flopped onto their forehead. "Do I want to know? Do I *need* to know?"

"No," Sloane insisted. "Nothing you need to know. Just show me her file. What's planned for this week?"

Robby snapped back into work mode, leaning over Sloane and typing into the laptop. And it was right there on the screen: Miller, Blake. Elsewhere Magazine. How had she missed this?

This grand opening had to go off without a hitch. She'd promised herself, and her cousin, Nico, that this was a sound investment. That her ideas were a sound investment.

And Sloane hadn't become a billionaire without a track record of sound investments. In less than ten years, she'd turned her uncle's mediocre vineyard into a thriving one. And then she'd bought the land next to it and together with Robby and Nico, they'd dreamed up the idea for Vella West Resort.

She really needed to call Nico. She had three missed texts from him this morning.

Work and her cousin had been her entire life for the last ten years. She drowned herself in work until there was nothing of *her* left in any of it. Until now. This resort had her pulse running through it. Every stone a piece of her heart.

Sloane had thrown herself into work to forget her heartbreak and grief. And it had worked. She replaced the emptiness Blake left in her heart with paperwork, planning and purpose. And now she was here—and the success of the resort depended on positive reviews and recommendations.

"And that's it. Just under a week. We conclude our contract with her Saturday night after the launch party. Then she goes home Sunday." Sloane looked up at Robby. They'd been chatting nonstop while Sloane was lost in thought. "You okay, boss?"

"It's Sloane." With a few key strokes she sent herself the pertinent details of *Miller, Blake*'s visit. She needed to do this herself. Nothing could go wrong. "I'll talk to her, okay. I'll apologize. I'll…think of something."

CHAPTER THREE

Blake

"THE HONEYMOON SUITE? Really?" Blake hissed at a wide-eyed Chloe on the other end of her FaceTime. A smile tugged at the corners of Chloe's mouth as she pressed her lips together, her eyes sparkling with suppressed amusement. "I had to sweep rose petals off my bed! Chloe, stop laughing."

Chloe's giggles subsided, replacing by a worrisome glint of amusement in her eyes. "Oh, come on. It can't be that bad."

Blake rubbed at her temples and frowned as she took in the oversized king bed, a bottle of red wine with two glasses and the 'congratulations on your marriage' card accompanying it.

"Chloe, there's a list of events in this folder." Blake waved the heavy folder with the itinerary at the phone and glared. "A list of *couples* events."

"Just bask in it," Chloe encouraged. "Who doesn't love a bathtub on their back deck? That place looks gorgeous."

Chloe was right, of course. The added surprise of seeing Sloane had sent her stress level to a ten, a headache building behind her eyes. But Blake wasn't going to tell

Chloe any of that. She narrowed her eyes at Chloe and pointed. "You did this on purpose!"

"Maybe I forgot to uncheck the couples' package? Maybe I thought you needed a little added luxury? Or, maybe it was all an honest mistake. I guess we'll never know." Chloe shrugged. "What I *do* know is you can't back out now. You're there. You have an article to write. And if you don't do it—then…"

She didn't finish her sentence. She didn't have to. If Blake didn't do this well, then the entire magazine was in trouble. *Elsewhere* needed her. Tara needed her. Chloe needed her.

"You're right," she sighed. "I hate when you're right."

"You love me. And you've got this. I'll make sure Tara knows you're right on track."

Chloe ended the FaceTime with a jab to the screen. Blake had to do this. She didn't have a choice. She was going to do these couple events. All by herself.

Blake did her best to forget about rose petals, and couples' hikes, and private cabana rentals by the pool. She especially tried to forget the fact that her first love—the woman who ghosted her ten years ago—was somewhere on this property. But memories of Sloane and their summer abroad played across her mind like a film montage of all her happiest moments—a highlight reel of something she'd never have again.

She'd tried to date, men and women, over the last ten years. But she never felt that inexplicable spark or connection with any of them. She'd never wanted to stay up all night just to keep hearing them talk. She'd never kissed someone for so long her lips grew swollen and tingly. And she'd never had someone look at her and see *all* of her. Not the way Sloane had been able to.

Blake groaned and rubbed at her eyes, trying to scrub away the memories. She grabbed the duvet from the bed and tugged until every last rose petal fell to the floor in a pile. She needed to put all thoughts of Sloane back into the box she'd shoved them into long ago. Blake let her frustration and anger settle over her like a shield. Sloane wasn't going to get to her.

Not this week.

By the time Blake had showered and dressed for dinner, she'd convinced herself that she would be just fine. She just needed to figure out her angle for the story, and then the romantic ambiance could morph into something else.

But the lingering look and the nod that seemed not so innocent when Blake had turned back around—that was familiar. Sloane would get that look before splashing her in the ocean or challenging her to a race along the sand. She'd get that look in her eyes before crawling into Blake's single bed in the middle of the night and wrapping their bodies so closely together Blake couldn't tell whose limbs were whose.

Okay, enough reminiscing. Blake had a job to do. She was going to represent her company well. She was going to have dinner in the five-star restaurant on the resort's premises. While the magazine would send a photographer out for the main shots, she wanted to include personal touches for sneak peeks on social media. She was doing two jobs this week, and she was going to do them both well.

"Ms. Miller, welcome to Niccolò's. We are so honored you could join us." A host with a crisp white shirt rolled up to his elbows and a long black apron practically bowed. So much for anonymity. "Please come with me. Your table is ready."

She followed him beyond the main restaurant and through an open set of wood and glass doors. The patio unfolded like a well-kept secret, alight in the warm glow of the early evening sun. The light slipped across smooth stone floors and glinted off glassware, turning every surface golden. Napa stretched out in the distance—vineyard rows brushed with light, the soft curve of hills disappearing into the haze.

Blake stepped out and paused. The space wasn't large, but it was exquisite—composed with a kind of precision that didn't announce itself—it just *was*. Tables were cut from travertine, raw oak or smoked stone, each paired with matching simple black chairs. The palette was warm and grounded—natural textures, soft lines, nothing overly designed. Just enough glass and brass to remind her this was money. Serious money.

She didn't need the full story to know the billionaire behind this had spent a fortune—not just throwing cash at it but investing in taste. Real, rare taste. The kind that didn't need to prove itself. Blake had been to her share of high-end restaurants, but this? This was restraint as luxury. Every detail felt curated down to the inch.

The glassware was impossibly thin. The ceramics had a hand-thrown look to them, each a bit irregular. Somewhere nearby, she caught the scent of grilled fruit, rosemary and citrus on charcoal.

She traced her fingers across the pale stone table, already cataloging questions in her mind. Robby would know who'd designed it, sourced it, styled it. And she *needed* to know. Whoever had created this space hadn't just built a restaurant—they made sitting down to a meal part of the experience.

Blake smiled to herself. She could get used to this.

"Ms. Miller, your table."

The host gestured to a small table in the corner of the patio—private, romantic and almost too perfect. A low centerpiece of freshly picked herbs and wildflowers looked as though it had just been gathered from the garden. Two place settings. Candlelight. Ambiance dialed to eleven.

Blake offered a polite smile. "Oh, it's just me. I'm dining alone."

The host blinked. "Oh? Is your partner not able to make it?"

She was going to kill Chloe. Beneath the host's perfect decorum, Blake still saw a flash of concern. She wanted to crawl underneath the perfect table scape to get away from the pity in his eyes.

"There was a mix-up with the reservations," she said quickly, her tone light. "It's just me this week. But it's beautiful—I love the flowers."

From across the courtyard, she caught a laugh. *Sloane.* Blake turned just in time to see her in conversation with a small group near the bar. She'd swapped her suit coat for something softer—a white button-down tank, almost sheer in the golden light. Black trousers, still tailored to perfection. When Sloane glanced over and their eyes met, Blake felt herself wilt a little in her seat.

God. Not like this.

The host had cleared the extra place setting with precision, stacking plates and utensils with just enough clatter to make Blake's cheeks burn. She sank back in her chair, resisting the urge to disappear under the tablecloth.

The couple seated nearby looked over with interest.

This was bad. Maybe she should just ask for the food to go.

"Blake, I'm so sorry I'm late." Sloane's voice drifted

across the restaurant. The host froze, quietly glancing from the place setting to Sloane before placing each item back with precision. He must know Sloane. And whoever she was, she was important.

"What are you—" Blake's words were interrupted by Sloane's.

"Is it still okay if we dine together?" Sloane looked at her meaningfully. Like she was trying to rescue her from everyone's stares. But she was leaving it up to Blake if she wanted to be rescued.

And against her better judgment, she did. Not by Sloane. In fact, Blake wished the person across from her was anyone but Sloane, with her effortlessly sleek hair, and her stupid long eyelashes and her frustrating way of making *everything* look easy.

"Sure," she said in a monotone. She gestured toward the chair across from her and raised a single brow. "Have a seat?"

Sloane nodded at the host and he finished setting the place. "I'm so sorry, Ms. Vella. I'll bring wine out right away."

Vella? Had he just called her Ms. Vella? But that would mean…no. This was Sloane Mitchell. Blake had seen her passport. Blake blinked, trying to hide the tsunami of emotions warring inside her. When did her name change? *Why* did her name change?

"Thank you, Vince. It's much appreciated." Sloane said the words soothingly. And the host, Vince, disappeared back into the restaurant.

Sloane stood across from her—quiet, almost careful. Like she wasn't sure she had the right, but had come anyway.

"I hope I'm not interrupting," she said, her voice low.

Blake looked up. Everything in her stilled as her eyes connected with Sloane's. Her heart was in her throat, which made no sense. Sloane didn't get to have this much say over her body. "It's fine," she managed to say.

Sloane hesitated, eyes flicking to the place settings. "Robby mentioned you booked the honeymoon package. Said you brought someone."

Blake shook her head. "I didn't. It was a mix-up with another writer." Sloane didn't need to know that this wasn't supposed to be Blake's story. And she certainly wasn't going to tell her that Chloe had purposefully booked up what was probably the resort's most extravagant package for just Blake.

"I wasn't sure," Sloane said softly. She didn't look away. "I wasn't sure if you'd want me here."

There was no judgment in her voice. No jealousy, no entitlement. Just something quieter—something Blake didn't have words for. Sloane didn't belong at this table.

A pause stretched between them—just long enough to feel it.

And it was as if that stretch of quiet held all ten years of silence within it. Blake's heart ached at the barely healed edges. How was Sloane able to sit down across from her so easily? She'd probably spent the last ten years coasting through life without a care in the world. Meanwhile, Blake had been barely keeping it together. She made sure her shield was locked in place.

Blake was not going to rile her up in the middle of a crowded restaurant.

"Just sit down already." Blake waved a hand at the other chair. The sooner Sloane sat down, the sooner they could get this dinner over with. Sloane could absolve herself of her guilt, and Blake could get back to work.

The silence settled again, looser now, but no less charged. Blake glanced down—the travertine tabletop, the hand-thrown ceramics, the delicate arrangement of herbs and blooms that looked like they'd been plucked from the garden seconds before sunset.

She was about to speak, when Vince returned, swiftly filling their glasses and disappearing again.

"So, what do you think of Vella West so far?" Sloane's eyes were wide and vulnerable, as if she was asking about so much more than a resort.

"It's beautiful," Blake said. She had to admit that at least. This place had a way of sweeping you up into the romance of it all. "Even the flowers feel handpicked just for me. Everything feels…chosen. Doesn't it kind of remind you of…"

"It does." Sloane's lips curved, barely. "And thank you."

Blake looked at her. "So, you *did* have something to do with all this?"

"A lot of it. I guess you could say I was inspired."

Blake could see Sloane's fingerprints—her perfect blend of old-world charm and modern elegance—all over this place. The restraint. The perfection. The way the space seemed designed to make you feel like the world was holding its breath just for you. It hurt to know that someone capable of such details could be so careless with Blake's heart.

Blake leaned back, letting herself look—really look—at the woman across from her. Years had passed, but something in her felt young again. Still undone.

Sloane was here. Sitting across from her. At a table for two lit like a love story.

It was too much.

It was not enough.

"How involved, exactly?" Her voice came out rough and low, scraping against her vocal cords. "I heard the server call you Vella. Is this all...yours? Are you married?"

Sloane didn't answer right away, but her gaze didn't waver. The smile that ghosted across her lips was soft. Sad. Like she wanted to tell her everything but couldn't. Or wouldn't. "No. Not married. My uncle had a vision for this place. I am just...helping to bring it to life. I took his last name to make it all—easier."

Blake's heart raced with a mixture of surprise and relief. She wasn't married—not that it would matter to Blake. Sloane could do whatever she wanted.

Sloane lifted the glass of crisp white wine to her lips and said just before taking a sip, "So, tell me about you."

"What do you want to know?"

"Everything."

"There isn't much to tell. After you, I mean, after that summer, I went back to New York. I interned for a terrible magazine. And then my boss, Tara, scooped me up. She quit and took me with her to a startup, *Elsewhere Magazine*. And the rest is...well, I'm here."

"So, you're a writer?" Sloane's eyes grew wide with something close to happiness.

Blake wasn't sure how to explain to Blake that she had taken a detour into social media nine years ago and never looked back. She'd embraced social media as if it was all she had left in the world, because at the time, it sort of had been. She was surprisingly good at content creation. Having something easy and dependable was nice. Blake was good at her job, and taking a risk hadn't paid off in the past. So, she was playing it safe. Until now.

"I'm a writer this week." She forced a laugh. "I'm ready to be dazzled by this place."

"Oh, this place will dazzle you, I promise." Sloane seemed to realize what she'd said because she sat her glass down and cleared her throat.

"What about you?" Blake asked. "What have you been up to? When did you start working your magic in hotels?"

Sloane laughed. Blake's cheeks flushed, but Sloane waved her away. "I'm not," she said quickly. "Not really. This is my first one."

"Well, you picked a good one to start at."

Sloane gave her a long look. Like she was trying to communicate something. But stopped. "I hope so," she breathed. "I spent years rebranding my uncle's vineyard. And now…now I get to do this."

Sloane had talked about her uncle a few times in Italy. He was a single dad with a struggling vineyard. Sloane wanted to help him. Apparently, she'd gotten her wish. "And what is it you want, Sloane?"

"I want to have dinner with an old friend. I want to drink good wine and stay in the sun too long. How am I doing?"

Friend. Old *friend*. The words were like a cool douse of water on Blake's speeding heart. What was she doing? Flirting with this woman after years and years. She was at work. This was business. Blake sat up straighter, mirroring Sloane's posture, and nodded once.

"Right," she said. She lifted her glass and waited for Sloane's to press against hers. "To old friends," she said brightly. And when their glasses clinked, Blake shoved their past into her memories, where it belonged.

CHAPTER FOUR

Sloane

BLAKE LOOKED GOOD. Time had made her softer and rounder, but also harder somehow. The Blake she remembered was open and adventurous. The woman in front of her was guarded. Now she eyed Sloane with, not quite fear, but definitely suspicion. But her cheeks still pinked at the top when Sloane smiled at her and she still played with her necklace when she was talking.

She forced her eyes away and took another large gulp of her wine. She needed to stop staring at Blake.

"So, you live in Napa?" Blake asked.

It was such a simple question, with a million ways to answer it. And all of them seemed wrong. Sloane *did* live in Napa. She'd grown up here until her parents sent her to boarding school. And she'd returned here during college to work on her uncle's vineyard. And now...well now Napa was very much home. And also, sometimes it felt like the loneliest place in the world.

Her uncle was gone. He'd been gone for ten years now, a terrible car accident on a winding road not too far from the property. Sloane still hated driving at night. Her cousin, whom she'd made her whole world, was off in college.

And her parents? Well, her parents barely spoke to her now. Which was fine by her.

Having Blake in front of her was overwhelming in a way Sloane didn't know how to handle. Just hearing her voice, seeing her face—it stirred something that Sloane had kept locked down for a long time. She wanted to let herself feel it, but the risk was too high. Sloane had survived these last ten years by keeping her heart safeguarded and locked away. Sloane had lost too many people already. She couldn't open up to Blake, not now when she was leaving at the end of the week.

People could hurt you even when they didn't mean to do it. Her uncle's death had been an accident, sudden and swift. But the hole he left behind never closed. Her parents had closed themselves off, with a selfish, cold retreat. And now her cousin—the one person she'd let herself love without fear—was gone too, chasing his future far from here.

So, she did what she always did. She pulled back from Blake.

"Yeah." She settled on a half-truth. "I have a place close by. The resort has been pretty demanding the last few months."

Sloane wasn't sure how much Blake knew—or how much she wanted to tell her. Sloane worked very hard to keep her identity under wraps because she didn't like the attention. She didn't want the press's pity. Her uncle's death still felt fresh and new, even ten years later.

But this was Blake, a woman who had seen all her most vulnerable parts. Could she share this, too?

"I can imagine." Blake gripped her cloth napkin tightly before smoothing it into her lap. She fixed her pointed stare on Sloane. "Too busy for phone calls even. Or messages."

Sloane winced. So, they were doing this. "Listen, I truly regret the way things ended. But I did what I had to do for my family." That was the understatement of the century.

She'd flown home from Italy like a zombie, and moved through a week of funeral preparations, then a week of settling into her new life. Sloane spent months barely hanging on, pouring what little effort and energy she had into Nico. Her cousin had only been twelve. Together they're learned how to pack a school lunch, survive all those first holidays alone. Together they learned how to laugh again, even through their grief.

By the time Sloane felt stitched together enough to reconnect with her friends, they were all gone. Off earning PhDs, running businesses or having babies. Sloane felt time slipping through her fingers. She'd wanted to call Blake. But so much time had passed and the missed calls from Blake had stopped. How was she supposed to call her with all her drama? Blake was the kind of person who wanted adventures and experiences and someone who could leave at the drop of a hat. Sloane was none of those things. Not anymore.

She couldn't say all that. So, she said, "I've been working hard these past ten years. And building a resort from nothing takes a lot of focus."

"Wait. This is yours? All of this is yours?" Blake blinked at her with wonder. She let out a low whistle. Sloane dug her fingernails into her palm to ground herself. It wasn't hers, not really.

"My uncle's," Sloane corrected. "But I'm in charge. Mostly. Unless you ask Robby." When her uncle passed away ten years ago, nothing felt like hers. She was a guardian, keeping the vineyard going in her uncle's name. Keeping it going for her cousin Nico. But this hotel was different. A tiny voice whispered to her heart that this place *did* belong to her.

"Oh. That's still really amazing." Blake took a sip of wine. And then another one. She watched Sloane with one brow raised over her glass. "So, this is what you've been up to all these years. Bringing a dream to life."

Sloane swallowed. Blake didn't know how close she was to the truth. How close Sloane *hoped* she was to the truth. Every time she chose a plate or a plant or a pedestal sink, she hoped her uncle would have been proud.

"Something like that," Sloane said with a crooked half smile. "This place is a dream come true. At least for me."

"Did you…did you know I worked for *Elsewhere*. Is that why…"

"No." Sloane practically shouted the word. Blake was a brilliant writer. She had no doubt the magazine selected Blake for her excellent work. And she didn't want Blake to think for one second she didn't belong here. "I promise. I had nothing to do with it. This was just a really, really wonderful coincidence. I do work closely with Robby. It's my job to make sure things run smoothly this week. So, I'll be around a lot."

There was that flush again. Sloane wanted to press her fingers against the hollow of Blake's throat and see if her skin was warm to the touch.

"I know Robby was expecting two people. I feel terrible having the honeymoon suite." Her voice wobbled a bit, and she let out an uncomfortable laugh.

"No, it's perfect. You should enjoy yourself. That's our best cottage. But, if I am remembering correctly, your itinerary is set up for two. I'll see what I can do to make arrangements—"

Sloane reached for her phone and began searching the

schedule for the week. Everything was full. It was full of excursions, leaving no wiggle room. She'd promised Robby she would take care of this. And here Blake was, already set up for disappointment.

"I'll be fine," Blake said, a sharp edge of indignation coloring her tone. She sat up straighter and tucked a lock of hair behind her ear.

"You'll be fine…going on a romantic horseback ride for two tomorrow?" Sloane raised a brow. She wasn't sure why she was goading Blake. She *needed* Blake to do these events. She sent Robby a help! text message under the table. Their response came back swiftly and punched Sloane in the chest: You'll have to do them with her.

"Are you saying I can't handle it?" Blake threw right back. Sloane loved when she was feisty. Her eyes widened and her mouth pulled into a flat line. A faint flush spread across Blake's collarbones.

"No, that's not what I meant." Sloane's pulse quickened. For years Sloane had dreamed of seeing Blake again. She stared at the message, willing the words to change. There had to be another way. They'd only been together ten minutes and Blake was clearly annoyed with her. "Robby said everything is booked. But I—" she chose her words carefully "—would be happy to join you on the excursions."

Blake laughed, a short bark of disbelief, before catching herself. She seemed to consider something before speaking again. Sloane wasn't sure, but the slight tremor in Blake's voice and the way her shoulders slumped suggested that admitting she needed help was painful for her.

"Are you sure you can handle that?" Blake sat up straight and cleared her throat. "You have time in your schedule to show me around?"

Sloane saw the question for what it was: a test. Sloane

had broken promises to her before. She couldn't do it again. If she was going to do this, she had to do it right.

"I will make time," she promised. "Friends?"

Blake tipped her head to the side and pulled her mouth into a tight smile. "Friends. And I expect you to be on time. Don't make me look foolish, Sloane." It made something churn in Sloane's stomach. Blake really had moved on. She could sit across from Sloane at dinner, agree to hang out doing romantic activities, and be completely unfazed by it.

"Good." Sloane took a long gulp of wine, desperate for a pause in the conversation. She needed to get it together. Blake's slight smiles and somewhat bossy tone couldn't make her stomach flip. Not this week. "I forgot how pushy you can be when you want to get your way."

Blake blanched. "I am *not* pushy," she laughed. "You just don't know how to ask for what you want."

A memory of their last days together came back to Sloane. Blake pushing, not so subtly, to know what was next for Sloane. Sloane dodging the questions at every turn. She didn't want to ruin her gap year by talking about her unknown future. She wanted to lie in the sun and kiss Blake and not think about tomorrow.

But then Sloane had gotten that call. And all thoughts of running away with Blake had soberingly come to a halt.

Sloane hadn't had a serious girlfriend in the last ten years. Sure, there had been a few meaningless hookups, but nothing that lasted more than a few days and definitely no one she introduced to Nico. Sloane had convinced herself that it was the pressure of work, or her protectiveness over Nico; but maybe it was more. Maybe this hidden hope that Blake would return to her somehow was the reason she never let anyone else in. Sloane didn't have the courage back then to say what she truly wanted. And it seemed she still didn't have it now.

Their dinner devolved into painful small talk and Blake looking like she regretted telling Sloane to sit down. Sloane wished she could rewind the last twenty minutes and begin with honesty. That she missed Blake. She thought of her every day.

She wanted Blake to know she'd left in a panic upon learning of her uncle's death. That she was scared to call Blake and tell her everything, only to have Blake tell her she wasn't interested with Sloane if she had responsibilities. Blake had fallen in love with a fun, carefree version of Sloane. And she was anything but that now. Instead, she spoke vaguely about work and dismissed anyone who walked her way.

But Robby appeared at the edge of the dining room and gave Sloane a signal that said, *actually boss, it's kind of important—you better get over here right now.*

"I'm so sorry." Sloane rose from the table, she felt awful leaving Blake there alone. "There's something I need to check on." She could see the way Blake's shoulders slumped, even if she tried to hide it.

Robby's words echoed in her mind. Blake's article could make or break this resort. They *needed* a good write-up. And Sloane had promised Robby that she could handle Blake Miller. If that is what it took to ensure a great opening, she'd do it. A knot of anxiety tightened in her stomach; she was facing a week with the woman she'd abandoned a decade earlier, a woman whose frustrated glare promised a difficult stay.

"But, Blake." She waited until Blake looked her in the eyes. "I'll go with you tomorrow. I'll see you in the morning for the first event at the edge of the lavender trail."

CHAPTER FIVE

Blake

A SINKING SENSE of dread washed over Blake as she flipped through the color-coded, annotated itinerary inside her embossed folder the next morning. Blake was accustomed to doing things alone. She had no problem attending local events, trying out a new restaurant or hiking with a group of strangers in San Diego.

But these events were *designed* for couples. She was looking forward to the horseback riding and lounging in the cabanas by the pool. But some of the events were marked as surprises, only noting a time and a location. She really didn't want to be crammed together with Sloane, close-bodied, while they worked with clay or some other ridiculous activity.

Blake's stomach dipped; a nervous energy buzzed through her at the idea of Sloane leaning over her, arms covered in clay slip. She shook off the image and tried to focus on breakfast. But she could barely eat the fresh pastries and tea left on her doorstep. Even if the pastries looked delicious, with their golden-brown crusts and sweet aroma, with the handpicked wildflowers adding a touch of rustic charm to the tray.

The lavender path outside her door took her away from

the main building and down a hill that led to a barn and stables. It was a rustic haven blooming before her out of the reedy yellow grass. A large wooden barn, a small cottage off to the side and a fenced meadow with two horses munching on grass.

The hills rolled up and around the grassy meadow, covered in precise rows of grapes growing on the vine. The creepers varied from young and thin to lush and overflowing. Blake knew nothing about wine making. But she loved the idea of seeing all these stages around her at once. A patchwork quilt of different hues of green—and a testament to patience and faith.

"How do you expect to ride in those shoes?" Sloane's voice felt rough as sandpaper on the back of Blake's neck. She hated that she knew what Sloane's morning voice sounded like.

"It's just a ride. These shoes will be fine." Blake turned to find Sloane brushing the hair of a gorgeous sable horse with a dark black mane. She glanced down at her tennis shoes and fitted jeans. "Will this not work?"

"Not for what I have planned." Sloane's brushing slowed and she flicked her heated gaze up Blake's body. "You still wear a size seven?"

Blake cleared her throat, pushing aside the odd sense of comfort that even though Sloane hadn't remembered to call—or write—in the last ten years, she somehow still remembered Blake's shoe size.

"Yeah."

Sloane tipped her head toward the barn and walked away, leaving the horse staring curiously at Blake. Blake didn't want to give Sloane the satisfaction of trailing after her, but she *did* want a pair of boots.

Sloane passed the stables and headed to the small building. There was a tiny black placard in the grass just next to the door. *Private Property. Please do not enter.* Apparently, rules didn't apply to Sloane, because she flipped up the latch and slipped inside the small house. Storage room? Cottage?

"Are you sure I'm allowed in here…" Blake's words trailed away as she stepped into the cozy space. There was riding equipment, yes, but there was also a small love seat. A desk. A soft mint-green wall with a brass bed pushed against it. Blake felt as if she had stepped into a dollhouse. A dollhouse with very expensive furnishings and a saddle.

"What is this place?" Blake asked.

"Just a cottage," Sloane replied, her tone suggesting the question didn't need further discussion. She opened a small cupboard and plucked a pair of well-worn but immaculate boots. She thrust them toward Blake. "There. Now you can ride."

Blake blinked at her. "Is this…yours?"

Sloane wiggled the boots, waiting for Blake to take them. "Yes? This is where I sleep usually. You can put them on over there." Her eyes flicked to the loveseat; a bright green thing that looked like shoots of summer grass sprung up inside this tiny house.

"Why do you have a tiny house here when there is an entire resort a five-minute walk away?"

"This just feels like home." Sloane looked around the space as if seeing it for the first time. Blake looked, too. Everything was simple, understated and soft. Luxury hidden beneath homey antiques, high-pile rugs and a homemade quilt.

Sloane winked at Blake and leaned against the wooden beam separating a kitchenette from the living room. "I can't tell you all my secrets, Miller."

"I don't think I know *any* of your secrets," Blake huffed. She dropped onto the couch and put on the boots, just so she'd have something to do. "I didn't even know you liked horses," she mumbled.

Sloane hmm'd to herself. "I don't. I like *one* horse. And she's going to be very mad if we don't get going soon."

"Where is everyone else?" Blake reached for her phone to triple-check the itinerary.

"The rest of the group already left. They're taking the easy trail around the pond." Sloane pressed her lips together as if trying to stifle a smile. "But I had something else in mind. Will you let me show you some of my favorite parts of this place?"

Blake bit back her frustration. Sloane loved to do this, surprises, adventures, unexpected little somethings.

Sloane must have seen the look on her face because she paused, tucked her hair behind her ear and said, softer, "Think of it as a behind-the-scenes tour. Still completely reviewable."

Blake exhaled deeply. "Fine." Once outside, she approached the gentle horse slowly, thoughtfully, and scratched at her muzzle. "I suppose a sneak peek and exclusive tour is kind of cool. But I get to ask some interview questions. Deal?"

"Deal."

"Good. Lead the way, Sloane."

Sloane

They'd only been on the trail for a few minutes when the questions started.

"So, how long have you been in California?"

How did Sloane explain this? That she'd always been in

California. That these hills were her backyard. And also that she hadn't really existed at all since she'd returned from Europe ten years ago.

"Practically my whole life. I went to college in New York, but otherwise I've been here."

That was an easy one, but Sloane didn't love the idea of Blake digging around in her past. The next few questions were also simple. Favorite kind of wine, best markets in the area, spa treatment recommendations. But then the real questions started and Sloane began to sweat.

"And when did you start working for your uncle?" Blake fired off questions like they were in a courtroom. Not unfriendly, but not familiar. Was she hiding a recording device somewhere? Blake's brow furrowed slightly as she waited for answers. Well, she was going to have to wait a bit longer.

"Sorry, not today, Miller. I want to talk about you now." Sloane looked back to see Blake absently threading her fingers between Winnie's hair, trying to hide her annoyance. "How long have you been writing for your magazine?"

"About a week," Blake said. There was something tense in her voice that made Sloane want to know more. Want to know everything.

"A week? How did you manage this assignment after a week?"

Blake's cheeks flushed. Or maybe it was from the morning sun. Sloane should have given her a hat. Or smoothed some sunscreen across her cheeks and down the back of her neck. Nope. She definitely shouldn't have done that.

"I've worked for the magazine longer than a week. I'm the social media manager. I post teasers and links to articles. That sort of thing." She paused for a moment, seeming to weigh whether she could trust Sloane. Sloane bit down on the inside of her lip, and tried not to give away how interested she was in knowing more. "But this is my… my chance to be a *writer*. I came here for a story. And I have to admit, this horseback riding experience certainly is good. Do all guests have access to the stables?"

Sloane turned back around and waited a few beats before responding. "No," she said finally. "I have a friend who brings their horses to us when we organize an experience. But Winnie and Rhett…they're mine."

Sloane had wanted Blake off the resort's property somewhere private, away from Robby's interruptions. She didn't think she could handle being part of a guided tour of her own hills, with resort guests asking questions.

She wanted to bring this new *walls-up* version of Blake somewhere safe. Somewhere she didn't have to be *Sloane Vella*, owner of Vella West. But out here, on the trail, with the vineyards rising around them like sentient chaperones—watchful, silent and unbearably aware—she realized how impossible that was.

This was her sanctuary, the one place she let herself breathe. Sloane had spent years hiking these hills, learning herself as well as the landscape. She was quieter now. Letting her actions and her management of the property speak for itself. She had hardened herself against the years of solitude.

Now Blake was in it, and the air felt thinner. The vines seemed to close in, not just watching, but reminding her exactly how much she stood to lose. Maybe Blake wasn't the only one with walls up.

"You know, if you want me to give this place a good review, you're probably going to want me to see some of the amenities that are actually available." Blake raised a brow. Sloane huffed out a breath that wasn't quite a laugh and shrugged.

Blake was right. She was here for a job, for a shot at something real. *A chance*, she'd said. And Sloane knew that's what she had to give her. She couldn't offer an apology, couldn't explain why she'd disappeared ten years ago without a word. But this—this opportunity—she *could* give her that much.

"Well, in that case, maybe we'd better head back." Sloane tugged gently on the reins, and her horse responded, though he turned his head as if questioning her decision. "I'm sure we can arrange a spa day. Or a wine tasting."

"Are you kidding?" Blake nudged Winnie forward until they were even again. She looked good in Sloane's boots. Good on her horse. She looked good in everything.

"You promised me an adventure, Sloane. I intend to hold you to it."

With a click of her tongue, Blake urged her horse ahead, slipping into the lead. Not quite a gallop—but fast enough that Sloane would have to move if she wanted to keep up.

Blake could ride. She could *ride*. This woman was going to be the death of her.

Sloane closed her eyes and bit back a curse. "Come on, Rhett," she murmured into the horse's ear. "Let's go get your girl."

Rhett had been on loan from a friend the summer Nico stayed with her after his freshman year of college. But by the end of that week, Rhett had made up his mind: he belonged to Winnie. He'd followed her across pastures, refused to eat unless she was nearby, once even cleared a fence just to stand beside her. It was ridiculous—how certain he was. How stubborn.

When it came time to send him back, she couldn't do it. It had cost her. But it had been worth it.

The horse seemed to side-eye her with quiet judgment. He was known to throw riders out of their saddle and Sloane usually left him alone. But he must have taken pity on her because he shook his head and took off in Blake's direction.

Blake was riding Sloane's horse, a gentle, but fabulous caramel-colored mare. And she looked damn good doing it, too. They chased each other through the hills. Sometimes Sloane would pull into the lead and other times she enjoyed trailing behind Blake. Sloane thrilled at having Blake here, laughing and asking questions, and pulling her hair up off her neck when she needed to cool down.

They wound up by a small pond at the farthest edge of Sloane's property, well past the resort's boundaries. The sun glinted off the water, painting the meadow in a late morning glow. Sloane hopped off her horse and walked over to Blake.

"It's going to be hot today, isn't it?" Blake asked. Sloane didn't respond. She walked closer and held out her arms. "What? You're going to help me down?"

"Obviously."

Blake scoffed as she adjusted the reins and prepared to dismount. "Sloane, I know how to get down from a horse."

"Humor me." Blake's stubbornness hadn't changed, at least. Sloane held up a hand and offered Blake one of her half smiles. "Winnie can be fickle."

Blake sighed but nodded. "Fine."

Sloane regretted the offer as soon as Blake's body pressed against hers. Blake slid down quickly, her body falling into Sloane's as she steadied her, digging her fingers into the soft flesh of her waist. Blake was warm and solid and smelled like every good memory Sloane had ever had. She'd wanted to bottle that summer up and bring it home with her.

"You can let go of me now." Blake's voice was a whisper in the hollow of Sloane's throat. This was the first time they'd touched in over ten years. Sloane forgot how Blake's mouth was right at neck level, in the soft skin of her throat. It used to drive her wild. It used to drive Blake wild, too. She'd told Sloane as much whenever she kissed the spot just below her jaw. She'd said she loved the direct access to the part of Sloane's body that turned her into a puddle.

"Right," Sloane said. She cleared her throat and stepped back. Space. She needed space. And maybe some water. Her throat was parched. Blake's probably was, too. "Here, have some water." Sloane reached into her bag and pulled out a canteen.

"Well, you're prepared." Blake smiled. "Thanks. Far cry from when we would head out for an adventure with nothing but our swimsuits and a few euros in our back pockets."

"It did lead to some great discoveries though." She took a drink from the canteen, realizing too late that Blake's mouth had just been in the same spot. The cool water did nothing to stop the blaze of heat in her belly.

"What else do you have going on today? I'm sure you're incredibly busy." Blake's words hit Sloane with a jolt. A quick glance at her watch reminded her she was ten minutes late for a meeting with a local vendor. She was going to lose the contract if she didn't get there soon.

"Yeah, we should get back." Sloane thought of Blake eating dinner alone tonight. The way she'd ignore everyone else in the dining room as she sipped her wine. She couldn't bear to think of it.

"There is a dinner tonight for some of the local vendors. Would you like to come?"

"That isn't on my itinerary. I'm supposed to go to the pool and then to a—"

"I would really love it if you'd come. It's not a big event. Just some local friends. It's strictly off the journalism circuit."

"I don't think that's such a good idea." Blake went quiet. "We can let the past be in the past, Sloane. You don't have to host me this weekend. I'll be fine. I know you said you would do some of the events with me. But we don't have to eat every meal together."

"No," Sloane said. "I want you there. I know I don't have any right to say this, but I want to see you again. I want to know more about what you've been up to."

"Sloane. You had ten years to do that."

"I know. I—" Her words cut off and she looked away. She wasn't going to get into this with Blake. Not when this morning had been sort of lovely, despite Blake's initial coldness and her own awkwardness. "I can't change the past, but I'd like to move forward. I told you I would do the events with you and I meant it. I want to keep this promise, if you'll let me."

Blake studied Sloane for a long time. Long enough that she felt her eyes everywhere. Then Blake shrugged. "Fine. What do I need to wear tonight? If it's another boots situation I'd like to be prepared."

Sloane bit down on her lip to keep from smiling. Blake looked good in her boots. Blake looked good in everything though. It occurred to Sloane that maybe Blake wasn't ready for an evening with the who's who of Napa Valley. Blake liked to be in charge, she wanted to know what was happening in every situation.

Sloane didn't want to overwhelm her, but she could at least ease this one burden. "Don't worry about that part," Sloane said. "I've got you covered."

CHAPTER SIX

Blake

BLAKE WANDERED TOWARD the pool, hoping that the warm air and sunshine would ease the restless thoughts swirling in her mind. She needed space—some distance from the weight of her emotions, the frenzy of her day, the quiet ache in her chest that wouldn't let her go. Blake knew this week would change her, but she certainly hadn't expected it to transport her back ten years.

The pool area was a work of modern elegance—a stark contrast to the vineyard's rustic charm. This wasn't just any resort pool; it felt like an exclusive oasis, the kind of place designed to make you forget that time existed outside its walls. Water shimmered in hues of aquamarine, the sun reflecting off it like a million tiny diamonds. Warm, golden light spilled across the space, kissing the edges of Blake's shoulders as she surveyed her options.

Tall cypress trees edged the perimeter, creating a barrier between Blake and the outside world. A few sleek white cabanas lined one side of the pool, each one a tiny sanctuary with thick, plush towels draped over loungers and small tables topped with chilled water and delicate sprigs of rosemary. The space was curated for tranquility—isolated yet welcoming.

Blake moved slowly, her feet cool against the stone as she walked, the soft scent of jasmine and fresh grass filling the air. Blake looked around the peaceful, open space. She wanted the quietest corner, the one that might hold her thoughts without judgment. The lounger she chose was near the far end of the pool, just a few steps away from where the water lapped gently at the stone. Kicking off her sandals, she let the weight of her day dissipate.

She draped the plush towel over the lounger, the fabric soft beneath her fingertips. Blake slid onto the chair, stretching out and tilting her head back, letting the sun bathe her in warmth. She closed her eyes, finding comfort in the murmur of voices, the breeze, and the water's gentle rhythm. For a few moments, she could exist in the quiet, letting the world spin on without her.

"Miss Miller?" A voice forced her to open her eyes and sit upright in her lounger. An unfamiliar staff member with a neat silver name tag and a crisp white polo shirt looked at her expectantly.

"Yes?" She shaded her eyes and looked up at the woman. She was young and held on to a crisp white envelope as if her job depended on it.

"This is for you," she said. "I'm so sorry to interrupt you. Is there anything else I can get for you?"

"Thank you so much. I'm good here." Blake took the envelope and the woman left. The expensive paper weighed heavily in her hands. If she hadn't seen her name printed across the front in Sloane's neat handwriting, she would have thought the woman had made a mistake.

The ink was blurry and imperfect where Sloane's pen had brushed the paper, as though she hadn't been entirely sure how to say what she was feeling. Blake hesitated at first, her fingers hovering over the edges of the letter. *Was she ready for this?* But she couldn't help it. She traced the words with her fingers as if the paper held something deeper—something unsaid, something both terrifying and thrilling.

The note, with its clumsy words, felt so…vulnerable. Sloane had written it by hand, and somehow, that small act of putting pen to paper made it feel more personal than anything typed on a screen could ever be. Blake lingered over the words as though they were a puzzle she couldn't quite solve, but wanted to.

> Blake,
> I had a really nice time riding with you this morn-ing. If you're still up for dinner tonight, I took the liberty of sending you a dress. It's waiting in your room. I'll meet you at seven in the lobby, if you're still open to it.
> Sloane

If you're still open to it.

That part kept echoing in Blake's mind. Sloane hadn't just written a note; she'd put her own hesitance on paper. Just when Blake had enough distance from Sloane to get some perspective, Sloane had to do something like this. A note. A handwritten note. She had to know what this would do to Blake. Sloane was playing dirty, and Blake couldn't help but smile at the thick paper in her hands.

And then there was the dress. If Sloane thought she could throw expensive clothing or lavish gifts at Blake and expect all to be forgiven, she was sorely mistaken. Blake's forgiveness didn't have a price tag on it. And she'd tell Sloane as much the next time she saw her.

She squeezed her eyes shut and let out a groan of frus-tration before glancing at the pool again, the water still and inviting. Maybe she could just let go of it all. Her anger and frustration at Sloane. Her worry about work. She could dive into the clear weightlessness of the pool and just…give in.

But the thought of that note—it's quiet promise and uncertainty—refused to let her go. It wasn't just a letter; Sloane had *written* to her. Sloane, who remembered she liked little notes and gestures, had taken the time to write to her. It was misguided at best, but at least it was a start.

She wasn't ready for tonight. But maybe she never would be.

Sloane

Sloane paced the lobby of Vella West, her eyes flicking to the door every few seconds. It was nearly time for dinner, and Blake was still nowhere to be seen. A familiar knot tightened in her stomach. Maybe the note had been a mistake. She'd picked up her phone to text Blake and realized that she didn't know her number. And before she could help herself, she was grabbing her favorite stationery and taking a risk.

But now she wasn't here, and Sloane was going to be late and she'd bought that dress. Sloane was just trying to make things easier…but she was pretty sure she'd gone and messed up any chance of redemption with Blake.

She had told herself she wasn't nervous, but that wasn't true. She was pacing, her breath a little quicker, her pulse a little too loud in her ears. *It's just dinner*, she reminded herself. *Just dinner.* But if she was honest, she knew tonight was about more than just food and wine—it was the first real opportunity to see if all the years between them had truly erased everything. To see if Blake still wanted to know her, when she knew everything about her.

When she had picked out the dress for Blake, she'd told herself it was nothing, just a small gesture. A way to ensure that Blake felt at home with the crowd tonight. But even as she thought that, her stomach twisted. What if Blake didn't want to be reminded of what they had been? What if all of this was *too much*?

Just as she was about to pace toward the dining area, the doors to the lobby swung open, and Blake walked in.

Sloane's breath caught in her throat.

Blake was standing there, looking like the ocean at high tide. The dress looked soft as silk under the lighting, the simple linen clinging to the rounded curves of her body, the hem just brushing the tops of her sandals. She looked stunning.

She looked perfect.

She looked smug—because this wasn't the dress Sloane had selected for her.

This dress wasn't extravagant, but it was perfect. Blake left her hair down; the soft curls framed her face in loose waves, her cheeks flushed from an afternoon by the pool. She looked *effortless*—stunning in that relaxed Northern California way that made Sloane's pulse race.

For a second, everything stood still. Blake wasn't the naive, young girl she'd been in Europe. She was confident, glowing and walking right toward Sloane.

Sloane shook herself from her stupor, her heart hammering in her chest. She quickly composed herself and walked over, her voice steadier than she felt. "There you are," she said, her smile pulling at the corners of her mouth. "You look…stunning."

Blake's eyebrow arched, and a teasing smile tugged at her lips. "Thank you."

Sloane laughed, the sound coming easier than she expected. "You didn't like the one I sent?"

Blake's smile softened, and for a brief moment they just stood there, gazing at each other. The years between them, the silence, the uncertainty—it all seemed to fade in that look. For a heartbeat, it was like nothing had changed.

"I don't know—I didn't open the garment bag." Blake's shoulders moved up in a soft shrug. It made her cinnamon swirl curls dance. "You can't buy me, Sloane. If you want to impress me, money isn't the way to do it."

A flush of heat crawled up the back of Sloane's neck, shame tagging along with it. That wasn't what she'd been doing…was it? She just wanted Blake to feel confident walking into tonight's dinner. That's all. So, she'd—okay, yes, she'd spent a ridiculous amount of money on a dress to prove she cared. Damn it.

"Well, probably for the best," she said, breaking the silence. Sloane swallowed back her pride. Blake's words were harsh, but not angry. This was progress. "This dress is a much better choice. I hope you're hungry," Sloane said, her voice low. She took a step forward, leading Blake toward the private dining room.

As they walked through the main lobby and then down another hall, Sloane could feel Blake at her side. Quiet but firm. The pull between them hadn't gone anywhere—it was still there, stronger than ever, and it made Sloane ache.

The vineyard's private tasting room was Sloane's third favorite place on the property, next to her cottage and the wildflower fields. It had a retractable wall of glass windows connected to the patio off the south side, with views of her stables and pond in the distance. Dining here felt intimate and wide-open all at the same time.

The table was grand, set with gleaming custom drink

ware and sophisticated silverware, each course meticulously presented. The air was fragrant with the aromas of fine wine, fresh herbs and expertly prepared dishes. The panoramic view of the Napa Valley vineyards past her own property stretched beyond the open doors, bathed in the warm glow of the setting sun.

Sloane couldn't help but look at all of it with new eyes. What must Blake think of all this? The Blake from ten years ago probably would have been unconvinced. But, then again, Sloane would have been overwhelmed, too. She took a deep breath and reminded herself that they'd both changed a lot in the last ten years. And she wanted to see what Blake had become.

As the night unfolded, the conversation at the table swirled around them—business deals, the latest vineyards and casual talk of family and life in Napa's bubble. It was all a bit too polished, too perfect for Sloane, who was always more at home in the vineyards, riding her horse or with her sleeves rolled up. But she could turn on the charm when she had to.

"Sloane, how's Nico? Why isn't he here?" Glenn was her uncle's best friend and friendly vineyard rival. When Sloane had taken over, he'd shown her the ropes and looked out for her and Nico. "I didn't think he'd miss a week like this."

He meant his question kindly, but it made Sloane tense. Her eyes darted to Blake, who pretended not to listen, but there was a hunch in her shoulders. She needed to tell her about her cousin. Blake deserved to know everything. But in the middle of a large dinner party was not the place to explain.

"He's still in school," Sloane responded. "His classes aren't done for a few weeks. I'll tell him you said hello."

"Tell him I said to come intern for me," Glenn's voice boomed. Sloane rolled her eyes. If Nico was going to do any work on a vineyard, it would be with her. "And bring this girl of yours around, too."

A thrill rushed down Sloane's spine. Blake wasn't *her girl*. But she didn't want to contradict Glenn. So, she let the words float around in the room, letting them drip down like legs on a glass of wine.

Still, Sloane couldn't help but smile as she watched Blake navigate the evening. Blake glowed with confidence, even if she didn't know a single soul in the room. She was doing her best—being polite, playing along—but there was a slight edge to her responses, a self-awareness that wasn't lost on Sloane.

Blake had a way of making everyone feel at ease while still holding on to her quiet, authentic self. And as the night wore on, Sloane noticed something else—how everyone, from the business tycoons to the local winemakers, seemed to love Blake. They asked her questions about her writing, curious about the behind-the-scenes of her career, all the while teasing her gently about her "Southern California ways" and wondering if she felt out of place among the Napa crowd.

One of the older women at the table, who had been friends with Sloane's family for years, raised an eyebrow at her. "I have to say, Sloane," she said with a knowing smile. "You two make a lovely pair. The way you look at each other—it's almost like you've been together forever."

Blake's cheeks flushed a soft pink, and she shot Sloane a quick, playful look. "Oh, we're not a couple," she said, but her voice was just a touch too defensive. "We're just friends. Old friends who found each other again."

The table erupted in knowing laughter, but there was

a warmth in their teasing. It wasn't mean-spirited. It was just *comfortable*.

"I don't know," another woman chimed in. "You two certainly seem like more than just friends. Come on, Sloane, you're glowing tonight. There's something in the air, don't you think?"

Sloane's heart twisted. She hadn't noticed how hard she'd been working to suppress that quiet glow—the one that came from more than just the wine. She caught Blake's eye across the table. There was something different in the way Blake looked at her tonight. Something that made her pulse skip, that made the air between them feel charged.

But she couldn't afford to linger in that feeling. Blake was leaving in just a few days. Letting herself believe in anything beyond this week was a luxury she couldn't afford—not again.

Sloane had promised Blake her time, not her heart. She hadn't agreed to relive what it felt like to love her. And certainly not to hope.

She forced her gaze away and smoothed her expression into something neutral.

"I'm happy," Sloane said, her voice light, the words almost convincing. "It's just nice to see you all again." She added, with a teasing lilt, "But I promise, there's nothing going on here."

Even as she said it, part of her wished it were a lie.

Blake raised an eyebrow and leaned back in her chair. "Sloane's right. Just old friends with an unexpected reunion."

She held Sloane's eyes for a beat and Sloane's pulse quickened with nervous excitement. With possibility. A small inkling that Blake was having the same confused rush of emotion as her. She didn't know what to do with the feeling, so she took another sip of wine and quickly changed the subject.

The laughter around the table picked up again, but Blake's voice, though light, had a softness to it that made Sloane's chest tighten just a little. The teasing had a warmth to it, but there was also an undercurrent of something *more*—an unspoken connection that had been simmering between them for years.

Sloane watched her, her heart swelling a little with pride. She'd always admired Blake's ability to weave a story, to make people see the world through her eyes. Tonight, in the midst of all the polished luxury, Blake was the most real thing in the room.

"So, Blake," a woman in a flowing summer dress asked, "what's the best destination you've written about? What's the one place that's stuck with you the most?"

Blake paused, considering the question. "It's tough," she said, her fingers lightly tracing the stem of her wineglass. "But I'd say one of my favorites was a small town in Positano. It wasn't on anyone's radar, but it was just *real*. The food, the people, the way everything felt untouched by the big tourist rush. It was…perfect, in its own way."

Sloane smiled softly. Blake's eyes sparkled as she talked—the genuine passion and curiosity always there. It was the thing that had drawn Sloane to her all those years ago, and it still caught her in a way she wasn't quite ready to admit.

"Remember that farmhouse?" Sloane shared the memory without thinking. "We were going to buy that place."

Blake's soft laughter seemed to reach across the table, a balm for Sloane. She remembered it, too. The dilapidated farmhouse that was supposed to become their future.

"That place was a mess. But it was gorgeous. I wonder if it's still standing? And if the vineyard next to it has produced anything."

"A farmhouse in Italy? Now, that's the dream," another guest said, and Sloane could sense Blake relaxing into the conversation now, the questions and teasing fading into background noise. It wasn't so much about the place—it was about how Blake made the world feel real. She always had.

The night went on like that—lighthearted, full of laughter, and a surprising amount of warmth. As the last course, a delicate chocolate mousse with a hint of sea salt, was served, the conversation drifted into softer tones, with people talking about their favorite memories of Napa. The laughter continued, but there was an easy feeling to it now.

Blake, though still a little out of her element, had finally relaxed into the night. She sipped her wine, a half smile playing on her lips. She'd navigated the evening well, despite feeling like an outsider at first. And somehow, Sloane had the sense that Blake was *starting* to let herself enjoy this—whatever *this* was—just a little bit more than she had at the start.

And as the night wound down, with people exchanging final toasts and goodbyes, Sloane felt her gaze drift back to Blake, who was now in the middle of a lively conversation with one of the other guests. The way Blake smiled, the way she fit into this world with her own quiet charm—it made Sloane's chest ache in a way she wasn't ready to fully unpack.

But for now, she was content with just watching her—glowing, real and entirely herself.

CHAPTER SEVEN

Blake

THE COOL MORNING air drew goose bumps along Blake's arms as she followed the short path from her cottage to the entrance of the resort. The moon was still low in the sky and she was going to give Robby an earful about this early morning wake-up call—who requires guests to be up before dawn?

The itinerary had only told her to dress warm, in layers and be at the front of the resort by four thirty in the morning. She'd thrown on some jeans and a sweater over a simple shirt. Blake wasn't worried about trying to impress anyone. She was certain she was alone on this adventure, since she and Sloane hadn't talked about it.

And maybe that's why the sight of early morning Sloane caught Blake off guard when she turned the corner and saw her standing by the entrance of Vella West. She wore fitted jeans and a tight black hooded sweatshirt and a beanie. She looked younger somehow, like the girl Blake had known before. Sloane was makeup free and sipping on a white to-go cup with a brown sleeve. When she saw Blake, she stood and strode toward her with purpose, never losing eye contact.

She held out a cup and Blake took it, even though she didn't drink coffee. At least it would keep her hands warm.

"What's this?" Blake asked as she took the cup.

Sloane shrugged. "A peace offering," she said. "I hope you don't mind, but I canceled the van pickup. I—well, I would prefer to drive."

Sloane's body stiffened as she waited for Blake's response. Blake wasn't sure what had her so nervous, probably the fact that the two of them were going to be alone together.

"That's fine with me," Blake said, her voice way too chipper for a before-dawn conversation. "Are you going to tell me what we're doing?"

Sloane offered her a secret, smug smile. "Nope. It's meant to be a surprise activity, according to Robby." She tipped her head toward the passenger door of her sleek black coupe. "First, we have to get there. Then you'll see."

They drove in the gray early morning light down the winding roads in relative silence. Blake's thoughts were a swirl of confusion and excitement as she peeked at Sloane out of the corner of her eye. Various resorts hidden behind high walls and gates flew past them as Sloane drove down the highway.

"Is something wrong with your drink?" Sloane asked. The coffee sat untouched in the cup holder, seeming to taunt Blake.

"No." Blake grimaced and grabbed the cup. She prepared herself for the bitter taste of coffee. But as she took a sip, a jolt of cream and Earl Grey hit her tongue. "Oh! It's tea."

Sloane scrunched her brow in confusion. "Of course it's tea."

"You remember how I take my tea?"

"Blake, you were insufferable in the morning until you'd had at least two cups of tea. I've probably watched you drink a thousand of those. Of course I remember."

Blake let the words settle low in her belly. Like most things with Sloane, it was an ache and a soothing balm all at once. Blake smiled down at the cup. She didn't respond, but she silently drank her tea and pondered the fact that Sloane remembered.

When Sloane pulled off the highway and onto a dirt road Blake noticed a sign that read Wine Country Tours in swoopy letters. Something prickled at the back of her mind. A memory. A dream.

Slowing down, Sloane turned into a dirt parking area, revealing the scene before them. There were six different wicker baskets large enough to hold at least ten people, arranged in a field. Even in the darkness, Blake could see ribbons of color spread out behind them. A breath hitched in Blake's throat and something tightened in her chest.

"Sloane—" The words cut off in her throat. "What are we…"

Sloane parked the car and turned to look at Blake. "Come on, we don't want to be late."

When Blake was younger, she'd stare at the hot-air balloons in the early morning sky. A trip was so far outside her budget she'd never even dreamed of booking a flight. But she had told Sloane about it. One morning Sloane had woken her before dawn, a steaming mug of tea in hand and they'd driven out to an open field.

Together they'd lain in the dewdrop grass and watched as giant orbs came into view. A kaleidoscope of color across the early morning sky.

"I'm going to do that someday," Blake had whispered into her mouth. "Just float away with nothing but heat and air and silence."

"Sounds terrifying."

"Sounds amazing."

"Maybe. If you're not afraid of heights."

"Well, yes, there's that." She'd kissed Sloane and let her fingertips trail up and down her spine beneath her sweater. "Are you saying you won't go with me?"

"I'd go for you," Sloane had promised between kisses. "I'll be terrified. And panicking the entire time. But let me be there. The first time you go."

"I will." Blake had said as Sloane pushed her back on the blanket and trailed kisses down her neck. "I'll wait for you."

And she had. Blake had had opportunities to try this, but she always turned them down or found an excuse. It felt right to be here now, with an older version of Sloane. There were a million promises they'd both broken to each other over the years, but she'd kept this one.

"I thought we were doing something from my itinerary?" Blake really wanted to go on this adventure, but it felt like too much. It was too special.

"This is on your itinerary," Sloane said with a wink. "I just tweaked it a little."

Blake was still trying to decide what to do about that wink when Sloane pointed across the field. "Come on, this one is ours." Sloane tugged on Blake's sleeve and Blake felt it in her stomach.

A wicker basket, much smaller than the rest, sat in the middle of the field. "Why is it so much smaller?" Blake had researched this. There were weight limits and balance requirements. And she realized now that she was going to be in that tiny basket with Sloane and a pilot and probably a few other strangers. Nerves coiled deep in her stomach like a spring, circling tighter and tighter until she was sure she'd be sick.

As they approached the basket, a man from the night before strode over. "It's all set for you, Sloane."

"Thanks."

He held up a fist, and she bumped it. Blake stifled a giggle at the sight of Sloane fist-bumping anyone.

Then he walked away.

"You first, Miller." Sloane gestured to the basket. Blake hadn't been nervous until now. Somehow, this tiny basket was going to hold at least three people with nothing but heat. There was no way.

"But we're missing our pilot," Blake protested.

Sloane climbed over the edge of the basket and stretched out her hand to Blake. She blinked at her. "Blake, *I'm* the pilot."

Blake stared at Sloane's outstretched hand like it was some kind of trick. The balloon loomed beyond them, the burner sputtering in rhythmic bursts, and still—still—she couldn't make the pieces fit.

"*You're* the pilot?" she said again, arms folded tight across her chest.

Sloane didn't flinch. "Yes," she said simply. "I got restless a few years ago. My entire life was mapped out for me and none of it felt like it was mine. I needed something just for me. And I know we promised to do this together one day. I guess it was my way of keeping that summer alive. That sounds ridiculous. I know."

A flash of electricity ran down Blake's spine and crackled along her fingertips, but whether it was anger or awe—or that dangerous space in between—she couldn't tell. Ten years of nothing. No calls. No texts. No quick, cowardly message on social media. Just silence.

And now this?

Sloane must have spent hundreds of hours getting certified, mastering the rules, learning the language of flight, just to—what? Carry some kind of torch for Blake? Sweep back in and dazzle her with a grand gesture?

It was infuriating. It was ridiculous. It was kind of… breathtaking.

The heat rising from the burner couldn't compare to the slow burn in Blake's chest. Maybe it wasn't really about the balloon. Maybe it was about all the things Sloane hadn't said, all the time that had passed. But it was also about the way Sloane looked at her now. Steady. Unflinching. Like she wasn't afraid anymore. Like she wasn't going to run.

Blake's throat tightened. The basket creaked slightly as Sloane shifted her weight. Her hand was still there, open between them, waiting.

Blake hesitated—just long enough to feel the gravity of it. Then she reached out and took it. Warm, calloused fingers closed around hers, and something settled in her chest like the quiet before takeoff.

"Okay," Blake whispered. "Then take me."

Blake forced her feet to move forward. She climbed into the basket, marveling at the fact that Sloane had done this, for her.

Sloane

When Sloane had shown up at Wine Country Tours three years ago asking for pilot lessons, she had needed a distraction. She'd spent seven years raising her cousin, and several weeks feeling lost once he left for college. The owner had laughed at her and offered her a ride instead. But she'd showed up the next day. And then the next. Finally, he'd agreed to take her on a private flight and explain the mechanics—if she paid.

It had taken three years, lots of money and hundreds of logged hours. But Sloane had gotten her pilot's license. It was one of her most prized possessions. Something she'd worked hard for just because she'd wanted it.

It had been a promise to herself that one day she'd get back to the woman she'd been before her world had shifted in an instant. Up in the air, she wasn't a caregiver. She wasn't a billionaire by horrible, horrible circumstance. She was just Sloane.

When they were secure in the basket, the team worked with her to get the balloon full and rising. They were the first to take off, the sky still inky black as they rose slowly and steadily off the ground. Sloane hated this part. The wobble, the uncertainty, the slow progression into the air. But with Blake next to her now, it was worth it.

Blake gasped when the basket jolted and her knuckles turned white as they gripped the edge. She let out a laugh, breathless and joyful, when they were just a few feet off the ground.

"How did you manage this?" Blake asked, her voice a little breathless with disbelief. Sloane snuck a glance at her and saw her staring—not at the balloon, but at her. Really looking. "I thought you were afraid of heights?"

Sloane's fingers clamped on the handle reflexively. She was *terrified* of heights. She gave the handle a firm tug, the burner roaring to life in response.

"I am," she breathed.

The fear hadn't gone away—it never did. It still crawled up the back of her neck, made her fingers twitch just before takeoff. But she'd stopped trying to push it down.

These days, it was familiar. Almost grounding. A steady reminder that some things were worth doing scared.

"Can I do that?" Blake leaned in, eyes following the line from Sloane's hand to the mouth of the balloon above them, bright and impossibly open against the sky.

"Technically? No. But, here." Sloane reached out her hand and pulled Blake closer. Up close, she smelled like rosewater and lavender. Like ten years hadn't passed. Blake's hair swirled around her, falling into her eyes. Sloane should have told her to wear a hat. She brushed Blake's hair off her cheek and Blake's breath hitched.

"Hold here," Sloane instructed.

Blake grasped the handle, and a bubble of laughter escaped her soft lips. Sloane gripped Blake's hip and held her steady. The air was cooler up here, the heat from the balloon kept them slightly warmer. But the heat pooling in Sloane's belly made the basket feel like an inferno.

"Okay, pull now." Sloane wrapped her fingers around Blake's and they pulled down. The fire burned bright above them and then there was a steady tug, like the earth going out from underneath her feet, as they lifted higher in the air.

"Sloane, this is amazing," Blake whispered. The sun melted over the horizon, spreading out like a layer of honey. The air came alive around them with mist and the promise of dew on the vines. Several hot-air balloons stretched across the sky in a patchwork quilt of color. Sloane wasn't one to take pictures. But she wished she was, just to capture the way Blake's chestnut curls whipped in the wind.

Sloane wanted to whisper all the things she hadn't been able to say. Maybe up here, where the world was silent and the ground was vineyards and hills and homes that looked more like pointillism than real life, she could say all the things she regretted. She should have called. Or that she sometimes typed Blake Miller into Google but never hit Search. Perhaps her greatest regret was not knowing how Blake had gotten a small scar on the knuckle of her ring finger. How many other things had Sloane missed?

"I know," she said instead, staring at the slope of Blake's neck where it dipped into her sweater.

"I want more of this, I think," Blake went on. "I've spent the last ten years in an office. I want to *live*. I want to travel and see the world again. Do you miss it?"

Sloane swallowed. She did miss it. And she didn't. She missed feeling like she didn't have a care in the world. And she also loved her cousin more than any stamp in her passport. "Sometimes," she said gently. "Sometimes."

"Can we see the resort from here?" Blake asked. She leaned over the basket and Sloane reached out to pull her back in on instinct. Blake's body fell flush against Sloane's with a thud.

"Easy there," Sloane laughed. "You need to keep your arms and legs inside at all times."

Blake nodded and pressed her body closer. Sloane allowed herself a moment to feel the weight of Blake's body before she inevitably pulled away.

"Over there." Sloane gestured east, and just at the base of a hill. The resort lay out like a map. The main house, the cottages, the stables. And the vineyards. The first time Sloane had seen it like this, it was still under renovations.

"Wow," Blake breathed. "It looks so small. How many times have you done this?"

"Too many times to count." Sloane smiled at Blake. Blake's eyes went soft.

"So, this is what you've been up to? Learning to fly?"

She said the words teasingly, but there was an edge to it. "Yup."

Blake had a million questions for Sloane as she took photographs of the world below. And she asked every single one. *How high would they go? How were they going to land?*

She leaned forward, rested her chin on Blake's shoulder and pointed. "We'll probably land somewhere over there." Blake followed her fingers to a light green patch of land. She nodded once, then snapped a photo before turning the camera on Sloane.

"May I?" she asked. She looked up at Sloane, a question in her eyes. Sloane nodded and pretended not to see the camera as Blake snapped a few more photos of them. Sloane's throat felt tight, wondering if every emotion showed on her face.

Because having Blake this close felt *right*. And she wasn't ready to come down from this moment.

CHAPTER EIGHT

Blake

AN HOUR HAD passed since the balloon had touched down in an enormous field somewhere in another county, yet Blake's thoughts remained suspended among the clouds. It had felt so right to have Sloane's arms around her, keeping her safe. And that terrified her.

She knew spending time with Sloane in any capacity would be tricky. Too many old feelings and old hurts to keep hidden behind polite conversations. But she hadn't expected the overwhelming surge of emotions that would follow, like a rushing river she couldn't contain inside the banks. Sloane had a way of infiltrating her mind and heart, blurring the lines between professional and past. Blake realized that had she declined Sloane's invitation and attended these events alone, she would have been the third wheel in some group, laughing and boarding a van to return to the resort.

Which would have been fine.

But she *wasn't* alone. She was with Sloane. Confident, poised and effortlessly charming Sloane Vella, who had dismissed the van caravan that was supposed to bring them back to Napa and assured Blake that a car would come for them later. With a nod, the van driver handed Blake a wicker basket with a blanket on top.

"What's all this?" Blake inquired, eyeing the basket as if it were a wild animal.

Sloane smiled. "I didn't have a chance to eat breakfast and thought we might be hungry after the flight."

Blake's heart tightened at the memory of Sloane always packing a small snack during their early morning hikes or train rides across Europe. She had always insisted it was for herself, yet would share with Blake when her stomach inevitably rumbled two hours into their adventure.

Blake rolled her eyes, suppressing the memory. She didn't need to get wrapped up in her better memories of Sloane. Or how they contrasted with her lavish displays this week. These elaborate gestures were simply a flashy display of wealth and privilege—or maybe they were just Sloane's way of controlling the narrative.

After all, Sloane was here to ensure Blake wrote a glowing review.

Despite her insistence on Blake's impartiality, she had arranged a private hot-air balloon ride for the two of them and was now spreading a thick blanket in the middle of an empty field. A gentle breeze stirred around them, and if Blake squinted, she could almost picture herself at twenty-two, two hundred dollars to her name and a single back-pack full of her life's contents.

She needed to get ahold of herself.

"Well, this certainly beats cheap granola bars and a shared bottle of sparkling water," Blake laughed breathlessly as she sat on the blanket.

"I don't know," Sloane replied, sitting beside her. She opened the basket and began unpacking the food. "I kind of liked those adventures."

Blake swallowed thickly. She didn't want to admit that she had enjoyed them, too. Because then she'd have to acknowledge how much it hurt to have it all taken away. How she had struggled to exchange her ticket and fly home alone, shattered, when Sloane had disappeared.

"Yeah, me too."

They sat in silence for a few moments. The sun crested the hill, casting a soft glow around them. Golden light caught the edges of Sloane's hair as she reached forward and plucked a strawberry from the wooden board.

"So," Blake said slowly, carefully, "did you always want to open a resort? I don't remember you mentioning it."

Sloane sighed. "Sort of. This was all my uncle's before he passed away. His name. His legacy. His fields. And I'm honored to continue his work. But the resort is my chance to do something I've dreamed up. And I want to make sure I get it right."

"Oh, Sloane. I'm so sorry." Her fingers twitched with the desire to touch Sloane. To hug her or comfort her somehow. But nerves held her back.

Something that resembled heartache crossed Sloane's face for just a moment. "It was a long time ago. But I'm not like you. I didn't get to pursue my dreams. I inherited someone else's. And it's my duty to make it right."

Blake had to stifle a scoff. Sloane had no idea what she was talking about. "I don't know that I'd call my job a dream. I create social media posts. I pitch ideas. This is my first assignment. I'm not a writer. Not anymore."

"You *are* a writer. You know that, right?"

Sloane touched Blake's wrist, and she felt it everywhere. How could the brush of Sloane's steady, thin fingers leave a trail of goose bumps on contact?

"I've always loved your words."

"You knew me for two months, Sloane. A lot has changed since then. You wouldn't even recognize my writing now. It's all hashtags and clickbait headlines."

That was a lie. Even though they'd only spent two months together, the connection they shared was something Blake hadn't felt with anyone since. She didn't believe in fate, not really. Soulmates? Definitely not. But if she ever were to believe, it would be because of Sloane.

From the moment their eyes met on that quiet, half-forgotten beach—both of them wandering, lost in different ways—Blake had felt something shift. She'd known. Or at least, she thought she had.

Within a week, they were inseparable. Their hearts and hands had tangled so tightly, Blake wasn't sure she'd ever fully untie the tethers they'd formed.

Sloane reached out again, gently brushing a strand of hair from Blake's face. Heat flared—down Blake's neck, across her collarbones, and curled low in her belly. Sloane's touch shouldn't be able to do that. Not after all this time. But, somehow, it could. Blake forced her eyes closed to fight against her desire to lean into the touch.

"I'd know your words anywhere," Sloane whispered. "I must have memorized every word you wrote that summer. I still have one of your notebooks—pages full of your doodles, half-formed verses, lines you tossed aside like they were nothing. It wound up in my bag and I didn't notice until I unpacked a month later."

"Well, I'm going to need that back," Blake said. She tried to push calm into her voice, but it still came out breathy. All the while, her heart beat rapidly at the revelation.

Sloane hadn't forgotten her. Not completely.

"Sure." Sloane gave her a lopsided smile and continued. "I whisper them to the vines sometimes, when they need some encouragement. Your words, Blake. They've carried me through…more than you can imagine. So don't tell me you're not the same. Even if you've changed—I still know you."

"Don't do that," Blake practically growled. "I'm supposed to be mad at you." Blake was mad. At least, she had been. Sloane had left her on read for nearly a decade. While she was, what, building an empire? But her touch combined with that confession made Blake weak. Sloane had saved her journal. She'd memorized her words. She saw her for who she really was. And it hurt.

"You can," Sloane breathed. "You can be mad." She tucked a strand of Blake's hair behind her ear. Sloane's fingertips on the shell of her ear sent fire coursing through her once again. "I'd be mad at me," Sloane whispered.

Blake's emotions clawed at her throat and rose up in pinpricks across her skin. She blinked rapidly. She wanted to storm off this blanket; she wanted to lay Sloane bare; she wanted to demand Sloane tell her why she hadn't called.

But one look into Sloane's wide, midnight-dark eyes made her question everything. This woman had endured the loss of her uncle, rescued a failing winery, built a resort from the ground up. She carried the weight of it all with quiet strength. Blake might've been angry, but she was also in awe. She wanted to pull Sloane close, to give her a place to rest—somewhere she didn't have to pretend.

Any chance Blake thought she had of staying strong fell away on the breeze like white puffs of dandelion spores. She leaned forward and pressed a soft kiss to the edge of Sloane's mouth, just to keep her from talking. It was barely the breath of a kiss. Not even a whisper. Still, Blake felt it in her toes.

Sloane froze, and Blake worried she'd made a terrible mistake. Maybe she'd misread the romantic balloon ride, the flowers, the champagne, and the sweet fruit bursting on her tongue. But then Sloane turned her head and opened her mouth to the kiss.

Sloane

Blake still tasted the same. Like Earl Gray and the hint of mint, and she smelled like a garden—rose and lavender and all of Sloane's better memories. She needed to catch her breath. She wanted to tell Blake everything.

She *should* tell Blake everything—about her cousin and her family obligations. But first, she kissed Blake tenderly, slowing down their frantic kisses to a measured dance. Blake kissed Sloane like she wanted to steal the secrets out of her. Sloane kissed Blake back like she needed Blake to know exactly why she couldn't.

When Blake tugged gently at Sloane's lower lip, it stung, but Sloane leaned down and into it, giving Blake exactly what she wanted.

She slid her body down next to Blake's on the blanket, fingers threading through the tangled curls now a mess from the wind and their frantic kisses. Her hands traced slow, featherlight paths over Blake's shoulder, then down her arm, lingering at the curve of her hip before ghosting over the swell of her breasts. Blake melted into the touch, nuzzling against Sloane's palm, pressing softly as if seeking to hold on to this moment before it slipped away.

Sloane loved that she knew how to tame the fire in Blake. They'd been through this before. She remembered how to talk her down, how to listen without judgment. Now she just hoped Blake could do the same for her.

But first, Sloane needed to steady her own breathing. She pulled away, just enough to clear her head. Sloane rubbed her thumb along the inside of Blake's wrist—back and forth, slow and soothing—until their breathing softened and the frantic energy between them mellowed.

"I'm sorry." Blake's cheeks flushed pink in the early morning sun. "I shouldn't have just kissed you like that. It won't happen again."

"Is that what you think?" Sloane asked, voice teasing. "That I'm mad you kissed me?"

Blake tried to look above her head at the wrists Sloane held gently but firmly. "Um, yes?"

Sloane chuckled softly, releasing Blake's wrists. The sudden absence of Blake's skin made Sloane ache in a way she hadn't expected. A way she shouldn't want.

"I don't regret kissing you," Sloane said warily. "I meant what I said. It's okay to be mad at me. It was awful of me to disappear on you. And I can't begin to tell you how sorry I am. I never should have left you alone, with only a note."

Blake sat up, frowning slightly. "Okay, yeah. I just got overwhelmed. This blanket, the breakfast… It feels like we're back in—"

"Sorrento." They said it simultaneously, then Blake laughed.

"I know, right?"

"I loved that place," Blake said, pressing her palms to her cheeks. "But we aren't there. I need to stay focused this week. I can't afford any distractions." Blake trailed off, the weight of responsibility seeming to settle over her.

Sloane nodded. "I understand." She was letting her fantasies run wild, but Blake was here on business. Sloane was trying to—maybe not win her back—but make amends somehow. She wanted to make sure they left this week on better terms. Maybe after all this, they could walk away not as friends, but at least not strangers.

Her phone chimed. She ignored it. Then it beeped again. It could be their driver. Sloane peeked and saw Nico's name flash. She sent him to voicemail and hoped he was okay. She'd call him back soon.

"Everything okay?" Blake asked.

"Yeah. My…cousin. I'll call him back."

"You have a cousin?" Blake said softly, mostly to herself. "There's so much I don't know about you."

"Hey, it's okay. Look at me." Blake didn't look up. Sloane tried again, softer. "We have a few days together. So, we got caught up in memories. It doesn't have to happen again. And we don't have to be embarrassed about it. I just know I had no idea how much I missed you until I saw you in the lobby two days ago."

Understatement of the year.

Blake snorted.

"And, you said so yourself—you need to write a review that will impress your boss. Which means you need to keep doing the resort's planned events."

"You're telling me this hot-air balloon ride was a resort event? Do you take all your guests on private rides?"

"Okay, fine. This one I got a little carried away with. A hot-air balloon ride was on the agenda—I just wasn't the pilot. But trust me, you don't want to see me as a bystander on one of those things. I'm much better when I'm in control."

"Yeah, you are." Blake blushed fiercely. "Oh my gosh, I said that out loud. See? See what you do?"

Sloane smiled wide. She adored seeing her so flustered, so alive. She loved Blake like this. No—not loved. What a silly word to pop into her mind. Sloane was careful, she had people depending on her. Nico, and Robby and the entire community. Feelings led to distractions. And distractions led to heartache and tragedy. She wasn't going to go there again.

"Blake." She said her name like a warning. Maybe for herself.

"So, what? We just keep doing these events and pretend this never happened?" Blake asked, raising an eyebrow.

Sloane sighed. "Well, I don't know that I'll be very good at that."

As if on cue, the crunch of gravel announced two cars approaching nearby. Sloane smiled at the sight of her sleek black coupe. Robby emerged, a giant cup of coffee in hand, their expression more scowl than smile. Sloane was going to have some explaining to do.

She waved. Robby nodded once before jumping into the waiting town car.

"I'm sorry. Did Robby just drop off your car so we can drive back?"

Sloane hadn't considered how it looked. She didn't get in cars with others. She couldn't tell Blake that. So, she said, "Yes. As a favor. They're not just the head of PR. They're kind of my only friend these days. Besides, I, um, don't get in cars with other people driving. And Robby knows that."

Robby truly was a good friend. Sloane had a panic attack the first and only time she'd tried to let someone else drive. Her uncle's death made it impossible for her to trust others behind the wheel. Robby had helped her through it. She'd avoid driving altogether if she could.

"Does that mean we need to leave?" Blake looked around the field as if suddenly realizing where they were.

"No, Blake. We don't have to leave. Not yet. We can stay as long as you want."

She flopped back on the blanket. "I'd like that."

Her sweater rode up slightly, exposing a sliver of skin at her waist, and Sloane groaned, looking away to hide her reaction.

"I missed you," Blake murmured. "I'm still mad at you. But I missed you. I'm glad you're okay. I'm glad I ran into you like this. Even if it still hurts a little."

Sloane's chest swelled with regret and frustration. Guilt and grief warred inside her. She thought she might cry. And Sloane didn't cry.

"I missed you, too," she finally admitted.

Blake picked up a muffin, breaking it in half. She offered the larger piece to Sloane, who took it tentatively.

"Here. Muffin peace offering."

Sloane scrunched her brows in confusion. "Is that a thing?"

"I think so. I'm pretty sure. Now we don't get to be angry anymore. We just get carbs."

Sloane's laughter rang out—big, bright and contagious. Blake snorted, nudging Sloane playfully, which only made her laugh harder. Within minutes, they dissolved into giggles. Blake wiped at her eyes and Sloane offered a napkin.

"You could always make me laugh," Sloane said.

"No, it's not me. It's us. The two of us together. Can we just have more of this?" Blake's voice softened, careful. "I'm tired of being angry. I don't want the hurt to take over the time we have. I just… I want to pause it. Just for a bit."

Sloane swallowed hard. Saying yes should have been easy. But nothing between them had been simple in a long time.

She didn't answer immediately. Instead, she reached

out slowly, tucking a loose strand of hair behind Blake's ear. Her hand lingered longer than it should have—as if afraid the moment might vanish if she let go too quickly.

"I'd like that," she whispered, voice low and steady as the breeze weaving through the field.

She reached for Blake's hand, not with the certainty she once had, but with a tentative, hopeful question. Their palms met, fingers intertwining—both familiar and new all at once. The kind of touch that remembers what was, and aches for what might be again.

Sloane went still, forehead dipping to rest gently against Blake's. Having her this close felt like something good she didn't deserve. Something she hadn't felt in a very, very long time.

Blake's breath caught and she pulled her fingers away. She took a small bite of muffin and chewed thoughtfully. "Okay, Sloane. This muffin is surprisingly good." Her eyes glinted with mirth. "Now, I *know* you didn't make it."

A derisive scoff that was awfully close to laughter escaped Sloane's lips as Blake playfully shoved her, their glee echoing in the air. It seemed Blake remembered everything, too. Down to the fact that the only thing Sloane could make was tea.

Sloane didn't know if that meant forgiveness—or simply that Blake couldn't bear to fight anymore. Sloane would worry about that bit later.

CHAPTER NINE

Blake

BLAKE WASN'T SURE what had overwhelmed her in that field—the sudden rush of feeling, the way her hand had caressed Sloane's cheek as if it was the only natural thing in the world. The kiss had caught her off guard, yet somehow, it was exactly what she needed. She hadn't realized how deeply she'd missed Sloane until she felt that pressure loosen and then swell again in her chest.

Being near her made everything else—the uncertainty, the weight of the past ten years—fade into a strange kind of lightness. Like a hot-air balloon slowly lifting inside her, expanding and carrying her somewhere higher, further than she'd been willing to go before. She was dizzy with it, nearly drunk on the sensation.

Now, alone in her room, the gauzy curtains stirred in the soft afternoon breeze drifting in from the southern-facing porch. Blake tried to imagine her life with Sloane back in it. How would they even begin to merge their lives?

Blake had worked too hard and for too long to move on from Sloane. She was really good at ignoring the ache in her chest whenever she saw a woman with sleek black hair or heard a laugh that was both soft and confident. Blake was just beginning to get back out there. She was ready to travel again. She was ready to prove to Tara (and to herself) that she was a professional writer.

As if on cue, Blake's phone buzzed rhythmically on the desk, yanking her from the moment in the field and back into the present. The screen lit up with another message from Chloe. Please send pages or notes. Tara is downing fistfuls of antacids and angry typing. Maybe she'll calm down if she hears from you. You can do this.

Blake bit her lip, hesitating. She and Chloe had become friends over the past few years. This wasn't just a friendly reminder—this was a warning from a friend. She needed to get something to Tara as a sign of good faith.

There was just one problem.

She had no pages, no neat notes—only scraps and half-formed ideas she already hated. Panic crept up the back of her throat. What if Tara hated everything she sent? Would Tara fire her mid-trip?

Maybe.

But she *was* a writer. That much Sloane had reminded her of just this morning, lying together on that blanket in the sun. The way Sloane had pulled that part of her up from somewhere buried deep, kissed it awake until it fluttered around them like something alive and urgent. Blake was a writer. She could do this. She had to.

She tapped out a quick message promising notes would come, then grabbed her pen and old, worn notebook. Sliding onto the chaise lounge on the balcony, she sank into its soft cushions, feeling the warm afternoon sun on her skin and breathing in the faint scent of jasmine carried on the wind.

The blank page stared up at her, daunting and open. What could she say? Half of her experiences so far felt like private moments, not something fit for a travel magazine. Writing it all down felt like exposing a secret that wasn't hers to tell. Maybe she'd invent a story about having a partner for this trip. None of the readers would know. But that felt disingenuous and not at all how she wanted to start her career.

Besides, she didn't want to do that to Sloane.

This morning, Sloane had been there, real and undeniable. The way the sunlight had danced in her hair, the quiet courage in her eyes, the way she'd reached for Blake's hand like it was the only anchor she had. Sloane was the reason everything had felt so perfect—so achingly perfect—even if she'd vanished the moment they returned to the resort, all mysterious and secretive about some urgent work.

A cold wash of reality settled over Blake, sharp and unwelcome. She knew Sloane was the owner of this place. Surely there were a thousand things for her to do. She didn't have time for horseback rides and hot-air balloon dates. Still, the fear squeezed her ribs, heavy and relentless. The sun sank lower beyond the hills, casting sharp shadows across the page and her thoughts. There was no one to tell this to, no one who understood this particular ache.

So, Blake let the words spill onto the page instead. She didn't censor herself. She didn't think of Tara, or the magazine or the careful professionalism she was supposed to maintain. She simply wrote—her frustrations, her hopes, the stinging loneliness she'd felt when Sloane had slipped away that morning. And how it mirrored the pain she'd felt ten years ago.

She wrote about the way she'd left behind the girl she used to be, the dreams and plans she'd had by the Italian seashore, ten years ago. How she'd come home a ghost of herself, resigned to believing the best years were long gone.

The pen scratched across the pages, sometimes fast and breathless, sometimes halting and unsure. For over an hour she poured out fragments of herself, messy and raw—some illegible, some surprisingly clear. Maybe this was just a jumble of ramblings; maybe one day it could become something. Maybe it would fade into nothing. But in that moment, Blake felt alive in a way she hadn't dared feel in years. The part of her that had gone silent was waking up, groggy and disoriented, but unmistakably present.

When she finally paused, she stretched her fingers and cracked her neck, the weight in her chest still lingering. She stared down at the pages filled with her tangled thoughts. She couldn't use them—not yet—but a warmth expanded in her chest at the relief of just getting it out. The words were hers to keep, to protect, to maybe one day share.

Her phone rang this time. Blake answered it without looking, still lost in the daze of getting words to the page. "Hello?" she said absently.

"Blake!" Chloe's whispered screech made Blake's stomach flip. "Words. Now. Your social media posts are great, but they aren't calming Tara down. If anything, they're having the opposite effect."

Blake swallowed thickly. Her posts had garnered thousands of likes. Especially the one she'd uploaded this morning with a view of the resort from above. "What do you mean? They're doing well."

"Exactly," hissed Chloe. "Don't remind her you're good at social media. Show her you are also a *writer*. Send her something to prove you can write this story."

"I'm on it," Blake lied. She glanced at her notebook, full of things she'd never print. "Five minutes. Stall her for me?"

"You got it," Chloe said with relief in her voice. "Five minutes."

The line went silent with static air. There was work to do. She opened her laptop this time and began writing again—this time with clarity and purpose. She described the resort in vivid detail, capturing the glamor, the rustic charm, the essence of a place that felt almost magical. It was honest, straightforward—the kind of writing her editor expected. And maybe, just maybe, it was a way to hold on to the day, the fleeting peace she'd found.

She didn't mention Sloane. Not the picnic, not the way her presence had changed everything. But as Blake shared the document with Tara and Chloe, she whispered quietly to herself, "Stay focused, Miller. Be professional."

Sloane

The large mahogany desk in the middle of the room had belonged to her uncle, even though Sloane was the one sitting behind it now. The room was a blend of old-world charm and modern elegance, with polished oak beams crisscrossing the ceiling and her mahogany desk cluttered with last-minute details. She'd let the designers have control of this space, thinking she could trust them. But it felt more like an homage to her uncle and less like her. As if the pressure of his legacy wasn't enough on its own.

Still, she loved the space. Through the tall windows, she could see the lush gardens below, dotted with guests enjoying the resort's amenities. To the left she could make out the stables beyond the luxurious cottages and the main resort's rooms.

Her phone buzzed, and she sighed, rubbing her temples before answering the FaceTime call. Nico's face appeared on the screen, his unshaved jaw and sleepy eyes a stark contrast to her polished appearance.

"Hey, kiddo," she greeted, forcing a bright note into her voice.

"Finally! What took you so long?" Nico's voice came through lively, a hint of playful impatience threading through. His lopsided grin filled the screen, his hair the mess of a college student who had just woken up mid-day.

Sloane straightened, brushing a stray strand of hair behind her ear as she shifted her weight on the leather chair. "I picked up on the second ring, thank you very much."

"Yeah, this time," he laughed. "I've been blowing up your phone for two days."

Her gaze drifted to the window for a moment, watching a group of guests laughing as they drifted by the pool. "Sorry, it's been busy around here," she admitted, glancing back at her cluttered desk, papers still waiting to be signed.

Nico's eyes narrowed slightly, his brow furrowing as he studied her face on the screen. "You look…different," he said, his tone shifting from playful to concerned. "Not bad, just… I don't know. Distracted? Flustered? What's going on?"

Sloane froze, her fingers stilling over the tablet she had been idly tapping. She hadn't realized how much her emotions were showing. Nico might be younger than her, but over the years, he'd taken care of her as much as she'd cared for him.

Both Nico and Sloane had expected her parents to get guardianship of Nico—and as a result—oversight of his trust. But Sloane's uncle surprised everyone when he left Nico, and everything else, to her. Her parents were furious, but when Nico told her he was pansexual, it made sense. Her own parents had been less than kind when she came out her freshman year of high school as a lesbian. Her uncle had been her safe haven, taking her in for the summers and loving her unconditionally. She was honored to do the same for Nico for all these years.

She forced a smile, trying to brush it off. "It's just the stress, you know? Big weekend ahead."

Nico didn't buy it. "Come on, Sloane. You're my cousin. I know when you're hiding something. What's going on?"

She sighed, leaning back in her chair, her eyes momentarily closing as she gathered her thoughts. She couldn't tell him about Blake. "It's just…everything's coming together, but it's a lot. I want this to be perfect."

Nico nodded, his expression softening. "It will be. It has to be." Nico shifted and held up his laptop. Sloane couldn't quite make out the words on the screen. "Because, I have news. I got it, Sloane. Look, the internship. I leave as soon as school's out."

Sloane's heart swelled with pride and cracked with nerves at the same time. An internship. In Italy. She'd helped him with the application. An entire summer learning about viticulture.

"Nico, oh my gosh, congratulations!" She kept her voice bright. An entire summer with him gone. He was twenty-two now. Next year he'd be graduating from college. He wasn't her baby cousin anymore. But Italy was half a world away. "I'm so happy for you!"

"Thanks," he said. He dropped the laptop with a thud onto his bed, his shoulders rising in a mixture of pride and embarrassment. "Anyway, I thought I'd come up. To celebrate."

She cleared her throat and folded her hands neatly on the desk, trying to pivot back to the weight of the conversation. "Nico…you know I want you here, but this weekend is going to be really busy. I won't have a minute to celebrate with you."

A pause lingered on the line, Nico's face softening, the excitement settling into something more thoughtful. "Fine…but soon? I want the full tour."

She smiled, reaching out to tuck a strand of hair behind her ear again, trying to steady her racing heart. "Okay, come next weekend. I promise. You'll get the full VIP treatment—and actual time with me."

"Deal. Just…try to have some fun this weekend, okay? Don't give me a reason to come up there!"

They said their goodbyes and Sloane sat back, eyes drifting again toward the window, feeling the overwhelming weight of everything—her uncle's legacy, her duties to Nico, the resort and the fragile hope she still held for herself.

But beneath it all was the niggling feeling that Blake Miller had shown up for a reason. Maybe fate had brought her here to remind Sloane that she had a life once, a life separate from raising her cousin, and saving a winery and taking on way more pressure and responsibility than she was ready for at twenty-two.

Blake's mere presence made Sloane want to try again. But that was very dangerous. Everything was riding on this week. Blake's positive review of the resort was going to launch Vella West into the world of luxury resorts. That, in turn, would increase the visibility of Vella West Vineyards. It was part of her next ten-year plan. Nico was counting on her. Robby was counting on her. Her entire staff was counting on her.

Sloane felt the pressure on her shoulders every day. A weight growing heavier and heavier as they led up to the grand opening party this weekend. Saturday night would be the lynch pin. If she could get through that night, then everything else would go into motion.

Sloane closed her eyes and rubbed at her temples, trying to forget the way it felt to have Blake next to her on that blanket. Despite the rational part of her brain screaming at her that it was impossible, Sloane desperately wanted to do it again.

CHAPTER TEN

Blake

THE GENTLE MURMUR of voices swirled in the air as Blake made her way toward the festivities the following evening. She wasn't sure what to expect. The itinerary had only said to dress in layers, bring a sweet tooth and leave your phone in the room.

She really hoped she wasn't in for some kind of cooking class or trivia challenge. But just east of the pool was an open area transformed into a cozy, romantic spot. It was all wood smoke and sugar in the air, with the glow of eight different fire pits, flickering in the growing twilight.

The staff had set out s'mores stations, complete with several kinds of gourmet chocolate and a smattering of different graham crackers, cookies and biscuits. There were long skewers and a variety of freshly made marshmallows in different flavors to choose from. The gourmet and luxurious upgrade of her beloved camping pastime from when she was a young girl made her heart all gooey like the marshmallows she intended to devour.

At the edge of the pavilion, musicians played acoustic guitars with familiar renditions of classic songs. It was one of Blake's best memories come to life, yet again.

Well, almost. She hadn't heard from Sloane all day.

Which was fine. Sloane had a multimillion-dollar resort to keep afloat.

And she shouldn't have assumed Sloane would show up. Maybe it would have been worse if she did. All the couples around the firepits seemed so cozy, cuddled up together and being generally adorable. Blake wasn't sure she was ready to roast marshmallows with Sloane like they didn't still have a million things to discuss. She lingered by the food station, selecting a fluffy strawberry marshmallow encrusted with tiny fuchsia sugar crystals.

She could roast it, but it looked so inviting and sweet she shoved it into her mouth, letting the hard granules of sugar dissolve on her tongue.

"There you are, Blake." Robby's voice grew louder as they moved into Blake's line of sight. They dressed impeccably and offered Blake a genuine smiled when they realized her mouth was full of marshmallow. "How are you enjoying the evening?"

She chewed quickly, heat creeping up her cheeks. A mouth full of sticky marshmallow was no way to greet the head of PR. "Oh, it's lovely," she mumbled. Robby looked at her with a knowing smile.

"May I?" they asked. Before she could respond, they led her to a luxurious outdoor seating area and sat down next to her. They brushed at their pants to ensure there were no wrinkles. Robby cleared their throat and turned slightly toward Blake. "I hope I'm not overstepping when I say that I know you and Sloane have some kind of history together and I'm sure it was very awkward to show up here and find…her."

Heat bloomed on Blake's cheeks. "Oh, no, we're not. I mean—"

"Blake, Sloane and I are friends. It's okay. And I know

she's doing everything she can to make this week as comfortable as possible for you, but I am still the PR manager. Anything you need, I'm here."

"I appreciate that, Robby. But really, we're just catching up. And since I don't have a guest with me, she's agreed to do some events with me."

Robby raised one brow with an air of amusement. "Well, that's very…nice…of her. Is she coming tonight?" Robby looked around as if Sloane was off grabbing more marshmallows.

"I have no idea," Blake answered honestly. The weight of the words pressed on her, making her stomach turn. "I've spent most of the day writing. I got sort of lost in my words."

"Working on the article?" Robby adjusted their sleeves and looked anywhere besides Blake's eyes. They seemed to keep a quiet composure, but under the surface, Blake sensed they were nervous. "You know what, never mind. The article is none of my business."

She needed to let them out of this conversation.

"You know, I think I've had enough firepit for tonight. I'm going to go for a walk and then head to bed." After a second, she added, "The bed is super comfortable." And then she cringed. *Now who is being awkward?*

"This also might be none of my business, but—I hear it's gorgeous down by the stables this time of night," Robby said softly. "At least that's what Sloane always says."

"Oh," Blake said. Her voice wobbled with embarrassment. Or maybe hope. Perhaps her heart had always known its destination for the evening.

They offered her a knowing smile. "Anyway, I'm off to check on other guests. And please, let me know if there's anything you need." They stood and handed Blake a thin blanket draped over the arm of an Adirondack chair. "In case you get cold. I don't like the look of those clouds."

The path to the stables was lit with tiny hidden lights, making the California poppies burst to life like fireflies lighting her way. The cool air, along with the smells of grapevines and earth, made her feel at ease. There was something about this place that made her want to carry her journal around with her and write until she ran out of ink. She wanted to commit it to memory.

Gray clouds gathered as she walked the path, and gratitude washed over her when she saw the barn in the distance. It was quiet down here. Blake reveled in the absolute stillness around her. She knew she was technically still on resort premises, but down here it all felt a million miles away. She ran her fingers along the edge of the railing that kept the horses corralled, the wood rough and steady beneath her fingertips.

How much of Sloane was in this setting? Did she design it herself? Blake couldn't help but let her thoughts drift to Sloane as she walked along the path. Maybe she shouldn't be thinking about that summer. Or yesterday morning. Or the way Sloane's hand had trailed up and down her spine like she knew her. Like they fit together perfectly.

Except they didn't. They couldn't. Not when Blake didn't know the whole story. Blake was going to find Sloane and she was going to ask for the truth. She was going to tell Sloane she needed to know why she'd left so suddenly ten years before. It would have taken two minutes to wake her up. Blake could have gone with her. Something. Anything.

Blake needed to know why she hadn't written, hadn't called, hadn't bothered to look her up *once* in the last ten years. She felt like she was losing her mind. Sloane was trying to pretend like nothing had changed.

But everything had changed.

Robby might be trying to bring them together, but they clearly didn't know the whole story. And if Sloane didn't want to tell her, after all this, then she would be okay. She could still write this story. She could still do the article. But whatever else was blooming between them would need to end.

Even if it hurt.

Blake turned in a circle, suddenly aware that the sun was beyond the hills and the lights from the resort didn't travel all the way down this path. She felt a raindrop on the back of her neck. And then another.

Out of the corner of her eye, a lamp flickered on behind the curtains of the tiny cottage—the same one she and Sloane had been in just the day before. The sight tugged at her, pulling her toward the house like a tide she couldn't resist.

Maybe this was her chance. A chance to get some answers. To see if Sloane was finally ready to talk.

Blake's heart kicked up. She was terrified Sloane would turn her away.

But at least then she'd know.

Sloane

The kettle rumbled with the beginnings of a whistle as Sloane clicked on her desk lamp. She tilted her neck to one side then the other, trying to work out the knot that had been between her shoulders since the call with her cousin.

Sloane never lied to Nico. Or told him to stay away. But Blake had crawled back under Sloane's skin messing everything up. From the moment she'd shown up in the lobby Sloane hadn't been able to think. And Nico would realize something was different if he showed up.

Thick rain drops splattered against the windowpane. Sloane ensured the window was closed and said a silent prayer that the outdoor events for the evening had wrapped up. What was it tonight? *Firepits.* Sloane closed her eyes and cursed under her breath. She had planned to surprise Blake, but she'd gotten too wrapped up in piles of paperwork.

She dropped into her chair and stared at the pictures framed on her desk. There was one of her with her parents (something she couldn't bear to throw out), a black-and-white photo strip of Sloane and Blake when they were at a fair in France (which she'd held in her hands so many times over the years Nico finally framed it for her), and one of her and Nico from fifteen years ago. When he was still a little kid and she was a moody high schooler.

She'd been staying with them for the summer, the way she had every summer since she was just a kid, and he was sticky with a popsicle dripping down his chin and she was laughing with her eyes closed.

Her uncle and Nico had been a safe space when her parents didn't even want to try to understand her. They'd spend their summers learning the language of vines and the earth, scattering wildflower seeds and singing classic rock. She remembered that day like it was yesterday. Bunches of grapes on the vine, dirt under her fingernails and love.

And now Nico was in college, older than she had been in the photo, and he still had her whole heart. She still worried about him. She'd still do anything for him. *Everything* for him.

She switched off the kettle and began her routine of making evening tea. It was the one pattern that hadn't changed for her in the last fifteen years. Peppermint tea, a book and ten minutes to herself. It didn't matter if she was traveling or working on the road, tucked away in city apartment or wrapped under an old quilt in this tiny home that felt more hers than anything else in the world. Ten minutes, peppermint tea and some deep breaths. Then she could go on.

She'd fix things with her cousin as soon as this week was done. She'd bring him up and they'd ride Winnie and Rhett and everything would be okay. Except, Sloane knew that wasn't true. Yes, she could fix things with Nico. But Blake's presence this week was rewiring Sloane. She'd never be the same after this. She wasn't going to be able to move on twice.

Maybe she shouldn't have kissed Blake on that blanket. She had wanted to. When Blake's hand brushed centimeters from her mouth, the air crackled with unspoken desire, and all it took was a slight turn of her head to press a kiss into the edge of her mouth.

It had been a terrible idea.

Hell, she probably shouldn't have taken her in the hot-air balloon to begin with. But Blake Miller had a way of turning Sloane inside out and making her want to do anything, *anything* to see her smile.

She had just taken her first sip of tea, the warm peppermint filling her nostrils with steam, when three knocks reverberated on the door. Sloane jumped, her tea jostling dangerously close to the edge of the cup and stared at the door.

Robby knew to leave her alone when she was down here. The other employees didn't even know this space was hers. Most assumed it held storage. Or maybe a second office for Sloane. She set her mug down and raced to the door, worried something had gone wrong tonight. Worried, she realized, about Blake.

She opened the door just as another knock came. And there, with rain water dripping down her neck, was Blake.

"Blake, what are you doing here? Are you okay?"

"I don't want you to disappear on me again."

She tried to pull her inside, but Blake stood firm. The rain picked up. But Blake didn't seem to notice. Her eyes flared wide as rain began to fall harder. Her curls were plastered to her neck and she was holding a blanket to her chest.

"I don't know what you're talking about. I'm right here."

"I know I said I needed space to write today. And I did. But I think I told you to stay away because I am scared. But I am also scared you're going to disappear on me again."

"Blake, I'm sorry. I—"

"You have your whole life up here. You have this place, and your friends and your plans. I've spent ten years wondering what happened to you and you've just been up here playing hotel."

"You don't know *anything* I've been through. I—"

"You're right. I don't. Because you never told me. It hasn't been easy for me, okay? I've been in the dark for ten years. When you disappeared, it wrecked me." She shivered and Sloane tracked a rain drop as it ran down her neck and soaked into her collar.

Blake shook her head and seemed to register for the first time that she was dripping wet. "Look, I didn't mean to barge in on you like this. I just need to say that I need more from you. Or…nothing at all."

Blake turned to leave and something snapped inside Sloane. Anger and heat and frustration all at once. That must have been why she reached out, grabbed Blake's wrist and tugged.

"Wait," she choked out.

Blake's pulse hammered beneath Sloane's fingertips. Her gaze met Sloane's with fire and heat and hurt. Sloane wanted to take it away. Even if just for a moment.

"What do you want from me Sloane?" Her chest heaved and her eyes flitted to the point where Sloane was still holding on.

"I don't know—I can't think. I just don't want you to leave," Sloane ground out. She shouldn't be doing this. "At least stay here until it stops raining."

"You can't just demand things. You can't take and take but never give—" Blake began. But then she stopped. Sloane must have looked wrecked because Blake took a step closer, her hand falling from Sloane's grasp.

"What do you *want*, Sloane?" she asked again. Her voice was rough with a hint of frustration. Or was it desperation?

All Sloane knew was that she was tired. She was tired of being strong. Tired of fighting the entire world. Tired of denying that she wished she could do it all again differently.

"Ten years ago…my uncle died." Sloane huffed out the words she still hated to say. "He was in a car accident. It all happened so fast. And I had to get back here. He put me in charge of this. Of everything. I didn't have a choice." Sloane felt her throat tighten as she fought back tears. "So, I've been here. And I was a coward. And I should have called—"

Blake reached out a hand and smoothed away the tears on Sloane's cheeks. When had she started crying?

"I should have called." Her voice was hollow. She couldn't look Blake in the eyes. Blake was right. About all of this. Sloane didn't know what she wanted.

"Hey, it's okay." Blake's voice was a whisper. "I'm sorry. I didn't mean to make you cry. Here, I'll come inside, okay? I'll come in."

CHAPTER ELEVEN

Blake

BLAKE WENT INSIDE. She was tired, and cold, and the rush of sugar was crashing out of her system. All she really wanted to do was collapse into Sloane's arms, but Sloane needed her now. Even if she didn't know how to ask for it.

Sloane's uncles death wasn't a surprise, but seeing the burden it had placed on Sloane definitely was surprising. She seemed hollowed out. A shell of the woman she'd been before.

"I can't talk about it—all of it—right now. It's too much. My uncle, my parents, my cousin." Sloane's breath came out with a hiccup and Blake shook her head. She didn't need Sloane to tell her everything *tonight*. She just needed to know Sloane wasn't going to run away.

For now.

Blake knew that days from now, when she was back home, she might regret this. When she was sitting at her desk, or walking along the booths at a farmer's market, or lying in her bed alone at night, she'd remember this exact moment.

She held Sloane in her arms, pressing kisses to the top of her head. "Thank you for telling me," she murmured. And "I'm here to listen." And "Oh no, I'm getting you all wet."

Sloane let out a small laugh at the last one before catching Blake's gaze. Sloane's eyes burned with a stubborn intensity; a fire ignited by some kind of decision. "I don't care about that. I'm just glad you're here."

"I'm pretty sure I have a puddle beneath me," Blake said with a little shiver. She was certain that she had smudged makeup at her eyes' edges, and that her sheer, wet top hinted at a lace bra underneath.

And Sloane had noticed it, too. Sloane's eyes, glassy and unfocused, met hers; Sloane's neck bobbed as she swallowed hard. A wave of warmth and delicious anticipation spread across her as she recognized her own desire mirrored in Sloane's eyes.

Sloane led her to the small sofa. The rain steadily pattered on the roof, but the cottage was quiet. They sat together, not talking, just taking in the moment. Blake rubbed Sloane's shoulders and murmured soothing words in a hushed voice. Soon the quiet turned into something more, something charged and undeniable. Blake shivered as chills ran down her spine.

They were alone, pressed together, practically clinging to one another. And Blake had never felt so vulnerable, and so certain she needed more.

"You're soaked. You must be freezing. Come here." The burn Sloane's fingertips left in their wake as they pressed into Blake's hips sent her reeling. Heat pooled in her stomach when Sloane's hot breath ghosted along the shell of her ear.

But even knowing how much this might hurt next week, Blake didn't stop. She just needed more. She needed the sharp dig of Sloane's fingernails across her shoulders. She needed more of Sloane's moans. She needed time to stop, and she needed to feel alive again.

"Sloane, I…" Blake needed to tell her. That it had been a long time. That maybe she'd forgotten how to do this. That even though she was hurting and maybe a little bit angry, she still wanted this.

"Shh," Sloane whispered along Blake's neck. A request. A demand. Maybe she needed this just as much as Blake.

"I just need to know you want this. That you want me."

Sloane ran her nose along Blake's throat. "There isn't a single part of me that doesn't want this, Miller. But say the word and I'll stop." She trailed the words like kisses up her neck, along her ear, into her hair. "Tell me to stop."

"Don't. Don't stop." The words tumbled from her mouth in a sigh. Sloane growled in agreement.

Blake decided to stop thinking. Later, she would catalog the quaint space they were in. The mug of tea still steaming on the edge of Sloane's desk. An old patchwork quilt folded across the top of a small sofa. The crystal hanging in the window that would no doubt throw a thousand rainbows across the room tomorrow morning when rain wasn't pelting against the window.

For now, she concentrated on the pressure of Sloane's mouth against hers. Blake cupped Sloane's face, wanting her to know she was in this. She was here. She bit down gently on Sloane's bottom lip, sucking it into her mouth and running her tongue along the edge. She felt Sloane loosen her grip, just a bit, and slump into Blake.

She remembered all the ways she could undo Sloane. Sloane liked to be in charge, but if Blake pressed just right, demanded just enough, Sloane would surrender. And she was surrendering now. "Take me to your bed," Blake demanded.

Sloane grabbed her hand and practically teleported to a small bed on the other side of the room. Blake wanted to laugh, but it made sense. All this luxury surrounded them, but Sloane had a hand-me-down handmade quilt and a single pillow. It was just so Sloane.

"I've missed this," Sloane said as she kissed along Blake's shoulder. "I've been thinking about you all day. I wanted to kiss you this morning. I didn't want to stop. I never want to stop with you."

"You can have me," Blake responded. She was pretending. She just wanted to be as close to Sloane as possible. For as long as possible. "Take it all."

Blake realized, for all the kissing they'd done, they were both still fully clothed. Blake in a long, rain-soaked skirt and cropped tank top, her hair spilling down around her. Sloane in a sleek pair of black joggers and a tank top she no doubt wore under her work shirts. It was tight, threadbare black, and she was braless, her nipples straining against the fabric.

She pushed Sloane down on the edge of the bed and Sloane sat quickly—willing and obedient. Blake thrilled at the idea that with one look she could demand anything she wanted from this woman. It made her feel powerful and also delicate, like she was being given a precious gift. She got to see Sloane like this, when no one else did.

Sloane's hand immediately ran up Blake's inner thigh, coasting higher and higher. Damn her for wearing a skirt. It made it all too easy to widen her stance, suddenly hungry for Sloane's fingers to move higher and higher.

"Can I touch you?" Sloane begged. She pressed her face into Blake's soft stomach and kissed absently. Blake loved how desperate Sloane was. Those words, along with the way her fingers teased at the soft cotton of her underwear, made Blake want to say yes.

Sloane was more confident now than before. She made

relentless eye contact with Blake when she spoke. It was unnerving and wonderful. Sloane looked at her like there was no one else in the world. Like she'd been waiting ten years to ask these questions. As if she didn't already know the answer.

Blake knew how much she wanted Sloane. She knew she'd say yes to anything Sloane asked. That her heart was right there for the taking, and that terrified her. Sloane could have it all. Blake knew it. She wanted Sloane to find out, too. "I need to feel you, Miller. Please?"

It was that word, that please, that made Blake break. There was no control when it came to Sloane. She would give her anything she wanted. She nodded helplessly, already pressing her body closer, giving Sloane the access she wanted.

"I want you," Blake panted into her mouth. "Touch me. See what you do to me."

Sloane

Sloane blocked out everything else in her life and focused on Blake's exposed stomach. Her soft curves had been driving her wild for the past few days. Well, the past decade, if she was being honest. And now that Sloane had successfully stripped Blake down to almost nothing, she noticed a smattering of freckles just above her right hip, the stretch of time across her belly and the goose bumps that ran up her thigh when she used her hands to spread her legs wider.

Blake was different, and also exactly the same. She brushed her fingers along the edge of her hip and bit back a smile. She felt the same, soft and responsive and inviting. Even with all the changes, she was still Blake.

Sloane had changed, too. In all the ways Blake had softened, Sloane had become harder. Her lean muscles were taught from hours of riding and gardening. Her legs sturdy from walking the vineyards. Her skin had a constant sun-kissed bronzing from hours outside. She wondered if Blake noticed, if she cared.

"Let me," she whispered. "Missed you." With a whimper Blake leaned down and covered Sloane's mouth with hers. Blake tasted like cabernet and the wild rain that still clung to parts of her skin. Like all the picnics they hadn't had yet. When Sloane delicately pulled Blake's underwear to the side and ghosted against Blake's skin, she gasped into her mouth.

"Please, Sloane. Please."

Sloane murmured her pleasure at Blake's request and pressed into her warmth. Blake wrapped her arms tighter around Sloane's shoulders and slumped into her a bit more. Sloane loved the feel of Blake's body giving itself over to her. She moved her mouth and her hands to all the places she knew would work for Blake before pulling back at the last minute.

Over and over again. She didn't want this to end. She didn't want to give either of them what they desperately craved too quickly. Because then this would be over. And Sloane needed Blake's body against hers for as long as possible. All night if she could.

Blake whined against Sloane's mouth in frustration. Blake must have realized what she was doing because she ground her body down into Sloane's lap, coaxing Sloane's hand to move toward her center. Sloane chuckled at Blake's not-so-subtle attempt to guide her to right where Blake wanted it most.

Yes, Sloane knew exactly what Blake was doing. Blake

didn't like to be teased; Sloane remembered that well. But Sloane absolutely *lived* for teasing Blake. And she was going to have to deal with it. Just this once.

"How do you remember me so well? How do you remember just what to do?"

"I told you," Sloane said, her voice barely a rasp. "I remember everything about you, sweetheart. Every freckle, every moan, every word you've ever written."

They stayed together like that for a while. Blake seeking more, more, more. Blake bit down on her lip and closed her eyes and then proceeded to explore Sloane's body. Her neck, the curve of her shoulder, the small space between her two breasts.

"Please, I need it," she whimpered. And Sloane would give it to her. Eventually. She'd give her anything she wanted.

When Blake got close to the edge, her moves becoming more frantic, her body seeking the pressure she so desperately desired, Sloane withdrew. She smirked up at Blake.

"Why did you stop?" Blake groaned. Her eyes were bleary and her body was still moving and she looked so gorgeous when she was pouting.

"Because," Sloane said. She stood and wrapped Blake in her arms, turning her so she was against the edge of the bed. She slowly sat her down and laid her back. "I want you like this when you come apart. I want to taste you."

Every one of Sloane's dreams for the last ten years couldn't compare to this moment. She was worried she'd built it up in her head. That she'd turned Blake into some kind of dream girl that reality couldn't compare to. But Blake in her bed, under her hands, was better than her memories. Blake was here. And she was real. And time had only made her softer, more tender and rougher all at once.

Blake ran her hands through Sloane's hair and talked her through what she wanted. For someone who claimed she wasn't pursuing her dreams, she knew exactly what to tell Sloane to do. Sloane pressed kisses up her stomach, up the curve of Blake's neck, and finally sealed her mouth over Blake's.

"I've missed you—I've missed us." Sloane's admission flew out before she could stop it. Sloane felt the lump forming in the back of her throat. Blake looked up at her, her eyes a bleary mess after bliss and maybe a little exhausted.

"Come here," she whispered with a gentle tug. She pulled Sloane down. And then Blake took her time. She touched every part of Sloane as if she were made of glass. As if she might disappear. No one had touched Sloane with this level of care in so, so long.

Blake looked at her like she might disappear. "I'm not going anywhere," Sloane whispered into Blake's hair. She wasn't sure what she meant by those words, but she needed Blake to know. She wasn't going to run. She wasn't going to disappear.

"Shh," Blake whispered. "Later." And then Sloane didn't think anymore. All she could register was the gentleness of Blake's touch, the softness of her lips, and the profound sense of forgiveness and understanding in their embrace.

And then she was close and then she was gone. Shattered into a thousand pieces and glad about it. Her eyes stung and she swore she wouldn't cry. Blake covered her in more kisses and pulled the quilt up around both of them.

Sloane's eyes kept drifting shut. Blake curled into her

arms, soft and warm. It made Sloane feel soft and warm, too. Pieces of her coming back to life that hadn't been pliable in over ten years. There was something about Blake Miller that made Sloane *want* to be soft.

Maybe that's why she had run away? She could have called Blake. She'd stared at her contact in her phone so many times. But she had turned to stone ten years ago. It was what her cousin needed. It was what her parents had demanded. If she let one crack show, they would have swooped in and demanded access to Nico. To the money. To everything.

If she had reached out to Blake, she wouldn't have been able to make it through. But maybe now she could melt, just a little. She could find a small part of her to be vulnerable. And let Blake see all of her.

Sloane fell asleep with her face pressed into Blake's hair, her mouth whispering unintelligible promises as Blake slept. Promises she hoped she could keep.

CHAPTER TWELVE

Blake

THE WALK BACK to the honeymoon suite was lit with the last moments of silver moonlight as the crickets serenaded Blake with their chirps. *Tell us everything*, they seemed to sing. But Blake just pulled the quilt closer as she continued up the path, past the main resort, and to her cottage.

She hadn't meant to fall asleep in Sloane's arms, but the bed had been so warm, and her body had been so thoroughly wrung out and the rain had lulled her into a deep sleep.

She woke in the last few moments when bottomless night transitioned to deep gray morning—maybe her body was still on hot-air balloon time—and inspiration had struck. She'd wrapped the blanket close and slipped away.

In the edges of gray dawn, Blake sat down at the table on her secluded porch and wrote. She captured the day, weaving moments into a tapestry, a history, a patchwork quilt of their memories stitched together like the orchards and vineyards from a thousand feet in the air. More words that would go nowhere. But still, writing them down made the moment seem more real.

She'd nodded off in her chair, the quilt around her shoulders, her eyes heavy and her hand no longer able to hold her pen.

When she woke, she was freezing, the furniture coated in morning dew and the entire world smelling alive, awash in the rain from the night before. Her body was sore in the most delicious way and she stretched out like a cat, searching for a patch of sunlight.

A soft knock announced her daily breakfast delivery, which was already waiting on the doormat of her front door. This was the kind of pampering that felt like too much. Like they knew her too well. A tray laden with an array of fruits, local honey and warm scones. There were fresh flowers arranged in a whimsical pattern. Wildflowers burst out of the jar haphazardly. Blake snapped a few photos on her phone to save them for a post later. She took the tray to her small table on the porch and drizzled honey over a scone.

I could get used to this. She knew that this wasn't what being a writer was like all the time. She knew one-week stays in luxury resorts wasn't the norm, but still. There was no shortage of things to write about. Or photos to take. Or reasons to swoon. Not that she would be writing about Sloane in her article.

Her article. She needed to buckle down and write some more words for Tara. She stared at her journal, bursting with all the things she couldn't say. All the things she couldn't put in a travel review.

Her phone chirped on the nightstand and she reluctantly left the morning tableau to see who it was. It could be Sloane. It could be her mom, trying to confirm plans for her end of summer visit. When Blake had come home that summer, she'd been too sad to visit her parents. But her mother must have known something was wrong. She'd shown up a week later with a carry-on full of face masks and romance novels.

She didn't ask any questions. She just sat next to Blake, side by side. She'd planned a girls' trip like that one every summer since. Blake always looked forward to them.

But it wasn't her mom. It was her boss. All the warm, fuzzy feelings Blake had stirred up vanished in an instant. The message read, Call me asap. She also had missed two calls. She must have read the notes.

Blake took a deep breath and messaged back, Ready when you are.

A video call immediately came through. *Crap.* Blake was not expecting a FaceTime from her boss at nine o'clock the morning after, well, after last night. But she couldn't back out now. She sat down on the patio and pressed the green answer button.

"Tara. Good morning—"

"Blake, I'm going to get right down to it."

This wasn't shocking. Tara always *got right down to it.* It was a signature phrase other people used in the office when impersonating her. Maybe Tara was going to give her more inches for the article. Maybe she wanted to make it a segment. Maybe Blake had impressed her so much she was going to give her her next assignment now.

"I'm going to need you to start from scratch."

"I'm sorry?"

"We can't use any of this. We're a travel magazine. Our readers want to know about the location, they want to feel like they're there. They don't want…this."

Blake's head spun with confusion. "Tara, I'm not sure what you mean. My notes *are* about the location. The options. What this place has in store. I thought the writing was okay?"

"Yes, Blake, the writing is fine. But this article needs more than fine. There's no heart here. It's like reading your grocery list. Or an edit list. Or—" Tara snapped her fingers and Blake flinched. "That's it. You're writing this like you're written a caption. I need you to write it with heart."

Blake felt her own heart in her throat. She couldn't write a story with heart and not tell the whole truth. Her feelings for Sloane would be apparent. She wouldn't be impartial. A story with heart…meant a story she couldn't tell. "With heart? I'm a journalist, Tara—"

"You're also someone who told me to take a chance. You told me you could do this. Are you telling me you *can't* do this? Because I can pull this. I can bring you back. If it's too much, tell me now."

Blake's stomach flipped. She couldn't give up on this. Not now. "I can do this, Tara. I have more notes. I have more…ideas. Give me a few more days."

Tara's lips pursed on the other end of the line. "You have two days. If I don't have something workable in my inbox in forty-eight hours, I'm pulling this. I gave you this chance because I saw something in you. Don't make me regret this. Vella West was a big enough name to pull in our advertising quota for the quarter."

"Okay, just send me my notes and I'll get going."

"Blake. There are no notes. My note is *start over*. Give me something I can leave notes on. Understood?"

Blake swallowed and willed her eyes not to water. "Understood."

"Good." Blake could feel Tara's stare through the phone. She was scrutinizing her the way she'd scour over layouts and spreadsheets. "And for goodness' sake, do something with your hair. You look like you were rolling around all night. I hope this isn't how you're traipsing around a five-star resort. You're an ambassador of our brand when you're there, Blake. Don't forget that."

And with that, the call ended. Blake slumped back in the chair and let out a shaky sigh. This was bad. This was really bad. Blake needed a plan. She would take a shower, make a list and head down to the lobby to see what else she could scope out.

Blake had been so careful to keep her emotions out of her writing. Because if she didn't, she knew anyone could see how her feelings for Sloane were all over everything she'd ever done. Why did Sloane have to work for this hotel? Why did she have to be here?

This wasn't doing her any good. Sloane *was* here. She *did* work for this hotel. And she wasn't going anywhere. Blake didn't *want* her to go anywhere.

Well, that was a sobering thought. Blake needed caffeine. She needed a reset. She would shower, review her notes, and then find Robby. Maybe they could tell her about some of these local products—she could include it in her write up. That would be sure to add some heart. She uploaded photos of the resort and got to work.

A few hours later as she entered the lobby, her phone pinged with a message from an unknown number. She opened it wearily.

I hope you don't mind, but your number was in your file.

I had a really good time last night. Unexpected. But good.

This is Sloane by the way.

Blake's stomach flipped.

I have meetings all day, but I'd love to join you on the train tonight. There are some things I want to tell you. I know I waited too long, but I think it's time we talked.

* * *

Blake didn't respond right away, but her heart surged with hope. The wine train had been included in the itinerary, but Blake had been too nervous to ask Sloane if she planned to attend what was essentially a Very Romantic Date.

Excited butterflies flittered through her as if she was the lavender outside. Sloane was finally keeping her promises.

Sloane

The pile of papers on Sloane's desk was so high it was leaning like a wobbly Jenga tower. Robby was going to kill her if she didn't get things under control, and fast. There were multiple requests for interviews, two vendors hoping to have their wine stocked in the restaurants and more than one reporter sniffing around. Sloane didn't do interviews. She didn't do public. If she could be a silent investor in this hotel, she would.

She just wanted to make it magical. And not get any of the credit. Her phone buzzed and she lunged for it. She'd texted Blake hours ago and still hadn't heard back from her. She was practically vibrating from nerves and caffeine. She'd felt a bit sweaty and a bit unnerved when she woke to an empty bed. Her sheets still smelled like lavender and rose. Being surrounded by Blake's smell was sweet, sweet torture.

Sounds great. She had responded. A new nervous wound around Sloane's chest.

"Why are you staring at your screen?" Robby's voice brought her back into the moment. She closed her messages and tossed her phone on her desk. They weren't going to get anything out of her.

"Come to think of it, you were smiling when you walked in earlier. This wouldn't have anything to do with the gorgeous woman staying in the honeymoon suite, would it?"

"Of course not," Sloane said, not meeting Robby's eyes. She felt them glare at her as she sorted the papers. "Just a good day, I suppose. Everything is on track."

Robby snorted and sat in the chair across from Blake with their legs crossed and a knowing scowl. "Boss, we've got a problem."

"Oh?" Sloane began staking papers into neat piles, ignoring the way Robby's glare was penetrating to her soul, as if they somehow knew what she'd been up to the night before.

"Yes. Someone sent room service to Blake's room this morning. And apparently there was an arrangement of flowers."

Sloane's shuffling paused for just a moment before she continued making haphazard piles. Of course, Robby knew about the breakfasts. Robby knew everything. "Well, that's thoughtful."

"It would be—if the hotel had done it." Robby took the last sip of their coffee before setting it down gently on the edge of the desk. "It's not part of the package. It's not in the agreement."

Sloane felt her body flush. She had just wanted to do something nice. Blake loved fresh flowers. Sloane could still remember the way Blake would daisy-chain together what were basically weeds, turning them into bracelets or flower crowns for the two of them in Italy. She'd spend hours weaving them into the perfect jewelry. Sloane felt cherished whenever Blake put a bright green stem around her finger or tucked a flower behind her ear.

She hadn't meant to become this secret deliverer of pastries and peonies. She'd snuck into the resort's garden and gathered some blooms together the best she knew how before sneaking into the kitchen and swiping some scones and local honey. And she'd been doing it all week.

"It's not a big deal. Just a simple breakfast. And, honestly, a really terrible floral arrangement."

"Terrible?" Robby raised a brow. "Now, I *know* it was you."

"I admit nothing."

"Well, I hope it *wasn't* you. Because then it could be seen as bribing a reviewer. You took her in your hot-air balloon. You ignored the group protocol. And now you're sending flowers. This could ruin us. If it goes sideways—"

"It's not going to go sideways."

"How do you know that?"

"Because, I—" Sloane opened and closed her mouth several times. "There's no way Blake would do that. Blake would know none of this was a bribe simply for a good review."

Robby smiled sadly at her. "Oh, babe. I really hope you're right."

"Right about what?" A cheerful voice called from behind Sloane.

Sloane's stomach fell to the ground. What was Nico doing here? He swept into the room with the air of an emcee, dropping his leather overnight bag into the chair and pulling off his sunglasses.

"Nico?" Robby raised an eyebrow and gave Sloane a look. "I didn't know you were coming."

Her cousin shouldn't be here. He should be in school. He should be studying. "What are you doing here?"

He scooped Sloane into a hug and pulled her close. He kissed the top of her head before lifting her in his arms and squeezing tight. She still remembered the day he realized he was taller than her. During his sophomore year, a sudden growth spurt brought him to six feet tall. It had him whooping with glee in the kitchen, teasing Sloane about how he could reach something on the top shelf for her. He was such a dork.

"I think what you meant to say was, baby cousin, I missed you. I'm so glad you're here for my big weekend."

She laughed as she held him at arm's length and took him in. He looked tired, but his eyes seemed focused and he seemed okay. "Yes, that, too. But I thought I told you to stay back and study."

"Pffft. And miss this? No way." He stared down at her desk and frowned. "Besides, I knew something was wrong when I called." He tugged on the front of her bob and tucked it behind her ear.

Dammit. Sloane, when stressed, had a habit of tucking and retucking her hair. He must have seen her nervous tic and now he was here, missing classes, just to check on her.

Nico studied her face, searching for answers. "Okay, that's it." He tugged on her hand. "We need to get you out of here. Why are you stuck at your desk? It's your big week."

Sloane was not going to tell her cousin that she'd actually spent the last forty-eight hours flirting and kissing and, well…she wasn't going to tell him any of that.

"Come on. I want to see my horse. I want to get some fresh air. Robby, you coming?"

"No. I have a lot to do. You two catch up." Robby waved them off as they took over Sloane's job of organizing papers. "Sloane, please don't forget about what I said."

Sloane swallowed thickly. Robby was right. She was putting everything at risk each moment she spent with Blake. But she just wasn't sure if she was going to be able to stop.

CHAPTER THIRTEEN

Blake

WHEN BLAKE ARRIVED in the lobby for the wine train, Robby greeted her with a town car. Worry crept up the back of her neck. If Robby had called for a car, then Sloane wasn't coming.

"Right this way, Ms. Miller."

Blake crooked her head at them. She didn't want to ask and risk disappointment flashing clear across her face.

"Don't worry. Ms. Vella is planning on joining you," Robby offered anyway. "She had some business to attend to and will meet you at the train."

Blake nodded and forced a smile. "Thank you, Robby. I appreciate it." She kept her tone light and didn't let her face drop until after she was tucked into the car. This is what she had been worried about. Sloane was a very busy person. Her life was full of obligations and commitments. And those things were more important than Blake.

When she arrived, a vintage train, completely renovated, waited on the tracks. Each car glimmered in the evening light, reminiscent of the old trains she'd seen in museums with formal dining cars and luxurious textiles.

Once inside, Blake realized she was in a private car. There was a couch, an elegant table setting and plenty of space to walk around. The windows were ajar, letting a soft summer breeze trickle through the windows. Everything looked custom selected: antiques in warm woods, brass fixtures and modern amenities. A bottle of wine chilled next to the table in an elaborate silver tub.

Someone cleared their throat from the far end of the car and Blake realized she wasn't alone. Sloane stood and walked toward her. Her hair was down and she wore a soft black camisole with wide white dress pants. She looked softer somehow, and absolutely gorgeous. The business suit was nowhere to be seen.

"Wow, look at you," Blake said in awe. "You look stunning."

A flash of pink crept up Sloane's neck. "Thank you," she murmured. Blake felt Sloane's gaze travel down her and back up again. "And I'm sorry about earlier. I had some family come in unexpectedly."

Blake bit the edge of her lip. Sloane had promised her she was a priority this week. And she wanted to believe her. But her tardiness had awoken worries from the past. "Family?"

"My cousin, Nico. He showed up unexpectedly and we spent some time catching up. But still, I should have called."

Blake's need to respond was drowned out by the train whistle. An announcer's voice came over the loudspeaker of the train. Blake wasn't even sure where the speakers were hiding. "We'll be leaving in just a moment. Please make sure you're seated and ready to enjoy the rambling vineyard hills, the incredible view and the romantic setting. Welcome to Napa."

Sloane gestured to the leather chesterfield sofa and the two women sat down. The train creaked and rumbled before starting on its path.

"This all feels so surreal," Blake admitted. "You, this train, this view."

Sloane poured her wine and passed her the glass.

"Tell me about your writing. I want to know more."

Blake knew she needed to be honest with Sloane. She just wasn't sure where to start. Or how much to share. "I'm not a writer. I mean, not anymore. Or maybe not yet? I've worked as social media manager for the last ten years. And I'm good at it. So, every time the opportunity arose to write, I didn't apply, didn't pitch my ideas. I love parts of my job. My colleagues are the best. But it always felt like there was part of me I was closing off. After you left—"

"Blake, I—"

"No, it's okay. You don't owe me anything. I did this to myself. After you left, I felt lost. I felt like I didn't deserve my dreams. So, I didn't pursue them. But seeing you this week, seeing what you've accomplished. It makes me realize my dreams are worth pursuing."

Sloane smiled sadly at Blake and shook her head. "Your dreams *are* worth pursuing. And I love my work now. I love my cousin. I can't regret how things turned out. But I wasn't pursuing a dream. I was cleaning up someone else's. When my uncle died, I had to hit Pause on everything of mine. It took years to untangle his finances. I was working my own job, managing his estate, and I became Nico's guardian. It was…a lot for me."

"Sloane, I didn't know." Suddenly, her cousin's arrival made a lot more sense. Sloane was practically a parent. Of course, she'd make time for her cousin. Blake tried to remember what she'd been like at twenty-two. There's no way she would have been ready to take on being a full-time parent on top of everything else Sloane had. The weight of it would have been too much for her.

But Sloane had managed it. Somehow.

"I know. I didn't tell you. I didn't tell *anyone*. I didn't want anyone to think I wasn't capable. Especially not my cousin. I'm all he has left. My parents were awful about it. They didn't understand why they didn't get custody of my cousin and oversight of the estate."

"I mean, that was a lot to put on you at twenty-two."

Sloane shrugged. "Maybe. But no one expected my uncle to go so soon." She took another sip of wine and pursed her lips together. "But we did okay. Nico and I. We figured it out together. And now he's in college. He's almost done. And I was able to open the resort."

"It is pretty amazing." Blake lifted her eyes to meet Sloane's. There were soft lines at the edges Blake hadn't noticed before. No doubt from years of trying to be everything to everyone. "*You're* pretty amazing. I can't believe you did all that."

"I'm so glad you like it. I have you to thank for all the details."

"What do you mean?"

Sloane fell quiet, her fingers twisting gently in her lap as if the truth had to be coaxed out of her.

"Every time I had to make a decision," she said softly, "I thought of you—of that summer. I'd ask myself, '*What would Blake love?*' The light in the room, the linens on the bed, even the shampoo. I think, without even realizing it, I was trying to bring it all back. Like if I could just recreate it, piece by piece…maybe you'd come back. Maybe your heart would recognize it and find its way to me."

She looked up then, her eyes full and open, golden sunset catching the tears she hadn't let fall.

"And you did."

The words settled into Blake like a warm breeze

through tall grass—soft and unexpected, stirring something she'd long tucked away. She had dreamed of this moment for so long that the idea of it had become abstract. But this was real. Sloane was here, speaking the kind of truth that tasted like late summer and first love.

And still—her heart fluttered with nerves, with disbelief, with fear.

It was so much to take in. So much to hold. This woman, this moment—it was everything she'd wanted. And yet, it made her feel fragile in the most exquisite way, like something delicate and treasured that might break from too much feeling.

She leaned in, closing the space between them with a kiss as soft as evening light on wine-dark lips. It was gentle, careful, full of memory and longing. She could taste the berries and the currants—the same ones they'd picked that first week—bittersweet and lush, alive with possibility.

"You didn't have to re-create the past," Blake whispered, her voice barely louder than the breeze. "You just had to pick up the phone."

"I know," Sloane breathed, her voice catching. "I know. I just didn't know how to say I was sorry. Or how to ask for another chance. I never really believed you'd show up."

Sloane

Sloane hadn't planned on telling Blake any of this—at least not in this order. She planned to start with: *My cousin is here.* And then, *by the way I was his guardian.* And then, *I sort of still am.* But Blake's floral dress wrapped around her body in the same way so many dresses had that summer. When they'd hopped a train and traveled from one side of Europe to the other. When they'd woken up in Rome and decided that they needed to leave for the coast immediately. Both of them giggling and shoving clothes into each other's suitcases, kissing and laughing and free.

Blake still had wild soft curls, a wide smile and eyes the color of the sea. Sitting with her tonight was like revisiting a dream. But better. Because Blake had a scar on her finger and a few silver threads in her hair and Sloane knew she was really here. This wasn't a dream.

A server brought them dinner covered in silver trays. They moved to a small rectangular table along the windows, draped in velvet and fine china. They spent time focusing on the now. Sloane told her about Rhett and Winnie. How stubborn he had been. And how he insisted on staying.

Blake's eyes sparkled with mirth as she teased Sloane about having so much in common with her horse. The conversation flowed as easily as the wine, and Sloane couldn't imagine a better way to spend a night. It was nothing like their stilted dinner less than a week ago the night Blake arrived.

"I like you like this," Blake said, hiding a smile behind her lips. "You're more confident now."

"It's Robby." Sloane sighed. "They won't let me get away with anything less."

"Well, good for them." Blake laughed with abandon and took a bite of dinner. "So, what's next for you, Sloane?"

Sloane felt nerves tense in her stomach. She didn't want to think about what came next. She knew what her uncle would have wanted. Expansion. She knew Robby and Nico were both depending on her to do whatever it took to ensure Vella West stayed profitable and secure. And she knew, deep down, that all she wanted was a quiet cottage, a cup of tea and someone to share it with.

She shook her head. "Nope. No work talk tonight." She dropped her napkin onto the edge of the table and stood, holding out her hand. "Come with me?"

Blake blinked at her before dropping her own napkin and taking her hand. "Where? We are on a train."

"Trust me."

She opened the door at the end of the car and the rush of air swept into the room. They weren't going fast; it was barely a ramble as they slowly passed by hills and groves of trees. They stepped into the neighboring car, which wasn't really a car at all.

When Sloane invested in the wine train, she'd insisted on creating this space. A private dining car with an adjoining courtyard of sorts. It was an open-air train car with live plants and strung lights and three-hundred-sixty-degree views of their surroundings. Soft music played around them, a slow, gorgeous Italian love song.

The music couldn't muffle Blake's intake of breath. "Sloane—I—this song." Sloane stepped closed and offered her hand. Blake took it and Sloane pulled her close.

"Dancing with you outside the Cafe de Sol was one of my best memories. Dance with me, again?"

Blake nodded, teary-eyed, and fell into Sloane's embrace. Sloane was just enough taller than Blake that her head rested perfectly in the crook of her neck. They swayed back and forth as the song played all around them.

The air was full of earth and vine and the edge of summer. The moment just before the harvest. Sloane knew that smell well. She inhaled deeply, also getting hints of Blake's shampoo and bodywash. Her heart clenched, knowing this was the moment she would remember most when this was over.

When Blake was gone, when she inevitably left for home, when her article went viral. Sure, she was in Sloane's arms now. But there was no promise of tomorrow. And Sloane couldn't even ask for it. She was the one who'd left ten years ago. She didn't get to request more. That had to come from Blake.

She just needed to make Blake want to ask. She pressed a gentle kiss into Blake's hair and felt her own eyes prick with tears when Blake squeezed her hand.

"This is so magical. Do all your guests get this special treatment?" Blake teased.

"No one else has ever seen this space," Sloane confided. "I had it remodeled about a year ago. Sometimes I take the train and just sit here. But no one else."

"Why not? It's beautiful. You could make it part of the resort. You could—"

Sloane shook their head. "Sometimes it's nice to have something just for you."

As if on cue, a faint buzzing filled the space. Blake pulled away, confused. Sloane tried to ignore it, but her phone buzzed again from her hip. She fished the phone out of her pocket and saw the obvious hurt on Blake's face.

Robby.

Why was Robby calling?

Sloane silenced the call and held it in front of her. "I'm so sorry," she murmured. "It's Robby."

"You can answer it." Blake backed away more, heading to the bench at the edge of the courtyard train car. She *should* answer it. Something could be wrong.

"Robby, unless this is an absolute emergency, I have

full faith in you and Nico to take care of things until I'm done with this date."

The phone was silent for a moment and then Robby's voice said quickly, "You got it, boss."

Sloane swiped the screen and turned her phone off before pocketing it again.

"What are you doing?" Blake said. "It could be important. What if something happened?"

Sloane strode over to Blake and wrapped her in her arms, she crowded her against the wall.

"Robby is very capable. They can handle anything for two hours. I want to be here with you."

"Are you sure?"

No, she wasn't sure everything would be okay. But it would get fixed if it wasn't. Besides, she was in the middle of a train ride. It wasn't as if she could stop the train and helicopter back to the resort. Well, to be fair, she probably could but she wasn't going to.

She was here, with Blake in her arms. And she intended to make the most of it.

"I'm sure. I'd like to introduce you to Nico tomorrow. If that's okay with you? But for now, there's nowhere else I need to be than here with you." She ran her nose along Blake's jaw and pressed a kiss just behind her ear. "Please Blake, can I kiss you?"

"You don't have to ask, Sloane. This mouth is yours. Do whatever you want."

Sloane raised one brow and kissed her. Slow. She drank her in. "We have about ten minutes before they show up with dessert."

"There's a lot we could do in ten minutes."

Sloane kissed her again; a smirk played at the corner of her lips. "Yes, I intend to find out."

CHAPTER FOURTEEN

Blake

BLAKE NEEDED A dose of reality. For days, she'd been swept up in a world of curated luxury—meals comped, spa treatments like dreams and views so flawless they looked staged. And Sloane. Sloane's lingering looks, gentle touches and constant presence in Blake's thoughts had been a welcome distraction.

She had to get off the resort. Everything around her was a carefully curated moment—the view from her balcony, the pastries at breakfast, even the plush terry cloth robe hanging in her bathroom. Now that she knew the truth behind Vella West's creation, it felt like the past was everywhere, pressing in from all sides.

Robby arranged for a car to bring her to downtown Napa. Buildings clustered closely together, a mix of classic brick architecture and bright windows. Custom-painted signs and open doors welcomed shoppers. It struck Blake how San Diego was less than ten hours away, yet it felt like an entirely different world as she walked the streets of Napa.

She turned down Front Street, passing a bistro with soft jazz spilling from hidden speakers and a couple clinking glasses on the patio. The river ran along the street. The slow and steady movement of water brought a sense of calm to her frazzled thoughts.

Sloane had a cousin. She had been his guardian. And she'd raised him for the last ten years. That was why she hadn't called. It was both satisfying and incredibly sad to know that Sloane hadn't meant to disappear. Blake hadn't done anything wrong either. But she'd spent the last ten years dissecting every moment to figure out why Sloane would disappear on her. It didn't make the hurt less, but it helped her understand.

As she wandered, an overhead sign caught her eye—the same insignia that adorned the shampoo and bodywash bottles from the resort's bathrooms. She ducked into the shop; her footsteps soft on the wooden floor. The air was warm and fragrant—lavender, cedar, something citrusy she couldn't quite place. Shelves were lined with soaps wrapped in linen and tiny bottles of custom scents, all catching the late afternoon light and glowing like little hidden treasures.

The shop was soft, inviting, the kind of place that made her want to curl up with a book and forget the rest of the world.

"Looking for something in particular?"

The woman's voice was soft with a bit of rasp, like a quiet breeze on a lazy afternoon. She stepped out from behind the counter, her round glasses catching the light. Her fingers were adorned with a smattering of silver rings and she waved them around as if each one held a story.

Blake hesitated, then pulled the brown glass jar from her bag and held it out to the woman. "I'm staying at the Vella West. Do you have more of this rose and lavender blend?"

The woman's smile softened, but there was a flicker

of something deeper in her eyes as she cradled the jar, turning it slowly.

"That one's special," she said quietly. "Not usually out on the shelves."

Blake raised an eyebrow, curiosity blooming alongside a sudden ache. "Oh?"

The woman glanced up, thoughtful. "It was made custom. A collaboration with the resort."

Blake's breath caught, though she didn't speak. She clutched the tiny bottle to her chest. Perhaps this woman could tell Blake something that would ease her anxious heart. "Do you know the owner well?"

The woman paused, then laughed softly, as if recalling a secret. "Sloane Vella? I've known her since she was a kid. Came out here every summer, riding horses, running wild in the hills with her uncle, rest his soul."

Blake's fingers tightened around the jar. The girl the woman was describing, that was the Sloane she remembered, too. A bit wild. A bit less controlled than the woman she'd been spending time with this week.

Sloane must have felt so lonely in those first few years. It must have been awful. To be twenty-two, your mentor gone, the weight of the world on your shoulders.

"She seems to have done just fine," Blake said, her voice barely a whisper.

"Well, yes she has," the woman agreed. "Grief has a funny way. It doesn't go away, just grows around you. Do you…know her?"

"I do," Blake said. "I mean, I did. Before."

"Well, in that case…" She looked Blake up and down with consideration before selecting a different jar from a shelf behind her. She placed it into a brown paper bag, folded the top carefully and handed it to Blake. "Take this one," she said softly.

Blake wasn't sure what to say, so she nodded, clutching the bag as she murmured thanks and stepped back into the golden light.

Outside, the sun was dipping low, casting long shadows across the quiet street. Blake wandered past shuttered bookstores and vibrant art galleries until she found a cafe tucked between two old stone buildings.

She ordered an tea she barely tasted and sat beneath the green canopy, pulling a worn linen-covered notebook from her bag—the one she carried everywhere but rarely opened. Its soft edges reminded her of the journals she'd kept during her younger, braver days, full of uncertain hopes and Sloane's name scribbled in the margins.

Her pen hovered for a long time before she set it down and huffed out an annoyed breath. She could do this. She needed to finish her article. She flexed her fingers. Maybe some lotion would help. When she unscrewed the lid, she was hit with peppermint, rosemary and…tea tree oil. She was hit with Sloane. Sloane up late at night sipping peppermint tea. Sloane, who would spend the mornings picking vibrant herbs, their scent a delicious mix of sweet and savory, but she was clueless about how to transform them into a meal. Blake rubbed a dab of lotion into the back of her hands before taking one more breath.

The scent, the memory, the fragile thread between past and present hit her all at once. Words poured out of her— anger, heartbreak, yearning and a quiet hope she hadn't dared voice. Page after page, her handwriting grew messier, ink smudged where her hand pressed hard. It wasn't a pitch. It wasn't neat. But it was hers. Honest and raw.

Maybe this was what she needed before she could figure out what came next. It hurt to rip open the past and sift through her memories. It hurt to think about returning from Europe, alone and heartbroken. Through blurred vision and a second round of tea, she wrote it all down.

When the sun slipped below the hills, casting the streets in amber and lavender, Blake tucked the notebook away and made her way back toward Vella West. The resort glowed like a storybook scene—warm lights flickering behind ivy-laced windows, the hills bathed in soft twilight.

The lobby was quiet when she arrived, the hush that settles at day's end when guests shower off sun and salt and settle with wine.

Sloane sat behind the desk, a tablet propped in front of her and a half-empty glass of sparkling water close by.

Blake hesitated, then stepped closer.

Sloane looked up and smiled, her eyes widening just a bit as she took in Blake. "How was your trip into town?"

"Good," Blake said, not knowing how to put the afternoon into words. Blake glanced down at the bag, thumb brushing the folded top. "Can I ask you something?"

Sloane spoke with no hesitation. "Anything."

"The flowers on the breakfast trays. The ones with herbs mixed in. Do you know where they come from? A woman at the apothecary gave me this scent and it reminds me of the herbs and flowers I get every day."

Sloane blinked once, like the question caught her off guard, then recovered, straightening a notepad on the desk.

"Well," she said, "some things are meant to stay a little magical for guests, Miss Miller."

"You said I could ask you anything," Blake challenged. There was a story here—not the kind for her article— something deeper. Something distinctly Sloane. She needed to know the answer. "And I want to know."

Sloane sighed and dropped her tablet. The look in her eyes was part defeat and part satisfaction, as if she had been hoping Blake would press the issue.

"Fine. There's a wildflower garden past the olive tree grove at the far perimeter of the property." Sloane leaned in close. "It's not really open to guests, but no one's going to stop you if you wander. Just…be kind to it."

Something settled deep in Blake's chest. This was a clue. A secret. Sloane was letting her in even more. She felt dizzy with the possibility and the promise. She needed to see this place. "Will you take me?"

Sloane

Blake was in her garden.

More than the stables, more than her tiny cottage, these wildflower fields were hers. The place she came when grief was too big to hold in her arms. She would come out here and wander and talk to the flowers. She'd whisper words to them and they never judged.

Sloane stood watching Blake from a distance, heart pounding with the weight of everything left unsaid. The olive trees swayed gently overhead; their twisted trunks bathed in the soft amber of evening light. Their silver leaves rustled like whispers in the wind, as if the earth itself was trying to comfort her. But nothing could settle the storm inside her.

Part of her wanted to walk away. She could leave Blake alone out here and retreat to the safety of her office. Or her house. She could have dinner with Nico. She could balance some books. There were a million things she could be doing.

But she crossed the distance and approached Blake.

"Well, this is it," Sloane said. Blake turned, her fingers brushing the fragrant stems of a lavender bush and smiled at the sight of Sloane. It made Sloane's heart feel too big for her chest.

"This is what?"

"My grieving spot. My…everything spot. This is where I come when I need to… I don't know. When I need to not be anywhere."

Sloane had left for Europe planning to soak in the wisdom of the world. She was going to wade into the waters of viticulture slowly, learning side by side with her uncle when she returned. But the universe had made other plans.

Blake reached out and took Sloane's hand. The simple gesture meant more than words. Sloane squeezed and then let go.

"I know I apologized for not calling you," she murmured to Blake, her voice barely more than a whisper. "But I don't regret it. I need you to understand why I closed myself off. I had to plan my uncle's funeral. Take care of Nico. Everything fell on me. I didn't want to burden anyone else. I'm *glad* I didn't put that on you."

She pulled her arms tightly around herself, as if she was still holding the fractured pieces of her heart together. She had felt broken, scattered, the life she'd built for herself disintegrating with every responsibility that had fallen on her. But Sloane never let anyone see just how shattered she was inside. She'd been strong for Nico, for her uncle's employees, for the land. And it was too much. It was all too much for someone to carry alone.

"You could have—"

"You wouldn't have wanted that," Sloane cut her off, the words slipping from her lips without thinking. "I couldn't ask you to be part of this. I couldn't ask you to help carry this weight with me. This weight I'm *still* carrying with me. Every day. I have hard days. I have days when all I want to do is cry. I can be messy. And mean. You don't want that."

Blake's sharp retort came swiftly. "You don't know that. You never gave me a chance."

Sloane's heart clenched, guilt and regret knotting in her stomach. Blake wasn't just angry—she was hurt. And Sloane had never meant to hurt her. Her responsibilities were hers alone; no one could blame her for not telling a girl she'd been kissing along the coast for two months. That would have been ridiculous.

"We'd only known each other for half a summer," Sloane whispered, the lie tasting bitter on her tongue. It had felt like more, so much more. They had connected in ways Sloane hadn't anticipated, and now that connection was back. And it felt like a life raft in a sea of chaos.

"I don't know how to do this," Sloane confessed, her voice trembling, vulnerable in a way she rarely allowed herself to be. "I'm used to things just being thrust on me. I never wanted to burden anyone. I just—I want to protect you. I thought if you saw all of this—this mess, this chaos—you'd walk away."

A decade of silence stretched between them; Blake stood motionless, the air thick with the scent of old regrets and unspoken words. The silence felt thick enough to suffocate. Finally, Blake's voice cracked through the stillness, quieter than before but sharp with emotion.

"You think I wouldn't have wanted to be a part of all of this?" Blake asked softly, her words falling from her lips like a challenge, raw with the pain Sloane hadn't seen. "You think I wouldn't have wanted to be there with you? I'm not the one who walked away, Sloane."

Sloane's chest tightened, and she stepped forward, not sure if she was seeking Blake's forgiveness or if she just needed her close. The gulf between them felt wide, and Sloane wasn't sure how to bridge it. She reached for Blake's hand, but the distance between them remained. "You shouldn't have had to be part of this," Sloane whispered. "I didn't want to burden you with *my* problems, with Nico, with everything."

Blake took a shaky breath before finally speaking, her voice thick with emotion. "You think I wasn't burdened too?" Her words hit harder than Sloane had expected, and they left a mark. "You think I don't know what it's like to carry everything alone?"

Blake's eyes glistened with unshed tears, and she took a slow, deliberate step toward Sloane, closing the space between them. "I had dreams, you know. I was chasing them with *you*. I was going to write about our adventures. And then you disappeared."

Blake blinked and let out a slow breath. Her next words came out softly, as if she was choosing them carefully. "When I got back to New York, my drive was gone. I didn't want to take on anything that wasn't a guarantee. So, I spent way too many years working as an intern, fetching coffee for the people who were taking risks and doing the writing. It took me ten years to work up the courage to try again. You're not the only one who felt abandoned, Sloane."

Sloane's chest ached at the admission, the rawness of Blake's words cutting through her like a knife. She reached out, trembling, brushing a tear from Blake's cheek, before cupping her face gently. "I never meant to make you feel abandoned. Never."

Blake closed her eyes for a moment, letting the cool air

wash over her, as if searching for the right words. When she opened them again, they were filled with something deeper—something Sloane could no longer deny. "You didn't trust me. Not with all of you. How can I trust anything now?"

Sloane took a steadying breath. "I didn't trust *myself*," she confessed. "I didn't think I could handle losing you. I didn't think I could handle—any of this."

Blake's eyes softened, but the vulnerability still lingered in them, raw and unspoken. "But you did. You did this all by yourself," Blake said, her voice barely above a whisper. "And you should be so damn proud of what you've accomplished. We were both so young, and stubborn and selfish. But we aren't those girls anymore. And you can choose. Do you still want to be alone? Or are you ready to let me in?"

"Blake, I—"

"It's okay, take some time." Blake pressed a kiss to Sloane's temple. Even then, Sloane could feel her pulling away. Putting some distance back between them. "I'm not asking you to have all the answers. Why don't we both take some time? I'll see you tomorrow night at the reception."

With a final glance, Blake turned and walked away. Sloane stood frozen in her sanctuary, the scent of rosemary, thyme and lavender thick in the air. Blake was asking for more than Sloane thought she could give. She hadn't wanted anything for herself in a long time, hadn't dared to hope. But Blake wasn't asking for promises—she was just asking if Sloane was willing to try, to imagine a future they could build together.

And that was terrifying.

CHAPTER FIFTEEN

Blake

BLAKE TOOK THE time to read over her notes from the week at the resort. There were a few pages she could use for the article. She had a collection of images, pages of handwritten notes, and she spent a few hours forming them into something readable before getting ready for the grand opening reception.

She sent them off to Tara with a brief outline for the article. She hoped it was enough to piece together when she got back. Now she had two stories. The messy, vulnerable truths scribbled into the margins of her notebook. And the polished, refined notes of a glamorous week in Napa. Neither felt complete. They were two halves of the same story. The best week of her life, the most complicated week of her life.

And she wasn't sure how Tara would react to the half she had sent. But she didn't have time to think about that now. She was already late for the culminating event of her week at Vella West: the Grand Opening Gala.

Blake had been nervous about tonight the entire week. Large crowds made her anxious, especially because she wouldn't know anyone. As PR manager, Robby invited the who's who of Napa Valley, San Francisco and beyond to debut the large reception area. She knew it would be lavish, and gorgeous and overwhelming in the best way.

She also knew this was it. After tonight, she returned to San Diego. She'd be saying goodbye to Sloane, to Robby, to Winnie and Rhett. And she wasn't ready.

As Blake stepped onto the smooth stone of the Vella West pavilion, the hand-laid tiles cool beneath her feet, she took a deep breath. She was done up in an ethereal blue dress that clung to her hips and strappy heels she would never have chosen herself, yet were somehow perfect for the elegant space. She knew this moment would forever be etched in her memory; a blend of unexpected harmony and unforgettable beauty.

Blake had wandered this terrace a dozen times over the past week, memorizing its lines, its angles, the way the light stretched across the stone in the late afternoon—but tonight, it was unrecognizable. Gauzy drapes caught the breeze like sails, casting fleeting shadows across the vineyard view. Lanterns flickered from the low branches of the old oaks, their golden glow warming Sloane's face as she chatted with someone across the terrace. Music drifted—low, lilting, familiar—and for a moment, Blake couldn't tell if it was the melody or Sloane's smile that made her chest tighten. The scent of night-blooming jasmine curled around them, and beneath it, the earthy sweetness of ripening grapes.

And above all, the people. There had to be hundreds—gliding through sunset-dappled courtyards and lingering beneath the branches of old oaks. The crowd was a curated kind of eclectic: soft linen trousers paired with vintage leather boots, silk skirts brushing the tops of scuffed Converse, wide-brimmed hats worn without irony. There were floaty dresses in desert pinks, sharp suits in rumpled cotton, bold prints that clashed just enough to feel intentional. Hair in every shape—slicked back, coiled in buns, left wild from the wind—framed faces that radiated ease. Northern California through and through. A little bohemian, a little luxury, all of it worn with ease.

Blake scanned the scene, a knot tightening just below her ribs. Everyone looked so effortlessly at home, as if they belonged here—laughing over glasses of pinot noir and chardonnay, all made from Vella West vineyards. Every hand held a stemmed glass, every smile seemed real. And for a moment, she wondered if she could belong here, too.

It had been less than a week since Sloane reentered her life, and already she was imagining them tangled up together again. Blake couldn't—wouldn't—be the one to ask. Yesterday, she'd asked Sloane to think about what she wanted. Blake could only hope that Sloane had listened. If Sloane wanted something with Blake, she was going to have to be the one to say it. Blake wasn't about to risk another rejection. Her heart wouldn't survive it a second time.

She searched for Sloane in the crowd, hoping she could find some kind of confirmation of Sloane's feelings with a look or a smile, when another person caught her attention. Blake had seen him earlier in the week, just once—from a distance, talking with Sloane around the horse stable. She hadn't expected to see him again tonight, let alone here, lingering near the edge of the lantern-lit terrace in a suit that looked custom tailored for his frame. He couldn't have been over twenty, with the boyish, unfinished look of someone still growing into himself, the kind of kid who tried to stand straighter when someone looked his way.

While everyone else looked dolled up for the night, he seemed at ease. His hair flopped to one side, and just the right amount of ankle flashed between the bottom of his pants and the cognac leather oxfords. But when he turned and the terrace lights caught his face, Blake felt the recognition land sharp and strange in her chest. The eyes. Dark as midnight, thoughtful, unmistakably Sloane's.

Nico, she realized. It had to be. Sloane had said she wanted to introduce them, but everything had gotten so hectic. The resemblance was too strong. And suddenly, in this dreamlike version of the place she thought she'd come to know, Blake felt time fold in on itself—past and present brushing close enough to stir something she wasn't ready for.

Her indignation with Sloane softened as she took in the way she cared for him. She wrapped herself around him almost protectively. He must have been so young. Probably still in elementary school when Sloane had become his guardian. This whole time Blake had been picturing a peer for Sloane. Maybe someone a few years younger. But this kid, he was a kid truly, looked at Sloane as if she hung the moon.

Sloane had shattered her heart. Given the way her chest ached now, she knew she'd always treat it like a healed break, covering it instinctively if danger came too close. Sloane hadn't meant to cause all this pain—she knew that now—but the ache couldn't be helped.

Maybe there was a part of Sloane that was still aching, too.

Blake wanted to run to her. To tell her she was sorry. That of course Sloane had done what she needed to do to survive. She wanted her to know she was proud of her, and proud to know her, in any capacity Sloane would have her.

Although she hoped it would be more. She wanted more.

Blake's heart cracked open with a sudden, brutal clarity: She was still in love with Sloane. Sloane, who was kind and selfless and always trying so hard to do the right thing. Sloane, who had shattered her heart in the name of someone else's healing. Blake wanted to go to her, to hold her, to say she was ready for whatever came next.

But the thought stopped her. Because whatever came next could be the moment it all fell apart again. She loved Sloane. That much was undeniable. And she understood why Sloane had left. She could trace every choice, every fear, and still it didn't quiet the ache that had taken root in her chest. Understanding didn't fix it. And love didn't protect anything. It only made the pain more precise.

Her heart pulled toward Sloane, desperate to close the distance and speak all the things she'd buried just to stay standing. But beneath that urgency, something colder anchored her in place. Because opening herself up again meant risking everything.

But before she could decide, Nico was walking toward her. Arms outstretched and smile wide. She braced herself for impact.

"You must be Blake," he said with a smile. A perfect smile. Sloane's smile. "I'm Nico, Sloane's cousin."

Blake held out her hand and shook his. "It's so nice to meet you," Blake said, her heart in her throat.

"Yeah, it's nice to meet you, too. Sloane wasn't going to tell me who you were, but I recognized you from your picture." He squinted at her and nodded. "You look the same. Plus, when you walked in and her eyes went all—" he held his hands up in front of his own eyes and mimicked little fireworks "—she didn't have to tell me."

"Oh!" Blake was a bit taken aback with how open and honest this kid was. Not at all like the Sloane she'd first met. Not at all standoffish. Maybe this was what having a loving and supportive parent figure did for someone? "Thank you?"

"For sure," he said. Nico exuded an aura of boundless loyalty and good cheer, like a golden retriever, all sunshine and warmth. Big smile, bright eyes, easily distracted. "Oh, look. They have my favorite." He motioned toward a woman with a larger platter. "These ones, with the little pieces of truffle and the fig jam. They're the best."

He took a napkin and placed four crostini haphazardly into his hand. The server smiled patiently before leaving, presumably to refill their tray. He held one out to Blake, but she waved him off. There was no way she was going to stand between Nico and his crostini.

He happily chomped down on the toasted bread before saying, "But I just wanted to introduce myself. And say thanks for being so cool about Sloane."

"I am very cool."

"Yeah, I told her not to come, but she told me that since I've never been before she wants to make sure I get settled."

Blake's brain whirled with so many questions. "I don't mind," she said, with absolutely no idea what he was talking about.

"I even told her to bring you with us, but she said no. I'm sure you have a bunch of stuff going on anyway. Who wants to repeat their European vacation with their kid cousin tagging along, right?" He rolled his eyes. "If you change your mind, I'm not that bad. I promise."

Blake's whole world whirled around her. Sloane was leaving for Europe? And she didn't want Blake to come with. Not that Blake expected Sloane to invite her. It wasn't like they were together. Even so, it stung to know they'd spent the entire week together and not once had Sloane mentioned travel.

"Sloane is going back to Europe?"

Nico shoved yet another crostini in his mouth and nodded as he chewed. "Yeah, I have an internship there this summer for viticulture." He held out a crostini to Blake and she waved it away. She couldn't eat anything. Not now.

She'd asked Sloane to take some time, to think about what their future could be. And she hadn't even mentioned a big trip. How were they ever going to have a chance at a future if she couldn't be honest with her. It wasn't the fact that she was leaving. It was the fact that, yet again, Sloane was leaving her in the dark. Prioritizing her own self-preservation over something they might build together.

Blake thought they'd had some kind of breakthrough in the secret garden. Sloane had been real and honest with her—or so she thought. Maybe she'd just been building up to the moment she'd leave again.

"I'm sure the two of you will have a great time," she said. She took a shaky breath and a sip of white wine, but she didn't taste it at all.

"Yeah, it's going to be great. But for real, I've never seen Sloane this distracted. And I mean that in a good way. She's usually all *work, work, papers, frown*. I think last night was the first time she's ever just…taken the night off." Nico looked almost dazed as he counted back in his mind. "It was kind of cool. And Robby totally handled it."

"I think you lost me," Blake admitted. This kid was hard to keep up with. Her brain was still fixated on this trip to Europe that Sloane had failed to mention. She felt her whole body tense with frustration.

"Never mind—it's all good. I need to go find more snacks." His eyes roamed the open space in search of another server. Blake was still trying to figure out the last thing he said. "Promise I'll get to say goodbye before I head out tomorrow."

"I will try. I'm heading out tomorrow, too," Blake said. She had regretted the early morning flight, but maybe now it was a good thing.

"Wait. You're leaving? Already?"

"Yeah, I live in San Diego. I'm just up here for work. For the article."

Nico frowned and looked Blake up and down like he didn't believe a word she said. "Well, I guess you better go find Sloane now then."

And with that, Nico waved and jogged off to a young woman in black pants and a crisp white shirt, holding a tray of tiny glass cups filled with a rainbow smattering of crudités.

Blake didn't want to be the person standing alone at a glamorous party, so she took off toward the outskirts of the pavilion, hoping a walk near the flowers would ease her racing mind.

Sloane

Nico was up to no good. Sloane could tell from the lop-sided grin and the way he kept flirting with one of the catering staff. She'd have to talk to him later about expectations. He was an adult and he'd have to start behaving that way. At least occasionally.

Listen to her. She sounded like her parents. No. She sounded like *a* parent. There was a difference.

And she was a parent in many ways, she supposed. Raising someone for ten years, even if they weren't *yours*, certainly meant something.

"Boss, this is all brilliant. Well done." Robby came to a stop next to Sloane and tipped their wineglass to her.

Sloane pressed her lips together. "It's Sloane. And we both know this event was all you. Especially last night. Thank you for handling the caterers last minute. And the electrical issues in the Hyacinth Cottage."

"Of course."

"Even if it did mean moving Nico into my tiny house."

Sloane had not been happy to come home after midnight and discover her cousin snoring on her couch. If she had known he would stay with her, she would have fixed up a proper bed. He'd requested a room at the resort so he could be close to the gym and the pool. But Robby hadn't set one aside for him since technically he wasn't supposed to be here for another few weeks.

But she'd taken one look at the six-foot water polo player on her couch and sighed before rousing him and moving him to her bed. Then she'd made up the couch and slept there herself. She still had the crick in her neck to prove it.

"Perhaps tonight, *you* could find a different room?"

When Sloane looked at Robby, their eyebrows were practically flying away. "Robby. I don't know what you're talking about."

"Oh, please, boss. Anyone can see the two of you are smitten with each other. And I was wrong. When I told you to be careful. She's clearly in love with you. And don't think I didn't do some detective work. That's *her*, right? She is the woman from the summer that—"

"I don't want to talk about it, Robby. That summer was a long time ago." When Sloane had taken over guardianship of Nico, she'd needed help. She was still finishing grad school, trying to juggle so many things, and Robby had answered an ad for a personal assistant. They were still in college, underqualified, blew the interview and crashed into a planter in the front yard. But they'd also made Nico laugh for the first time in months.

Sloane hired them on the spot. And then got them the training they needed.

"Frankly, boss, I don't care what you want. You saw something in me ten years ago. You gave me a job, you encouraged me to grow and now I get to manage PR at a world-class resort."

"And you're qualified to do it."

"I know, but that is not the point. The point is, let me return the favor. I see something in you, when you're with her. She brings you to life in a way I've never seen before. If you have even a small chance to keep this going, you have to try. You deserve to be happy. You deserve to go after the things you want."

"Even if I wanted it… I'm not ready. You heard Nico. He got into his internship program. In less than a month he's leaving. He needs me. I can't just—"

Robby silenced Sloane with one pointed stare. "Taking a few weeks off to go to Europe is not an insurmountable challenge. Nico wants you to be happy. Your uncle would want you to be happy."

Sloane took a deep shaky breath and swiped at a tear. Nico *needed* her. She couldn't let him down. Not the way her own parents had let her down when they dismissed her sexuality and her dreams. This was a chance for her to get it right. "I just want to do right by him. I want him to know I'll always be there."

"And you will be, but he's twenty-two now. And you're only thirty-two. It's okay. Let her in."

Sloane nodded once. She thought of all the things she'd

been through in the last ten years. Taking over guardianship. Overseeing her uncle's estate until it could become her cousin's. Knowing she was thrust into a world where she wasn't sure she belonged. Knowing she had a million things to prove.

She'd been strategic with investments, she'd done her part, and then she leveraged them to open this resort. And in four years, he would be twenty-five. He would get his inheritance. And then maybe he wouldn't need her anymore. At least not in the same way.

And it also filled her with hope. Nico was an adult now. He'd always need her, but not in the same way, not as much. And admitting that meant admitting she *could* be with Blake—if she was willing to fight for her.

But the thought of losing Blake. Again. After how they'd reconnected? That was just as unbearable. Was it possible that there could be a world where she could have it all? She could be there for Nico, take care of this resort and make room in her for life for Blake?

"Maybe you should go talk to her, before she goes?"

"What are you talking about?"

Sloane's eyes snapped up and she searched for Blake in the crowd. But all she saw was golden brown curls bouncing up and down as Blake left the party.

CHAPTER SIXTEEN

Blake

BLAKE GRIMACED AS she made her way along the lavender path and back to her cottage. The broken heel of her strappy sandal dangled pathetically in her hands. She should have known better than to wear these shoes in the uneven terrain. But they'd gone perfectly with the dress Sloane had sent her earlier in the week, and she couldn't resist. It was worth her current hobbling situation.

And, she had to admit, the wardrobe malfunction did give her an excuse to step away for a moment. Nico hadn't held back when he'd told her all about Sloane's plans to leave town. She was still reeling from the news when a group of partygoers had accosted her with questions about the resort and her connection to it. Blake had felt the creep of embarrassment in her cheeks when she remembered that technically her connection was through her employer, *Elsewhere Magazine*.

The group had *loved* that. They had tons of recommendations, many for their own vineyards or businesses, and Blake wasn't sure how to handle the attention. She was used to being behind the camera, behind a screen, not people-ing at a grand gala.

Blake had worried she wouldn't fit in tonight. Sloane's

friends were used to the polished, sun-soaked world of Napa's luxury resorts, with their manicured vineyards and carefully orchestrated parties. Maybe she was just a stranger who'd stumbled into Sloane's life ten years too late, an uninvited ripple in waters Sloane had fought so hard to calm.

Blake's thoughts churned, heavy and tangled. *You showed up ten years later at a resort she created based on memories of you.* The thought echoed inside her chest, complicated and aching. But Sloane's life was messy. Wrapped in layers Blake hadn't yet fully peeled back. Sloane had carried so much for so many years—all on her own. And she wasn't ready to let Blake help. Blake wasn't going to be the one chasing or pleading. She was the one who'd come back, unexpectedly, and maybe that made her the intruder. The one who had to respect the walls Sloane needed to keep up for now.

Lost in those swirling thoughts as she sat on the edge of her bed, Blake barely noticed the knock at her door until it pulled her back, sharp and urgent. She blinked and opened the door without bothering to check who was knocking. And there she was.

Sloane.

Disheveled. Eyes wild and trembling like a storm barely contained. Her usually sleek bob was windblown and messy, and every movement thrummed with desperate energy.

"You left the party," Sloane said, voice breathless, stepping inside as though she couldn't bear to let Blake escape. "I don't know what I did to upset you, but please—I'll make it right. Tell me what's wrong."

Blake's chest tightened at the raw vulnerability in Sloane's voice. This wasn't the poised, guarded woman she'd known earlier, but someone real—fractured, but wanting to be understood.

"Sloane, slow down," Blake said gently, reaching out, her hand brushing Sloane's arm, stilling the trembling in her hands. "It's okay."

"It's not okay." Sloane's words rushed out in a near whisper, a jagged edge to her tone. "You show up to the grand opening, wearing that dress—" Sloane's eyes dipped to Blake's waist for a moment.

Blake bit the edge of her lip. She hadn't worn the dress originally because she didn't want Sloane to think she could be bought. But when she'd finally unzipped the garment bag this morning, she knew she couldn't leave without at least trying it on.

"Do you like it?" Blake asked.

"It's gorgeous. *You're* gorgeous. But that's not the point." Sloane shoved a hand through her hair. She stared off in the distance as she seemed to reorganize her thoughts. "Dammit, Blake. I don't want you to go. I'm a mess. A giant mess with a million things I don't know how to fix. But if you're okay with messes..." Her voice cracked, a shaky, hopeful smile breaking through. "I kind of think you are. Please don't go."

Blake's heart stuttered, her breath hitching. Sloane's confession felt like being swept into the air in the world's biggest hot-air balloon, yet there was something raw and familiar in it—something that made her want to pull Sloane close, to ease the ache in her voice. But she didn't move.

Instead, Blake laughed softly, a nervous sound, caught somewhere between disbelief and relief. She'd waited ten years for this. And this was how Sloane found her. Barefoot and considering the best way to leave.

She held up her broken shoe, the heel swinging limply in the air like a fragile flag.

"My shoe broke when I stepped off the lavender path,"

Blake said, voice softer than she intended. "I came back to change. But, Sloane...you...want me to stay?"

Sloane's cheeks flushed bright. Her eyes flicked down to the shoe, then back to Blake, her gaze unreadable for a second too long. Finally, she cleared her throat, a nervous chuckle escaping her lips. "Oh. Your shoe. That's... I see. Your shoe." She quickly tried to recover. "We can just go back to the party now."

Blake shook her head, the smile widening despite the tug of vulnerability in her chest. She stepped closer to Sloane, feeling the gravity of the moment pull tight between them. There was something trembling in Sloane's eyes now, something unsure. And Blake's heart—her heart that had been full of *doubt* and *fear* for so long—felt soft and open.

"Sloane," Blake whispered. "Look at me."

The air seemed to shift. Time itself seemed to hold its breath. Sloane leaned back against the door frame, small and vulnerable—like Cinderella just before midnight, like the magic might slip away any second.

Sloane's eyes met hers, shimmering with unshed tears, blinking rapidly to hold herself steady. "Of course, I want you to stay," she whispered, her voice so quiet, it felt as though it could break. "I've always wanted you with me, even when I didn't know how to be. Even when I was so lost in all this...all this mess. And now I'm terrified you'll leave. That I'll lose you again. But maybe that's just me. Maybe I'm too broken to let anyone close. But *you*—you're worth the risk, Blake. You're worth all of it."

Blake's breath caught, the weight of Sloane's words making her heart skip like smooth stones across water before finally sinking in. It was too much, and yet, somehow, it was everything. She stepped closer, closing the remaining distance between them until the air was thick with unspoken tension. She could feel Sloane's pulse under her skin, her body trembling slightly as though the world outside might come crashing in at any moment.

"Don't be scared," Blake murmured, her lips barely brushing Sloane's forehead. "You don't have to be perfect, Sloane. I never needed perfect."

Sloane let out a shaky breath, her hand trembling as she reached up, threading her fingers through Blake's hair.

"You don't understand," Sloane said softly, voice breaking. "I did have to be perfect. Nico deserves perfect. My uncle should still be here. But he's not. And it's my job to hold all of it together. It's my job to make sure his legacy continues."

"Is that why you're leaving?" Blake asked, her voice soft as silk.

"Leaving?"

"For Europe. Nico told me you're leaving with him." Blake worked to keep her voice calm. She had no right to be mad about it. Sloane could go wherever she wanted. Sloane *should* go with Nico. Even if Sloane leaving again, leaving *Blake* again, was the exact thing she was trying to protect herself from. Blake's heart crumbled to pieces in her chest, but she kept her chin from wobbling, and she was proud of that.

Sloane blinked. "He told you that?"

That wasn't a no. Blake got the next words out even if they hurt. "Yes. And he asked me to go, too." She choked out a breathy laugh. "I can see now how you've had your hands full with him."

Sloane took in a shuddering breath, her shoulders dropping. "Yeah, I hope I'm doing it right. I know I'm not my uncle. I could never be. But I want to do right by him."

Blake reached up, gently cupping Sloane's face, grounding her in the moment. "It's not your job to be your uncle. You get to decide how this all happens. You get to decide what you want."

"I'm sorry I didn't tell you," Sloane said as she leaned into Blake's touch. "I just found out, nothing has been decided. And I just—"

Blake reached forward and wiped at a tear threatening to spill over Sloane's lashes. Sloane sniffed and nodded. Blake stepped closer, the space between them evaporating in an instant. She closed the gap, pressing her lips gently to Sloane's mouth. It was a kiss that spoke of years of silence, the burning need to *finally* let go, the longing to believe in something real.

Because this was real. Even if it was messy and they were still figuring it all out. This week had been a gift. A precious slip back in time. Blake had Sloane in her arms, and she was real and soft and hard at the edges, and Blake intended to keep her there.

"It's okay, Sloane." Another kiss to her cheek. "It's okay." And to her temple. Her hairline. And back to her mouth. "We're okay. We can figure it all out."

It wasn't rushed. It wasn't frantic. It was slow, tender and full of every ounce of emotion neither of them had allowed themselves to feel. Blake's arms slid around Sloane's back, pulling her closer, feeling the tremble in Sloane's body.

Sloane

Later, Blake led Sloane out onto the secluded wooden porch of her cottage. The night air was cool and crisp, a gentle breeze rustling through the nearby olive trees, their silvery leaves shimmering faintly under the moonlight.

It was the kind of night that felt suspended, as if time itself had slowed down just to let them exist in it, just the two of them.

In the distance, the party carried on—a murmur of laughter, clinking glasses and the steady rhythm of the live band filtering softly through the dark. But here, on the private terrace, there was only the quiet hum of the evening and the warmth of the space surrounding them. The world felt far away, and yet it felt as if it were pressing close, holding its breath.

The bungalow felt like a world apart—quiet, intimate, a sanctuary from everything swirling inside Sloane's head. She had spent so much of the last few years fighting to keep everything under control, to manage every moment, every decision, with perfect precision. But here, with Blake beside her, that constant need to *control* seemed to dissolve, like the last traces of daylight slipping away into night.

The warm glow from the porch light cast soft shadows over Blake's face, highlighting the vulnerability and strength Sloane saw there. Blake was always so open, so unafraid to be seen. It made something inside Sloane ache—something she had hidden deep, tucked away under layers of duty and responsibility.

"Do you want to go back to the party?" Blake asked, her voice low, almost hesitant. There was an edge of uncertainty to her, as if she was afraid that maybe she was pushing too much, too soon.

Sloane shook her head slowly, her eyes fixed on the fading lights of the resort below. The laughter, the music, the buzz of the crowd—they all seemed so distant now, like echoes from another world. "Not right now," she whispered, the words barely more than breath. It felt like an admission. A release. She didn't need the noise. She didn't need the spectacle. Not when she could feel Blake's presence next to her, steady and warm, like the first light of dawn after a long, dark night.

Blake moved closer, sitting down beside her, the motion fluid, instinctive. She leaned gently onto Sloane's shoulder, the weight of her touch soft but firm, a quiet reassurance that no matter the mess or the chaos, she wasn't alone.

Sloane let herself settle into the moment, the weight of Blake's presence anchoring her. It was simple, this closeness, and yet it was everything. It was the first thing that felt real in a long time.

"I think I know what I'm going to write for my article," Blake said softly, as if sharing a secret, her voice just loud enough to reach Sloane's ear.

Sloane glanced up at her, surprise softening her features. She had thought Blake would be too caught up in the celebration to even think about work. "But your stay isn't finished. I was still planning to wow you with the resort's brunch tomorrow."

Blake shrugged, a shy smile tugging at her lips, the corners of her mouth lifting in a way that made Sloane's heart beat just a little faster. "It's already done. When you know, you know."

And Sloane *did* know. She knew it in the way Blake's eyes lingered on her, the way she didn't rush to fill the silence, the way her mere presence calmed the storm inside. For the first time, Sloane understood that there was no real need for grand gestures or promises. She didn't need a private train car or an entire morning sky. This quiet moment was enough. The honesty, the rawness of just being in each other's space—it was more than enough. It was everything.

Sloane's chest tightened, a rush of emotion flooding through her. It was fierce, tender—something sharp and soft all at once. She reached out, her fingers brushing lightly against Blake's cheek, feeling the warmth of her skin. And then, slowly, as if the very act of moving closer required all of her courage, she pressed her lips to Blake's in a kiss.

It was slow, deliberate, full of promise and quiet determination. There was no rush. No need to prove anything. Whatever storms they still had to weather, whatever fears or doubts remained, they would face them side by side. Together.

The kiss lingered—soft and full of everything that had remained unspoken. It was the kind of kiss that made the rest of the world fade into the background, until all that mattered was the warmth between them, the steady rhythm of their hearts and the hopeful silence of the night around them.

When they finally pulled away, neither of them moved far. They stayed close, shoulders brushing, sharing a silence that was deeper than words. Outside, the music still drifted faintly through the cool night air, but here, in this moment, there was only them. The party could wait. The world could wait.

For now, this was all they needed.

CHAPTER SEVENTEEN

Blake

SUNLIGHT SPILLED ACROSS the honeymoon cottage in thick, golden ribbons. It pooled on the floor, warmed the sheets, caught in the loose ends of Sloane's hair. Blake stirred slowly, then all at once, blinking into morning with the sudden, full-body awareness that she wasn't alone.

Sloane was pressed against her, still asleep. Her breathing deep and even. Her face turned slightly toward Blake's shoulder. Their legs tangled beneath the sheets like they'd been searching for each other even in sleep.

She hadn't slept like this in years. Not next to someone. Not safely. Not like her body had finally remembered what peace felt like.

Sloane didn't stir when Blake moved, didn't even flinch as Blake gently extricated herself from the bed. She was such a heavy sleeper. That hadn't changed. Blake smiled to herself—little forgotten memories of Sloane returning now in fragments. The way she hogged blankets. The way she muttered nonsense when nudged awake. The way she kissed like it meant something.

Blake pressed a kiss to Sloane's temple and padded to the door, expecting to find the usual silver tray waiting in the hall. She braced herself for the scent of tea and citrus scones, for the single flower in a bud vase, delicate and fragrant.

Except today, there was nothing.

No tray. No flower. Just a quiet, empty hallway.

"That's odd," she murmured, frowning as she stepped back inside.

Sloane was awake now, still lounging lazily beneath the sheets, one arm tucked beneath her head, the other thrown wide like she owned the room. The morning light made her skin look like marble and gold. Blake tried not to stare. Failed.

"What's odd?" Sloane asked, eyes soft with sleep.

"The breakfast tray," Blake said, confused. "It's not here. They've brought it every morning like clockwork. Always the same—fruit, pastries, Earl Grey with cream. And the flowers…they're this haphazard mishmash of the most gorgeous wildflowers. But somehow, it works?"

Sloane was quiet.

Blake looked at her. "What?"

Sloane let out a slow breath. "We don't have a breakfast service, Blake."

Blake blinked. "What do you mean?"

"I mean…there's no one delivering those trays. That was me."

The world tilted.

Blake stared at her. "What?"

"I know you like Earl Grey," Sloane said softly, almost like it was a confession. "And you hate melon. And you always loved lavender shortbread. I just thought… I don't know. I wanted your mornings here to feel good. Even before…everything else."

Blake sat slowly at the foot of the bed, as if her legs

couldn't be trusted to keep holding her up. Her throat tightened.

"You were doing that even before we talked. Before we figured anything out. Before I knew you even wanted me here."

Sloane nodded, looking suddenly shy. "I wasn't sure if you'd stay. But I knew you'd wake up."

Blake let out a shaky breath. Her vision blurred. "You brought me breakfast. Every morning?"

Sloane nodded again, quieter this time. "With flowers. From my garden. You used to pick them in Florence. I remembered that."

The flood hit Blake all at once—memories, feelings, the impossibly tender ache of being known so completely by someone she thought she'd lost. Her chest ached in a way that felt both sharp and astonishingly good. Like something healing beneath the skin.

"You didn't owe me anything," Blake whispered. "You could've ignored me. You should have."

"I didn't want to ignore you," Sloane said simply. "I wanted to show up for you. I didn't know how else to say it yet."

Blake pressed her hands over her mouth, overcome. The breakfasts, the tea, the lavender—she had thought it was just hospitality. Some polished luxury offered to all guests. But it had been Sloane. It had always been her.

All those mornings…before the apologies. Before the kisses. Before they were even speaking fully like people who used to be in love.

She wasn't sure if she wanted to cry or laugh or climb back into bed and never leave.

"God, Sloane," she said, voice breaking. "You were already taking care of me. And I didn't even know."

Sloane reached forward, gently hooking her fingers around Blake's wrist and tugging her closer. "I've always wanted to. Even when I didn't know how."

Blake leaned in, their foreheads resting together. "I still can't believe you remember how I take my tea."

"Too much cream. No sugar. Always Earl Grey." Sloane grinned. "You used to dip your toast in it. Like a heathen."

"Still do."

Sloane tilted her head. "Come back to bed."

Blake nodded; eyes still glossy with unshed tears. She slid beneath the covers again, curling into Sloane like it was instinct, like she had never left at all.

"I can't believe it was you," she whispered again.

"You believe it now?"

Blake smiled against her shoulder. "I believe everything now."

And they stayed that way, skin to skin, breath to breath, as the sun climbed higher. Breakfast could wait. The rest of the world could wait. But this—this quiet, powerful truth—was finally here.

Sloane

This was why brunch existed—because it was almost noon, but Sloane could still order an omelet and drink something sparkly in public.

The morning air was soft around the poolside patio, dappled through pale umbrellas, scented with rosemary and citrus, and punctuated by the gentle murmur of other guests enjoying their last hours of the weekend. A server had just dropped off a new pot of Earl Grey, and across the table, Blake was stirring in cream—her hair still damp from a shower, face clean and open, bare feet tucked beneath her chair.

Sloane barely touched her mimosa.

The *Santa Ynez Valley Chronicle* lay folded in front of her, creased where she'd been gripping it too tightly.

"Vella West Grand Opening: Boutique Luxury with Heart and Vision."

They'd written a glowing feature, more expansive than she'd expected. It praised everything—architecture, wine, staff, food—but it was the final paragraph that got her. The writer described the resort as *a place you could come to feel like yourself again. A home, dressed in elegance.* It was the kind of praise she'd dreamed of.

And it didn't mean a thing without someone to share it with.

She stole a glance across the table at Blake. Her sleeves were rolled, a gold ring glinting faintly on her middle finger as she cradled the teacup. A familiar ache tightened behind Sloane's ribs. She knew Blake had to leave today, but she couldn't escape the desire to move that tiny band of gold one finger over, asking her to stay forever.

But before she could get carried away, Blake's phone chirped on the table between them—a terrible reminder that life still had obstacles for them, even though they seemed to be on the same page for the first time in ten years.

Blake tapped something out on the phone. "My car. I told the hotel to send it at one. I totally lost track of time."

"Wait," Sloane said. "Can't you push it? Just an hour?" She needed more. She'd offer to charter a plane for Blake if she thought she'd accept it. She'd offer to go with if she thought she could get away with it. Blake had her entire heart—and it was going to be torture to live without it until they got this all sorted.

Blake stood. "I wish I could. I've got a debrief call with my editor as soon as I land, and a meeting first thing tomorrow. I wasn't even supposed to stay this long."

Sloane stood, too. "I thought we had more time."

Blake's voice softened. "I did, too."

Sloane looked at her, really looked—at the shadows under her eyes, the hopeful pink of her cheeks.

"I'll walk you to the car."

They didn't speak much as they headed through the garden path, past the vines and wildflowers, the scent of lavender caught on the breeze. Guests were checking out, the world moving forward while Sloane wanted time to stop.

Outside the front entrance, the town car waited. Blake's bag was already loaded. The driver leaned on the hood, scrolling through his phone.

Blake turned to her. "I'm glad I came."

Sloane nodded, but her voice caught. "I wish you didn't have to leave."

"I wish I didn't either."

They stared at each other. The moment a breath away from cracking open.

Then Blake stepped forward and pulled her into a hug—longer than expected, her face pressed into the crook of Sloane's neck. Sloane wrapped her arms around her waist and held on.

"I don't want this to be the end," Sloane said, the words thick in her throat.

Blake leaned back just far enough to look her in the eye. "Then don't let it be. Think about what you want. Think about what you're willing to give. And then find me. We both have things we need to take care of. I'll be waiting for you."

Sloane kissed her. Just once—soft and lingering. Something slow enough to say what she couldn't.

"I'm not trying to fix everything. I just don't want this to be another goodbye. I don't want to wait another ten years."

"You need to finish opening this resort. Robby needs you, the town needs you. And I need to figure out my next steps with writing. This isn't goodbye. This is…pause."

Sloane bit back tears as she pressed her forehead to Blake's. "Okay." She wrapped her in a hug. She knew she was right. They weren't twenty anymore. They had responsibilities and things that needed sorting out. They couldn't just run away together.

But it still scraped her heart out to watch Blake Miller drive away.

CHAPTER EIGHTEEN

Blake

BLAKE KNEW COMING home was going to be hard, but it wasn't in the ways she'd imagined. She sat down at her laptop, ready to finalize her edits in preparation for the meeting the next day.

Her apartment was compact. Okay fine, it was small. Probably not much bigger than the honeymoon cottage she'd spent the last week in. But it also felt flat. Her home didn't have any photographs adorning the walls. She had some prints of local places, but nothing she could look at and pinpoint to a memory.

Not like Sloane's small home, full of pictures of Nico and her uncle from every stage of life. She didn't even have an old photo of her and Sloane. Not mismatched mugs or hand-stitched quilts.

Blake sighed and opened her laptop. She had a million notifications on her work's social media. She opened it as a way to ease back into work. She'd address a few comments and upload a few final photos before turning to her write-up of the resort.

She clicked on the home icon and her website flooded with vibrant images from the past week. To any stranger these photos would look like a luxurious stay in the bespoke vineyards of the Napa Valley. A farm to table breakfast tray, the sunrise over the hills from hundreds of feet in the air, a picnic in a meadow with homemade jams.

Catchy phrases and targeted hashtags accompanied each photograph, subtly advertising the resort and related products while appealing to those seeking adventure, luxury and travel escapes.

But there were other hints there, too. A hazy, backlit photo showed Sloane's form leaning against the railing of the honeymoon cottage, her features lost in shadow. No one would know it was her. Winnie and Rhett in their corral, noses together in the midday sun. Blake's novel splayed open at the foot of her lounge chair in a cabana. She'd tried different captions here. Lines from her journal. Snippets of poems half remembered. She'd snuck them in between advertisements disguised as art.

Her heart caught in her throat as she read the comments. People wanted more. She thought she'd been capturing small moments, but she had told a story in photos. She'd let the world watch her slowly fall back in love over the course of the last week.

Her followers had noticed. *Who is that woman in the photo?* And *since when did you start writing poetry?* The edge of her journal peeked out in a photo. Blake had let people in, a lot of people in, without realizing it.

Blake tapped her pen against her mouth and frowned. She had almost finished the write-up. But she knew there was another story here. She scrolled through the comments again. She liked them all and responded to some, each response a tiny hot-air balloon of hope in her chest.

Her phone buzzed beside her and she happily answered when she saw Chloe's name.

"Welcome home, Blake!" Chloe's chipper voice rang out

on the other side of the line. Blake didn't have a chance to respond before Chloe plowed through the conversation. "We are meeting on Friday for coffee at nine. You can't say no. I want to know all about the mystery woman on your feed. You didn't tell me you *met someone* on the trip. Who is she? Another guest? I need *details*."

Chloe's voice, a familiar and slightly chaotic melody, reached Blake's ears, reminding her that she wasn't completely alone in San Diego. Even if she hadn't realized it until now. And even if that friend was a bit overbearing, it was nice to know she had someone she could talk to.

"Actually, I was wondering if Tara had time to squeeze in a meeting with me on Friday?" Blake tried to keep her voice steady. "I want to talk to her about the article. But we can get breakfast afterward?"

"You don't have it, do you?" Chloe's voice dropped to a whisper. "Oh god, we're all getting fired. I can't work at Java Bean again, Blake."

Blake stifled a laugh. "Don't turn in any applications just yet. I have the article. But there's something else I want to show Tara, too. And I'd like to meet with her about it."

"Okay, I can do tomorrow morning before her first meeting. Bring her an oat latte. It will loosen her up a little."

"Thanks, Chloe. You're the best."

With that, Blake hung up and pulled out her tattered notebook with thousands of words already penned. It was time to finally let it all out. It was time to tell her story. Sloane's story.

That Friday, Blake sat stiffly in the high-backed chair across from Tara's desk, the tips of her fingers tapping nervously against her blazer. Her hair was pulled back into a tight ponytail—sleek, controlled, the antithesis of the woman she had been when she'd first stepped into the world of travel writing.

She glanced around the office, feeling the weight of it all—white walls, chrome furniture, an overstuffed bookshelf filled with trade magazines and bound volumes of past issues. Tara's domain was always immaculate, the kind of place where everything had its place. Everything was curated, even the air. Blake hated it. The space was sterile. The office felt as devoid of warmth as she felt inside.

Once, she'd been excited about this job, eager to write about new places, experiences and the world beyond her cubicle. But now, months later, she could barely recognize the person who had walked into this building with wide eyes and an open heart. She'd given up parts of herself to fit the role. The work was fine. The job was fine. But Blake didn't feel *right* anymore.

She was the magazine's social media manager. She posted; she curated content; she engaged with followers. It was supposed to be her way in—the backdoor to the writer's room, the place where her real ambitions lived. Tara had promised her that if she proved herself, if she could show her potential, she might just get a shot at writing those glossy travel pieces.

But now Blake knew something—*really* knew something—that she hadn't before. She wasn't meant to be here. Not like this. Not doing this.

Tara finally looked up from the draft of Blake's latest article, her sharp eyes scanning Blake with the practiced gaze of someone who could read the room in a heartbeat. Tara didn't waste time with pleasantries or unearned compliments. She was precise, concise and ruthless when it came to business. It wasn't personal. It never was with Tara.

"Blake, I asked you to write a travel review," Tara said, her voice smooth, devoid of inflection. "I trust that's what you have for me?"

"Tara, I—" Blake was great at writing words down, but not so great when she had to say them out loud, on the spot, to her boss. "I did write one. And it was *fine*. But it wasn't the complete story. You can still print that one. It's in your inbox right now."

Tara frowned at her computer screen and clicked around for a moment. She nodded curtly before looking back at Blake. It was now or never. Blake took a deep breath and handed a stack of papers to Tara, her heart and soul were on those pages and as they slipped from her hand, she knew there was no going back.

"But I also have this. I know I was supposed to stick to the review. But this story? It's *better* than a review. It's the entire reason Vella West exists as it is. And I think our readers will want to read something like this." Blake took a deep breath. "You asked for my best work. And, well, this was it."

Tara narrowed her eyes at Blake, but Blake didn't care. She was proud of that article, dammit. No matter what anyone said. Tara held up a finger, asking for a moment. Blake cleared her throat and said nothing.

Tara scanned the pages, her narrowed eyes giving away nothing. Blake hadn't expected her to read the entire thing right then, while Blake sat there silently watching and sort of wanting to disappear into the ether. Her entire heart was literally in her boss's hands.

When Tara finished reading she shuffled the papers, tapped them into a neat pile and stared at Blake.

"If it isn't the right fit, I understand. Maybe we can post it as a separate blog on social media? Or maybe we can—"

"Blake, are you quite finished?" Tara asked, her voice a bone-chilling monotone.

"Yes?" She hated that it came out like a question.

"Good." Tara dropped the papers on her desk and smirked. "Some free advice? Don't self-reject. You just handed me an amazing story and then cut it before I shared my thoughts."

Blake wanted to argue, but Tara was right. That was exactly what she had done. "I understand." Blake cleared her throat and sat up straighter. "Good advice."

"I know," Tara responded. She leaned back in her chair and crossed her arms. "It certainly isn't on brand. And it needs some editing. Our readers might hate it. But I didn't become editor in chief of this magazine without taking risks."

Hope swelled inside Blake like a morning breeze rustling the poppies in the vineyard. Her story was worth the risk.

"Tara, I don't know how to thank you."

"Well," Tara said with a frown. "Don't thank me yet. But in for a penny, in for a pound. We've got to try something. And this might be just what we need. You're sure she'll sign off on this?"

"Who?" Blake assumed Tara would do the editing, but maybe she was wrong. She'd work with anyone Tara assigned. Her story, her and Sloane's story, was going to be published.

"Sloane Vella. She'll need to sign off on the story's accuracy. She has to be okay with her story being in print. We're going to need her to corroborate the details."

Blake bit down on the edge of her lip. She hadn't considered what this might mean for Sloane. For her vine-yard. For Vella West.

"I'm sure," Blake said. And she hoped she was right.

Sloane

Robby slid the stack of reviews across the desk, then nudged one final page toward her without a word.

Sloane's eyes caught the byline before she even saw the column heading: *Blake Escapes*. Her heart lurched, a familiar sense of dread sweeping over her as she glanced down. The travel magazine's logo loomed at the top of the page.

"You'll need to take a look at this one." They tapped the edge of the page. "It needs you to sign off on the facts."

Her fingers shook when she finally reached for the page, but she didn't pull it closer. It was Blake's story. Blake hadn't told her much about it and by the way Robby was looking at her now, she knew it couldn't be good. Had Blake given the resort a bad review?

Sloane let out a laugh, though it was more like a stran-gled sob. "If it's bad, just tell me now. I can handle it."

"Have you even talked to her?" Robby set down their stack of papers and leaned on the desk. "How have you not seen this?"

"A little." Sloane tucked a chunk of her black bob be-hind her ear and sighed. "I'm giving her space."

"Space? Nico leaves for Italy tomorrow. How much more time do you need?" Robby nudged the paper again, their voice louder this time. "Come on. Read it. Stop being so stubborn."

Sloane sat there for a moment, staring at the article, be-fore Robby stormed out of the room. She was leaving for

Europe tomorrow—everything was set. The hotel was in good shape, business booming. But something was wrong. She could feel it, that dark pull in her chest that had nothing to do with logistics, and everything to do with Blake. And whatever this was.

But she couldn't escape the pull. She shoved the paper aside for a while, distracted, but when the silence grew unbearable, she finally picked it up.

"Nowhere Else," by Blake Miller.

Her heart skipped a beat. That was it. The same Blake.

Sloane's hand shook as she touched the page. The years she had buried, the pain she'd tried to move past, rose to the surface like an unexpected wave.

She took a deep breath and began reading. Her eyes lingered on the opening lines:

I never believed in forever—until I fell in love with her in Italy, ten years ago. We were young, reckless maybe, but what we had was real. Deep and raw enough that even now, a decade later, it still aches to think about her. So, you can imagine my surprise when I walked into Vella West, fresh-faced and ready for my first job as a travel writer—and came face-to-face with my gorgeous, heartbreaking past.

Sloane couldn't breathe. The words hit her like a freight train, and she had to blink back tears.

But this isn't just a story about a chance reunion or lost time. It's about the silence that stretched between us, the years swallowed by mistakes and misunderstandings. It's about the quiet spaces filled with regret—and the faint, stubborn hope that maybe some things don't have to end. That love, no matter how tangled, can find its way back—like a secret whispered beneath the golden glow of a fading afternoon, hidden along winding vineyard trails, and carried softly on the breath of a dew-kissed morning.

She read it again. And again. By the third time, she was crying. And by the fourth, she was already halfway to her house.

This was terrible timing. She was leaving tomorrow. For Europe. With Nico.

"What happened to you?" Nico's voice cut through the haze of her thoughts as he dropped his duffel bag onto the rug.

Sloane sniffed, brushing the tears away. She waved absently at the papers. Nico picked them up and sat down at the table, reading the article quietly. The silence stretched between them, charged and full of unspoken words.

After a few minutes, Nico spoke, his voice soft but firm. "Sloane…you have to go to her."

Sloane blinked, almost startled by his directness. "What are you talking about? We leave tomorrow. I—"

Nico rolled his eyes, his tone growing impatient. "I can get myself to an internship, Sloane. You don't need to come."

Her breath caught. She swallowed hard. "I know you think that. But I can't just—"

Nico leaned forward, placing a hand on her shoulder, his voice gentle but resolute. "I know you, Sloane. I know you've put everything on hold—*everything*—for so long, and you've held this place together for years. But if you love her, you can't ignore what is *very clearly* a love letter back to you."

"It's not a love letter, it's an arti—"

"Sorry, cousin. You're wrong. This is top-tier love letter. You can ignore it, but is that really what you want? A chain of hotels, endlessly working? What do you want?"

Sloane wiped at her eyes and pulled her knees up to her chest. A decade of emotions that she'd stuffed down for so long came bubbling to the surface. "I don't know."

"I think you do. I think you want her. I think you want a chance to slow down. I think you should take it. This will all be here when you're ready. I'll be here. Robby will be here. Let us take care of you for once."

Sloane stared at him for a long moment. Nico wasn't a kid anymore. He wasn't the one who needed her to fix things anymore. The quiet realization hit her like a wave— maybe it was time to stop holding everything together for everyone else.

"I know you've always been there for me," Nico continued, his voice soft. "And I'll always need you—but not the way I used to. Let me go."

Sloane felt the weight of his words settle in her chest, a lump forming in her throat. She opened her mouth to protest, but Nico was already shaking his head.

"You've done everything for me, Sloane. You've done enough. Go to her. Please."

The weight of his words pushed Sloane further into the corner she'd been avoiding—the realization that if she didn't make a choice, she'd be stuck with the what-ifs forever. Nico wasn't a kid anymore, and Europe could wait. But the chance with Blake? That was something she couldn't put off.

Sloane took a deep breath, letting go of the final thread of hesitation. "What if she doesn't want me?" she asked, her voice barely above a whisper.

Nico's eyes softened. "But what if she does?"

Sloane nodded slowly, the fear still tight in her chest, but now, underneath it, there was something else. A spark of possibility.

"I have to go, don't I?"

Nico smiled, the same knowing grin from years ago. "Yeah, you do."

She laughed—a soft, shaky laugh—and grabbed her bag. "How did you get so smart about this love stuff?"

Nico rolled his eyes. "I am so not doing this with you," Nico laughed. "Now, go! I'll call you when I get there."

CHAPTER NINETEEN

Blake

THE CAR BARELY came to a stop before Blake stepped out in the early morning light, her flats landing softly on the warm stone of the circular drive. Summer had settled in like a heavy golden fog—thick with sunlight, soaked in heat that clung to her skin and made the world feel endless, as if the days would never slip away. Everything looked just as she remembered—maybe even sharper, more vivid. Or maybe it was just her, seeing the past through eyes that had been broken and rebuilt.

The antique doors loomed ahead, framed by ivy that had thickened and darkened under the relentless sun. The lavender was wild and rampant, spilling over the stone walls, heavy with scent—honeyed and sharp. Bees flitted between blossoms like they'd been invited to a secret party, carefree and buzzing with life. A butterfly drifted past her shoulder, fragile and unhurried, as if it knew she was coming home.

Blake adjusted the strap of her bag—a lighter load than last time. No laptop. No voice recorder. No backup outfit for wine tastings or fancy dinners. She hadn't even packed a swimsuit. This trip was different. It wasn't about work anymore. Not really.

Earlier that summer, she had come thinking this was just an assignment—a story to tell about a breathtaking, over-the-top resort that seemed too perfect to be real. Work. That was all. But she hadn't expected Sloane. Hadn't expected the flood of memories, the sharp ache of a laugh shared across a vineyard dinner table, or the ghost of a touch on a terrace railing. Their goodbye had never felt like an ending—more like a question mark hanging in the air, waiting for an answer.

Now, here she was. Not sent by an editor. Not chasing a deadline. Chasing a feeling. A hope. The part of her that still believed they weren't finished yet.

The heat wrapped around her, heavy with rosemary, lavender, and the bittersweet scent of memory.

Her fingers brushed the worn wood of the ancient doors. She swallowed hard and let a small, shaky smile slip free.

"Okay," she whispered to herself. "Let's try this again."

She stepped inside.

The lobby hadn't changed much—still the same soft light, the same polished floors—but there was a new floral arrangement on the large center table, lush and fragrant, like a silent promise of new beginnings. Behind the desk stood Robby, whose smile was warm but carried something else—something like a quiet sadness.

"Ms. Miller," Robby greeted, voice gentle but with a knowing edge. "I wasn't expecting to see you again so soon."

Blake forced her voice steady, even though her heart hammered in her chest. "Hello, Robby. Is Sloane here? I need to see her. I have to—"

Robby cut in with a teasing smirk. "I read your article."

Blake blinked, confused. "I'm sorry?"

"You didn't mention me once," Robby said, mock stern.

Her throat tightened. If Robby read the article, then maybe Sloane had seen it, too. "You read it? I told Tara I wanted to do this in person. Did…did she sign off on it?"

"Actually, I'm not sure. She took it with her. But I thought it was good. Except for forgetting to mention me—I'm kind of an important part of this place."

A small laugh escaped her lips. "I'll make sure to fix that next time."

Robby nodded. "Thank you. But Sloane's not here right now."

Her heart dropped. "No? But I thought she wasn't leaving until tomorrow."

Robby shrugged. "She hasn't been in the office since this morning. If I were you, I'd check the stables—she always says goodbye to the horses before she goes anywhere."

Blake pressed a quick kiss to Robby's cheek. They both blushed, but the warmth of the gesture steadied her nerves.

"Thank you, Robby. Really."

"I know."

Blake took off down the path, her hair streaming behind her in soft waves of caramel and gold. She was glad she wore flats instead of sandals—she needed to be quick. She wanted to call out Sloane's name until it echoed across the estate, wanted her to stop, turn around, come back. But when she rounded the corner, she saw it: a black car pulling away from the driveway.

"No, Sloane," she cried out, voice breaking like a fragile thread.

But the wind carried her words away. Sloane couldn't hear her. She hadn't called—hadn't reached out—and Blake hadn't even saved her number. The things Blake wanted to say couldn't be whispered over the phone. They needed to be said face-to-face, heart to heart.

Now Sloane was leaving for Europe without her.

Blake kept walking toward the house, not sure what she was searching for anymore. The ache inside her was a raw wound, open and bleeding.

Near the meadow, the two horses stood silently, watching. Blake stood beside them, tears spilling freely. She scratched at their noses, the familiar softness grounding her.

"I love her," she whispered, voice cracked. "I love her so much, and I don't want to say goodbye."

The words hung in the air, fragile and heavy.

And then, almost like a voice from within, a whisper answered: "So don't."

Blake's hands clenched into fists, nails digging into her palms. She closed her eyes and made a silent vow. She wouldn't let her go. Not like this. Not without a fight.

Because love wasn't about perfect timing or neat endings. It was messy. It was hard. It was painful. But it was real.

And if she had to chase Sloane halfway across the world, if she had to break down every wall and tear down every doubt—she would.

Because some things were worth every risk.

Sloane

Sloane had never been good at goodbyes. In fact, she had been a master at avoiding them. Her life, the mess of it all, had been full of those—so many little departures that had added up to one giant, painful absence. She had thought it was easier this way, walking away before someone else could.

Nico was going to be fine. He was studying abroad for the summer, not leaving forever. He would love Italy, just as she had. And he'd come home with a stronger sense of what running a vineyard might be like. If that was what he wanted.

If not, that would be okay, too. Blake wasn't going to force her dreams on Nico. She loved running this place. She especially loved the thrill of restoring and getting it up and running. Robby was the one who was good at keeping it going. Blake would love to see it. She could still hear Blake's voice in her head, so clear it might have been a whisper in the room with her.

Sloane turned away from the window. She'd packed all the things she thought she'd need, but none of it felt right. She didn't need a passport or a suitcase full of memories that no longer fit. She needed one thing.

Blake.

The thought crashed into her like a wave, sweeping away all the plans she'd made for herself, for Nico, for the future that she had thought would be hers. What was she doing? She couldn't leave. Not with everything left unsaid again.

Sloane grabbed her bag and tossed it into the corner, pulling on her shoes with shaky hands. She didn't care about running anymore. All she could think about was finding Blake. She'd go to San Diego. She'd find her on her next writing assignment. Whatever it took.

When she reached the stables, she noticed someone talking to her horses. No, not *someone*, Blake. There she was, standing tall in the morning light, her face bathed in a glow that almost made Sloane believe this was a dream. A second chance.

Blake's eyes met hers and the world seemed to stop. The horses shifted restlessly behind them, but for Sloane, there was only Blake—everything else faded away.

"I was scared," Sloane whispered, her voice trembling. She didn't care anymore if Blake understood. She needed to say it all. "I ghosted you not because I didn't care, but because I was terrified. Terrified you'd see my family's mess. Terrified you'd think you had to help me raise a kid when we were still just kids ourselves."

Blake's gaze softened, and Sloane's walls—built so high, so carefully—cracked, and everything she had tried to bury came rushing forward.

"I read your article. Blake, it was beautiful," Sloane said, her voice breaking. "I'll sign off on it. I'll sign anything you need."

Blake let out a soft laugh. "Thanks. I don't know what's next, but I do know this—I'm done letting other people write my story."

Sloane took a step closer, her heart pounding. "What about me?"

Blake's hand reached for hers, soft but steady. "What about you?"

"Is there room in your future for someone like me? Someone stubborn and still full of grief?" Sloane asked, almost afraid to hear the answer.

Blake's fingers traced light patterns up Sloane's arms. "Someone kind? Fiercely loyal. Someone who'd give everything for her family."

Sloane swallowed hard. "Blake, if you keep touching me like that, I'm going to kiss you."

Blake leaned in, voice low and daring. "If you kiss me, I might tell you I love you, Sloane Vella."

Sloane closed her eyes, breath catching. "Good, because I love you, Blake. I think I've loved you this whole time. I just didn't know how to carry it all, so I hid it away." The world had narrowed to just the two of them—the thundering beat of her heart, Blake's hand on her skin, the pull between them undeniable. For a moment, everything else disappeared.

"I love you, too." Blake said. "We'll figure it all out. Together."

But then Sloane pulled back just enough to whisper, her voice full of trembling hope, "I'm not leaving for Europe, Blake. I stayed because I had to find you."

Blake's eyes widened. "You...you stayed?"

"I was going to go with him because I was afraid to let him to do it alone. I was afraid to admit that he didn't need me anymore," Sloane admitted, "but my heart has always been here. With you. I was scared, Blake. But I'm not running anymore. I want to be with you."

Blake

Blake's breath hitched. The raw emotion in Sloane's voice made her chest tighten. Slowly, Blake cupped her face, eyes brimming with tears, and leaned in for a kiss. It wasn't just any kiss—it was everything. It was the apology, the promise, the hope for what could still be.

"I love you," Blake whispered, her words barely a breath.

Sloane's lips curled into a smile as she kissed Blake again, deeper, letting everything else fall away.

"I love you, too."

They stood there, wrapped in each other, letting the kiss say everything the words couldn't. The world outside—the perfect world of the resort, the carefully planned events, the polished image—faded to nothing. There was only this: the quiet, the warmth, the certainty that they were finally, finally here.

Sloane's arms curled around Blake as if she would never let go, her fingers pressing into Blake's skin like a silent promise. Blake's chest tightened with an overwhelming tenderness, and for the first time in what felt like forever, she didn't feel *lost*. She felt home.

When they finally pulled apart, breathless and wide-eyed, the moment stretched out around them. It wasn't *just* about the kiss. It was about the understanding, the unspoken bond that neither of them had realized was so desperately needed until now.

Blake cupped Sloane's cheek, her thumb brushing over the softness of her skin. "I'm not going anywhere," she said quietly. "Not this time."

Sloane smiled, a small, fragile thing, as she nodded. "Good."

They didn't need more words. Not yet. Not now.

There was only the gentle, slow pull into the cottage. Into each other. And the quiet, inevitable way they moved together, no longer held back by fear, by time, or by the walls they'd built around themselves.

EPILOGUE

Blake

THE EVENING SUN sank beyond the last hill as Blake and Sloane watched from a blanket in the grass. Winnie and Rhett drank from the stream nearby as crickets began their evening chirp in the mid-July sunset.

"Alright, Miller. I'm done with work for the day. You've dragged me all the way out here. I know you have something to tell me. Spill it." Sloane dug her fingertips into the soft flesh at Blake's hip, making her giggle.

"The numbers are in." Blake held her breath. They'd been waiting on the magazine's sale numbers. The numbers that held Blake's writing career in her hands.

"And?"

Blake blew out a breath. "Consistent overall. Tara said that the initial spike in sales due to the originality of my article helped counterbalance the...dip in sales after the first few days."

"So, what does that mean?" Sloane leaned forward and pressed a kiss to Blake's temple. She tucked the hair behind her ear and kept nuzzling, kissing.

"I can't think when you're doing that," Blake chided. Sloane nuzzled in closer before her soft laughter tickled Blake's neck and she relented. "It means no more articles like this one. Tara said if I want to write for *Elsewhere*, I'll need to change my tactic."

"Blake, I'm so sorry," Sloane said. And Blake knew she meant it, too. They'd had some time to talk about their future. Blake wanted to keep writing. But she knew now, she didn't want to write bite-sized social media posts and travel articles.

"I think I'm okay with it," she said, sighing. "The good news is, there was a big uptick on social media followings. For some reason, the algorithm loved me. Loved *us*. They especially liked your wildflower fields."

Sloane bit her lip. "You know I'm going to have to ask Robby what all this means later right?"

"It means… I quit." Blake felt a giant weight lift when she said the words. "I think I'm going to take my journals, my notebooks, and see about turning them into a blog. I want to be my own boss and write about…whatever I do next. Whether it's traveling, or…"

"Or?"

"Well, you know how you've been wanting to give Robby more responsibility?" Sloane nodded and Blake felt hope bloom in her chest. It was now or never. Last time they had a plan, Sloane had bolted. But it was different now. She hoped.

"I was thinking that maybe, if you did—if you turned over the resort to them, just for a little while…maybe we could finally do the Italy trip. Again."

"You want to go back with me?" Sloane's eyes looked wet with tears.

"I want to go everywhere with you, Sloane Vella." Blake leaned forward and pressed a soft kiss to Sloane's mouth. "Will you go back with me?"

"Yes," Sloane whispered when she finally broke their

kiss. "It will take some time. I need to get everything organized, and train Robby on some of the protocols. But, yes. I'll go anywhere with you."

Six months later

The road twisted, narrow and uneven, winding through the verdant hills as Sloane's hands gripped the wheel, her jaw set in that quiet determination that always made Blake's heart flutter. She didn't know where they were headed, but Blake did—every curve of this road, every shift in the landscape felt like a pull from the past, a thread she was about to tug.

Blake had never imagined it would be like this. That she would return to this place—the one they'd found together so many years ago when everything felt possible and no dream was too big. The farmhouse was still here, still waiting for them.

"Just up ahead," Blake said, her voice thick with emotion. She looked out the window, trying to ignore the flutter of nerves in her stomach. She had to get this right.

They were nearly there. The vineyard was spread out before them, the vines twisted and aged, but still strong. The house, nestled among them, stood just as it had all those years ago: tired but full of potential, like a forgotten dream ready to be revived.

As the car rounded the final bend, the farmhouse appeared in full view, surrounded by fields of grapevines that were wild and overgrown. The stone walls were cracked in places, but they held a quiet kind of strength. The windows, dusty and boarded up, had an air of mystery—like secrets were waiting to be discovered.

Sloane didn't say anything at first, her gaze caught by

the sight of the place, but Blake could see the recognition in her eyes, the flicker of memory that passed over her features.

"I remember," Sloane murmured, her voice hushed, almost reverent. Her hands relaxed on the wheel, and Blake watched as her lips parted in disbelief. "We used to talk about it. About fixing it up. Living here."

Sloane shook her head, a laugh slipping past her lips, tinged with wonder. "I didn't think it could ever be real."

Blake's heart swelled; her chest tight with the weight of everything that had come before this moment. The years apart, the distance they'd created between them—this house was the one thing that had always remained, a promise unfulfilled, a dream they'd shared on a blanket under the stars.

"I didn't either," Blake said softly, her gaze steady on Sloane. She reached over, her fingers brushing against Sloane's, an unspoken reassurance. "But it's for sale now. And it's ours if we want it."

Sloane's eyes widened, a flicker of something deep—hope, maybe, or fear—crossing her features. She turned to Blake, her expression unreadable, but Blake knew. She knew the weight of that question. This was it, the choice to step forward, to take the leap.

"I want it," Sloane said, her voice low but steady. "I want it with you."

Blake smiled, the kind of smile that was full of promises. "Good. I was hoping you would say that."

She opened the door and stepped out into the warm Tuscan air, the scent of earth and vines mixing with the distant sea breeze. The sun was beginning to dip low in the sky, casting long shadows across the property. There was so much to fix, so much to rebuild, but there was something about the place—about the history of it—that felt right.

Sloane followed her, her boots crunching on the gravel path as they moved toward the house. They walked through the overgrown garden, now untamed but still filled with beauty—wildflowers peeking out from the weeds, vines climbing over forgotten trellises. The house loomed ahead of them, the stone steps cracked but sturdy, the wood of the shutters weathered and worn.

Blake reached out, tracing her fingers over the wall, her touch lingering as though the house itself was alive, holding memories of the past. This was where their future could begin.

"We'll fix it," Blake said, her voice soft, almost reverent. "We'll make it ours."

Sloane turned to her, eyes full of affection and something deeper—something she didn't need to say, because Blake already understood. They would do this together. Just like they'd always dreamed.

Sloane

The warmth of the stone under her palm grounded her as she took in the familiar sight of the farmhouse. The same house that had been a dream so many years ago. Back then, it had felt like a wild, impossible idea—an abandoned place that existed only in their shared fantasy, a dream whispered between them under the blanket of stars.

But now, here it was. And it was real.

Sloane's pulse thrummed in her ears as she looked at Blake. She could still see the girl she'd fallen in love with—unpredictable, wild, full of hope and promise. She saw it in the way Blake's eyes shone when she spoke about this place, the quiet confidence that radiated from her as she laid out the future they could build.

They'd talked about this when they were younger— before life had swept them in different directions, before they'd been torn apart by circumstances they hadn't yet learned to navigate. But this farmhouse, this life, had always been there, waiting for them to come back. Waiting for them to choose it. Choose each other.

And Sloane was ready. More than ready. She had been dreaming of this moment her entire life—of settling into a life that felt like home. But now, standing here with Blake, the weight of it all settled on her chest.

It wasn't just the farmhouse, the vineyard, the life in Italy. It was *this*. It was the way Blake made her feel alive in a way no one else ever had. It was the way Blake made the impossible seem like the most natural thing in the world.

Sloane turned to her, her heart in her throat. "I've spent my whole life running," she said, her voice thick with emotion. "But this…this is what I've always wanted. With you. This. *Us*."

Blake reached out, cupping her face, her thumb brushing gently over her skin. "I've always known that Sloane," she whispered, her voice low, full of meaning. "This isn't just a house. This is home."

Sloane leaned into the touch, her heart pounding as she looked up at Blake. The sky above them had turned a deep violet, the first stars twinkling in the evening sky. It felt like a sign, like the universe was aligning.

But there was one more thing she needed to say. One more thing she needed to ask.

"Sloane," Blake murmured, stepping closer.

But Sloane wasn't waiting anymore. She took a step

back, dropped to one knee in the soft grass, and held out the ring that had been waiting for this moment. The sapphire gleamed in the fading light, a symbol of all they had been through and all they still had to look forward to. She could feel the weight of it in her hand—the weight of the years, the heartache, the hope.

"Blake," she said, her voice steady but full of love. "I'm ready for one more adventure with you. The kind that lasts forever. Will you marry me?"

Blake's eyes filled with surprise, then joy, as she knelt in front of Sloane, taking the ring and slipping it onto her finger. "Yes," she whispered, her voice breaking.

Sloane closed the distance between them, pressing her lips to Blake's in a kiss that sealed everything—the past, the present, the future. This was home. This was everything they'd ever wanted. And it was just the beginning.

* * * * *

If you enjoyed this story,
check out this other great read
from Jenny Lane

Her Fake Wedding Date in Sicily

Available now!

FOR BUSINESS...
OR PLEASURE

JOSS WOOD

MILLS & BOON

PROLOGUE

Ten months ago...

WORKING IN THE intimate bar of St Croix's Reyes Luxe hotel, adjacent to its world-famous wellness centre, Judah Reyes placed a mojito in front of the woman sitting at a high table closest to the bar. Her eyes didn't leave her phone, and she didn't register the drink or his presence. He took in her lovely profile, her straight nose and stubborn chin, and frowned. Judging by her rigid back and pale face, he wasn't sure when she last took a full breath.

Her screen was in his line of sight, and he saw a masculine hand resting on the inside of a slim tanned thigh, the faint tan line on his finger suggesting a recently removed wedding ring. Pointed red fingernails held a glossy brochure for the Reyes Luxe wellness centre. Maroon and gold, it looked a little old-fashioned, and very uptight. When he reached Reyes Luxe's marketing department, he'd suggest a corporate rebrand of their marketing assets to something less jaw-breakingly boring.

Actually, he had a lot of thoughts about Reyes Luxe's branding, the message they were promoting and the overall direction of the company. But that was a fight for later.

'He's like a toddler who can't be left alone for a minute. What a bastard.'

Her voice sounded disembodied, almost robotic. He'd served enough drinks to enough people to realise she was seriously rattled. 'Are you staying at this hotel?' he asked.

It took a couple of seconds for his words to land. She looked up at him, her pine-green eyes moving from his face to her drink and back again. 'Oh, hi. Thanks for bringing my drink over.'

She lifted her drink, and sucked. In the low lights of the bar, her long tawny hair—thick waves tumbling down her back—shimmered. She was small, petite, almost delicate, but she didn't need height to command attention. Pretty, sure, but it was a diluted word. She was effortlessly lovely, and heat-drenched desire shot down his spine.

Yep, and that was what made women like her extremely dangerous.

'Yes, I'm staying here for a few days, I have business here.'

Judah nodded at her phone. 'That doesn't look like business,' he said.

'My ex and his new girlfriend are here to, once again, mess with my life,' she replied bitterly.

Judah winced. While his parents had been happily married—they got hitched before the big money started rolling in—he'd grown up in and was part of a world where love was often linked to a business plan. When big money was at stake, relationships were often carefully negotiated contracts—strategic, sleek, and PR friendly. Few people married for love or for forever. They often married for the photos, to become a power couple, to maximise and merge brands.

He'd seen too many people stand at an altar, hand in hand, all smiles and designer tailoring, saying 'I do,' when what they really meant was, 'This will look good in a press release.'

Yeah, marriage had never been on his wish list. Not because he didn't believe in love, but because the real kind—messy, mutual, unfiltered—probably didn't exist. Not for someone like him. Not when your last name was Reyes and came with dollar signs and expectations.

Looking for a reason to hang around, Judah pulled a kitchen towel from his waistband and wiped the already clean table.

'How long have you worked as a bartender?' she asked.

'Here, a couple of months,' he replied, straightening. After earning his MBA at LSE a few years back, his dad had tried to slot him straight into a high-paying, decision-making executive role at Reyes Luxe. Judah immediately slammed on the brakes. What the hell did he know about running a global empire? Titles meant nothing if you didn't understand what powered and influenced them. So he'd opted for the long route.

It had been his choice to work within every department across the Reyes Luxe line—and because there were a lot of departments across multiple companies in ten or so countries, he might have a handle on the business in, hell, twenty years or so. Currently, he was gaining practical experience working in the food and beverage department of their St Croix hotel, and moonlighting as a bartender, a job he actually enjoyed.

The bonus? Being back on the island. To him, St Croix was more than just palm trees, clear sea and luxury villas—it was childhood summers and salt in his blood. It was home, even if he didn't live here full-time anymore. Judah looked around the bar, saw that no one needed his attention, and took in her beachy, floral dress, which dipped low to reveal the edges of a sexy midnight blue bra. Up close, he noticed her carefully applied make-up and curled hair. 'Are you waiting for him?' He nodded at her phone, still showing the photograph.

She snorted. 'As if.' She ran a finger around the rim of her glass, eyes fixed on the swirl of liquid inside.

'Hair, make-up, pretty dress,' he pointed out.

'Why do men automatically assume we dress up to look good for them?' she asked. Right. Fair point and he was an arse for assuming otherwise.

'Sorry,' he said. 'That was an asinine comment.'

She nodded, her eyes locked on his. She sighed, and her shoulders slumped. 'But you're not completely wrong.' She lifted her chin, green eyes flashing. 'If I run into him, and I probably will, I want him to know I'm thriving.'

'Are you?' he asked, not convinced.

She lifted one shoulder in a jerky shrug.

'I'm working on it. But he caused me a lot of grief, so I'm as good as I can be.' She wrinkled her straight nose. 'Why am I telling you this?'

He'd worked as a bartender through college and learned how to tune in to the vibes from his customers. He sensed their mood and instinctively knew when to speak and when his customers needed silence. 'People tend to talk to bartenders,' he reminded her. 'We're part magician, part therapist, part friend. I'm Judah, by the way.'

'Calla.'

'Judging from your accent, I'm guessing you are from New York.'

'And you're British.'

He'd been educated in the UK, but his childhood had been split between his parents' homes in New York, Lon-

don and the Far East. And St Croix. 'Why are both you and your ex on the island at the same time?'

'Jack and I are both bidding on an island-based project,' she replied. Her eyes flicked past him, toward the door. Judah turned, the back of his neck prickling.

Blond. Early forties, and fit in that over-polished, personal-trainer-on-speed-dial way. Judah recognised the type. Confident swagger, expensive watch, the kind of smug smile that announced that he was an entitled rich son-of-a-bitch. Judah hated him on sight. Not because he was unfamiliar—but because he was *too* familiar. Judah'd grown up with boys who became entitled men—cocky, privileged, relying on their instantly recognisable surnames and family money. He'd watched them slip and slide through life, dodging their commitments and responsibilities. And through his dad, he listened to stories about how their fathers charmed, schemed, manipulated and broke situations and people. Hell, he'd seen his father use money, power and influence to get a desired result.

He'd been, was still, terrified he might be tempted to lean into the unearned privileges that came with his instantly recognisable name. Call him stubborn or stupid, but Judah didn't want to be lumped into the same rotting heap of trust fund arrogance and entitlement. He refused to be another rich boy who'd earned nothing, who traded off his name, who'd had everything handed to him.

Screw that.

So yeah, his reaction to him was visceral. It was bone-deep irritation that rose like steam before reason could take hold. Right, it was definitely time for him to walk away.

'Enjoy your drink,' Judah said, pushing down his protective instincts. What was wrong with him? She was, at least, five years older than him, definitely in her mid-thirties, and she didn't want or need his protection. But something about her reminded him of a once glorious wilted rose whose petals were one breath from being blown away.

Judah slid behind the bar and positioned himself at the end, close to her table. He glanced at his watch and saw he was five minutes from the end of his shift. With luck, he wouldn't have to serve Mr Slick. Standing back, he smiled as the next shift's bartender slid behind the bar. He quietly greeted her and silently thanked her for coming in early. She could take over...

But, because his curiosity remained, he'd stand there, just for a few more minutes.

Calla was the first to speak, and when she did, her voice was stronger than he expected. 'Where's your latest conquest, Jack?'

His smarmy chuckle drifted over to Judah. 'She was tired after we...*after*.'

Judah gritted his teeth. *Prick.*

'I'm sure I know the answer to this question,' she said, her voice cool and even, 'but why are you here, in St Croix?'

Judah dropped his head to hide his smile, appreciating her tone and detachment. He hoped it was a verbal slap across Jack's smug, self-important face.

'Same reason as you, darling,' he drawled. 'Along with two other designers, I'm meeting with the owner of Reyes Luxe, hoping to secure the redesign for his island property.'

Sol House? *Hell, no!*

His voice scraped across Judah's nerves—too smooth, too rehearsed, nails dragging over a blackboard. 'I did warn him,' the man added, voice dropping into fake sympathy. 'I told him you weren't suitable and not experienced enough for a project like this. But Mr. Reyes insisted on seeing your work.'

Judah thought fast, recalling his father saying something about meeting interior designers to revamp Sol House, but he'd been rushing to be on time to make his shift and hadn't paid much attention. Judah didn't move, didn't speak, heat building behind his ribs. This jerk-off had no idea just how badly he'd overplayed his hand. He was far down the food chain at Reyes Luxe—his choice—so Judah rarely stuck his nose in his father's business. But Sol House had been his mum's personal property—a sanctuary filled with his best childhood memories, the one place where he could breathe easier and be wholly himself. There was no way he'd let that smug, Armani-clad jackass set foot in the only house he truly loved.

Yeah, *no.*

Not happening.

He tuned back in to their conversation. 'You've obviously forgotten I interned on a project for Mr Reyes years ago, before I made the crucial mistake of marrying and starting a business with you.'

'No, your biggest mistake was thinking you could leave without my permission.' His smile was slow, lacking humour and stolen off a snake. 'You had no right to walk away from me, from my name and from the life I gave you. No right to think you can operate in my world without me.'

Whoa, narcissistic much? Who the hell did this guy think he was?

'Why am I even sitting here listening to you?' she murmured, looking more fragile than she did before. Broken, a little lost. And her ex, the man who'd promised to love her, was enjoying every second of her pain and discomfort.

Calla picked up her phone and slid out of her chair. She swayed a little and gripped the edge of the round table, a rag doll about to collapse in on itself. There was no way he could leave her looking like that...

Thinking fast, Judah ducked into the bar's tiny stock room and pulled his black button-down shirt over his head, revealing a black, body hugging tank. He tugged it out of his black pants. Looking in the mirror behind the bar, he ruffled his slicked-back work-appropriate hair, and nodded when it fell over his forehead and into his eyes. He looked younger than he actually was, early twenties rather than late, ready to go bar hopping or clubbing, the tank showing off his muscled arms and chest.

It was time to put the good looks he'd inherited from his stunning mum to good use...

He shoved his wallet and phone into the pockets of his pants and ambled out from behind the bar, with what he hoped was a charming, anticipatory smile on his face. Walking straight up to Calla, and in one smooth move, he slid his arm around her too-thin waist and cupped her face in his hand. She was so warm, and she smelled like lime and lilies. Intoxicating.

He slid his hand to her lower back and tucked a long curl behind her ear, aiming to project a sense of familiarity, of shared intimacy. Calla opened her mouth to speak—the jackass looked both shocked and pissed off, and he didn't want her undoing all his good work—and he lowered his head to rest his lips on her ear. 'Let's give him some of his own medicine, huh?'

Pulling back, Judah handed her an easy grin. 'I've been looking for you. Are you ready to go, gorgeous?'

He held out his hand, not sure if she'd take it or slap

him. He desperately hoped for the latter, because he might punch Mr Slick if he smirked.

She blinked, her eyes wide, and Judah found himself mentally begging her to take his hand, to walk out of the bar with him. Many seconds later, her fingers met his, and he gave her hand a reassuring squeeze. He hauled air into his lungs and, pulling her as close to him as possible, led her out of the bar and into the warm Caribbean night.

CHAPTER ONE

TEN MONTHS LATER, in her Reyes Luxe hotel room on St Croix, Calla tossed her bag onto the white linen–covered double bed and walked over to the huge window dominating the space. The hotel overlooked Teague Bay's sun-drenched beaches and swaying palm trees. She'd forgotten that St Croix was a slow, honeyed sigh of an island, emanating a casual charm that seeped under the skin. The sea shimmered—emerald and sapphire light dancing on every swell and dip, bold, brilliant and utterly unapologetic. The colonial façades of the buildings were faded just enough to be romantic, and the scent of salt air was everywhere. It instinctively made her want to relax, to be a cat stretching out in the sun.

The memories of long-ago warm nights and hotter glances rolled over her, and she tasted the tang of lime and his kisses on her lips, remembering a tanned masculine body moving over hers. Part of her longed to be stretched out on a beach blanket beside someone she had no business wanting but couldn't stay away from—whispering midnight confessions between intense kisses, while the ocean listened in, shameless and uninvited.

Calla rocked back on her heels, the pretty hotel room fading, giving way to the still sharp, golden memory of him. The bartender with the crooked smile and sexy voice.

The younger man who'd made an outrageous suggestion, and then, with complete aplomb, knifed Jack—metaphorically, obviously—between the ribs by walking her into the night. Outside, instead of dropping her hand and walking away, he'd looked at her like she was ice cream on a steamy day and expected him to suggest they find a bedroom. But that hadn't happened.

Not then anyway.

He'd simply held her hand—hers small and cool, his much larger and tanned—and led her down a stretch of moonlit sand. The surf bubbled over the sand, a crab dodged the waves and his voice soothed her as he told her stories of island lore, of rebels and pirates and forgotten kings. It was absurd and magical—and somehow he managed to push the tense run-in with her ex, the one who'd left a decade's worth of scars, far, far away.

And then, when the glow of bars and restaurants gave way to darkness, he'd stopped and cupped her face, holding her like she was something precious. Without hesitation, he'd lowered his head and kissed her, slow and deep and thorough, as if he had all the time in the world.

Later, he'd walked her to his motorbike, no helmet, no hurry, and driven her across the island, showing her his personal playground. She pressed her face to his back, hair flying, arms wrapped tight around his wide chest or ribbed stomach, feeling alive in a way she hadn't in years. Calla knew he kept driving long after they should've stopped, just because she said she loved the wind and the rhythm of the engine. She hadn't been brave enough to tell him she'd, most of all, loved feeling him between her legs.

Later, when the rising sun kissed the sea good morning, they finally tumbled onto the bed in that one-room, ramshackle surf shack by the sea where he loved her like he meant it.

Again. And again. And again.

The sex had been, was still, the best of her life. It was also the only sex she'd had since her divorce. Calla placed a hand on her stomach, aching for that magical time when time stood still. Where was he now? Was he still running free, kissed by the sea and the sun? Still smiling like a man with no weight on his shoulders?

She glanced at herself in the ornate mirror across the room, the antithesis of that beachy woman whom he'd loved so well. Her curly hair was ruthlessly pulled back, sleek and straight. Her make-up was flawless, her outfit impeccable. She exuded control, professional distance.

Beneath her polished exterior, she saw faint lines at the corners of her eyes, a tiny strand of silver near her temple. Her neck ached, and the tightness in it, and her shoulders never really went away. She worked harder for everything now—her body, her business, her sanity. That woman on the beach? Barefoot, windblown, laughing in the dark? Calla barely recognised her. In some ways, she was as much a stranger to that version of herself as she was to that gorgeous man she'd spent too little time with.

Calla shook her head and mentally snapped herself back to the now. She wasn't here to daydream or for a vacation, she was here to work. To take another shot at a once-in-a-blue-moon project, a commission that would supercharge her business, boost her career and hopefully, rehabilitate her reputation. Or at the very least, restore it to what it was before.

She couldn't afford to waste time or be distracted by St Croix's loveliness or by remembering that sexy deep-voiced bartender who'd made her body sing, and her soul sigh. She might be at a honeymooner's dream destination, but her focus would be, as it always was, on her work. On landing the commission to redecorate and update Sol House. Calla kicked off her heels, opened the button on her fitted jacket, feeling the pull of her tight pencil skirt. She considered changing into a pair of cotton shorts and a T-shirt, but since she was due at Sol House in fifteen minutes, it wasn't worth the hassle.

After snatching a bottle of water from the bar fridge, she sat down on the bed and picked up her phone. As soon as she connected to the Wi-Fi, her phone started beeping with text and email notifications. Some from her assistant, one from her ex-husband.

She opened it and skimmed his words.

I hear you are in St Croix, and that you've been given an opportunity to submit a proposal to revamp Sol House. The project was abruptly put on hold last year, then shelved. Why are you getting the first crack at the commission?

She really should've deleted Jack's number months ago. Every time his name popped up on her screen—usually late at night, usually loaded with just enough nastiness to make her stomach twist—she thought, *Enough now. Cut him loose. I'm done.*

But she never hit that delete button.

Yes, she knew she was being perverse, and that she was clinging to the thin whispers of what remained of a toxic relationship. She didn't miss him, *God. No.* She kept reading his messages because those smug, casual, caustic, acidic messages—interspersed with demands she return to work for him at Atelier Abernathy—reminded her of how he'd ripped her apart with a smile on his face. Jack was the vehicle by which she'd learned a dozen lessons, both big and small, all of them hard. He'd taught her how not to trust, about the cost in giving too much, believing too easily, loving too deeply. He was the reason she didn't let people in.

One moment, she'd been a rising star in New York's competitive interior design scene; the next, an outsider and a liability. Thanks to Jack and his influential family, her work dried up, and clients stopped returning her calls, and the truth settled into her bones: if you didn't protect yourself, no one else would. Love wasn't a partnership; it was playing Russian roulette.

So, no. She didn't delete his number. Because every time his name flashed across her screen, it reminded her why she had rules now. Why she kept her emotions locked down, her life airtight, her business above reproach. Why she never let herself lean. Never on clients. Not on colleagues. Not on lovers.

And especially not on men.

But Jack, as always, had impressive connections and somehow had learned that the managing director of the Reyes Luxe wellness brand wanted to know whether she'd be interested in revamping Sol House, his impressive mansion on the east shore.

She should've felt flattered. Proud, even. But instead, the offer made her suspicious. Like Jack, she was curious why she was the first designer through the door. After the past few years of hell—a toxic divorce, public embarrassment, a stalled career, clients ghosting her—she couldn't work out why she was here. On merit? She doubted it. Jack had torched her reputation as a rising-star interior decorator, especially among those who awarded the kinds of commissions that attracted attention and built careers.

And, dammit, she couldn't rid herself of the persistent, insistent voice whispering that she wasn't quite good enough. That she didn't belong in Jack's world of elite and old-money properties and projects. She tried to fight her inner critic, but it was exhausting. But, bottom line, she *needed* this job. Not only for her career, but to prove to herself that she could still create. That her work still mattered. That *she* mattered.

Calla sighed, squared her shoulders and took a breath. Obsessing over the past wouldn't get the job done. Whatever the reason, being the first one in the door was a hell of a coup for a small designer operating a lean, independent studio out of a shared space in Brooklyn. While her name was, she hoped, quietly gaining traction again, she wasn't an A-list designer anymore, someone the owner of Reyes Luxe would normally contact. Maybe, because he was British, he wasn't au fait with what was happening in the NYC design scene and hadn't heard about her fall from grace.

But, because the email hinted at future work with Reyes Luxe if she satisfied the owner's expectations, she wasn't going to look a gift horse in the mouth. Or a commission that would give her immediate legitimacy, her career a life-changing boost. It was a lifeline, a high-profile, international contract that had the power to reset her entire reputation—under her own name, on her own terms.

Of course, she was going to take a shot at it. She wasn't an idiot. Or, to be scrupulously fair, she wasn't an idiot *anymore*.

According to his board of directors, his CFO and upper management, and his two assistants, there were a thousand things Judah Reyes should've been doing—in London, Singapore and New York. Instead, he stood barefoot on the veranda of Sol House, hands in the pockets of his chino shorts, staring at the horizon like it held the answers.

The sun was hot on his back, burning through his cotton button-down and making his skin prickle. The sea, far below him, rolled up onto the small private beach bordered by rocks, quietly relentless. Judah stretched and yawned. He'd had a fitful few hours of sleep and couldn't remember the last time he'd slept through the night. Definitely not since his father died, collapsing in the middle of a board meeting last year. One moment a titan, the next he was gone. His death had been the event that split life into before and after, a mental rift in Judah's psyche.

Judah before had been laid-back, happy to work behind the scenes and to be underestimated, perfectly content with taking his time to learn the family business, knowing that he had years, *decades*, before he needed to step into his father's too-large, too charismatic shoes. He'd been learning the business, taking his time, preferring to prioritise having a work-life balance rather than working the consistently long hours his father did. Though, looking back, it was fair to say that the work-life balance had been tilted toward having fun—working a little, surfing, travelling and partying more. His dad—larger than life, self-made, soft with Judah in a way he wasn't with the world—had encouraged it. *Take your time, son. There's no rush.*

He'd lied.

Instead of running the company for the next ten, twenty years, David succumbed to a massive heart attack and handed Judah a legacy, an international company and a harsh spotlight. He'd stepped up because he had no choice, not because he felt ready. And ten months on, he still didn't. He'd become a master of keeping his expression neutral as he signed off on multimillion-dollar deals, but under his tie and suit, his throat was tight and his heart careered off his ribcage as he second-guessed every decision. Would he ever feel like he belonged at the helm of Reyes Luxe? Would his father approve of and be proud of the job he was doing?

Out of the office, he smiled for the cameras on red carpets and magazine covers, but he didn't recognise the man wearing his face dressed in Thom Browne and Zegna suits, hair carefully styled.

St Croix and Sol House were the only places he could still breathe—just a little. Sol House held most of his memories of his mum, and was the only one of his properties that felt real, where he could remember his father as being just a dad. The house still smelled like his dad's cigars and sun-dried linen. This was where his father taught him to swim, to paddle, to surf. Where they sailed and swam and talked about everything and nothing. After his mum passed, and for a month every summer, they'd spent time here, just the two of them. He hadn't been back since his death, and the house felt lifeless, cold, abandoned, filled with silence and the echoes of happier times.

The sea beckoned him to come play, but he'd yet to walk down the path to the secluded cove. He'd arrived the day before yesterday, and all he'd done was work. He put his foot down this morning, telling his assistant he didn't want to be disturbed unless the markets crashed or aliens landed. The reality was that he might have today, Friday, and this upcoming weekend to himself. If he was lucky.

Judah pushed his hand through his hair and released a frustrated sigh. He also needed to figure out where to take the company, what he wanted from it. He'd just finalised his dad's last planned project and from now on, the direction of Reyes Luxe was his alone—every win, every loss, every person's job, share prices, returns and dividends were on him.

It felt...heavy. Overwhelming.

After his father's death, he'd avoided St Croix and the house, telling himself he was too busy to visit. And he had been, initially, he'd barely had time to breathe. But as the shock faded, he started questioning everything— where he was going, what the company stood for, who he was, what he wanted—and he started craving silence and salt water. The urge to feel like' himself, not the face of Reyes Luxe, burned through him and threatened to consume him. He craved authenticity and to reconnect with who he was before...before he became an icon, an heir, a brand. But that version of himself—unguarded, unpolished, whole—felt like a stranger he couldn't quite reach.

The last time he truly felt like himself was ten months ago, right here in St Croix—a few days before his dad died, when he was laughing with and loving Calla. It was the last time he'd felt fully relaxed, completely at ease in his skin. Lately, for some strange, irrational reason, he couldn't shake the feeling that being with her again might help him find that version of himself. It was bizarre. Nuts. But the thought lingered. Then it hit him— Calla was a designer, and the only reason she'd come to the island in the first place last year was to pitch for the Sol House renovation.

Sure, the house needed upgrading, but it was low on his priorities and, truthfully, it was an excellent excuse to see Calla again. So he'd told his assistant to make her an offer to be the first person to submit her designs for the revamp. He wasn't committing to anything just yet; depending on whether he liked her ideas, he might hire her.

And she was arriving—he glanced at his Breitling—shortly. His breath caught in his throat, and his heart rate accelerated. He didn't believe in lasting connections and relationships were too risky. He'd lost his father between one heartbeat and two. Love was just another way to be gutted by grief. And really, no one was able to see him beneath the gloss and money. But Sol House held the version of him he missed, the man who didn't carry the weight of a billion-dollar empire on his back. And during those thirty-six hours with Calla, he'd been the best version of himself—unfiltered, open and fully alive.

And maybe—if he was lucky—these next few weeks with Calla would show him the way back to being the man he used to be.

Sol House stood behind a private gate on St Croix's northeast shore and was exactly as Calla had expected—elegant, expansive and quietly breathtaking. Calla stepped through the columned entrance, past the murmuring fountain and into the great room, where crystal chandeliers caught the Caribbean light like diamond drops. The bones of the house were beautiful—vaulted ceilings, French doors, curated art she'd presumed would be kept—but the interior was stuck somewhere between the '80s and death.

She remembered the photos she'd been sent by the CEO's PA: the kitchen was a black granite shrine, the heavy old-fashioned dining table sat twelve, and the bedrooms? Bland and boring and in desperate need of charm and soul. The east wing was all size and shine—spa baths, gold-veined marble, walk-in closets—while the master suite within the west wing boasted a lounge, terrace and more bland and boring. The library cum office, separating the master bedroom and lounge, was a gem, with soft light and comfortable furniture, and an exceptional view, all perfect for daydreaming.

Despite its mishmash styling, the house was a love letter to old-style Caribbean living. Just a little worn, a little faded. The design brief she'd received from his PA—if it could be called that!—was to make it sophisticated enough for upscale entertainment, but it still had to feel like a home. Sure. *Easy.* She'd solve the Middle East crisis while she was at it.

Calla's heels click-clacked on the Italian marble as she crossed the great room, walking behind a casually dressed woman who introduced herself as Bella, the part-time housekeeper. She wanted to stop and inspect what she thought might be a Jim Lambie on the wall, a Nicholas Hlobo sculpture in the far corner. Reminding herself that she would be spending the next two weeks—at least!—in this house and on the island, and to be patient, she checked that the zip of her pencil skirt was in the middle of her back, and the pendant of her necklace rested in the centre of her throat. Yes, she was detail oriented, but in her job, she had to be.

Details, control and self-reliance, along with independence, were the four cornerstones of her life.

Her thoughts stopped as she caught sight of the view off the expansive balcony. Calla placed her hand on her heart and simply stared, her lungs forgetting how to haul in air. The ocean was so endless, compelling, and an indescribable shade of blue, not turquoise or sea-green or aqua, simply undefinable and delightful. Sea and so much of it. She glanced at the blue infinity pool extending a little way off the cliff and easily imagined her arms on the edge, feeling she was about to fall into the sky and sea.

She'd admired houses before—even coveted a few—but she'd never fallen head over heels for one. Not like this, and not until now. The view was *everything*. The kind of everything that made her brain misfire and her heart stutter.

'Everybody loses their breath when they first walk onto the veranda.'

Instant recognition stiffened her spine and caused her heart to flutter, then shudder. That voice…deeper, darker, more compelling—it was the same one that painted compliments on her skin, whispered dirty, delightful suggestions against her lips and called her name when his orgasm rushed over him. Calla felt her knees weaken and clenched her fists, telling herself she couldn't pass out, couldn't gasp or sway or act like a fool.

Couldn't…*holy hell*. What was she supposed to do? Say?

Biting down hard on her lip, she half turned and, as casually as possible, slipped her Audrey Hepburn glasses onto her face, hoping the gesture would give her a couple of seconds to gather her composure. But how was it that her sexy bartender was standing on the terrace of Judah Reyes's luxury St Croix house…

Unless…no! Unless he was the owner, the CEO…

No. Way.

Way.

Calla resisted the urge to bite her lip as she took him in. He looked taller, bigger, meaner…older. His shoulders were as wide as she remembered, his chest as broad. The face she remembered had been open and ready to smile, but now his expression held shadows. His lips were thinner and pressed together. She couldn't see a hint of his dimple, and his eyes were darker, flatter, lacking the warmth from before. This was, but wasn't, the same person.

'It's been a while, Calla. Have you been well?'

He sounded like he was ordering coffee, like they'd met last week, like he hadn't buried his head between her legs, making her crash and burn, like he hadn't made her laugh. Or think. Or wish she could give up her New York life to live in a one-room surf shack beside the sea.

'What? I don't understand—'

He lifted one bigger shoulder. 'It's pretty simple, really. Last year, my father wanted this place revamped and invited three or four designers to submit designs, yours being one of them. The following week, he died of a heart attack.'

Calla grimaced. 'I heard that. I'm sorry for your loss,' she murmured. She'd received a generic email from someone last year informing the designers of his death and that the project to revamp Sol House had been shelved.

He nodded briefly. 'Sol House needed revamping then—it needs it more now.'

Okay, she understood that much. 'Your PA told me I'm the only one who's been asked to submit designs to upgrade your home. I don't understand why you haven't asked other designers to pitch their proposals, as well.'

He hesitated, an action so brief that Calla wasn't sure if she'd imagined it or not. 'I'm trying to take a vacation, and I didn't want a gaggle of designers invading my space, so I thought I'd start with you,' he told her.

His reply made sense, but... Calla tilted her head, trying to read the flicker in his eyes. What did it signify— challenge? Regret? Something else entirely?

'If I like what you do,' he continued, smooth as glass,

'it could lead to more work with Reyes Luxe. A few of my wellness centres, including the one here on St Croix, are due for a refurbishment.'

Damn, that was one hell of a carrot. For a small designer, landing Sol House would be impressive, working on a Reyes Luxe property would be career defining. His name on her portfolio would put her on the map in all the right ways. It would also shut Jack the hell up. That would be a huge bonus.

But something still tugged at her gut. The offer was golden, yes—but why did it feel like there was more beneath the surface than what he was saying? Like he wasn't just handing her an opportunity but also daring her to take it. Like his offer was the tip of a massive, concealed iceberg?

Her mind reeled, trying to make sense of the past few minutes. 'Sorry, you've caught me off guard. I thought you were a bartender, a surfer, not the CEO and owner of one of the world's most recognisable brands.' Over the past few months she'd been too busy keeping her head down and working herself to the bone to stay afloat to pay much attention to the news, business or otherwise.

His eyes darkened, and his lips thinned. 'When we met, I was a bartender, I did surf, all the time, and I wasn't in charge. That all happened after...' He pushed his hand into his hair. 'After.'

His frown didn't lift. Stepping closer to her, Judah used his finger and thumb to pull her sunglasses off her face. Well, there was no hiding now. His eyes darted across her face, and wherever they landed, she felt their impact, a tingle, a buzz. Her cheeks reddened as she remembered him looking at her like this just before he...

Okay, can't think about that now, he was her client. Her

very rich, very influential, very sexy client. Dear God, she'd slept with her client. Potential client...*whatever.*

'I prefer your hair curly, and you wearing a loose dress and being barefoot,' he said, handing her her glasses. Their fingers brushed, and sparks skittered up her arm, into her core.

Oh no! No! No! No! She still couldn't be attracted to him. That wasn't, on any planet or in any galaxy, acceptable.

She knew where that road led. Mixing business and romance had already blown up, rather spectacularly, in her face. Jack had made sure of that. She'd trusted him with her heart, her future, her career—and when he was done with her, he'd dismantled all three with the efficiency of a nuclear strike.

She'd been left with a crater where her confidence used to be.

So no, she couldn't go down that road again. She was in a never-ending battle to restore her professional credibility. She couldn't risk the progress she'd made for a man who made her stomach flip every time he smiled. The human equivalent of—she glanced at the ocean beyond his big bicep—that yacht skimming out to sea and disappearing from view.

Attraction was dangerous. And trust wasn't something she believed in anymore. Calla swallowed and gripped the handle of her tote bag tightly. 'I came dressed for a business meeting, to meet a potential client.'

Not you.

'It's good to see you again.' If it was, why had he never bothered to track her down before this? It wouldn't have been hard to do. Calla pushed that thought away, annoyed with herself. She knew very well that a one-night stand was all he'd offered, and that any further conversation or connection hadn't been part of the deal.

Besides, she'd been a mess last year and would've been horrified if Judah rocked up in Brooklyn, looking to reconnect. She hadn't had the mental capacity back then—didn't have it now—to pay attention to anything but work, to rebuilding her name and her company. He would've been an unwanted and unwelcome distraction.

So why was she disappointed? Stupid. And illogical.

Judah pushed his hand through his too-long hair, and the ends brushed the collar of his cotton shirt. Then he gestured to the chairs sitting under the roof of the veranda. 'Let's get out of the sun,' he suggested. He looked at the lady who let her in, and Calla caught a small smile on his lips. 'Bella, could you bring us something to drink?' He turned to Calla, his eyes connecting with hers. 'Freshly squeezed juice, iced tea or water?' he asked.

How could he ask her about liquid refreshments when her brain had been deep fried? She forced herself to concentrate. 'Anything is fine.'

Judah ordered iced tea and gestured for her to take a seat. Calla placed her bag and portfolio case on the seat beside her and licked her lips. What was the protocol when your potential client also happened to be the hottest mistake of your life? Or maybe not a mistake—just a memory you'd replayed too many times, always in the dark, always alone.

Calla decided to bite the bullet. 'What's this all about, Judah?'

He took a moment to answer her. 'Last year, you—and one or two other designers who probably didn't hear about my father's death—sent in your renovation plans for this house, just like my father requested.' When Judah slipped into that formal tone, Calla could picture him in a sharp suit, behind a massive desk at Reyes Luxe, running the show. 'I've finished the business projects he started before he died—I'd like to finish this personal one too. So I looked at those designs.'

Calla waited for him to say something about her work, to compliment her designs, but he just looked at her, silent and sombre. He wasn't the carefree man she'd spent the night with, the one who complimented her easily and frequently. He was her client, and this was a professional situation.

It would've been a lot easier to get her head around that concept if she could stop replaying the way he'd lifted her like she weighed nothing, holding her steady against him as he kissed her absolutely senseless. She shook her head, trying to concentrate on the here and now, but, behind her eyelids, images of him whipping off his shirt, acres of tanned skin exposed to her touch, flickered, then burned. The way he looked at her, with reverence and appreciation as he undid the clasp of her bra, his fingertips sliding over her nip—

Work, Calla! You are here as a professional decorator, not as his one-time, brief lover. That was in the past... way in the past.

Calla wiggled in her chair, grateful when Bella placed a glass in front of her. She thanked her, lifted it to her lips and sighed at the combination of mint, lemon and ice. She drained half and leaned back in her seat, and tucked her foot behind her calf. It was time to stop remembering and start business-ing. *Compartmentalise, Calla. You're good at that.*

'Something about what I did back then must've resonated with you for you to invite me back.'

He didn't drop his eyes from hers and, once again, she felt like she was missing out on a fairly significant puzzle piece. Something that would bring the picture into focus.

'Is that what happened?' she pressed.

He took a long time to answer her. 'Something like that,' he said, not giving anything away.

Calla didn't believe him.

CHAPTER TWO

JUDAH RAN A hand through his hair and stared out over the infinity pool, where the horizon blurred the edge of the Caribbean sky and sea. He'd done the right thing by bringing Calla here. The second he saw her standing in the foyer—tote bag in one hand, proficiency wrapped tight around her like armour—he'd known.

Calla was the only choice. Professionally, sure. But also…inexplicably, personally. It didn't make any sense—it was something that no one would understand…it simply was.

He allowed his eyes to wander over her, taking in what remained the same, the changes. She was older, but then, so was he. This Calla was sleeker, sharper, spikier. Harder. But he'd caught something familiar in her eyes, the flash of curiosity, the spark of excitement as she took in his dated, but still glorious house. She stirred something in him he hadn't felt in a long time. Something reckless. Something real.

The moment her fingers brushed his, when their eyes first connected and he inhaled her light perfume, he experienced an unfamiliar pulse in his veins, something he hadn't felt since…well, *her*. It was need, and want, the thrill of taking a risk. The time they spent together was a looping movie playing on his mind's big screen—high-

lighting her laughter, her unfiltered honesty, the occasional flashes of vulnerability and insecurity she probably
thought she hid. He still remembered the creamy heat of
her skin, the salt on her lips, them sharing stories like they
had all the time in the world, their out-of-control passion.

But he never expected her to *still* affect him as much
as she did.

Judah exhaled and rubbed the back of his neck. She
hadn't known who he was then. She'd simply seen him.
Just him.

No one had—not truly—for almost a year now. But a
small part of him, the piece that still clung to ideas like
fate and magic, couldn't help but wonder if he'd been…
God, he mocked himself for even thinking it…*guided* to
bring her back into his life. He recalled how he felt, just a
month ago, flat and uninspired, burdened, while he unen-
thusiastically searched for an old set of plans on his dad's
laptop. The folder labelled *Sol House Revamp* on the system jumped out at him and curiosity got the better of him.
He clicked—and there it was. Her name. Another impatient click later, and he was staring at her work.

He'd scanned her proposal, then went back for another,
deeper, look. While he hadn't loved everything about her
submission, it was immediately obvious she understood
the soul of his house. Its wear, its warmth, its history. Its
wounds. The other designers had seen a luxury property,
but she'd seen a home.

Her vision, back then, wasn't about making Sol House
something it wasn't, and her proposal centred around bringing it back to life. Then he started wondering about what
it would be like to be with her at Sol House, watching her
work on ideas for revamping the house. The idea of bringing
her to St Croix had taken root and refused to be dislodged.

He told himself Sol House needed someone like her—a designer with sensitivity and restraint. That he needed to be there to answer her questions, to oversee things. But deep down, he knew the renovation wasn't the real reason he'd reached out. If he was being honest—truly honest—he was looking for something in himself. Chasing a version of the man he used to be, the one he'd last been with her: barefoot, sun-kissed, free. A man he could barely even remember.

He hadn't brought Calla here just to restore Sol House.

Admitting that to himself was hard enough. Telling her? Impossible. Not now. Maybe not ever. So he'd keep it professional and keep their attention focused on the project. Whatever was going on in his head, it was his to carry. He wouldn't lay the weight of his issues on her—or anyone.

He drained his glass of tea and crunched through an ice cube, lightly banging the base of his glass against his thigh. 'Sol House hasn't been updated since God knows when, and it desperately needs work.'

Calla tipped her head to the side and he was grateful when she didn't rush in to agree with him. This house was like a sibling; he could criticise it, but didn't like others doing the same. 'It's huge and every room needs an upgrade of one sort or another. Have you tackled a project this big?'

Calla rocked her hand up and down. 'Not a house, but I was involved in the renovation of a historic inn, which isn't that different. But big or small, my process is still the same.'

'Which is?'

'Nailing my client's vision, understanding his or her lifestyle, and wants and needs. Obviously, that would require us to sit down for a detailed briefing.'

Judah shifted, tension creeping into his shoulders. 'Can't we just walk through the house and call it good?' he muttered, his tone sharper than he intended.

It wasn't about curtains or couches. It was about *her*. About being here with her—*in this house, on this island*— and being bombarded by memories. Of his dad and his childhood. Of him and Calla together. Of the person he used to be.

Bringing Calla here had been great in theory, but it suddenly felt like too much. Like she might see too much. He'd brought her here to help him reconnect with the parts of himself he'd buried—but being this close to her was more challenging than he'd expected.

Calla crossed one leg over the other and rested her forearm on her knee. 'You're assuming that I'm going to take on your project, Judah. I'm not sure I am.'

Judah was fully aware of the power of the Reyes Luxe name, and he frequently used it as a carrot and a stick in business negotiations. He knew that if this project went out to tender, he'd have the best designers chomping for the chance to revamp Sol House, for a foot in the Reyes Luxe door.

He might be in St Croix, in casual clothes, but this was just another negotiation—he was simply doing another deal. Yeah, and the sea below them was made of whiskey. He schooled his features and kept his expression imperturbable.

'Everyone in the industry knows that whoever lands the contract to design my house has a serious edge when it comes to future design work for Reyes Luxe—because they've already managed to impress me on a personal level. There's so much work that it would be a full-time position.'

Back then, she'd pleased him on an ultra-personal level, but he couldn't think about that now. Sure, inviting Calla here wasn't purely a business decision, but it wasn't fully personal either. He liked her designs, liked her work and thought she might be a designer he could work with. But she was also the woman he'd never been able to forget— the one who'd appeared shortly before he'd faced a major crossroads in his life, making him wonder if Fate was just messing with his head. But she didn't need to know any of that.

'You'd be a fool to turn down one hell of an opportunity because we slept together, Calla,' he said, keeping his tone bland.

'I'm not even sure I want to work for anyone or be a corporate designer, Judah,' she shot back. 'I like being my own boss.'

He respected that, and he also liked calling the shots. It might be stressful and lonely, and he might second-guess himself daily, but now that he was used to power, he couldn't imagine giving it up or taking orders from someone else. The only difference between what he and Calla did was the amount of money involved and the scale.

'But what you can't deny is that your being here, after being asked to submit a proposal, is bound to get people talking. Right now, they are wondering what I know that they don't, whether they missed out on something special by not hiring you, and whether you are going to be the next big thing. If I like your proposal and hire you, you will be on everyone's lips, and the offers with roll in. The PR and publicity factor will be considerable. That's the power of Reyes Luxe, Calla.'

'When you put it like that...' she murmured, running her fingers across her forehead, the unconscious action suggesting she had a headache. He wasn't surprised since her hair was tight against her head and her clothes were more suited to corporate boardrooms. He looked down at her feet scrunched into tight two-inch heels and winced. She needed the wind in her hair and her toes in the sand...

And there he went, crossing the line from professional to personal.

'You're right—it's not an offer I can walk away from,' she said, sounding glum.

'I'm not leading you to an execution, Calla.'

She raised her eyes to look at his and cocked her head. 'No, of course you're not. So why do I get the feeling there's a lot more to this offer than what you're letting on?'

He knew what she was asking, whether he expected them to roll back the months to when he last saw her, naked and lovely in his bed. Whether that was part of the deal he was offering. Annoyance bit, but he forced it away. He couldn't blame her for thinking that way...

For centuries, millennia, men used their power over women to get their way, and the power balance was often tipped in their favour. He might've been a surfing bartender last year, but now he had the power and influence to change her life for the better. And she wanted to know what he wanted in return.

It was a completely fair question. But if he told her the truth—*please help me reconnect to who I was, take me back to a simpler time, hell, rewind time for me*—she'd run a mile. All he could do was reassure her that he expected nothing from her that wasn't work and design related.

What he hoped for was another story. 'You're here to do a job, to suggest a new look, to convince me it's what I want. I'm not going to pressurise you for more. It'll be strictly business for as long as you want it to be.'

Her head jerked up, and her gaze smashed into his. 'What does that even mean?'

'Exactly that. Nothing more. Nothing less.' Judah rose to his feet and slipped his hands into the pockets of his shorts. 'Spend the next few hours exploring the house, getting a sense of the scale of the project. Then come and find me and I'll take you on a tour of the grounds. Later this afternoon, you can give me your impressions and broad ideas for how you think it should be updated. If I like what you have to say, we'll move on to the next step.'

Well, on the plus side, she wasn't bolting for the door. Calla nodded and unfolded her long legs to push her way to her feet. 'Is there any room you'd prefer I didn't see at this point? A private place?'

He swallowed his snort. 'You've seen me naked, so seeing my bedroom or bathroom isn't that big a deal.'

She flushed, heat crawling into her cheeks, and he silently cursed. *Not helpful, Reyes. Professional, remember?* He looked down and frowned at her squished feet in her black heels, and just like that, made a new rule. 'Also, I'm not a fan of shoes in my house, so I'd prefer you remove yours.'

Because, damn, her feet needed a break.

Calla looked adorably confused as she removed one shoe, then the other, her head now not even reaching his shoulder. He'd forgotten how petite she was. 'Sorry, I didn't know.'

'It's the Caribbean, there's no need to be formal.' Would he be pushing his luck if he suggested that she remove the tight band holding her hair back, to pull her shirt out from her skirt? Probably.

Definitely.

'As I said, find me when you are done. I'll be around.'

He felt his phone vibrate and then heard the personalised chirp telling him his assistant was looking for him. He walked away from Calla, hard to do, and pulled his phone from his pocket. That his PA was reaching out so soon after their last conversation meant that there was a crisis somewhere. *Crap.* Could he not have one day off?

Just one?

Calla wiggled her toes and sighed when she felt the blood flowing back into her cramped digits. She savoured the sun-warmed stone tiles beneath her feet, then walked over to the wall keeping her from falling the hundred feet down the cliff. Leaning on it, she rested her fore-arms and clasped her hands. She wanted to run, to catch a taxi back to the airport and return to Brooklyn, where she knew what she was doing. Well, sort of knew what she was doing. She hustled for work, tried to ignore her ex and did far more than she was asked for the clients she did manage to land, so that neither Jack nor Candice had any ammunition to use against her. So that she could al-ways defend her work with complete conviction.

She turned around and lifted her eyes to take in the multilevel house. The tri-level Tuscan-style villa blended old world elegance with Caribbean appeal. Terracotta roof tiles, arched windows and weathered stucco walls gave the exterior a sun-warmed, Mediterranean vibe. This outdoor entertainment area, running the length of the house, was magnificent. It had three seating areas, couches in nineties flower prints close to the entrance, chairs under huge um-brellas next to the Jacuzzi and six loungers, two of which were double size, dotted around the pool. A sixteen-seater dining table occupied the space next to the Mexican-inspired outdoor kitchen, and next to it was a modern-looking bar with mirrors behind the fully stocked shelves.

It was a mishmash of styles and Calla wanted to get her hands on it. Desperately.

It was a crime to turn her back to the ocean, but she had to keep her eyes on the prize as she tried to make sense of her morning. She placed her hand on her too-fast heart and knew it was racing from a combination of excitement and confusion. Judah, the man who shattered her emotional equilibrium so easily ten months ago.

The same but so different: calm, commanding, flexing his confidence and wearing his power like a second skin. The contrast between the man he was then and now made her feel off balance and, yeah, rattled. Back then, with him, she'd felt weightless, like she was stepping into light and laughter. She'd found it so easy to talk to him, to let go, to *be*.

But the stakes were higher now, and she wasn't someone desperate to step out of her life. She wasn't as lost, as vulnerable. Scrabbling to reestablish her business, hustling for clients, working long hours had hardened and focused her, and she wasn't easily distracted. Yet he just needed to look at her from those lapis lazuli eyes and the ground shifted, rocking and rolling, beneath her.

It annoyed her that he still had an effect on her. Sure, he was a very good-looking, ripped, tall guy, but there had to be more to her reaction than a woman's appreciation for a hot man. She wasn't a teenager, for God's sake! So why did he still get under her skin? And why, dammit, did she desperately want to crawl into his arms, rest her head on his chest and *connect*?

She couldn't; that was impossible. And mixing sex and work would be a stupid thing to do. He was right—revamping Sol House would catapult her back into the big leagues. While she wasn't tempted (much) by the idea of becoming Reyes Luxe's in-house designer, a high-profile, international contract with Judah had the power to reset her entire reputation—under her own name, and on her own terms.

Stomping back to her tote bag, she pulled out her tablet and, still standing, jabbed the power button. After it booted up, she pulled up her old submission she sent to Judah's father last year. She scrolled through the images and renderings, wincing a little. They weren't bad; they had potential, but they were so damn *safe*. They lacked confidence and were tentative, a reflection of who she'd been at the time. With the distance of time, she knew they weren't good enough, and she wouldn't have, even if David Reyes hadn't collapsed, been awarded the contract. But she wasn't that designer anymore. She'd honed her skills, sharpened her pencils—metaphorically and literally— and was up to the challenge of Sol House. She could now handle anything life threw at her.

Including Judah Reyes. She'd be stepping into his world again, but this time she'd have boundaries. She'd keep their relationship purely professional, and her heart locked down and unaffected, her libido in check. She had to stay detached. And controlled. She couldn't afford to make the same mistake twice—not after Jack. Not after the humiliation of mixing business and love and having it blow up in her face. She'd lived that once. She would not allow that to happen to her again. And definitely not with Judah.

She was here to work. To prove to herself—and to everyone watching—that she could regain what Jack ripped from her and rebuild everything he tried to destroy. That she was still worthy. Still in control.

She was definitely not here to fail. Or to fall.

Well, there was no time like the present and no point in putting this off. Calla slid her tablet back into her tote bag and looked down at her discarded shoes. She loved the smooth stone of the floor under her feet. Judah's '*no shoes in the house*' decree meant she'd have to explore barefoot, forcing her to feel the house. She was very okay with that.

And, God, what a house.

Inside the great room, it was cool and quiet, reminding her of a grand old lady taking a nap. Even asleep, she oozed personality—hints of faded glamour, stubborn beauty and unapologetic originality.

Calla trailed her fingers along the edge of the antique sideboard and took in the grand chandelier hanging from the ceiling. It was far too large and a little absurd in this Caribbean light, but somehow, it worked. Maybe it was the contradiction that made it interesting. Much like the man who now owned it.

This first walkthrough, without notes or a camera, was, despite everything that had happened, her favourite part of the process and the one thing Jack never managed to touch or taint. She cocked her head and listened to the house breathe, allowing it to be. To speak to her, if it wanted to. At the bottom of the staircase, a side table showed a long-forgotten deep white water ring. She could see the vase that once stood there: overflowing with lilies, lilacs, maybe garden roses. She could smell the floral scent trailing up the stairs behind someone barefoot and laughing, their tanned skin bearing hints of sea salt and sun. Someone happy. Someone *home*.

Despite everything, there was still joy in connecting with a property. She adored the house's soaring ceilings, the wrought iron details and the eclectic collection of art, from both Titans in the art world and those she thought might be island based. The upper-level guest suites were elegant but in need of attention. The gym boasted sleek top-of-the-line equipment. The wall panelling, however, needed to be ripped out and burned. It was dark, masculine and suffocating. Working out was hard enough; you didn't need to look at ugly walls while you punished yourself.

The kitchen—well, the less said about that, the better. And, ugh. It was all black stone and stainless steel—it felt like a catering kitchen. She opened one of the two eye-level ovens and frowned at its pristine condition. It didn't look like it had ever been used. She wrinkled her nose and climbed the staircase to the master suite.

Judah's scent hit her the second she stepped into his space.

It was still so familiar, an indefinable combination of spice, citrus…cedar? It was masculine, expensive and, infuriatingly, still the same smell she remembered from all those months ago. Trying to ignore the memories threatening to suck her in—of her putting her nose to his neck and inhaling him—she took in his bedroom, empty but for the absurdly large bed facing a wall of glass doors leading out onto a wraparound deck. From his bed, he could watch the ocean in all its moods.

Calla peeked into his walk-in closet and blinked. The man had more clothes than she did. Far too many shelves were dedicated to board shorts and even more to T-shirts in what she could only describe as designer monotony: navy, black, white, charcoal…

Shaking her head, a little amused, Calla walked out onto his private deck through the open glass doors next to the right side of his bed. Below her was a tropical garden bordering an immaculately maintained swathe of green grass. Walking around the corner, she put her back to that huge bed, and tried not to remember another bed in another place, a lot less opulent than this, but as sexy.

Don't go there, Calla. Sunlight dazzled off the sea, and the ocean breeze playfully tugged at her blouse. She rounded the corner and caught a glimpse of the stone terrace below, halfway down the cliff to the beach. On it, Judah's tall, broad frame moved with easy purpose. He was shirtless as he waxed a surfboard lying on a concrete table with wooden benches.

Her breath caught before she could stop it, her body remembering how he touched her, something her brain was desperate to forget. She narrowed her eyes, squinting against the glare. He looked relaxed, content. Not like a man who controlled a global company worth more millions than she could imagine.

He looked out to sea, and Calla followed his gaze, seeing the waves breaking offshore. Not the biggest, but surfable. If she didn't interrupt him now, she'd be stuck here until he came back. Which, judging from the memory of the last time, was long enough for her to wonder if he'd been swept out to sea.

If she was going to bid for this project, she had work to do and couldn't wait hours for him to come back. Her sketchbooks were still in her suite at the hotel. Her laptop, her pens—everything she needed was back there. But, before she could start, she needed to formally accept Judah's offer to submit her ideas.

Calla took a breath. Then another. Then marched barefoot back through Sol House and down to the terrace, hoping she could keep her spine straight and her heart in check.

Calla's pulse pounded as she wandered down the path that would eventually lead to the private beach cove. She

stopped at the edge of the stone terrace halfway down, her eyes on Judah standing next to a long, well-used surf-board, applying wax with slow, practised strokes.

The breath snagged in her throat. She knew what she was doing with paint samples, and fabrics, with textures and perspective, but she had no idea how to handle this muscular man with shadows in his eyes. His skin glowed warm and golden, the ridges of his back flexing with each movement. He didn't look like a CEO. Nor did he look like the man who'd handed her a massive opportunity in an '*Iced Americano to go*' voice. Right now, he looked like he did that night. Like the man who'd walked her out of the hotel and kissed her like he already knew how she'd taste.

He looked up, eyes shaded by the sun, but that crooked half-smile she remembered, the one she found so sexy, lifted the corners of his mouth.

'You were a while,' he commented.

'Mm. There was a lot of house to explore.' She folded her arms, ignoring the way her fingers itched to brush the swoosh of sand off his left shoulder. His damp board shorts suggested he'd already taken a dip. She was jealous; the sea looked cool and inviting. But then she remembered it was June, the height of summer, and would probably be the temperature of barely heated soup. 'I didn't expect to find you out here.'

Judah wiped his hands on a towel and stood, tall and barefoot, lifted the board off the bench and planted its tip in the sand next to his foot. 'I took a call, sent a few emails and decided that it was too beautiful a day to be inside.'

'How often do you get to come out to the island?' she asked, running her toe up and down the back of her bare calf. She felt a little silly standing barefoot, her shirt still carefully tucked into the band of her tight-fitting skirt, with strands of her hair escaping from her sleek tail. She tucked them behind her ears.

He glanced out at the horizon to where the water shimmered like a sheet of polished blue glass. 'I haven't been back since that weekend.'

She waggled a finger between his chest and hers. 'Since we...'

'Yeah.' He sighed and rubbed his shoulder blade, the one free of sea sand. 'I flew in a couple of days ago.' Yet instead of taking the time to settle in, he'd invited her out to get working on his house. Why so soon? Why hadn't he taken a few days to decompress?

'I'm still getting into the rhythm of being here, the pace of the island,' Judah added.

She lifted her hand. 'The island has a pace?' she asked. 'What is it called? One beat faster than sleepy?'

He smiled, and Calla's stomach flipped over. God, the combination of his quirking lips, flash of white teeth and the shallow dimple in his stubble could liquefy knees at fifty paces.

'I've decided to take your job offer,' she said, hearing the tremble in her voice and hating it.

'I'm sure that you'd prefer your client to be anyone but me.'

She bit the inside of her lip and forced herself to meet his enigmatic eyes. 'A client is a client,' she murmured.

'Liar,' Judah softly retorted. 'You hate the personal connection.'

She couldn't deny it, and a part of her wanted to insist that nothing personal remained between them—that she'd feel the same way if he were any other man. She didn't have time for complications, romantic or personal, because she had to focus on growing her company and proving Jack and the Abernathy clan wrong. That she was talented, reliable and responsible. That she belonged in the world they ruled. And the only way she could do that was by landing a big whale client. They didn't get much bigger than Judah Reyes.

'So you're willing to give it a shot?'

'Yes, despite the surprise reunion. Despite the...' She sighed, looking for the right words. 'Despite everything.' The memories, the potential emotional landmines she'd have to dodge. She couldn't pass this up; she'd regret it forever if she did.

Something flickered in Judah's gaze. Relief?

'Good.' He handed her a sharp nod. 'Professionally, I'll give you all the input you need. I want you to bring the house back to life.'

By qualifying his statement, by sliding in the word *professionally*, he made her think of that iceberg again, of strong currents underneath a calm surface. What was she missing? The best way to find out was to ask. She narrowed her eyes. 'And personally?'

He stepped closer, careful, and she wondered where he'd go next, whether he'd tell her the truth or brush over her question. He was now so close she could feel heat rolling off him, see the faint scar on his collarbone, the exact line where the stubble on his neck stopped, his individual, surprisingly long eyelashes. But up close, she could also see his exhaustion, and the muted emotion in his eyes a direct contrast to the amusement and mischief she remembered.

'Personally,' he said, voice lower now, 'I remember every moment we spent together—I remember how you were. Open. Unfiltered. Real. I'm wondering if that woman

I met is simply buried behind your straight hair and businesslike clothes, or whether she's gone forever.'

He didn't need to know that when she returned from St Croix, she, very deliberately, very systematically, took her beach clothes, the bikini she wore, her flip-flops and every memory of Judah, and the person she'd been with him, and packed them away. She'd had a life to rebuild, pride to salvage, and she hadn't wanted to be distracted by recollecting a never-to-be-seen again blue-eyed surfer who'd rocked her world.

Guess she was super wrong about that.

Her heart kicked against her ribs. 'A lot has happened since we last connected, Judah. And that weekend was a way for me to step out of my life. I didn't have anything to lose back then.'

And if they got personal, if they decided to re-explore their attraction—and when he looked at her like that, she knew he was as attracted to her as she was to him—she would carry the majority of the risk. If it ended badly— and these types of situations always ended badly—Judah could, very easily, find another designer, but she'd fail to restore her reputation and she'd lose future work. She was the one carrying all the risk.

'Can we forget what we did, who we were?' she asked, stepping back and hauling in a deep breath. 'I can't go back, Judah. I *won't* go back.'

He exhaled and pushed a frustrated hand through his hair, his lips thinning. 'Sorry, *shit*.' He grimaced. 'I told myself I wasn't going to bring it up—I was going to leave well alone—but seeing you all buttoned up annoys me. I'm trying to be more of this—' he gestured to himself, bare-chested, board at his feet, wind tugging at his hair '—and less of the Reyes Luxe version.'

He'd lost her. 'I don't understand.'

He managed a small smile. 'I don't blame you. I barely understand it myself.' He took a moment, obviously trying to make sense of his thoughts. 'This island is my favourite place, the place where I can *be*. As my designer, I'd like you to embrace the island and the house. And I don't want you designing for the brand. I want you to design for *me*.'

The words landed hard, too close to vulnerability. They were too intimate.

'I also want you to stay on the property.'

He wanted her to live and work in his house? She stared at him, and a warning light whirled in her brain, red and flashing. No, she needed the distance and safety of being able to leave each day, to return to her hotel room to recalibrate. How could she work, concentrate, when she had to spend so much time with her sexy client and the ex-lover she'd tried so very hard to forget?

Calla looked away, toward the water. 'That's not a good idea, Judah. You *know* it's not.'

Stubbornness jumped into his eyes. 'I'd like you to live on-site. I asked Bella to make up the guest cottage for you.'

The guest cottage was one step removed from staying in his house, but still…

'Judah—'

'That's the deal, Calla.'

'You keep changing the goal posts,' she cried. 'You're making me jump through hoops because you know how much I want and need this project.'

He didn't back down and, once again, despite his bare chest and sand-and-sun-dusted shoulders, she saw the determined man who operated an international empire. 'You can either stay in a guest suite in the house, or in the guest cottage. Your choice.'

Calla knew there was no point in arguing; he wasn't going to back down. And this wasn't a hill she was prepared to die on. She silently cursed him before pushing her words out between gritted teeth. 'I'll move into the guest cottage.'

But she needed to remind him of her boundaries and where they were. 'We need to keep this clean, Judah.' A memory flashed in his eyes. She knew it—something that reminded him of the wonderfully dirty-in-the-best-way-possible sex they'd shared. She needed to clarify her statement. Immediately. 'We need to be professional.'

He tipped his head in a gesture that might, if she tried hard to see it that way, be one of agreement. Calla's breath caught at the heat in his eyes. She was very out of practice, but she recognised desire and lust when it burned super brightly. And all for her. And damn her for wanting to slide over to him, to hoist her thigh over his hip, to place her hands on his shoulders and kiss him stupid.

Stop. Enough now.

Calla turned away. She needed distance. Space. Boundaries. She glanced at the guest cottage, set a little way apart from the main house. It wasn't enough, but it would have to do.

She started to climb the stone path back up to the house, away from him and her attraction, but couldn't stop herself from glancing back at him, once.

And of course, he was watching her, his gaze heating her skin as it always did.

'Calla.'

She turned. Judah leaned the surfboard against the table and put his hands on his hips. It was a classic warrior pose and was accompanied by a frown and a hard jaw. 'As I said, it's strictly business for as long as you want it to be.'

He covered this distance between them in a couple of strides, stepped into her personal space and ducked his head. When he spoke again, his breath tickled the hair at her temple and drifted over her ear. 'But do let me know if you want that to change.'

Calla cursed the heat in her cheeks and wished she could be half as direct, as confident as he was. She might be older in years, but he had her beat when it came to self-possession. 'I don't know what to say to that,' she admitted.

Judah smiled, walked away from her, and Calla watched him go, her bottom lip caught between her teeth. What the hell had just happened? And why did her heart feel like it was beating at a thousand beats per second? Why did crazy things always seem to happen to her?

But most of all, why did she feel like running into Judah Reyes here in St Croix was utterly, illogically *right*? Like meeting him again was going to change her life in ways big and small?

CHAPTER THREE

STANDING TO ONE side of Judah's entertainment deck, a little apart from the rest of his guests, Calla sipped her mojito and sent a wistful look toward the guest house. She'd been at Sol House for two days, sleeping in the cottage for one, and she didn't want to spend the evening socialising with people she didn't know. What she most wanted to do was to change into a bikini and amble down to the beach for a night swim. Or to lie in her bed next to the open window, under the fan, listening to the waves roll up onto the rocks below the cliff as she studied the summer night sky.

This party was, so Judah informed her when he arrived at the cottage yesterday to issue the invitation, an island tradition, one his mom started over thirty years ago and which had grown into an annual affair. Judah'd said he could still picture them, his mother radiant as she greeted guests, his captivated father never far from her side. Calla imagined that Sol House, and his childhood, had pulsed with joy on those warm St Croix nights, the air tinged with sea brine, champagne and expensive scents.

Judah's guests were a mixture of islanders, expats and business friends. Some guests had flown in just to attend his summer party—a clear reminder of how influential he was. There had to be over a hundred people in attendance, scattered through the house and gardens, drinking his champagne and keeping his hired-for-the-night bartenders and caterers busy.

There were some big names here—some Calla hadn't expected to see—and it reminded her that while Judah was based in London, he was as influential in New York. She watched an important art curator glide past, her hand tucked into the arm of a Manhattan power player rumoured to dabble in black market art. A few former clients had recognised Calla—people she and Jack had once worked with—and their curiosity was obvious. She and Jack had each been a half of Atelier Abernathy— they'd started the business together, but in their divorce, Jack treated it like it was all his—but in a world that made sense, Jack should be here, not her.

Throughout the evening, she'd sensed eyes on her, saw how people abruptly stopped talking when she looked their way. She'd somehow become the talk of the party, a huge curiosity. Calla sighed. People loved unanswered questions, and when it was accompanied by a hint of scandal— the dissolution of their marriage and the interior design studio they owned together had been gossip gold and kept tongues wagging for the best part of a year—all the better.

Her phone buzzed in her hand, a sharp interruption to the low hum of music and laughter floating over the pool.

She glanced at the screen. There was one new message.

Are you enjoying Reyes's party? Have you found someone to talk to? Probably not—because we both know you don't belong there. You belong here, working behind the scenes, under me. *For me.*

Calla exhaled slowly through her nose. Jack. Naturally. Having lived with her for so long, he knew exactly how to weaponise her insecurity. He'd always had an uncanny talent for finding the softest, rawest part of her and twisting the knife. She locked the screen without replying, shoving her phone back into the pocket of her wrap dress.

What was it with Jack and his inability to let go? Why couldn't he just...unhook himself from her life and fade away? Why was he still obsessed with her, with what she was doing? More importantly, why hadn't she blocked him? Why did she keep hanging on to him, even if it was by the messages he sent?

She'd told herself it was strategic—that through his messages, Jack frequently dropped hints about what was happening in the design world she ached to be a part of and cutting him off meant cutting herself off from that world. But maybe, deep down, she wanted to believe that one day the man she'd married, loved, would turn out to be better, kinder. Nicer. Maybe she was looking for a reason to justify giving him a decade of her life.

Calla slipped into the shadows, partially concealed by a column and a huge ficus tree, happy to separate herself from the too-brittle laughter and the rising noise. Through the leaves, she scanned the crowds of threes and fours, looking for Judah. Because he was so tall, she found him quickly. She liked his outfit. The lightweight, milk chocolate–coloured trousers, sockless brogues and a cream linen shirt, sleeves rolled up his forearms, suited him.

Sometimes when he tipped his head to the side, when he half smiled, she saw the younger man she spent the night with, the carefree surfer who made her laugh, sigh and scream. But he was definitely more distant than before, cautious and careful. The past months had changed him: he'd aged. Oh, not physically, but mentally, emotionally.

He'd taken an emotional battering. Having been through one herself, she could recognise the signs from miles away.

Back then, he seemed much younger than her, the six-year gap between them so much wider than it was today. Now it seemed inconsequential. If anything, she felt like he was older, definitely harder, tougher. Not prepared to take any shit. And damn, that made him more attractive, not less.

'I've wanted to kiss you since the second I saw you. I kept thinking, no way it'll be as good as I imagine...'

He leaned in, and moonlight emphasised the light stubble on his strong jaw. 'You're like sailing through the Drake Passage during an Antarctic storm, thrilling and dangerous. Kiss me again.'

Nothing could stop her, and she did.

Her hands slid up his chest, fingers splaying over warm solid muscle, and her body moved instinctively into his. And oh, God, this man could kiss.

Judah kissed like a man who knew he was good at it. He took his time, kissed her deep, then light, then deep again, alternating between devastating hunger and exquisite tenderness. It was maddening. It was glorious. He built her up until her skin vibrated with tension...and then he pulled back, just enough to keep her right on the edge. Frustrating, yes—but soul-tinglingly, deliciously right.

This was what she hadn't even realised she was missing. Not just from her marriage but from the few men she dated before Jack. None of them had made her feel like this.

Like her skin was too tight for her body, and her heart was warm honey. Everything in the world contracted to where their bodies met—their mouths, hands, his warm, masculine body, his hard erection, pressing against her stomach. Judah made her feel intensely, astonishingly feminine. *More herself than she'd ever been. Younger, hotter, cooler, he made her feel everything she should as a woman.*

And everything she shouldn't.

Annoyed with herself for falling into the memory, Calla turned her back to him and rested her arms on the veranda railing, her eyes on the sea far below her. The colour of the night sky was an inky, deep vibrant blue, the same shade as Judah's eyes. It was a colour she wanted to use as an accent shade. In the library, maybe? Or the master bathroom?

'Why is she here and not Jack Abernathy?'

Calla stiffened as the coated-with-spite words drifted over to her. The speaker was standing off to the side and hadn't noticed her. In her black dress, she blended into the shadows.

'I can't understand why Judah would employ a talentless nobody whose only claim to fame is marrying Jack. Everybody knows that Jack carried her, that he's the design genius behind Atelier Abernathy. His design for the Metfords' mansion was a work of art.'

Calla slapped her hand over her mouth to keep her snort from escaping. Yeah, Jack's contribution to that job had been to flirt with Mrs Metford and to explain Calla's ideas. She'd been the one who'd burned the midnight oil, who'd tracked down the unusual architectural elements, commissioned the once-off furniture and designed the fabrics. But Jack, because he was a master manipulator and the King of Spin, took all the credit for her hard work.

'His pro bono upgrade of the kids' paediatric ward at Cummings Hospital was also genius. It was part fantasy, part practical, all fun.' Okay, that comment hurt more. That project had been a heart tugger, something she poured everything she had into.

Calla heard a distinctively feminine sniff. 'And what

did she do? Messed up on contracts, cheated on him and rode his coattails. God, how did he hook up with such a talentless hack?'

Calla dropped to her haunches and placed her head in the crook of her arms. She'd been talked about incessantly ever since the divorce and company break-up, and she knew people had said worse about her than this. But, God, why did it still hurt so much?

Jack had stolen her work, sabotaged her reputation and painted her as unstable, and she was still suffering from his emotional brutality. Was it any wonder that she'd vowed never to trust again, that she'd never risk losing everything again? Love was the most destructive weapon out there.

More importantly, what should she do now? Stand up and make her presence known? Keep her position and hide?

'Ladies.'

Calla lifted her head at Judah's pointed drawl. She stiffened. Did he know she was here? Still on her haunches, she shuffled backwards, closer to the railing, deeper into the shadows. She could just see his bare ankle, his big foot, the cuff of his fashionably short pants.

'What a lovely party, gorgeous champagne. We're having a lovely time.'

Yeah, that voice was pitched lower than before and carried a great deal of flirt. Judah took a moment to respond. 'That's strange—I didn't think you were enjoying yourselves.'

Calla's eyebrows lifted at his comment. Judging by the feminine gasps, they were equally surprised by his observation. 'Really? Why on earth would you think that?' one of them asked.

'People having fun don't stand in dark corners gossiping about their fellow guests.'

The silence following his statement was thick with embarrassment. 'Ah...*um.*'

Judah's tone dropped a couple of degrees. 'You're an art curator, right? And you're a gallery owner?' he said, his tone silky. Calla shivered. Why did she feel like she preferred to be hiding in the shadows rather than standing in front of him?

'Yes, we are,' Viper One replied, introducing herself and her companion. 'It's so nice to meet you, Judah.'

'Did I invite you?'

'Um, we tagged along with the Streatfields—they own a villa on the North Shore. We were just talking about your art, and were wondering if you'd—'

'You were not talking art—you were trashing one of my guests, who happens to be my super-talented interior designer, Calla West.'

Calla's eyes widened. Instead of apologising or even acknowledging Judah's accusation, the blonde took her shot to make her pitch. 'I'd love to talk to you about loaning some of the art you inherited from your father to my gallery—'

Viper Two wasn't about to be outdone and outmanoeuvred. 'And if you are looking for something special, I am deeply connected to the art world.'

Wow, they weren't shy.

Judah stepped back, and Calla leaned forward, just a little, to see him. She took in his hard, you're-dead-to-me death stare. He jerked his head toward the exit. 'You have five minutes to leave. If you don't, I will get my people to escort you out. I will make it obvious you are no longer welcome here.'

Under their perma-tans, they paled. They looked at each other, confused. 'But why?'

'Nobody insults *my* people in *my* house at *my* party. Leave. *Now.*'

They scuttled away like beach crabs caught beneath the light of a handheld torch. Calla watched as Judah closed his eyes, gripped the bridge of his nose and sighed. 'Will this damned party ever end?' he muttered.

Her thoughts exactly. Calla watched as he rolled his shoulders and tipped his head from side to side, as if trying to gather some energy to keep going. Then he swivelled around and walked over to her, holding out his hand. Judging by his lack of hesitation, he'd known she was there the whole time.

When she placed hers in his, so much bigger, he tugged her to her feet. 'Are you okay?' he demanded, his tone low. Calla was grateful his big body shielded her from the guests behind him.

She pushed her hair behind her ears. 'I'm fine,' she replied, embarrassed.

He narrowed his eyes, disbelief crossing his face. 'You are not,' he disagreed. Liking her hand in his a little too much, Calla pulled it away and folded her arms across her chest. Whether she was fine or not didn't matter; she was here to do a job and she couldn't let him see how rattled she was.

'Want to tell me what that was all about?' Judah demanded.

She'd rather have her fingers smashed. 'It's nothing.'

'Don't treat me like an idiot, Calla.'

There was a hard, don't-mess-with-me note in his voice she'd never heard before. Something lethal and unforgiving. 'I don't like being lied to,' he stated.

She didn't either. She wrinkled her nose. 'I have what some would term an ugly relationship with my ex-business partner and husband,' she explained. 'He has his supporters.' Which would include pretty much anyone with any clout in Manhattan.

'Mr Slick from the bar?'

His gaze sliced through her—cool, steady, unblinking. His expression remained implacable, but his eyes told a different story: the holes in her explanation were wide enough to sail a container ship through sideways.

'Thank you for standing up for me,' she said. It had been so long since someone had taken her side, and she felt tears burning her eyes and the back of her throat. 'I appreciate it.' His defence of her had been quiet but lethal, and he'd handled the ugly situation with sharp efficiency and subtlety.

'I don't need to be thanked,' he brusquely replied, jamming his hands into the pockets of his pants. 'And don't you dare cry—you're too strong and have too much pride to let those hyenas affect you.'

His words were bullet harsh, but she lifted her chin to meet his eyes. He held her gaze for a few beats, then nodded. 'Yes, there's your spine. Good job, Calla.'

Calla pulled in some air, unable to break his intense stare. She was so drawn to his steadiness and liked that he could see both her vulnerability and her strength. But then fear rolled over her, a cold North Atlantic storm surge. She'd allowed a man to see those sides of her before, allowed him into her heart and mind, gave him her body, and he'd stomped all over her in his Guiseppe Zanotti shoes. She'd never allow a man that much power over her again.

Judah sighed. 'And she's gone.' He rubbed the back of his neck. 'I liked the woman I met last year. Can I have her back again?'

'That was one night and a day, never to be repeated,' Calla told him.

'Pity,' Judah drawled. 'I liked her. A lot.'

She'd liked that person too. But that night had been a step out of time; it hadn't been real life. They'd shoved the world away and had played, laughed and loved in an alternate reality. Those golden hours could never be sustained long-term. Open, eager, chatty, quick to laugh, she'd let her guard down, piece by piece, and lived like there had been no tomorrow. But when she woke up from an afternoon nap, sunlight streaming in from the window and the cries of the gulls fighting over a crab, she knew that it was over. Real life needed to be faced so as she dressed, she picked up the bricks and the barbed wire and re-created all her emotional barriers. With one last look at Judah, naked, lying on his stomach, all golden skin and ripped muscles, she'd walked away, knowing he'd only ever be a brief, amazing experience, an incredible memory.

But here he was, having hauled her back into his life, back to this place. And this time she couldn't leave. This time, for the sake of her company, her pride and her reputation, she had to stick. And stay.

'I'd love to know what you are thinking,' Judah murmured.

Before she could answer, someone called his name. He lifted his hand in acknowledgement and sighed. 'Go to bed—get some sleep. It's been a long day,' he told her, his tone suggesting she not argue. Man, he'd perfected his ordering-his-underlings, CEO-in-charge voice. But Calla found herself nodding. There was nothing she wanted more.

Well, maybe to have him in her bed with her...no! *Jeez, Calla, get a grip.*

Immediately!

CHAPTER FOUR

THE NEXT EVENING, Calla sat in the corner of a couch in Judah's great room and watched her first tropical storm batter the cliffs and the cove below them. Just an hour ago, Judah tracked her down and insisted she come up to the main house, telling her that a tropical storm had abruptly changed course and its outer edges would slap this side of the island and Sol House. It wasn't safe for her to be alone if the storm intensified. She'd tried to protest, but Judah remained firm; he wanted her in the big house.

She'd thought he was overreacting, but the sea, which glittered playfully that morning, turned a sullen grey-green, spitting restless waves onto the rocks and Judah's private beach. The air slowly grew heavier, thickened with humidity and electric tension. Clouds gathered, a slow-moving army—thick, low and slate-coloured—dragging gloom across the sky. The gusty wind tossed branches, rattled shutters and bent trees. It wasn't a storm at its strongest, ugliest or angriest, but it was enough to set her nerves on edge. She winced as lightning slashed the sky wide open, white-hot and furious. A beat later, thunder boomed, and she slapped her hands over her ears, her heart punching her ribs.

Judah nudged her shoulder with the foot of a wine glass. 'The storm is still offshore,' he said. 'But even being on the edges of it can feel like standing between chaos coming in and chaos going out.

'Here, it's decent red—it'll calm your nerves.' Calla took the glass, her fingers grazing his—warm, callused, familiar—and turned her gaze to the roiling sky.

Chaos in and chaos out. That was a good description of their relationship. They were suspended in the in-between. Memory and want behind them, questions and confusion ahead. Too much history to go back. Too little certainty to move forward. And no map for what came next.

Judah sat down on the opposite edge of the couch and propped his bare feet up onto the glass, steel and wood coffee table in front of him. They'd lost power a half hour ago, and then the generator immediately kicked in. But Judah killed all the lights, telling her that the best way to watch a storm was with the house in darkness. She didn't tell him that the last thing she wanted to do was sit in the dark and watch nature throw a temper tantrum.

Good things never happened on stormy nights.

'You're more tense than I expected you to be,' Judah said, looking relaxed. But his sharp eyes were on her face, and Calla knew he was looking for an explanation as to why her shoulders were up around her ears and her hand was tightly clenched around the stem of her wine glass.

She couldn't tell him that she'd once loved storms, that she'd been the girl who'd run out into the rain to dance, the thunder the only music she needed. She'd whirl and twirl and kick puddles of water, arms akimbo, a huge smile on her face. But then, a few weeks after she turned nineteen, her dad died during a storm and, many years later, Jack, his voice raised above the sound of hail and thunder, told her he was divorcing her, that there was no money left in their joint personal and business accounts, her beloved company was a hollowed-out empty shell and her reputation was in tatters. She'd wanted to howl, but the wind outside did it for her, a wild animal caught in a situation with no escape. Each lightning strike was a knife in her heart, each roll of thunder spiking her soul. Jack just sat there, a smirk on his face, enjoying the havoc and destruction.

She recalled wondering why she never knew how much he hated her, how much he resented her. She hadn't seen it...no, she'd *chosen* not to see it. He'd snowed her, but she'd let him.

She was no longer the girl who loved storms; she would never dance in the rain again. Calla lifted her wine glass to her lips and took a long swallow, then another. A lightning strike, closer this time, made her glass wobble, and the red wine sloshed in her glass. Judah's fingers covered hers, and he slid the glass from her grip and placed it on the table in front of her. He scooted closer to her and half turned to face her. 'The storm is about five miles from here. We're only experiencing the outer edges. The lightning is a long way away, the thunder too. When dawn breaks, it's going to be another stunning summer's day in the Caribbean, utterly calm.'

Yeah, but it was a long time between now and then. And anything could happen.

'It's also moving away from us.'

'It doesn't feel like it,' she muttered. Sheet lightning threw light onto the shadows in the room, and the sea roared below them. Thunder rattled the glass in the windows, and the wind skittered over the house, making the shutters shudder.

'Tell me what you remember about that night we spent together,' Judah said, placing a hand on the foot she'd tucked under her thigh. She sent a fearful glance out the window. Calla thought about pulling her foot out from under his hand, but his touch settled her, made her feel safe. And grounded. Like nothing could happen to her while Judah held her, his fingers wrapped around her slender foot, his thumb sliding over the skin on the arch of her foot. But as his words settled, she squirmed.

There was so much else they could talk about, so why was he going there, going back?

Why couldn't they ignore it and pretend it never happened? And why was it that the one night she let her guard down—really let it down, his-kisses-on-her-skin, laughed-so-hard-she-cried, was-thoroughly-loved kind of down—was with him?

Judah *bloody* Reyes.

And just like before, he still affected her. His mouth. The way he walked, looked and smiled. The way his voice wrapped around her like a heated blanket and made her think stupid things, like *maybe you're safe here*. She wasn't safe anywhere, nor with anyone.

That old version of her? The one tangled in those sheets, whispering to a stranger with cobalt blue eyes? She didn't exist outside of that one night. Calla couldn't afford to. Too much was riding on her being professional, emotionally distant and in control.

This person she was now wore heels, severe suits and three layers of emotional protection. She read every email, contract and memo twice, and didn't believe in fate or chemistry or whatever nonsense that made women fall into bed with men like him. But Judah was back in her life looking at her like he knew something. Like he'd seen her without the mask and remembered the woman underneath. He'd seen her in ways no one else ever had. Him looking at her like *that*, and the way she reacted, was dangerous. She couldn't go back to that night, and wouldn't allow herself to go to him again. Not when everything she'd built was hanging on her staying in control. She cleared her throat and told herself—again—that she had to focus on the job. His high-profile, make-or-break, life-changing opportunity. Offered to her by the only man who ever made her forget her name.

Why was life messing with her?

'I don't see the point of looking back, Judah,' she said, pulling her foot out from under his hand and placing her feet on the floor, her knees pressed together.

'You're like a prickly hedgehog who curls up into a spiky ball when it's threatened.'

It wasn't a bad analogy. Not that she'd tell him that. 'I just think we should keep our relationship confined to business,' she stated, wincing at her too-prim voice. God, was this how she sounded all the time? Uptight and prissy and unapproachable?

'That's difficult to do since I clearly remember what you look like naked, the sounds you made as I loved you, the way you called my name when you fell apart.'

Calla lifted her hand to her forehead, heat starting as a small flicker and exploding into a supernova. Why did he have to remind her of how good they'd been together? Memories rushed over her, recollections of him holding the side of her face with his big hand, his eyes locked on hers as he pushed into her, the perfection of that moment, the suggestion that she'd been created to be loved by him, just like that.

Her eyes crashed into his, and electricity, borrowed from the lightning, arced between them, as powerful as anything nature could generate. It took all her willpower not to lean against his broad chest, his arms around her, to rest a minute within the safety of his grasp. But she wouldn't allow herself to be that weak, to fall apart.

She couldn't trust him to hold her. Not for long anyway.

Calla pushed to her feet and slid her feet into her sandals. She pressed her fingers to her thumb—index, middle, ring, pinkie—and the repeated motion soothed her, bringing her back to the moment and what was important. The storm, both inside her and on the other side of the massive windows, was dying down, and her moment of weakness, of temptation—an old-fashioned word but apt—had passed.

She was back in control. And control was everything.

As if to put an exclamation mark at the end of that thought, the hum of the generator disappeared, telling her the power had been restored. Calla raked her hair back and pasted a small smile on her face. 'I'm going to head back to the cottage and get some work done,' she told him, ignoring his penetrating gaze.

'Is this who you are now?' he softly asked.

'What do you mean?'

'Do you simply ignore the uncomfortable because it's exactly that…uncomfortable?'

Well, yes. Because she didn't know how to answer, Calla just shrugged. 'Doesn't everyone?'

'Sit down, Calla, and finish your wine.'

Judah leaned back, trying not to make it too obvious that he was watching her, because the last thing he wanted was to spook her more than she already was. But damn, keeping his eyes off her felt like he was asking the tide not to turn. There was something magnetic about her, something in the way she held herself that made it impossible to look away. Like she'd packed her whole damn history into her petite, compact frame and dared the world to guess how heavy it was. He wouldn't pretend to know the weight of it. He just knew she carried it like it didn't cost her anything, which probably meant it cost her a lot more than she'd wanted to pay.

She resumed her perch on the edge of the couch, a skittish bird about to take flight. She was, but wasn't, the same woman from that night. This Calla was the edge of a sharpened blade, the fine tip of a fountain pen. The Great Wall of China in human form.

But she was still her. Or was he simply hoping, praying the woman he remembered still existed under all her many layers? Because if that held true, then there was a chance that the man he used to be, joyful and relaxed, quick to laugh, was also still buried—barely breathing but alive—under the layers of expectation and responsibility and the Reyes Luxe brand.

He reached for his wine glass. Sipped it slowly and said nothing for a while. The sound of the storm moving out to sea filled the silence.

She turned to look at him, her shoulders and back stiff. 'Why are you doing this, Judah? Why are you raking up the past?' she demanded, sounding a little desperate. 'Why did you even ask me here? What do you want from me?'

He rubbed his forehead with his fingertips. Wasn't that the question? It had been, still was, irrational and absurd, but he couldn't shake the idea that being near her again might help him claw his way back to that version of himself. Being back in St Croix—with Calla at his side—felt like he might finally stumble across the answers he'd been looking for.

'That's a difficult question to answer.'

Judah resisted the urge to run his thumb over those too-deep lines between her arched eyebrows.

Her deep eyes slammed into his. 'I need to know… How much is my being here, on the island, about the time we spent together? Is this about work or what happened back then?'

He'd been dreading this question and didn't know how to answer her. And he had to be careful; if he messed up now, their working relationship—any relationship—would be over before it started. He ran his thumb over his jaw, his stubble scratchy.

'I wouldn't have asked you to submit a proposal if I didn't think you were the right fit,' Judah said, his voice steady. 'This house…it means something to me, it's been in my family for decades. My mother used to fall asleep in that hammock in the garden during the summer heat. I learned to swim right off this beach. It's more than a building—it's part of me. I wouldn't hand it over to just anyone.' He paused, his eyes holding hers. 'I've seen your portfolio, and I looked into your past work. I liked what I saw—more than liked it. You've got talent, Calla. Real vision. And that's what Sol House deserves.'

'Then why won't you let me do my job without complicating it with references to the past? Why do you keep dragging it up?'

Because it was a compass point, something he held on to, a lighthouse when the swell rose and the winds whipped. Because it was the memory that comforted and consoled him, that anchored him.

Judah resisted the urge to scrub his hands over his face. They were still finding their way back to each other, not yet comfortable, and the months since he'd last seen her seemed like years. Calla crossed her arms, her fingertips digging into her biceps. She wasn't ready, or prepared, to broach their past, or to hear about his other reason for wanting her in St Croix. Then again, he wasn't ready to tell her.

Because he hadn't worked out how to say, 'That thirty-six hours with you? That was the last time I felt like myself.'

And maybe a part of him wanted her to see him as controlled, together, an adult. Back then, he'd let her believe he was just some barefoot bartender. A man with no ambition or direction. He'd treated her like he did everyone else, thinking it was safer to be underestimated than to create expectations that, as the son of David Reyes, he couldn't meet.

He was a Reyes. The only Reyes of Reyes Luxe. She now knew he was responsible for the company his father had built. But she didn't know that most days he was holding on by his fingernails, trying not to get chewed up by it. And if he explained, would she be disappointed? Worse, far worse, would she pity him? He couldn't handle that. He wanted her to see him as solid. Capable. Completely confident. Not the guy who sometimes still felt he was surfing a monster wave, waiting to be crushed.

'I need to get going,' she said. 'I still have work I want to do tonight.'

It was blatantly obvious she wasn't ready to remember, to go back. So he stood there, hands in his pockets to hide his clenched fists, and gave her what she obviously wanted, the polished and professional version of himself. Judah Reyes in all his CEO glory. 'Right, we're keeping things professional.'

Judah gave her a tight smile, knowing that it didn't reach his eyes. 'The storm has moved out to sea, and any danger has long passed,' he said. 'Do you want me to walk you back to the cottage?' He knew she'd refuse, but manners dictated that he ask.

'I'm fine.'

Of course, she was. 'I'll see you in the morning.'

He lifted his chin and pulled up his most implacable expression. By the time she murmured a soft goodnight, he'd slipped back into his corporate skin, back into being the version of Judah Reyes who didn't show his hand, who'd never let anyone see he was off balance. Someone determined to learn how to wrangle his empire, isolation and uncertainties alone.

Calla curled up on the overstuffed daybed in the guest house, her coffee cup resting on her thigh. The distant thunder and the occasional howl from the wind reminded her that the storm still swirled somewhere out to sea. But the storm in her soul was louder. Messier.

She exhaled, emotionally and physically whipped, and stared out into the smudgy darkness. Damn, Judah. What was all that about?

His question put her on a remote highway in the dark, about to be run over by an eighteen-wheeler truck. She hadn't the first idea how to react. Then, when she'd tried to pull them back to work and business, he shut down immediately, pulling back and away.

His expression haunted her. He hadn't tried to argue or explain, hadn't pushed for more. He'd simply...*stopped*. Shut down and retreated. She exhaled and stared out into the smudgy dark. And wasn't she being a hypocrite? On one hand, she wanted him to push her, on the other, she wanted him to be professional. That wasn't right. Or fair.

But she vacillated between the two with all the enthusiasm of an out-of-control bungee rope.

Calla wrapped her hands around the coffee cup, trying to absorb its dwindling warmth. She hated the unreadable look in his eyes, his tight smile, the way he'd offered to walk her back as if they were strangers—the prick was sharper than she wanted to admit. He'd uttered that line about being professional, handing her what she asked for. Professionalism. Distance. Detachment. So why did it feel like a door had slammed inside her chest?

It was for the best. She needed to keep a healthy distance between them because there was too much at stake. Her career, her reputation, her need for control.

Calla stood up, walked to the tiny kitchenette, tossed her cold coffee into the sink and placed the cup in the dishwasher. She should've walked away from him, refused to listen and kept it professional.

'Judah, you and I...we were a moment, a step out of time. An anomaly,' she whispered, her chest tight. She hoped saying the words aloud would make them settle and lodge in her soul. 'A bright, burning blip.'

So then why did she feel she was standing in a hot, too-bright spotlight? She wanted to be furious and dug deep to find her anger. When she did track it down, it was muted and laced with regret, confusion and a gnawing question she couldn't shake: Was he really as emotionally composed as he wanted her to believe? And why, *really*, had he brought her to St Croix?

And why did a part of her want to remember the woman she so briefly was? The one who could laugh easily, talk openly and be emotionally available? Calla walked into the bedroom, feeling like a zinc bathtub riding the white water rapids of a too-fast river. Judah—an emotionally available alpha male, a rare and dangerous breed—wasn't someone she was ready, or able, to deal with.

'Next time, let's keep it professional.'

She tested the words, hoping to sound like she meant it. She didn't, the tremble in her voice too distinct. Going forward, could she do that?

She didn't know.

CHAPTER FIVE

A COUPLE OF days later, Judah placed his hands on the long dining table outside and stared down at her sketches, taking in her mood board and her colour combinations. Calla could read his body language and knew he wasn't connecting with her work.

'I'm not convinced.'

To be fair, neither was she. She looked down at the cool greys and blues, the muted colours and couldn't take offence. She liked elements of the brand-new design, but her core concept remained vague. After days of trying to crack the design, she was creatively stuck. Sharing her half-formed ideas with Judah wasn't confidence—it was a silent plea for direction, for anything he liked that might spark her inspiration and give her direction.

'Sorry, Calla, it's just not me.'

Ugh. She sighed and wrinkled her nose.

He folded his arms across his chest. 'What's the problem?'

Well, since he asked. 'You haven't given me much to work on,' she told him, trying to keep her tone professional. 'You don't have any strong feelings about colours, or a style or finishes. You gave me a few photographs from when you were a kid, but they were photos of you and your parents, not of the house. And you said that you wanted me to capture the vibe, not necessarily the décor.'

Judah frowned. 'I gave you carte blanche.'

What clients didn't realise was that creative freedom wasn't as much fun as people expected it to be. Anything and everything was on the table, and she didn't know what he liked or was even drawn to. And when she asked what he liked about his apartment in London—or flat as he called it—he told her it was decorated per his father's taste, and he hadn't had time to update it. So no help there. But she couldn't ignore the fact that she hadn't pushed him harder, interrogated him about what he wanted in a home, what he liked and hated. Maybe she hadn't *wanted* to ask the tougher questions because it would've meant digging deeper—getting too close. Given their history, digging was emotionally dangerous.

Still, she couldn't play it safe. If she was going to do this properly—if she was going to reclaim her professional reputation and rebuild her business—she had to bite the bullet. She couldn't design a home for a man she was too afraid to understand.

She scowled and blew air into her cheeks. She needed to go back to the drawing board. Literally.

Judah reached into the under-counter fridge, pulled out a beer and offered her one. Shrugging—it was after five—Calla took the drink and slid onto a bar stool tucked beneath the freestanding marble-and-wood island. The outdoor kitchen and bar were far nicer than the actual indoor kitchen; in fact, the whole entertainment area functioned as an outside room. And with its ceiling fans and incredible vista, it was her favourite place to be.

Judah took a pull of his beer and reached back into the fridge to pull out a long fish. 'I caught it earlier while trawling off the kayak,' he explained. 'I was going to grill it for supper. Do you want to join me?'

She should say no, but she didn't want to return to the cool, quiet, but oh-so-empty guest house. But she needed to push her attraction aside, and if she could make this meal about work, maybe she could grill Judah over his design decisions while he cooked and they ate.

Oh, Calla, be honest. You're just looking for an excuse to spend time with him. But who could blame her? In chino shorts, an untucked mint green button-down shirt, cuffs haphazardly rolled back, and bare feet—his nose a little sunburned and his lips chapped, he looked like the surfer-bartender she'd met ten months ago. Seeing him like this, she'd never believe he was the CEO of one of the world's premier wellness companies.

'Are you working at the moment or taking a break?' she asked.

'I wish I could switch off,' he said, pulling a filleting knife from the block behind him, 'but I still had to give the company a couple of pints of blood today.'

'It's that demanding?'

'It's that demanding,' he admitted. 'I always knew I'd be doing this someday. I just thought I'd have more time to prepare.' He brushed a lock of hair off his forehead with the back of his wrist. 'I thought I'd have my dad to guide me while I gained experience.'

Underneath his words, she heard a note of anxiety, even desperation. Was she letting her imagination run wild? She scratched the side of her neck. 'Why do I get the sense that you hate being the CEO?'

He didn't raise his eyes from his task. 'I hate that my dad died. I don't hate that I'm the CEO.'

'I don't believe you.'

Judah laid down his knife and placed his palms on the counter, the muscles in his forearms tensing. 'Hate...

well, *hate* is a strong word. I just feel, I don't know, out of sync—like this is surreal.'

Despite knowing she shouldn't, that she should change the subject back to something, anything, work related, Calla leaned forward, curious for more. 'Talk to me, Judah.'

His intelligent eyes slammed into hers. 'It veers from the professional into the personal, Calla.'

Well, later she couldn't squeal that she hadn't been warned. She nodded. 'Unfortunately, I just realised that, as much as I want to keep our relationship business based, in order to do my job, I'm going to need to get a little personal now and again.' She saw his frown and winced. 'I know, I don't like it either.'

'You're putting words in my mouth again, Calla.' Judah picked up his knife and sliced into the fish. Their eyes caught and his half-smile was gently reassuring and some of the tension in her neck and shoulders eased.

'One of the reasons I came back to St Croix is because I'm looking for something real. Something that makes sense again.' He exhaled, the confession seeming to catch in his throat. He cleared it, but when he spoke, his voice still sounded scratchy. 'The truth is, and as much as you don't want to hear it, the half weekend I spent with you? Well, that was the last time I felt like me. Not the version of myself people expected, not the Reyes heir, the CEO, the largest stockholder of an international company. Just…me.'

He shrugged. 'And I guess I've been chasing that feeling ever since.'

Shock flickered through her, and bright sparks seared her skin. A part of her, the part in charge of protecting herself, wanted to argue—but no words came out. After a couple of beats, she cleared her throat, desperately thinking of something to say.

She didn't understand.

'I'm confused,' she admitted.

'The company was my father's. I never established it or was part of its vision. I've spent the past few months completing projects my father planned and initiated. Nothing I've done since inheriting the company has my stamp on it. I feel like I own it but have no connection to it.'

She could understand that. 'It must've been quite a shock going from being a bartender to a boss.'

He handed her a grim smile and nodded. 'At the time we met, I was working my way through the company, spending time in all the Reyes Luxe departments to get a handle on the business from the ground up. I just happened to be working in the St Croix hotel at the time and was helping out by doing a few shifts behind the bar.'

She leaned forward, fascinated. 'I presume your dad wanted you to learn the business by starting at the bottom.'

He shook his head. 'No. He wanted me in the office next to him, wearing two-thousand-dollar suits, receiving a fat salary and a title I hadn't earned. It was my choice to learn the business from the ground up.'

Her respect for him rose. Most of his peers would've taken the easy route to the top of the food chain.

'So…now that you have the corner office, you're doubting it's where you should be?' she prodded, fascinated by this glimpse into his psyche. He came across as so stoic and unflappable, but beneath his calm surface churned a wide, silent whirlpool.

'I don't have the luxury of doubt. I have to suck it up and make it work,' he muttered. 'My biggest challenge is where do we go from here?' Judah flipped the fish over to fillet the other side. 'The Reyes Luxe board, and my executives, have many ideas on where they want the company to go, what they want to do with it, and how to expand our footprint. I get a hundred ideas a day, none of which I connect with.'

'Can you give me an example?' Calla asked.

'Well, everyone thinks I should acquire ForgeRitual, a male-slanted wellness company. I'm not sold on the brand.'

'Why not?'

'It leans into promoting machismo, and I think even a whiff of hyper-masculinity can be toxic. I don't believe anyone should dictate what masculinity should look like in the twenty-first century. Everyone around me disagrees with me, mostly because acquiring the company would be very good for the company's bottom line.'

Calla bit the inside of her cheek. 'Can I state the obvious and say that you should follow your gut?'

He released a small snort. 'My gut and I have stopped communicating, mostly because the past ten months have been crazy, and utterly surreal. I feel like an actor who has been shoved into a play and hasn't had time to read the script. I badly need a reset, to recalibrate, and I thought being back here in St Croix was a good way to do it.'

There was more of the iceberg to uncover, but she wasn't going to push him. He'd already given her so much more than she'd expected. And by opening this door, treating him as a client was going to be so much harder. And all her fault. 'I'm sorry, Judah.'

He managed a small smile. 'It is what it is.' He hooked his finger around the neck of his beer bottle and lifted it to his lips, his eyes on Buck Island. 'But working from Sol House is much nicer than working from the company HQ in London or at our offices in New York or Singapore.'

She looked around, took in the playful sea. 'It's not too shabby,' she agreed, tongue in cheek.

'Is this where you feel completely comfortable?' she asked, tapping her index finger against the neck of her beer bottle. 'Relaxed and utterly at home?'

'There's only ever been one other place where I've enjoyed as much.'

She leaned forward, intrigued. Another island? A city? 'Where?'

His hands stilled, and he looked up, transferring his attention from the fish to her. His eyes were a fire blue, a small smile played on his lips and she sensed his answer before he spoke. 'When I walked into my friend's surfside shack with you, I felt instantly at home,' he murmured.

Calla did her best to ignore the heat in her veins, her suddenly erratic heartbeat. She tipped her head to the side, intrigued. 'Is it still around?' she asked.

Judah shook his head. 'No. Sadly, it was destroyed in a hurricane last season,' he replied.

Calla thought back, trying to push aside memories of Judah taking off his shirt, the way he kissed her, held her, unable to recollect what the shack looked like. She'd barely taken her eyes off Judah, and little about the seaside shack, except for the way the light streamed in through the sea-facing windows onto his spectacular body, registered.

'I don't remember much. Can you describe it for me?' she asked, placing her chin in the palm of her hand. She was only asking because it might inspire some design ideas. Yeah, and a purple pig just flew across the endlessly blue sky.

'It was a cluttered mess,' he told her, smiling. 'Surfboards lined the walls, the floor was concrete and paint-splattered and it had been used as a painting studio by the previous tenant. The couch was huge. I was able to stretch out on it, battered but so damn comfortable. The bed was against the back wall…'

Yes, she remembered the bed. She swallowed and played with the silver bangle on her wrist. 'Colour scheme?' she asked.

'Mostly white, hints of blue. The artists left an abstract mural in bold pink and orange on one wall.'

'I remember that mural—it was amazing. Depending on how the light caught it, it was bold and brilliant, a Caribbean sunset, or muted and lovely, a gentle sunrise. How could I have forgotten?'

Because remembering one thing meant unlocking all the rest, and that would've left her aching for an impossible *something*. Unlocking one memory led to others— his hot skin over hard muscle, the way he said her name like it was something precious, the reverence in his touch. His clever mouth painting kisses across her belly, over her hip, his hands streaking down her thighs with an urgency that made her feel worshipped and wanted.

The warmth in his eyes, the way he looked at her like she held all the secrets to the universe. Like she was enough. Like she *mattered*.

It was too much; he was too much. Needing to regain her equilibrium, Calla slid off her seat and walked over to the opposite wall, her eyes taking in the twenty-plus framed photographs on the wall. Some were from the past five or ten years—there were a couple of Judah and his dad holding surfboards and standing on paddleboards, in a restaurant—but others were of a young Judah and a stunning-looking woman with the same eyes and shape face. She tapped the woman's face. 'Your mum?'

Judah looked up. 'Mm. The super-cute kid with her is me.'

'It's a pity you grew up to be ugly,' she quipped, relieved when Judah smiled at her joke. She was out of practice and had forgotten how to gently tease. Had she ever teased Jack? No, she'd never felt comfortable enough.

Calla returned her attention to the photographs. The last photo of Judah and his mum together was when he was around ten or so. 'Did she die?' He nodded.

Calla winced. 'When?'

'When I was eleven.' He wrapped the fish in foil, paying the fish far more attention than it deserved. 'She was diagnosed with pancreatic cancer in March and was gone by July.' He walked over to the sink to wash his hands, and Calla watched his profile as he looked out at the sunset gathering its colours on the horizon. 'It was a grim time.'

She could imagine. She'd lost her only parent, her dad, in her late teens—her mum took off when she was a baby—and she still missed her father so much. She couldn't pull her eyes off another photo of Judah, and his mum and dad. They looked so happy, a complete unit. Her dad had been her person, all she'd ever needed and she fell apart when he died. Was it her desperation to belong, for a family, that made her leap at the chance to join the Abernathy clan? Maybe. She'd never thought about it like that before; it was something to unpack. She looked at the next photo, one of Judah and his dad, looking so similar, laughing. 'You and your dad look close,' she commented.

He turned to face her, drying his hands with a kitchen towel. 'We had a couple of rough years after Mum died, and he didn't spend much time at home. But we got closer when I got older. Spending weeks here every summer helped. He taught me to surf, to paddleboard.'

Judah asked her to open a bottle of white wine. After pulling the cork, Calla resumed her seat and tipped Chardonnay into their glasses. She'd veered off course, leaving the professional behind and heading into personal; but in this particular tug-o-war, curiosity kicked caution's butt. Besides, asking a few questions didn't have to mean anything. It wasn't a sign she was losing control. It couldn't be. There was no reason they couldn't be friends.

And the more she understood him—what made him tick, what resonated with him, the memories he held on to—the better she'd be able to shape Sol House into something that felt like his. Well, that was what she was telling herself, *begging* herself to believe. 'I'm sorry you lost him, Judah.'

Judah pulled salad ingredients from the fridge and reached for a platter.

'Yeah, it was a shock. One moment I was doing shifts as a Reyes Luxe bartender, learning the ropes, the next I was the boss of bosses.' He shrugged and leaned his hip into the counter, the salad forgotten. 'It was such a crazy time,' he admitted, his voice low. 'I had to arrange his funeral, fly back to the UK, meet with lawyers and board members, wrap my head around the fact that, as the major shareholder of Reyes Luxe, I was expected to, per my dad's wishes, run the company.'

Calla bit the corner of her lip. 'Did you have time to grieve him?' she softly asked.

Judah lifted one shoulder. 'I don't know. The first three months were a blur, the second three not much better. In a way, I still feel like I'm on autopilot, just following the blueprint my dad left for me.'

Calla placed her wine glass on the island and snagged a baby tomato destined for their salad. 'What do you mean by that?' Judah took a while to respond, and she knew he was debating how much to tell her. She waited, expecting him to deflect or steer the conversation somewhere safer— toward her designs for the house or logistics or the weather. That's what she would've done, what she always did when someone asked for more of her than she was willing to give. Vulnerability was too big a risk. She either deflected the conversation or threw up walls—along with being a good designer, she was a master builder of emotional walls.

'As the new face and voice of Reyes Luxe, I became very newsworthy very quickly, and that was difficult, for many reasons. I was this golden heir, portrayed as someone who had a great education, wealth and decent looks.' Calling his looks 'decent' was like calling an iceberg an ice cube. 'Everyone quickly forgot I was in this position because I'd lost my father.'

Right. When she thought about it that way, it cast his grief in a different light.

'And God, it's such a pain in the arse being the "face" of a wellness empire,' he said, pulling a face. 'If I look tired, and I often look tired because I suffer from insomnia, our range of vitamins don't work. If I'm not seen at my regular gym, I'm either sick or lazy. If I talk to a woman, even casually, we're dating.'

That was the problem with being young, gorgeous and eligible. And carrying the name of a fitness, wellness and nutrition empire. 'All I want to do is once, just once, walk down a street eating chocolate-drenched ice cream.'

'Do you like ice cream?'

Judah smiled, and it felt like the sun had slipped out from behind a heavy cloud to shine on her. 'I bloody love ice cream. And chocolate. And anything able to give me cavities.'

She couldn't help it, she laughed. Judah smiled at her, and Calla placed her fist into her sternum, feeling the warm glow in her stomach, the boom-boom of her heart. Just like before, this man could make her feel, make her laugh and crack her façade.

'My dad had been vociferously against anything containing sugar. He'd hated anything sweet, including honey and xylitol so when my friends were sneaking weed and beer into their houses, I was sneaking in chocolate bars and tubs of ice cream. I still make furtive late-night runs to the store and then pay for it the next morning by adding thirty minutes to my gym workout.' He saw the question on her face and grinned. 'And yes, it's always worth it.'

Calla gave him a long up-and-down look. 'The occasional ice cream binge hasn't hurt you, though,' she told him. 'You look fitter, harder, than you were before.'

'Have you been checking me out, Calla?' he teased, blue eyes glinting.

Calla waved her hand, knocked her wine glass, and she just managed to catch it before it tipped over. She sucked wine off her hand and wrinkled her nose at the drops on her shorts. Judah handed her a kitchen towel, and she wiped the counter, desperately hoping for a sea breeze to cool her face.

Judah leaned his hip against the counter, folded his arms and his sexy biceps bulged. 'Technically, I work out for the sake of my employees.'

Calla tilted her head. 'How so?'

He nodded, straight-faced. 'If I don't exercise, I get cranky. Nobody wants a cranky boss. Basically, my abs contribute to my employees' mental health.'

She snorted, trying to hide her amusement. 'Wow, your generosity knows no bounds. But are you sure they are as sexy as you think they are?'

With complete confidence, he lifted his shirt. His shorts hung low on his hips, and her fingers itched to dance over his stomach's defined ridges. She released a loud sigh, and Judah bowed.

Calla's laugh burst out before she could stop it, and heat rushed to her cheeks. 'God, you are insufferable!'

He leaned, just a little, enough for her to smell his sexy sea-and-spice scent. 'You're blushing, West.'

Of course she was—a sexy, younger man was flirting with her. And she was loving it. Not that she'd let him know that. She pointed her wine glass at him. 'You're imagining things.'

Those blue eyes glinted with mischief. 'Maybe. But I'm not the one knocking over wine glasses.'

Calla rolled her eyes and took a sip. 'Be careful when you walk back into the house, Reyes. I'm not sure the big rooms and high ceilings are expansive enough to accommodate your enormous ego.'

Judah chuckled and clinked his glass gently against hers before returning to assembling the salad. 'Let's eat, I'm starving.'

Calla wasn't sure whether she was relieved or sad that he'd changed the subject and ended their brief bout of flirting. Their attraction still flickered between them—light, flirty and dangerous.

She picked up her glass again and took a deliberate sip, breathing deeply.

How was she ever going to put their relationship back on a professional footing? Did she even want to?

Later that evening, Calla sat beside Judah, their feet dangling in the warm water of the pool, glasses of red wine resting on the tiles behind them. The air was thick with humidity but fragrant, carrying notes of jasmine and sea brine. The rhythmic chorus of tree frogs competed with the soft jazz drifting from hidden speakers.

It was a stunning night—warm and still. And she'd had a lovely, unpressured evening. She and Judah had caught up, silently agreeing to keep their conversation light and non-confrontational as they'd eaten his fried fish and salad. The meal ended with simple bowls of vanilla ice cream. Judah's portion, naturally, had been three times the size of hers.

She circled back to their earlier conversation, picking it apart. One question still lingered—one Judah had carefully avoided answering.

'Why aren't you sleeping?' she softly asked.

She looked at his profile and sensed his tension.

'I employ over ten thousand people across six countries. I own gyms, spas, meditation centres and professional sports facilities. I have a life coaching franchise, a vitamin line and a mindfulness and wellness app. I've got a lot on my plate and it keeps me awake.'

It sounded a lot, *was* a lot, but Calla knew he was capable of juggling the demands of a huge company. He had an excellent degree and was whip-smart. His inability to sleep went deeper than his day-to-day work pressures. 'And I'm pretty sure you could do all that with your eyes closed,' she told him. 'What's the real reason?'

Judah's eyes slammed into hers. 'You're pretty curious for someone who never talks about herself.'

Calla lifted one shoulder. Being emotionally isolated was the only way she could protect herself from being emotionally battered again. She didn't have anyone to stand between her and the world and could only rely on herself. So she had to be her own advocate and protector. It was a matter of survival.

Understanding the power of silence to get people to talk, Calla simply waited. Maybe he'd talk to her, maybe he wouldn't. She couldn't force him. Nobody, she suspected, could force Judah Reyes to do anything he didn't want to do.

Judah gripped the edge of the pool. 'Since he died, I've been following my father's vision for the company. I've completed projects he started, finalised deals he negotiated, bought and sold assets and melded companies as per his five-year plan. He died in the middle of it, so I've done my best to complete it.'

Calla had no doubt he'd done everything required of him. He'd fulfilled his dad's wishes. What more could be asked of him? 'So what's the problem?'

Judah twisted his lips. 'The problem is that I need to figure out *my* five-year plan, work out where I want to take this company, and what my vision for the company is. I don't have a blueprint to follow anymore. How much do I want to carry over from the past? What do I want to do that's new?' He hesitated, looked down at his hands. 'What's authentic?'

He'd used that word before, and it seemed to carry more weight with him than the rest.

'Does it not feel like it is?' she asked.

Agitation had him kicking his foot, making the pool water ripple. Knowing how rock-steady he always was, the calmest port in a storm, she knew she'd touched a nerve.

'I don't know how to answer that. Or, rather, I don't *want* to answer your question. Because if I say no, then I'm invalidating my father's work, work he was immensely proud of. If I say yes, then I'll be lying to myself and you.'

'So it's a little of both?'

'It's a *lot* of both. I need to plot a way forward, and I

know it's not going to be the same way as my dad's. I feel guilty about that, because he put in thirty years of slogging to get Reyes Luxe the way it is. What right do I have to change it?'

He stared in the direction of Buck's Island. 'But if I do change it, what do I change it to? What feels right to me? What can I live with?'

Judah's words hit a little too close to home.

For ten months, she'd thrown herself into salvaging her career without ever asking why. Watching Judah struggle with a legacy he hadn't chosen, she saw herself—lost, uncertain, maybe chasing something out of habit or pride.

Was she rebuilding to prove something to herself? Or was it just an exhausting *up yours* to Jack and everyone who believed him?

Did she really, truly still want this career—or had she simply forgotten how to want anything else?

But this wasn't about her; it was about him.

He was torn between what felt right and what he felt he owed his dad. What he should keep, and what he should let go of. Where he could make his mark. And how to do it. Because he was so steady, so thinking, and so very confident, she frequently forgot he was still young, only thirty-two. He still had so much time. He was putting more pressure on himself than he needed to, but Calla knew he would not appreciate her saying so.

But how could she help him? What could she say? 'When last did you feel truly authentic? Like you were fully and utterly yourself?' she asked.

Judah's head snapped up, and his eyes slammed into hers. His gaze intensified, and his eyes turned to lasers, slicing through her carefully constructed walls, looking deep into her soul. He surprised her when he dropped into the pool fully clothed and, because he stood in the shallow end, she could look directly into his eyes. He placed his hands on the warm tiles on either side of her hips, effectively caging her in. In the warm glow of the underwater pool lights, she clocked the flickers of deep gold in his eyes, his stubby dark eyelashes, the scar running along his jaw. The scent of him, olive oil and sea, spice and citrus, made her feel a little swoony, and her nipples tightened. The space between her legs heated, and her womb throbbed.

He was the only man, ever, who could shut down her brain and stop her synapses firing, who could transport her to bed with one look. God, if he kissed her, she would be in serious trouble.

It was trouble she didn't need. But it was also the trouble she craved.

Judah lowered his head, and his lips whispered along her cheek bone, down to her jaw and the side of her mouth. His lips slid across hers, light, feathery, and Calla had to clench her fists to keep from reaching for him, from sliding her hands up and under his shirt to find ripped muscles under his tanned, hot skin. She wanted him. For the first time in months, the first time since him, she wanted to be horizontal and naked with him.

Any type of naked with him.

'I answered your question earlier, Calla,' he whispered, his soft breath and his words hitting her ear.

Had he? He was so close, and her need was so great that she couldn't remember what he'd said. Or what she'd asked. 'What were we talking about again?' she asked, a little breathlessly. She wished she could act cooler, be more sophisticated, but she'd only had two lovers in her life, one a lot better than the other.

She didn't know how to play the game. Never had.

He didn't answer her, but instead covered her lips with his clever mouth, and Calla felt herself dissolving, fully immersed in his kiss. He didn't move his hands off the tiles, didn't do anything but kiss her, softly, reverently, like he was rediscovering a previously lost, longed-for land. It was a kiss full of soul, of secrets, hot and sweet and far more seductive than she'd expected.

And it was over far sooner than she wanted. Or expected.

Judah pulled back. 'The last time I felt truly authentic was with you, Calla. In that surf shack last year. I'll keep reminding you until my words sink in.'

Oh.

Oh...

Calla went still, every muscle contracting, as reality rolled over her. She couldn't afford to let his words sink in, to let them resonate. Honesty was his weapon, and it always left her vulnerable. So she did what she was good at—what kept her safe. Her hands slid up to his shoulders, her palms flat against the hard muscles of his chest. Then she pushed.

And when he stumbled back a step, she scrambled up and ran.

CHAPTER SIX

SHE'D RUN OFF. Again.

Judah linked his hands behind his head and released a long sigh as he watched Calla's slim frame move across the entertainment area, her body tight with tension, leaving wet footprints behind. She didn't glance back but just skipped down the stairs to the garden like she needed to get as far away from him as quickly as possible.

After hauling himself out of the pool, he walked over to the wall, looked down and watched as she hit the path bisecting the manicured lawn, moving quickly across the stone pavers. She pulled open the door to the guest house and disappeared from view.

She was very good at shutting him out. Mentally and physically.

It happened every time he got too close or too real, when she clocked his desire for her or when their heat became too much to ignore. The second he showed her that his attraction hadn't faded—not even close—or that she might feel the same, she hit Eject without a moment's hesitation.

He gripped the wall with both hands and allowed his head to drop. The taste of her was still on his tongue, and he could sense her breath on his lips. That kiss—God, that kiss. He couldn't call it a mistake, nor was it something he could regret. Touching her was both a pleasure and a privilege. She'd responded, and for too brief a moment, she'd fallen into him. Her lips moved against his, soft and sexy. He'd definitely felt her body soften, lean, give in to the madness flaming between them.

But then she'd remembered who she was. And why she was here and what was at stake. Then she'd stiffened and pulled back. And bolted.

He knew what she was doing right now, and that was pacing the guest house, mentally composing a list of reasons why she was right to shut down their kiss, to keep things between them professional. To keep their fire contained and controlled.

Frustration flared, and Judah dropped a series of F-bombs. He could've deepened the kiss, taken more, and she might've—would've—followed. But he didn't want her like that. Oblivious, and carried away. When they came back together, he wanted her to make a deliberate choice to be with him, to take what he offered, to enjoy the heat and the flames. He didn't want her off balance and resentful after they'd slept together.

He knew she'd been through something—maybe many somethings—both during her marriage and in the months since he'd last seen her. She didn't need to explain; the signs were everywhere. It was obvious that money had been tight; he saw it in the outdated phone she used, in the too-slow laptop with the crack in the corner of the screen. He presumed every cent went back into her business. She'd told him she needed this job, but he instinctively knew there was more than money on the line.

He scrubbed his hands over his face. He understood her need to keep their relationship on a business footing. The power dynamic between them was unequal and firmly tipped to benefit him. She needed to keep him happy, professionally, and didn't want to mess up her chances of future work by muddying the waters with a sexual affair. Calla was smart to be wary, and, understandably, didn't want their attraction to taint her work. She wanted to earn it. On her own merit. And, damn it, she deserved to.

The problem was now that he'd touched her again, he didn't know how he was supposed to keep from doing it. They were back where it all started, and the island held so many memories of her, memories he was desperate to revisit. Did they ambush her too? Did she remember the way they'd kissed like people did after dicing death? Rolling together in the surf, sand sticking to their skin? Teaching her to surf and how she'd laughed every time she fell? Undressing each other in the moonlight? So little time, but chock-full of moments.

That weekend was burned into him. It was the happiest, most uncomplicated stretch of time he could remember. Was it any wonder he wanted to re-create it?

But what if he was still on the first page and she'd finished the book and had moved on?

What then?

Frustrated, Calla threw down her pencil and scowled at the bright pink paddleboard making its way across Solitude Bay, skimming the surface of the calm, stunning sea. Why couldn't she transfer the fleeting images flashing across her mind onto the empty page of her sketchbook in front of her? This had never happened to her before, and there seemed to be a block between her mind and the blank page in front of her. She'd been here for ten days now, and she'd accomplished nothing.

Was Judah *that* big a distraction? Was her mind so full of him that she couldn't concentrate on anything else? Or was she so worried about her business and her career, her future, that she'd created a mental block? Calla pulled her feet up onto the seat of her chair and wrapped her arms around her knees. Being in Judah's arms last night, feeling his lips on her mouth, had been pure heaven. She'd felt both intoxicated and protected, safe and turned on. How could he pull so many emotions to the surface at the same time?

This was exactly why mixing business with pleasure was a terrible idea. Romance in the workplace was a minefield—messy, distracting and full of regret. Sex blurred boundaries, scrambled one's focus and made people forget the damn job. How was she supposed to concentrate when the GPS in her brain kept rerouting to imagining Judah naked—in the shower, in her bed, pressed up against her, touching and kissing her like it was the only way to keep the world turning? *Argh!*

'What did the sea do to you?'

Calla looked up to see Judah standing at the edge of the veranda, dressed in board shorts and nothing else, sunlight bouncing off his tanned, bare chest. The light hair on his chest was more golden than she remembered, and his abs more defined. His board shorts hung low on his hips and showed off sexy hip muscles.

'Calla?'

Calla tapped the side of her head with the heel of her palm to kick-start her brain. Right. What had he asked? She looked down at her sketchpad. 'I'm frustrated because I can't seem to translate my vision to paper.' She scowled at the empty page.

Judah held the point of his gleaming white surfboard. 'Maybe you need a break, to step away for a while. Why don't you come to the beach with me?'

Calla shook her head. She was already working in shorts and flip-flops, and at a dining table outside instead of a desk. Her standards were slipping, and she couldn't play hooky either. 'Judah, I'm already so far behind it's not even funny. You wanted an initial proposal in two weeks—that's three days away, and I don't know how I'm going to make that deadline.'

'So do you think it will help to sit there and force your brain to cooperate?' he asked. Calla was glad he didn't say something asinine like 'I'll extend your deadline' or 'take your time'. Statements like that would've been an insult. She was a professional, dammit.

'Well?' he asked, raising his eyebrow when she didn't answer his question.

'No, I'll probably just get more frustrated and more annoyed,' she admitted. 'But that doesn't mean I should go to the beach instead.'

'Take some time off, Calla, make up for it later.' His mouth lifted in that sexy half-smile, half smirk she adored. 'Nobody is going to report you to the productivity police.'

Calla wrinkled her nose. It wasn't that. Or only that. She didn't think that spending non-working time, especially when they were half naked, with Judah was a good idea. Their chemistry was constantly bubbling, ready to ignite. One touch, one kiss, and she suspected they might self-immolate. They should be keeping their distance, not trying to find ways to spend more time together.

'The sun is shining, and the sea is warm,' Judah coaxed. 'Get your pretty butt out of the chair and go change into a bikini.'

'I'm thirty-eight years old, I think I'm far too old for a bikini,' she whipped back.

'Sweetheart, that body was made to be shown off,' he

drawled, igniting baby fireworks on her skin. 'Besides, you made that stupid rule? If you feel confident in a bikini, no matter your age, wear whatever the hell you want.'

He had a way of cutting through to the heart of what was important, of clearing away the extraneous and finding the simple truth. In so many ways, she had a lot to learn from him. Calla placed her pencil in her case, closed her sketch pad and pushed back her chair. She sent Judah a quick glance and sighed.

From the moment he uttered his invitation, she knew she was going to join him, that she would say yes. Oh, she could B.S. herself, throw up a couple of mental roadblocks to make herself feel better, and more in control. Did she want to recapture some of the feelings from those heady days she spent with him last year? To feel the way she did back then? That would be a solid, hell, yes!

She should work. She wasn't going to. And if that meant a sleepless night wrestling with her creativity, then that was the price she'd pay.

'Shall I meet you out front?' she asked.

Judah nodded and loosely held his surfboard against his side. 'Sounds good. Ten minutes?'

Calla nodded, caught by the intense expression on his face. She waited, knowing he had more to say. 'But Calla…if you come to the beach with me, you come as you. Not as my interior decorator. As you.'

She heard his unspoken words…*as the woman you were back then*. She leaned back in her chair and watched him walk away, big, solid, in control. She knew she should stay put, knew she was taking a risk, but he was the only man who could tempt her into exploring life at the end of her comfort zone, like she was standing at the end of a cliff. There was a good chance that she would fall, end up emotionally splattered on the rocks below, but the urge to recapture those sunshine-and laughter-filled days, when the world stopped and only the two of them existed, was too tempting to resist.

Don't cry later, Calla. You knew what you were getting into. So don't you dare cry.

Judah held his surfboard under his arm, a backpack on his back and a cooler in his other hand. He picked his way through the rocks and turned back to look at Calla, scrambling over a boulder behind him. She wore black board shorts over a lime and pink bikini, her hair bundled up under a black baseball cap. Her sunglasses kept slipping down her nose and her towel kept falling off her slim shoulder. She looked like she was in her early twenties.

Her age had never been an issue for him, and he thought it a stupid barrier people threw up to avoid getting hurt. Who cared if she was six years older? To him, it wouldn't matter if she was ten or even fifteen years older; he just... liked her. Always had. Attraction and connection didn't stop to ask for birth dates or age differences, it just looked at the other person and said 'yep, her'.

Besides, if the situation were reversed and he were older, nobody would blink. And that was hypocrisy at its finest. Sometimes, in certain situations and at certain times, others would immediately ascertain that she was older than him; at other times, like now, they'd assume she was younger or, at the very least, the same age as him. The thing was, it didn't bloody matter. It never would.

'How much longer?' Calla called, and Judah grinned at the hint of a whine in her voice.

'You should exercise more and eat better,' he replied, ducking his head to hide his smile.

'Oh, shut up,' Calla shot back. 'I walk when I can.'

'But I bet you grab ready-made meals, slices of pizza and Chinese when you are in a hurry.'

'Not always Chinese. I try to keep things balanced by eating Thai, Korean and Vietnamese food, too,' she whipped back.

'My point is that you should be cooking for yourself more, eating fresh vegetables you've prepared yourself.'

'Like you do?' she asked, jumping off a rock onto the beach. She immediately kicked off her flip-flops and dug her toes into the sand, closing her eyes as she found joy in the simple pleasure. 'You probs have a chef or a house-keeper who leaves perfect meals in the fridge for you. I don't. Besides, when would I have the time to cook? I work fourteen-plus hours.'

He didn't like the idea of her working so hard for so little return. 'I'm just saying, you need to look after your-self better.'

Calla patted his bare shoulder, sending waves of elec-tricity through his system. He was acting like he was thir-teen, and it was the first time a girl had touched him. What was wrong with him? Oh, nothing, except the woman he'd dreamed of for the better part of a year was standing in front of him, half dressed, looking gorgeous with a small, sexy smile on her lovely face.

'Stop nagging me about my eating and exercising habits, Reyes,' she told him, skipping ahead of him. 'I'm taking a few hours off from real life. And in the little bubble I'm creating, there are no calories, sun doesn't cause cancer and stress doesn't exist.' She dropped her beach bag and planted her pretty butt in the sand and bent her shapely legs.

She looked around. 'The beach is empty,' she stated, sounding satisfied.

'It's one the locals use,' he explained. 'It'll get busy later.'

She smiled up at him, and Judah was sure his heart stopped beating. He dropped to balance on his haunches in front of her. She'd opened the door, and he was a fool not to walk right in. He stroked the back of her cheek, then her jaw, with his knuckle. 'In this bubble you've created, can we roll back time and be the two people we were back then?'

She stared at him, her eyes wide. But she didn't say no, so he pushed the rim of her cap to the back of her head and lowered his mouth to hers, picking up where they last left off with a hot, demanding open-mouthed kiss. Calla stiffened, for just a heartbeat, second thoughts nipping, but then she lifted her hand to touch his jaw, to run her fingers down his neck, over his shoulder. He ravaged her mouth, and her tongue joined him in that age-old dance. This... God, *this* was what he needed.

Hauling her to her feet, he banded his arm around her waist and lifted her to her toes, and her arms tightened around his neck. A hand under her butt boosted her up his body, and her legs wrapped his hips, her feminine core against his hard, need-her-now erection. Her mouth tasted of mint and coffee, and he couldn't remember when last he felt so alive, so utterly lost in the moment.

Judah walked her towards the ocean, his mouth not leaving hers. The warm water hit his ankles, then his calves, then his thighs. Calla, lost in their kiss, didn't react when the water soaked her shorts and lapped her waist. Their kiss was so hot that Judah was surprised steam didn't rise off the water. Calla crossed her ankles behind his back and clenched her thigh muscles, her expression blissful. She tipped her head to the side, and he scraped his teeth along the cords of her neck, over her collarbone and shoulder. Using one fingertip, he pushed the strap of her bikini down her arm to nip at the ball of her shoulder, loving her soft and smooth lime-scented skin. Pulling back to look at her, Judah smiled at her closed eyes, her parted, slick lips. She looked relaxed and turned-on, lost in this moment.

He couldn't resist seeing more of her, so he pulled the cup of her bikini top down, his eyes feasting on her budded nipple, softly pink in the sunlight. Ducking his head, he pulled it into his mouth, flattening it against the roof of his mouth with his tongue. Calla arched her back, her fingers spearing his hair, making those sexy sounds of want and need.

He liked her like this, loose and letting go.

Talking of letting go...

While this beach was currently empty, it wasn't private, and if someone should come along, he'd give them a show. He had to stop now, before they went too far. Reluctantly, he released her and, in one swift movement, pulled her bikini back into place. Burying his head in her neck, he closed his eyes, trying to push back the wave of desire threatening to buckle his knees. He was a good sailor, a better surfer, had spearfished and spent a good portion of his life on the ocean, and very little scared him. But Calla was on another level. She, on so many levels, exhilarated and terrified him.

Calla's legs dropped from his hips, and she found her footing, her feet digging into the sea floor. She tried to pull away, but there was no way he was going to let that happen, so he pulled her to him, turning her so that her back was to his chest, his arms criss-crossing her torso, his still-hard erection pressing into her back. 'No, don't pull away,' he said in her ear. 'I stopped kissing you because this isn't a private beach and I don't want you to be embarrassed.'

She relaxed and sagged, just a little, against him. He raked back her hair with wet fingers. 'I've imagined kissing you so many times, but it was a million times better than I imagined,' he murmured.

'Maybe you have a really terrible imagination,' she said, her voice a little shaky.

That wasn't possible. 'Better,' he insisted.

Calla gripped his forearm, her fingernails digging into his skin. 'What do we do now, Judah? How do we go forward?'

She was someone who needed a plan, a way forward, preferably signposted. 'We swim, I surf, we lie in the sun and eat,' he said, keeping it simple. 'We chat.'

She sighed. 'I don't know what we have to talk about,' she said.

'We both know that we could talk for days, years, and not run out of things to say, Calla,' he replied, striving for patience. She was scared, he could feel it vibrating through her, knew it like he knew his signature. Scared of what she was feeling, the passion between them, mixing business and pleasure, her future. But he'd do anything he could to make her fear go away.

And if that meant giving her the damn contract to revamp his house, he would. She could mess up his house, paint the walls lemon green and the skirtings pink, cover the couches with flamingo or leopard prints and he wouldn't say a damn word. Not that he thought, for one moment, she'd screw up that badly. But he'd sacrifice his house to give her a little financial breathing room.

Not that she'd accept any charity from him.

'I'm not very good at compartmentalising, Judah.'

He nuzzled his nose into her hair, kissed her temple. 'Try it for the next three hours, Cal. Just one hundred and eighty minutes.'

He felt her stiffen, knew she was thinking too much and would talk her way off this beach and back to work. There was no way he was going to let that happen. So he placed his hand on top of her head and, as she opened her mouth to talk, pushed her head under an incoming wave.

Lying back on her elbows on a huge beach blanket, Calla tipped her face up to the sun and closed her eyes. She'd needed this, needed the sea and the sun and the way it made her skin prickle. Or was being with Judah what she needed? Maybe both?

She adjusted her bikini top, which had the tendency to slide to the side, and watched Judah rustle in the cooler box, looking for more to eat. They'd already demolished a couple of sandwiches, some johnnycakes and fresh mango slices. How could he still be hungry?

Calla felt a cold can against her shoulder, and she saw the can of beer Judah offered her. She couldn't manage another bite of food, but she could murder a beer. Sitting up, she took the can, thanked Judah and clinked it against his before taking a long, refreshing sip. There was something amazingly wonderful about downing a cold beer in the hot sun, the ocean just a few feet away.

She squinted at the foot-high waves. 'You're not going to get any surfing done today,' she told him.

Judah echoed her previous position and leaned back, his elbows taking his weight. He didn't look worried. 'Surfing is a lot better in the winter months. I'm happy to just sit here.'

Calla picked up a handful of sand and allowed it to fall through her clenched fist. St Croix in late June was hot, hot, hot, hot, and she could see a thunderstorm building up on the horizon. She hadn't checked her weather app today and didn't know how intense the storm would be. 'We're not expecting anything crazy weatherwise, right?' she asked.

'Nothing but an afternoon storm. No cyclones or tropical storms are expected anytime soon.'

That was a relief.

'Why do you hate storms so much, Calla?' Judah asked.

She'd been expecting the question, but now that he'd voiced it, she couldn't remember the pat answer she'd normally handed out. Besides, she didn't want to lie to Judah. 'A couple of bad things happened to me during thunderstorms,' she quietly told him.

'Like?'

'Well, the night my dad died, there was the most incredible thunderstorm, with lightning and thunder that was loud and intense.'

'Worse than the other night?' he asked, sitting up and resting his forearms on his bent knees.

She nodded. 'Yeah, worse. He died as the storm petered out.'

He placed his hand on her thigh and squeezed, a quick gesture of support. 'Anything else?'

Unfortunately, there was. 'My ex ended our nearly decade-long marriage during a thunderstorm. But before that, about two years after we got married, I came home after finishing a job early in Washington, DC. I wasn't due home until a few days later. But I missed my husband, and I wanted to surprise him. It was storming when I arrived home, and I didn't have an umbrella with me. I got soaked running from the taxi to the front door, but I was planning on luring him into the shower with me when I got into our apartment.' Judah's dark expression suggested that he knew what was coming next, but she kept talking.

'You caught him.'

She wrinkled her nose. 'No, our place was empty.' She looped her arms around her knees. 'After I showered, I emptied the room's small bin, and while I was tying the bag, I saw an empty lipstick box. High-end, not my colour or my brand.'

Judah's eyes darkened in anger, and his jaw and fist tightened. He wasn't angry at her, but for her. A novel, slightly weird situation.

'Why didn't you leave him then?' Judah demanded. 'Why did you stay with him? Why did you let him do that to you?'

It was a question she'd asked of herself so many times and in so many ways. She drew her finger in the sand and frowned. The squiggles made no sense. 'While I knew he'd cheated on me, I couldn't toss away everything we had built on such flimsy evidence. We had a business together, and I couldn't walk away from it. I'd given it my everything. We had joint accounts, projects we were working on, he needed me, and I, sure as hell, needed him,' she explained. And Jack had been her *family*. It had been small, dysfunctional, but hers and that was a reason why she'd stayed so much longer than she should've. 'Would you think less of me if I told you that it was easier to push it aside, to ignore it, than to make a big deal of it?'

'It *was* a big deal,' he insisted.

Of course it was. But how could she make him understand? 'Jack was the only person I had in my life, Judah. I never knew my mum, my dad was gone, and I was an

only child. I didn't have any extended family and because
I worked such long hours, I didn't have any friends. He
was my person. I didn't think I could live without him.'

'You were wrong,' he muttered, sounding annoyed.

'I was wrong,' she admitted. 'But it took me a while
to realise that, and to realise I'm fine on my own. That I
can take care of myself. Honestly, if I can survive being
married to and divorcing Jack, I can pretty much survive
anything.'

'Was it brutal?'

Brutal? What a tame word for what he put her through!
'He froze me out of the company we created, badmouthed
me to our clients, destroyed my reputation and moved
money out of our business accounts. Embezzled money
from me.' Yeah, it had been brutal. Jack hurt her in every
way he possibly could.

She recalled the text message she'd received from him
that very morning, and his demand to know when she was
returning to the city, and why she was staying so long in
St Croix. For some reason, Jack still wasn't done with her
and was unable to let her go. He still needed to punish
her, to control her, to use her as his verbal punching bag.

But that weekend last year with Judah had been the
turning point. It was when she realised that she didn't
have to play by Jack's rules anymore, and was reminded,
by Judah, that men could be kind. Judah hadn't demanded
anything from her. He hadn't pushed or pried—just sat
beside her in quiet companionship, letting her breathe.
Letting her be.

Back then, she'd told Judah more about herself than
she'd shared with anyone in years. Her job. Her past. Her
life in New York. What she loved. What she missed. She
hadn't mentioned Jack at all.

And when he made love to her as the dawn kissed the sea, she didn't hesitate to follow where he led. Loving him, being with him made perfect sense. Just like it did now.

The urge to kiss him, to run her hands over his perfect body, was almost overwhelming. How far was it to his open-top Jeep? How long would it take them to head back to his house and his bed?

Or any horizontal surface.

Calla sighed, forcing herself to be sensible. They now had ties that bound them, contracts and money on the line, and future projects to consider. They weren't two random strangers who could shed their clothes and inhibitions, believing they'd never see each other again. This was real, grown-up, far-reaching. She had to tread carefully. But she also needed to acknowledge how consequential that weekend was, how his attention, in some strange way, encouraged her to gather her strength and finally move on from her train wreck marriage. Just being with him gave her the confidence to gather her wits and courage to start again.

'Thank you for being there for me that weekend,' she said, unable to look at him.

'Rescuing you from that prick was the least I could do,' he muttered, frowning.

'You rescued me from more than just being in his presence,' she explained. 'You told me I was strong and capable and that I deserved more. In the months following that night, when things got really tough, and they got really tough, I held on to your words, and often reminded myself that somewhere in the world, some hot guy thought I was courageous. And strong and worthy of more.'

Judah stroked her hair, her bare back. 'You forgot sexy and gorgeous.'

Was it the heat from the sun causing her cheeks to

bloom, or was it the way he looked at her, like she was a much-anticipated birthday gift he couldn't wait to unwrap? His eyes dropped to her mouth, and Calla swallowed, longing to straddle his thighs and lay her mouth on his. She wanted him, wanted more of him, wanted more...

But wanting more was dangerous, and she didn't know how to want without considering the consequences. She was risking her independence, all the work she'd done on herself, for herself, to get to this place in her life where she felt capable and strong. She couldn't allow a man to slide back into her life and take over. And Judah, despite being younger than her, was a take-charge type of guy. He wouldn't sit on the sidelines, waiting for her permission to walk into her life, happy to leave it when she felt the need for solitude. She could never risk allowing anybody to mess with her psyche and soul. She couldn't even suggest a one-night, or couple-of-nights stand with Judah, because she knew that the closer she got to him, the more she'd want. Her imagination would start working overtime, and she'd start to want more than she could have.

Lovely things. Impossible things.

'It's not a good idea, Judah.'

He didn't pretend to misunderstand her. 'Probably not. But I can't stop myself from wanting you.'

Having such a big, masculine, alpha man look at her with desire-fuelled fire in his eyes made her feel powerful and feminine, like she was channelling every goddess throughout the centuries. She knew it was a siren's call, a way to madness, but she couldn't help leaning sideways, her mouth finding his.

Judah cradled her face in his hand, his thumb stroking her cheek bone. 'Stop overthinking this, sweetheart.' His deep voice was low, coaxing, and a little wistful. 'Let's pretend, just for a couple of hours, the rest of the day, that we are who we were back then. I'm just a bartender, and you're a woman who walked out of the bar with me.'

Calla's heart lurched. His soft request was ridiculous. And dangerous, but so, so intoxicating. She should say no. She should scoot away, thank him for the trip to the beach and ask him to take her home so she could get back to work. Once there, she would sit at a desk and wait for inspiration to strike.

But she didn't move.

She looked into his eyes and felt her resolve dissolving. He dropped his hand and lifted an eyebrow, but she didn't feel pressured or manipulated. He was just asking, and Calla knew that if she found the strength to say no, he wouldn't sulk or curse, he'd simply respect her decision. Unlike Jack, he was a grown-up.

As the seconds ticked past, she found it more and more difficult to distance herself from him. She'd wanted him back then; she wanted him now. Wasn't she allowed this? One little (or big) indulgence? She was, generally, a good person, someone who worked hard, played fair and did her best to be nice. Was responsible. Surely she was allowed a moment where she got to take and feast? She wasn't asking for forever or for a promise of something more. She just wanted him. For a little while. And when the time came, she'd be able to let him go. She had to.

Calla closed her eyes. 'Okay,' she whispered. 'Let's pretend.'

CHAPTER SEVEN

JUDAH ABRUPTLY BRAKED, exited the Jeep and ran around to the passenger door, ripping it open. He'd kept hold of Calla's hand the entire journey home, terrified her rational, careful brain would talk her out of letting him take her to bed.

He wrenched her door open and unclicked her safety belt, her perfume going straight to his head. Pulling back, her mouth inches from his, he watched her eyelids lower as she looked at his lips, her clenched fist resting on her thigh. She wanted him…

Just to make sure, he covered her mouth with his and slid his tongue between her teeth, lightly growling as he took her mouth, spicy and fresh, on fire for him. Knowing he needed nothing but her, only her, he slid his one hand under her thighs, the other around her back and easily lifted her out of the car, hurrying to the front door of his house. Holding her easily, he walked her inside and up the stone staircase to the master suite, a place he'd longed to take her since first seeing her.

Judah laid Calla on his big bed, pulling back to take her in. She still wore her board shorts and her bikini, but she'd lost a flip-flop somewhere between the car and his bedroom. Her hair tumbled over her pink-from-the-sun shoulders, and her eyes were wide and full of heat and want. A deep, dark green that reminded him of mystical and ancient forests, a place where druids worshipped and spirits roamed. She lifted her hand and traced the ball of his shoulder with her index finger, and she followed its path down his pec and over his nipple. He closed his eyes.

Her touch felt like home.

'Your body is perfection, Judah,' she said on a breathy sigh that sent a bolt of heat and electricity straight down his spine. Oh, his body wasn't perfect, he knew that—he had scars on his collarbone, chin, a nasty one on his shoulder from surgery, more scars on his thigh from a car accident. But he wasn't going to argue with her...

'So strong, so masculine, so powerful.' Calla sat up and linked her hands around his neck. 'Kiss me, Judah. I like it when you kiss me.'

His liking started with her breathing, and it just got worse from there. 'Are you sure this is what you want, Cal?' he asked. It was so hard to check in when all he wanted to do was take and take and take. But he needed her fully on board, and yes, his ego wanted to hear that she wanted him as much as he wanted her.

'Mm,' she said, lifting her left shoulder. He couldn't resist her soft, smooth skin, so he dropped an open-mouthed kiss on her collarbone.

Not good enough. He needed more. 'Is that a yes, Calla?'

She planted a series of small kisses on his jaw. 'It is,' she said, and he noted the lack of hesitation in her voice. Judah pushed her back and lowered himself to her, keeping his weight off her by digging his elbow into the mattress. He stroked her hair away from her face and smiled.

'You are so goddamn beautiful, Calla,' he murmured, before placing his mouth on hers. He simply rested his mouth on hers, happy to let their anticipation build, knowing that gratification would be so much hotter and sweeter later.

Calla, more impatient than he, pushed her tongue to trace the seam of his lips, to tempt him with tiny nibbles that tested his resolve. The urge to take nearly overwhelmed him, but he knew he had to go slow, or else this would be all over far too soon. Calla needed, deserved more. They both did. They were both in the ring, punching it out with circumstances and life. Calla was fighting the memories of her past, trying to plant her feet, and he was trying to reclaim himself, the pieces he'd lost over the past few years. Fighting to figure out who he was while trying not to be drowned out by the noise of the world shouting who he should be.

But for tonight, for however long he had to love her—because God, being with her was *everything*—he'd make sure they forgot the mental wars they were waging. They would, as the many lifestyle coaches and yoga instructors he employed instructed, be present.

'Judah.'

The way she said his name, holding a little bit of wonder, a lot of need, skittered through him, and he pulled back to take in her lovely face. So pretty, the only woman who'd ever managed to slide beneath the surface, the one he couldn't hide from. Or not completely. Man, he wanted her.

Sliding his arm under her waist, he pulled her up and into him and covered her mouth, unable to go slow, needing to take, and give. His tongue twisted around hers; Calla released a moan and dug her fingernails into his shoulders. Sweet pain. Her hand drifted down his back, and she pushed her hand under the band of his swim shorts, frustrated when the barrier of the fabric impeded her progress. Oh, he'd shed his clothes, but not yet.

Today, with her, the journey was as important as the destination.

Lowering her back down to the bed, he moved his mouth along her jaw, down her neck and across her collarbone, pulling aside the straps of her bikini top as he went. He was about to undo the clasp when Calla half sat and did it for him, pulling the top away and flinging it to the ground. Judah immediately rewarded her by locking onto a perfect, already hard nipple, lathing it with his tongue. His fingers covered her other breast, testing its weight, his thumb teasing her nipple. How was it that her skin tasted so sweet?

He'd never been this hard, this desperate to be inside a woman, longing to experience her wet warmth. With hands that were less assured than normal, his breathing more ragged, he pushed her shorts down her hips, taking her bikini bottoms with them. This... Calla...naked. Lying on his bed as the dappled sunlight hit the bed, just as he'd dreamed. His.

For now.

Judah rolled off the bed and stood up to shuck his shorts, his eyes on her face. He liked that she lay there and looked her fill. He did the same. Long legs, round hips, a mole on her right hip. His eyes locked on hers, and he fell into all that green, another walk through that ancient and mysterious forest. What was she thinking? He was desperate to know.

Calla sat up and encircled him. 'You're so beautiful,' she told him, sounding serious. 'I look at you and all the moisture from my mouth disappears.'

Judah wasn't used to compliments from his lovers; they generally expected to hear them, and rarely handed them out. A little dazed by the emotions skipping through her eyes—so much lust, a little affection—he placed his hand on top of hers to keep her from stroking him. 'If you keep doing that, I'm going to come.' He wasn't lying; when it came to her, he had minimal self-control.

He placed one hand next to her head and slid his other hand down, over her stomach, between her legs, finding her sensitive spot without hesitation. She arched off the bed, closed her eyes and released a long, huffy breath. The fantastic combination of sea, her perfume and sex wafted over them, and Judah groaned. He was a grown man, experienced, but he didn't know how much longer he could keep himself from plunging into her, from losing himself in her. He was on a knife's edge here.

But he needed to make Calla come first. Two for her, one for him...that was the deal, a silent promise to every woman he made love to. If they were gracious enough to give him their bodies, it was the least he could do.

Judah rested his thumb on her. Her breathing was as ragged as his. Calla's mouth dropped open, and he was about to kiss her when she rested her fingers on his jaw, her face and body flushed with pleasure.

'I'm so close.'

He was aware and loved that she was so responsive. 'No more,' she said, pushing his hand away. What the hell? Why was she stopping now? Judah hesitated, unsure why she was slamming on the brakes. Calla rubbed her thumb over his bottom lip.

'It might sound corny, very uncool, but I want us to come together, like we did back then.'

He loved her honesty and didn't care about being corny or being cool. And, well, he wanted that too, obviously. But that would break his rule of two to one. When he hesitated, Calla narrowed her eyes. 'I'm not sure what you're thinking right now, but if you don't get a condom on in the next two seconds, I might scream. And not in pleasure.'

Right. God. What was he waiting for? This was Calla, not a casual hookup. There were no rules when it came to her, he was stumbling around in the dark. Shocked into action, Judah managed to open the bedside drawer without looking and found a strip of condoms. He pulled it out, ripped one off and tossed the rest on the bed, or maybe they landed on the floor. He didn't care; he'd look for them later. Calla, impatient, took the packet, removed the condom and slid over him. He loved her hand stroking him. She felt…right. Hot and exciting but comfortable too. Safe.

Weird to be feeling that right now. He was about to cover her, to finally, finally, slide home, when Calla pushed him onto his back and threw her leg over his hips. She closed her eyes as she rocked against him. All doubts about whether she was ready evaporated as he took in her expression, a combination of warrior want and feminine power. She lowered herself onto him, inch by fabulous inch, biting her lip every time a wave of pleasure rippled through her. He could feel her every reaction, and pleasure spiked through him. She rocked, he lifted, the room faded away, and all that was left was Calla.

Knowing he couldn't wait a second longer, Judah rolled her over and in one fluid move, made her his. He checked once, quickly, to see if she was okay and still with him— her glazed eyes and open mouth told him she was—and then started to move, Calla following where he led. Hot and strong, hips lifting in sync, they reached for and gathered every last molecule of concentrated pleasure. Energy rocketed down his spine, but he wouldn't go there without her.

'Calla, now,' he commanded. He needed her in this moment with him.

'Now?' she asked, breathless.

He dropped an F-bomb and clenched her hip, digging his fingertips into her soft skin. He was holding on by a thread now.

'Okay,' Calla said on a breathy laugh, and he felt her ripple, heard her pleasure-filled sob. Thank God. He could let go, so he did, diving in again, chasing that special high he hadn't felt since her. That added extra, something indefinable, and only experienced with Calla. The room filled with colour, an aura pulsed behind his eyes, and then he shattered, coming hard. All that was left was a vortex of sensation, and Calla standing in the middle of it.

Somewhere, from a place far away, he felt Calla's hips lift, her back arch, her small whimper, her body rippling as pleasure rolled through her a second time. He rested his forehead on her collarbone and smiled.

Two for one. Yeah. The way it should be.

This was straight out of a romance movie.

Calla, her back to Judah's chest, her head on his bicep, his leg over hers, looked out of one of the two glass doors that formed the walls of the master suite. Across the bay, Buck Island looked greener today, the sea a more intense shade of blue. A speedboat flew across the slightly choppy waters, and a yacht with sails unfurled headed out to sea. Where were they going? To the Bahamas or Jamaica?

Talking of…where was she going? Where was this going? She and Judah spent the rest of yesterday and most of last night making love—they hadn't been able to stop, well, feasting was an accurate description—and they'd only fallen asleep a few hours ago. But it was morning now; she'd woken at her normal time, and the reality of her situation strolled back in and parked its arse down.

And while spending concentrated, naked time with Judah had been lovely, nothing had, fundamentally, changed.

She still needed to protect her business, and herself, from Jack's never-ending insinuations and manipulations, and to establish herself so firmly that nothing he or his family said or did could undermine her or her business. That meant landing a high-profile client, a client that screamed 'she'd arrived' and 'don't mess with her'. Judah was that client, her one shot. And she'd jeopardised everything by sleeping with him.

Oh, he'd promised their personal history wouldn't affect any business decisions—and she wanted to believe him. But reality was that, by giving in to temptation, she'd added a layer of unneeded complication. She'd put everything at risk to be with him.

How stupid was that? She'd done that with Jack, and look where that got her. She'd lost her share of the business, all her savings, and had her heart stomped on. And he was still trying to hurt her in any way he could. But here she was, in Judah's arms, practically begging life to test her again.

When would she learn?

She needed to get out of his bed, leave his room and reset their relationship. Get back on track. Now. Immediately. And it would be so much better if she could do that without hashing it out, without any explanations. She'd leave, and when she saw him again, she'd treat him like her client and be super professional and polite. With luck, he'd get her '*this was a mistake*' message.

Calla, hearing his deep breathing, pulled her leg from under his and lifted her head off his arm. She wrapped her hand around his wrist and lifted his arm—man, it was heavy—off her chest, rolling away from him. Landing on her feet, she stared down at him, holding her breath. When he didn't move, she released a long stream of pent-up air.

So far, so good.

Spotting one of his shirts lying over the back of an easy chair, she pulled it over her head, the soft hem hitting her thighs. Where were her clothes? Her bikini top lay at the end of the bed, and her bottoms and shorts were on the floor. One flip-flop, where was the other?

She couldn't find it and decided to look for it later. Her main objective was to leave his room without him realising she was gone, without having to talk to him. Because if he looked at her with those marvellous blue eyes, if she saw his sexy half-smile, she might be tempted to climb back into that ridiculously big bed and play hooky for the day, the week.

She had work to do, a company to run, a design to submit, a future to secure. No man, not even Judah Reyes, would knock her off course again.

Calla tiptoed to the door, the light wood floor silky beneath her bare feet. Grabbing the handle to slide open the door, she turned back to look at him and gasped. Judah rested on his elbows, his hair mussed and his eyes narrowed. 'Were you seriously going to sneak out?' he demanded.

Calla wrinkled her nose; she was so busted. She rubbed her foot on the back of her calf. 'I—um—I thought I'd let you sleep.'

He rubbed his hand over his stubbled jaw, unimpressed by her obvious lie. 'No, you're leaving because you're trying to put distance between us, distance between the person you were last night and the person you're trying to be.'

What did that even mean?

Judah left the bed and walked over to her, supremely comfortable in his nakedness. And why shouldn't he be?

He was gorgeous. He stood in front of her and placed his forearm on the door above her head, caging her in. It took everything within Calla not to lay her cheek on his chest, plaster her body against his. No, she had to be strong. This was another one-night thing, just two ships passing and all that. They were ships that should never have collided…and what was with the references to ships? *Honestly.*

'Why are you running, Calla?'

She wasn't, precisely, running. Maybe walking fast? But she couldn't tell Judah she was terrified of how he made her feel. He sparked her imagination of what could be, of the future she'd dreamed of when she was young and naive. She could barely admit it to herself, never mind to him, that he made her feel loved, cherished and protected.

But protecting her wasn't his job; it wasn't anyone's job. She was her own protector, her biggest advocate, her only cheerleader. Asking anyone else to do that for her, to give them that much responsibility, was asking to be disappointed.

She'd write her own story. Create her own life. Live it alone.

She forced herself to meet his eyes. They could both benefit from some honesty. 'I slept with my client, Judah. What does that make me?' she asked, her voice breaking a little.

'The hell you slept with a client, Calla!' Okay, so he wasn't going to let that stand. 'You slept with *me*. The man you met ten months back, the one who walked you out of the Reyes Luxe bar. You did not sleep with the owner of Reyes Luxe. That's what we agreed yesterday.'

She threw up her hands, frustrated. 'We just used that as an excuse to sleep together! We both know we can't separate the two!' Calla cried. 'It doesn't work that way.'

His eyes hardened, and she caught a glimpse of the determined businessman who made tough decisions involving millions of dollars and affecting thousands. 'It does if I say it does,' he said, not yielding an inch. 'Your work has nothing to do with what we did last night. Our personal interactions are between you and me. Do *not* confuse the two.'

How could she not when so much was on the line? 'That's easy to say when you're not the one who's risking everything, Judah, when it's not your butt dangling over the fire. You hold the power—I have none.'

His jaw tightened, and she suspected he was grinding his teeth. 'It's not about power, Calla.'

She released a sharp sigh. 'Of course it is, Judah. Everything is about control and power. You have it, I do not. You can change my life, businesswise, but nothing I do or say will affect you. You hold all the cards. And that's why this,' she waggled her index finger between them, 'will never happen again.'

The problem was that he just had to look at her and her knees weakened, and her body throbbed from wanting him. Tough. She'd just have to suck it up and remember the big picture. He held her future in his hands, and she'd jeopardised their professional relationship by taking a stroll through the past and hooking up with him again.

Stupid. This was why her body and heart should never be allowed to make decisions.

'I'm going to shower and get to work. I already lost too much time yesterday.' Calla ducked under his arm and, when she was out of his reach, turned back to look at him. 'And I'd appreciate it if we could forget this happened. I'd like us to go back to being client and decorator.'

Keeping his hands on the wall, he turned his head to

look at her, his blue eyes lasering through her. 'Let me think about that…mm.' He waited a beat before speaking again. 'No, we're not going to do that.'

Right. She was on her own, fighting their attraction. That was okay; she'd fought bigger battles than facing down a sexy man who wanted her. She could do this.

Maybe.

She hoped.

One step forward. Six back.

Judah pulled on a pair of shorts, sat on the edge of his bed, his forearms on his knees as he listened to Calla's retreating footsteps. He hadn't expected her to stay all day, but he'd at least hoped for the morning. He'd had plans for her; he'd wanted to see her sleep-soaked eyes turn limp and liquid with desire, wanted to wake her up with slow morning sex. He'd wanted to drink coffee with her on his bedroom balcony, as they watched the activity in the bay. Wanted to take her back to bed for a mid-morning nap.

But she was gone—already slipping back behind her walls.

He exhaled hard and scrubbed a hand over his jaw. He got it. He did. Still, it didn't stop the sting.

With Calla, he felt like himself. Just Judah. With her, he felt like he did last year, like he was wholly, completely himself, not a satellite of his father or Reyes Luxe's highest-paid minion. Back then, she hadn't known who he was, and he'd loved the anonymity. He had been seen for who he really was, not what he owned, ran or represented. She'd made him feel that way again last night, and something inside him had readjusted. Like his heart could finally beat without being squeezed tight.

Losing his father had thrown everything into chaos.

David Reyes had been a good father in many ways, but he'd also been a lot to deal with. Bigger than life, relentless in his vision and driven to make Reyes Luxe the number one wellness brand in the world.

And then his father died. And the world expected him to take the reins of the company, ready or not. After ten long, exhausting months, he was remembering what it felt like to have loose lungs, shoulder blades that weren't tight with tension, how it felt to move through the day without a dull, just-there headache. To think. To dream about the future, not to just worry about it. Ideas were starting to bubble, and thoughts about where he could take Reyes Luxe and how he could put his own mark on the company, flitted in and out of his mind. They were still nebulous, unformed, but it was his vision, not his father's. Something quieter, a brand that was less in your face. Something more real and accessible.

Calla, as he somehow sensed she would, reminded him of who he was and the man he wanted to be. Reconnecting with Calla had shifted something in him. He hadn't realised quite how numb he'd been until she walked back into his life...until her laughter warmed the rooms, her voice soothed his soul and her smile kick-started his heart. Now that they'd slept together—and he'd seen her briefly drop her guard—he couldn't pretend nothing had changed.

She saw beyond the brand and his CEO image, had told him to trust his gut, and to stop chasing his father's version of success. But she wasn't living her life that way. She was still letting fear run the show, keeping it all strictly professional like that might protect her from feeling too much.

But he also understood her hesitation. The power imbalance between them was real. And like any other professional with a sense of pride, she didn't want his charity and wanted to keep her talent separate from their chemistry. Just like he wanted to keep himself separate from Reyes Luxe, from his dad. He respected her stance.

But did she understand how good her designs were? She had a great eye for colour, and a clean but expressive style with an audacious edge. Just like he'd wanted to earn his place at Reyes Luxe, Calla wanted the commission to redesign Sol House because she nailed the brief, not because they nearly set the sheets alight.

Still...*shit*. He liked her. In a deeper, harder way than he had back then. He liked her mind. Her stubbornness. Those flashes of vulnerability that seeped out when she wasn't careful. Her courage and her strength to keep going. Sure, there was a part of him that ached to protect her— with his money and connections, he could make life easy for her. But she'd hate that. And it would make her hate him. Calla didn't need a white knight, she needed a man who believed in her.

Could he be that person?

Judah pushed both hands into his hair, tugged. He'd only recently reconnected with her, and was trying to figure out his way forward. Right now, he couldn't offer her much beyond great sex. He was in a state of flux himself, his own road unclear. But, despite saying that, he knew he wasn't just looking for another one-night stand with Calla. And he couldn't pretend their chemistry and attraction would go away just because she wanted it to.

But for now, maybe they did need to hit Pause. That was the sensible, adult choice. Just until the ground under his feet stopped shifting, until a clear path opened up ahead. He knew what he should do...but after a night like that, how was he supposed to just walk away?

CHAPTER EIGHT

JUDAH HELD CALLA'S tablet and squinted at it. The colour palette was shades of white, with splashes of island colour, reds and tangerines, hot pinks, all the colours of a Caribbean sunset. It radiated easy comfort—plush, sink-right-in sofas, a coffee table sturdy enough for sun-kissed feet, and lush, vibrant indoor plants. It was a space he could live in, the kind that made his shoulders drop, his tension ease. And yet, somehow, it still felt elegant. Stylish enough to impress, but warm enough to unwind in. God, she was talented. He tapped the screen with his index finger before angling the screen so Calla could look at it.

'I like this,' he said.

Calla, standing opposite him at the head of the outdoor dining table, pulled her bottom lip between her teeth. He ached to soothe the slight pain with his lips. It had been two days since they'd made love. Calla had holed up in the guest cottage, seldom leaving. He saw the light on in the cottage late at night, and he knew she was burning the midnight oil. There were also dark stripes under her eyes, and she looked a little pale. He wanted to take her to bed but knew that as soon as he got her horizontal, she'd probably slide off into sleep. He was more than happy to hold her while she slept and was prepared to be any type of pillow she required.

He jammed his hands into the pockets of his shorts. 'Stop biting your lip, Calla. There's no reason to be nervous.'

Her lip popped out, and she folded her arms, rocking on her heels. 'I really want you to like them,' she said, and Judah picked up the anxiety in her voice. 'I mean, I want all my clients to like my designs…'

He sighed. Why was she avoiding him, wasting the little time they had? It was stupid, and asinine. They were adults, they liked each other and wanted to sleep with each other. Why did this have to be more complicated than that? Why was she throwing work into the mix, and why was he worried about what came next? Why couldn't they live in the present?

'This is close,' he told her, tapping the screen. 'Maybe fewer white couches?'

Calla nodded. 'I can do that. It was my favourite too, but I thought the pinks and reds would put you off.'

Not even close. He half sat on the table. 'This is going to be a once-in-ten-years overhaul, so I want it to be able to withstand people coming in and out, and them using the furniture. And white isn't practical for a beach house.'

'You want it kid and dog proof,' she murmured. She kept her eyes on the mood board, but her cheeks flushed with a shade of pink similar to the swoosh on the mood board. Was that her way of asking whether he wanted either, or both, in the future? A way for her to take a few steps back to him?

'I want both, at some point,' he told her. He gestured to the great room and then pointed to the pool. 'I want them to play Lego on the floor, swim in the pool.'

'The kids or the dogs?'

He smiled. 'Either. Both,' he replied, then grinned. 'A

Lego-playing dog would be cool.' He folded his arms, enjoying her laughter. 'Do you want kids?' he asked.

'I did...' She hesitated. 'I do. But I've been consumed with my business for so long that I haven't spent much time thinking about it. Also, I know how hard it is to be a single parent, so I don't want to do it alone. But I'm nudging forty, so I'm running out of time.'

No, she wasn't, that was nonsense. Plenty of women had children in their early to mid-forties these days. The image of Calla, her tummy round with her child, grinning at him, flashed behind his eyes, and it was so strong and so perfect that his knees jellified.

Judah rubbed his hand over his face, around the back of his neck, feeling hot and clammy. He'd spent the morning paddleboarding, maybe he'd spent too much time in the hot sun and was suffering from a little heat stroke. Kids weren't on his radar, and since he was only in his early thirties, he had lots of time. After he sorted out Reyes Luxe, reengineered it and reshaped it, he could think about settling down, being a dad.

But that would only be in about ten years or so...

And while he had time, ten years was pushing the boundaries of Calla's fertility. *God...enough, Judah. You're jumping too far ahead. You've only slept with the woman a few times. Maybe you should sort your professional life out first before planning your personal.*

Judah's phone vibrated, bouncing slightly against the wooden surface of the table, and he looked down at the screen. Grateful for the distraction, he answered his assistant's call. 'Yeah, what is it?'

He listened to Brent's explanation for his call, his blood icing. After five minutes, he spoke. 'Let me get this straight.... The board isn't prepared to wait for my decision about acquiring ForgeRitual?'

'They are demanding a decision within a week.'

'I am the bloody CEO and the major shareholder of this company,' Judah muttered, his words gritty. 'I'm not sold on their brand, I think it flirts with toxic masculinity.'

'They disagree and they think this is too good an opportunity to lose.'

Judah swore, and his eyes connected with Calla's. She cradled her tablet to her chest, her expression concerned. 'Are you okay?' she mouthed.

Obviously all his irritation was reflected on his face. It seemed he lost his ability to look unaffected around her. He shook his head, and she winced.

'Also...'

Oh, crap, he instantly recognised the anxiety in that one word. What else had gone wrong? 'Did you see the email from Harmony Green?' Brent asked.

Reyes Luxe's head of research was emailing him? Harmony, a close friend of his dad's and one of David's first hires, called him directly when she had an issue. 'What does the email say?'

'Look for it. I'll wait while you read it.'

What was going on, and why did Brent sound so deflated? Judah read the email. He turned hot, then cold, and goose bumps covered his skin. What fresh hell was this?

Calla walked over to him, carrying two beers in one hand and Judah's sunglasses in the other. After abruptly disconnecting his phone call, he'd walked up to the railing, his face white and his lips bloodless.

Had someone died? Did the bottom fall out of Reyes Luxe's stock price? Was his enormous workforce going on strike? She tapped his arm with one of the bottles, and when he looked at her, she pushed the beer into one hand and his sunglasses into the other.

'Thanks,' he said, his voice hollow. Judah placed the bottle on the railing, his fingers white against the bright green bottle. Yeah, something had rocked him. But what? Judah was normally so unreadable, so calm and collected—okay, except when he made love to her—so it was a surprise to see him with messy hair and turbulent eyes, his expression frustrated and a little uncertain.

She needed to comfort him, but didn't know how. Scooting closer to him, she pushed her shoulder into his arm and tipped her head to rest her temple on his shoulder. 'What happened?'

Judah didn't answer her, choosing instead to look at his phone. He swiped his thumb over the screen and shoved it at her. Calla took it and saw that it was an email from someone called Harmony Green. Judging by the domain name at the end of her address, she worked at Reyes Luxe.

Calla skimmed through the email...

We've had several conversations about the future of Reyes Luxe and your intention to honour your father's legacy...

However, I've recently learned that Reyes Luxe is seriously considering a partnership with ForgeRitual. I want to be clear: I believe this would be a serious misstep for the brand....

Over the past few years, I often challenged David's choices as the company veered toward scale over substance, and I came close to resigning. I ultimately chose to stay because I believed in your leadership and your potential to steer the company with authenticity.

But your willingness to even entertain this partnership has shaken that belief…

Regrettably, I no longer feel I can continue with the company under this direction.

Wow. Calla tapped the side button to turn the screen black. She placed the phone on the dining table and walked back to where Judah stood, his jaw clenched, still looking out to sea. He'd yet to put on his sunglasses or take a sip from his beer.

She placed her back to the railing and the sea. 'I remember you mentioning ForgeRitual, Judah. It's a men's wellness brand, right?' They promoted men's-only gyms and spas, vitamins to boost testosterone and leaned into 'reclaim your masculinity' branding.

'The business plan says acquiring it is a no-brainer. We'll recoup the investment in a year and will double profits in eighteen months. My board members keep telling me it will honour my father's legacy as a man's man who built his body and his business.'

'Is that what you think?' Calla gently asked.

'They keep reminding me of our investors, that we need to keep expanding into new markets, of my father's legacy.'

'But this won't be his legacy, Judah, it will be *yours*,' Calla pointed out. 'It'll carry your name, and it will be your signature on the deal.' The whole concept sounded dreadful, and she instinctively hated it. But this wasn't about her—it was about Judah and how he saw his company and his role within it. Would he chase profits? Did he care about what people thought about him, what he'd leave behind as a legacy? How much did he owe his father, and how far would he go to honour the man he loved and adored?

'My father trusted the board, trusted his advisers,' Judah stated.

'But?'

He finally looked at her.

Judah's grip on the beer bottle finally loosened. He slid his sunglasses over his eyes and lifted the bottle to his lips. After a few swallows and a long moment of silence, he spoke again. 'The men on the board, my father's friends, chase profits. That's what they do.' He nodded at his phone. 'This would be a very profitable venture.'

'But you're not convinced.'

'How do you know that?' Judah asked, half turning and leaning his hip into the stone wall. The sun turned the stubble on his jaw and the hair on his arms golden. In his polo shirt and chino shorts, he looked every inch the rich millionaire he was. But there was tension in his thin lips, and in the tight muscles in his neck and shoulders.

'Well, you mentioned as much before. You've delayed making the decision because you aren't certain, not because you are. I think your first impression was right, Judah.'

'And what was my first impression?' Judah asked, knocking his bottle against his thigh.

'That you absolutely bloody hate it.' Calla was surprised by how certain she sounded, how convincing. Judah didn't believe in toxic masculinity. Of course he would hate the idea.

Instead of answering her, Judah slid his arm around her waist and pulled her into him. What else could she do but clutch his shirt and rest her cheek on his hard chest? How could she stay professional when he needed comfort and connection? She felt his lips in her hair, the light kiss he placed on her temple. His hand on her lower back pulled her closer, and her stomach hit the hard ridge of his erection…he *wanted* her. No, he wanted her a *lot*.

She stiffened, and Judah released a half-laugh, half snort. 'I can't hold you and not want you, Calla. That's asking too much of me.'

Calla leaned back to look up into his gorgeous face, frowning when he simply held her, not speaking. Not pushing.

That was all? Why wasn't he demanding more, kissing her, coaxing her back into his bed? And why did she feel so disappointed? If keeping things professional between them meant so much to her, if it was so important, why did she keep digging into his thoughts and life, and listen when he spoke about his problems? Why couldn't she keep any decent sort of emotional distance between them?

And why did she want to kiss him again, make love to him, here in the sunlight in the middle of a scorching July day?

'Your eyes…' Judah murmured, his hand coming up to caress the skin under her right eye. 'They're warm and full of heat. They tell me you want me, Calla.'

She should protest, deny his words, but her tongue refused to cooperate. It couldn't form the words.

'Being apart from you, not being able to touch you, has been hell, Cal. Tell me you want me to take you to bed, Calla.'

She should pull away, insist that she needed to go back to work, to keep their relationship on a business footing. But she couldn't. The only thing she wanted was to get naked with him, right here and now.

Don't do it, Calla, it'll be another mistake.

But it was a mistake she could live with, would have to live with, because she wanted this memory. One day, when she was old and wrinkled, and sex was a distant memory, she wanted to recall making love with Judah in the sunlight, the Caribbean glinting blue beneath them, sunlight dancing on Judah's skin as he pleasured her.

She wouldn't deny future Calla this memory...

Standing on her tiptoes, Calla slid her hands under Judah's shirt, finding hot skin covering hard muscles. After brushing her mouth across his, she tugged his shirt up and over his head, exposing his tanned chest and abs, his big arms. His shirt dropped to the floor. His shorts rode low on his hips. So hot. So sexy.

And for now, the next hour, day, week or two, he was hers.

'Make love to me, Judah,' she murmured. His eyes darkened with heat and need, and when he dipped his knees to scoop her up to carry her inside, she stepped back and put a hand on his shoulder. When his eyes slammed into hers, she shook his head and smiled at his cocked eyebrow.

She nodded to a double bed lounger half in and half out of the sun. 'We're completely alone. Why not here? And why not now?'

He pushed back a strand of her hair that had escaped her functional ponytail. Needing to feel it wrapped around his hand, he tugged the band from her hair, and her wavy hair spilt down her back and over her shoulders. 'I need to go inside to get a condom, but I'm scared to leave you alone in case you change your mind.'

Sweet of him, but she had a solution for that problem. Her hand skated across his chest, over the ball of his shoulder, down his big arm. 'I'm on the pill and haven't had sex since you last year.'

'I had a physical a few weeks ago. I'm clean.'

'If you want, we can—'

'I want.'

Calla squealed when Judah banded his arm around her waist, lifted her off her feet and walked her over to the lounger, where he placed her on her feet. He gently turned her around, found the zipper to her sundress and slid it down her back, his lips following the path of the zip as he lowered it, his lips hot against her skin.

He kicked her dress away and turned her to face him, and traced a finger over the edge of the cup of her sky blue bra. Thankfully, her panties matched today; they didn't always. 'I missed you. Sometimes I look at you and everything disappears.'

She knew what he meant, sometimes it felt like they were the only two inhabitants on earth, that the world and everything in it had faded into insignificance. It was so terrifying being so in tune with someone.

Because she wanted to lighten the atmosphere, to bring them back to the moment, and the pleasure they were about to enjoy, Calla reached behind her back and unsnapped her bra. The cups fell away and Judah gently pulled it from her body and let it land on her sundress.

'Yeah, this is going to be one of those memories I keep forever,' he murmured, his hand covering her breast, his thumb rubbing her nipple into a hard, tight peak.

They were in sync again. What was she going to do about it?

Dressed in Judah's shirt, Calla rolled onto her side on the two-person lounger and placed her hands under her cheek. Judah had pulled on his shorts and lay on his back next to her, one hand under his head, his other hand resting on her hip.

She should feel guilty about sleeping with him again, but she didn't. She felt like a woman, at ease in her skin, appreciated and adored by her lover, satiated and relaxed. She knew she should be working, but she'd worked so hard for so long. Surely she was allowed to take an afternoon off now and again?

'Cal?'

'Mm?' She was feeling a little dozy, and could, without any effort at all, drift off to sleep.

'Tell me what happened with your ex.' Calla frowned. That was an out of the blue question. She was now fully awake and deeply uncomfortable. She hated talking about Jack. He was a reminder of how she'd been, how naive, how she thought love would solve all her life problems.

'Why do you want to know?' she asked, sitting up and crossing her legs. Judah didn't move, he just looked at her with eyes that could laser through her.

'I want to know you,' he said. 'You are the person you are today because of the things that happened to you. I've picked up bits and pieces, things you told me back then and now, but I want to hear the full story, all at once.' He frowned. 'And I want to know whether I should've hit him when he walked into the bar.'

His statement raised a small smile, but it quickly fell away. 'It's not a pretty story, Judah.'

'Marriages that fall apart usually aren't,' he agreed. 'That doesn't mean the stories aren't worth telling.'

Calla looked down at her hands twisting together in her lap. She needed to be honest with him, because it was the only way to make him understand why this could never go anywhere, why she would never allow herself to be in a relationship again.

But telling him meant more than just recounting her history. It meant showing him how weak she'd been. How easily Jack had broken her down, that it had taken so very long for her to realise he didn't love her but just wanted control over her. She had clawed her way to find her self-respect, but to lay it bare for someone like Judah? Someone smart, self-possessed and capable? She didn't want him to see her like that.

She had her pride. And pride was the only thing that had kept her going. And her pride still didn't want to tell him the truth. That Jack eviscerated her, and that the idea of depending on and trusting someone still made her flinch. If she told him, he'd understand the depth of her resolve, but he'd also see that she'd been naive. And so damn weak.

She didn't want him looking at her and seeing those cracked and battered parts of her.

He squeezed her knee. 'I think you desperately need to tell someone, Calla, and it might as well be me.'

Calla wrinkled her nose. Nobody, apart from her divorce lawyer, knew of the hoops Jack made her jump through, the levels of hell he made her walk through. Her lawyer even went so far as to urge her to have therapy, but she'd chosen to shove away the pain and disillusionment and bury herself in her work.

But Judah was here and willing to listen and wouldn't, she didn't think, judge her too harshly. 'While I was working to midnight every night, designing homes that got us noticed, that even won some awards and accolades, Jack was spending his time cheating on me and embezzling funds from our joint business account.'

'Bastard,' Judah muttered.

'Worse, he used my designs—my ideas—to secure contracts under a new design company he quietly established. Over a few years, he moved our jointly owned assets into shell companies by duping me about what I was signing, sometimes even by cleverly forging my signature.'

Judah sat up and ran a hand over her hair, his touch immediately dropping her rising anger levels. 'Then he locked me out of business decisions. When I couldn't ignore it any longer, I demanded a divorce. During those negotiations, his legal team painted me as being—how did they put it?—emotionally unstable and professionally incompetent.'

'He's the human version of a haemorrhoid,' Judah said, his words a low growl.

'The fallout was devastating. I lost my stake in the company, the one I grew and nurtured. I lost my talented staff, who I'd trained and mentored. My client list.'

She swallowed and swallowed again. 'Worst of all, I lost my reputation and my credibility. I wasn't just heartbroken—he humiliated me. I'm furious that he did that to me, that I *allowed* him to do that to me.'

It wasn't until Judah gently wiped away a tear that she realised she was crying. She used the balls of her hands to remove the moisture from her cheeks and chin. 'I hate crying,' she muttered.

'I think you haven't cried enough, sweetheart,' Judah told her, banding his arm around her waist to pull her onto his lap. Clasping her head to his bare chest, he wrapped his arms around her and kissed the top of her head. 'He doesn't deserve your tears, but you're allowed to cry. You must've felt so alone, so hurt, like you were caught under a tsunami of betrayal.'

He got her, like no one had before. Calla felt a sob

build, tried to push it down, and another rolled over it, stronger and wilder, and up her throat. Calla tried to pull away from Judah—quiet tears were one thing for him to witness, her losing it was another—but he just tightened his arms, just a little, and rested his chin on the top of her head. 'No, you're staying here and you're going to cry. As long and as hard as you need to. You need to get it out of your system, sweetheart.'

'I can't,' she sobbed, her throat burning as she tried to repress the bubbling emotion.

'Yes, you can, Cal. And you will, because you're not going anywhere.'

She was so tired, tired of holding it back, sick of being brave, of being strong. Crying, *sobbing*, was self-indulgent and useless, but maybe she did need to let go, to release all the emotion she'd kept bottled up for so long.

But whether she wanted to let go or not, there was no stopping the tears. Somehow, she'd released a high-pressure cork, and a loud, guttural sob broke the silence between them. Then another. God, how was she making those weird sounds? A part of her, disconnected from the sobbing woman sitting on Judah's lap, watched her cry, tears dripping from her cheeks and chin onto her hands, turning his light T-shirt a deeper shade of blue.

Judah simply held her and listened to her snort and sob, his grip on her not easing, his support unwavering. After many minutes—five? Ten?—her tears dried up, and her sobs turned to the occasional hiccup. She felt exhausted and empty, and lighter than she had in years. Clean, like she'd taken a mental shower. So that was why people advocated for crying jags. She got it now.

Judah stroked her hair off her damp forehead and dipped his head to look at her. 'Better?' he asked, in the same tone he would use to enquire whether she wanted a cup of coffee.

Calla nodded.

'Can I say something?'

Calla nodded.

He held her face, his fingers on her neck, his thumb on her jaw. 'I don't think anyone has told you how damn courageous you were, how incredibly strong. Most women would've curled up in a ball and retreated, but not you. You didn't. You kept going, kept fighting. Maybe you were fuelled by rage, but you chose to move forward, to plant your feet. That takes guts and grit, Calla. And I'm so bloody proud of you for choosing to fight rather than flee.'

Compliments weren't something she'd received often, infrequently from her clients, never from Jack. Judah's sincerity was... God, it was *everything*. It made her feel seen, valued and respected.

'Thank you,' she murmured, touched. She'd always remember making love to him in the sunlight, but she'd remember this moment more.

His arms briefly tightened around her, before he released her. 'You must be hot—I know I am.' Still holding her, he swivelled, placed his feet on the floor and easily stood, her in his arms. She instinctively hooked an arm around his neck.

'Where are you taking me?' she asked, tipping her head back to look into his strong, sexy face. She couldn't resist this man anymore, not for a second. And yes, she was falling for him again. Or maybe she'd fallen last year, and she'd simply resumed her spiral. It didn't matter how it happened. Neither did she know how the future would unfold, where they went from here, but she didn't want to let a day pass before she spoke, touched or kissed him again.

Right now, nothing mattered. Not the difference in their ages—so inconsequential—not the fact that she worked for him, not her company or her clients. In this moment and in his arms, there was only Judah and the way he made her feel. Strong, capable, talented, treasured. Seen. So very seen.

Calla was happy to go wherever he led her. But she didn't expect him to walk her into his infinity pool.

CHAPTER NINE

A WEEK LATER, Judah helped Calla out of his doorless Jeep, taking a moment to admire her tanned legs and arms in her thigh-length, short-sleeved brown-and-white-patterned dress. She'd been in St Croix for nearly three weeks now, and she looked so much better than she did when she first arrived. The dark stripes under her eyes were gone, and the frown between her eyebrows had vanished too. She often walked on the beach while he jogged, swam while he surfed, and she was fitter and stronger, her muscles looser.

Whether it was from the sun, sea or the sex, or a combination of all three, she was now quick to smile. The quality of her work had also improved; her designs were more relaxed and a great deal more playful. He'd told her a few days ago that he was happy to go to contract for her to revamp Sol House, but she'd demurred, saying she needed more time to finalise her design, to make it perfect.

His lover, it turned out, was a perfectionist and was never satisfied with 'good enough'.

Outside one of St Croix's best restaurants, tucked inside one of the many eighteenth-century Danish-style buildings that lined Christiansted's cobblestone streets, Calla slid her hand into Judah's and looked up at him. 'It's nice to be out and about. Apparently, this restaurant is fantastic.'

He nodded, taking a moment to scan the street for paparazzi. They rarely bothered him on the island, but he wasn't naive—the locals were curious. Rumours about Calla being his lover were making the rounds, especially within the expat community. The Vegas rule—what happened there, stayed there—applied to St Croix, as well. But he couldn't count on their discretion lasting forever. Eventually, he and Calla would end up in a gossip column. It was unavoidable. He'd ordered his PR team to monitor the situation, and he would know as soon as a story about him and Calla broke.

He glanced at Calla, so small next to him. Should he drop her hand? Then again, why the hell shouldn't he hold it? They were both single, both consenting adults. They weren't breaking the law. Yet he still, before following Calla into the restaurant—a tiny thirty-seater serving divine food—looked up and down the street one more time. Why did he feel like he was being watched?

He shook his head. He was being paranoid.

Judah greeted the owner, introduced her to Calla and stood back as the two women chatted about the restaurant and Crucian food. When she was relaxed, Calla was quietly charming and sweet.

Judah followed Calla and the hostess to their table, pulled out her seat and waited for her to settle before taking his own. Calla ordered chardonnay, and he asked for a beer. David had been a lifelong teetotaller and preached against alcohol, but Judah enjoyed the occasional beer, whiskey or glass of wine. He was, however, careful about sending the wrong message to his customers and rarely drank in public. But he was in St Croix, on holiday, and… *sod it*. It was a beer, not a line of cocaine.

'You're mulling something,' Calla said, pulling his attention back to her. Her hair was in a loose plait, pulled to one side, and it hung over one shoulder. She wore minimal make-up—she didn't need much—and she'd swapped out her normal gold hoop earrings for a long earring falling in a long, smooth sparkle to her shoulder.

'You look lovely, by the way.'

He loved how pink stained her cheek bones when he complimented her.

'Thank you. You seem a little distracted. Is everything okay?'

She was the only one who could see through his mask of implacability. And he still found it unsettling. He gestured to his ear. 'I like your earring thing,' he said. 'And the way you've done your hair.'

She narrowed her eyes, waved his words away and leaned her forearms on the table. 'Thank you, again. Now stop trying to change the subject, and tell me what you're thinking about,' she said, her eyes locked on his.

He might be marginally better at opening up than she was—neither of them found baring their souls easy—but he did want to run his thoughts about Reyes Luxe past her. He never did that with anyone else, not even his most trusted employees. But he knew he could trust Calla. She wasn't the type to blab.

'I decided not to buy ForgeRitual,' he told her. Without engaging with the board or even reading their written demand, he'd issued an internal statement ditching the project and instructing everyone to move on. To say the board wasn't pleased was an understatement. 'I need to start coalescing my vision for the company, where I want to take it, and what I want to focus on. I'm thinking of taking it in a new direction and doing a complete rebrand.'

She placed her chin in the centre of her palm, her attention wholly on him. He liked it. 'Tell me more.'

Could he? Should he? He waited while the waitress delivered their drinks, and when she walked away, and after they'd clinked glasses, he spoke again. 'I've also realised I'm not happy with our core message,' he said.

'Which is?' Calla asked.

'That health is everything, and if it's not your everything, you're wrong and ignorant.'

Calla shook her head. 'I think you are being a bit harsh, Jude.'

He loved it when she shortened his name; nobody else ever had. It warmed him and made him feel more connected, and made it easier to talk to her. She wasn't only his lover, but his friend. Possibly his best friend.

'What comes to mind when you think about Reyes Luxe?' he asked.

'Mm,' she murmured. 'I think of wealth, that it's an exclusive club of glossy, fit people who have the time and money to spend at the gym, at spas and at wellness centres.'

'Exactly.' He took a sip of his beer. 'And I think that's what I'm struggling with, the glossy, the wealth. And the idea that you have to be fit and gorgeous and rich to be a part of the Reyes Luxe world.'

She pursed her lips, thinking. 'If you wanted to take the company in another direction, it would mean an entire rebrand of the company, Judah. Part of its appeal is that it's aspirational, that it's for golden people and that you, as a client, are part of an elite club.'

She was so smart, and he liked that about her. Judah took a sip of his beer and scratched an itch on his cheek. 'Did you know that my dad only got into the health and wellness industry because of my mum?' he asked.

She shook her head, her eyes on his face. All of her attention was on him, and he loved it. Loved the way their eyes connected, the way her fingers occasionally brushed the side of his hand, grounding him and reminding him of the physical connection they shared.

'She was a runway model, but into alternative health, organic foods, walking barefoot and communing with nature. A complete free spirit.' He smiled. 'My mum was a punk rocker activist with the soul of a sixties flower child.'

Calla gifted him with a soft and sweet smile. 'I love that.'

'Apparently, when they first met, my dad was overweight, completely stressed out and he never exercised. My mum changed his diet, got him exercising, and he lost the weight, and he got fit. Then very fit, and his weight and how he looked became an obsession. Reyes Luxe was born from his "transformation".'

Judah looked out of the window, saw a man standing in a doorway opposite, dressed in black pants and jeans. He frowned. Who wore black on a summer's evening in the Caribbean? He turned his attention back to Calla. 'It's ironic that my two health-obsessed parents, obsessed in completely different ways, both died from what the experts call the scourges of modern-day life, cancer and a heart attack.'

'It happens more often than we like to think to super-fit people.' She leaned back in her chair and rested her hands in her lap. 'While I love hearing about your parents and would like to know more, we've veered off the subject of Reyes Luxe. Tell me about the new direction and Reyes Luxe's rebrand.'

It was his first time putting his thoughts into words and, ridiculously, he felt a little nervous. 'I feel like I've been wearing someone else's shoes for months now. I think it's time I kicked them off.' Calla didn't look surprised, she simply nodded, her expression encouraging him to continue. 'But it would be stupid to shrug off the Reyes Luxe brand entirely, too much work and money has gone into making it what it is. But I'm considering making it smaller, even more exclusive, more expensive.'

As he expected, her brow furrowed. 'That's not what I expected you to say. Aren't you trying to get away from the glitz and glam?'

He nodded. 'Yes and no. If I'm going to cater to the rich, then I'm going to target the very rich and market only to them, through exclusive channels. I'm going to make Reyes Luxe products exceptionally high-end and exceptionally exclusive. That'll make the line *exceptionally* profitable. I'm going to only have one Reyes Luxe spa and club per city instead of many, and I'm going to make them extremely difficult to access. It'll be the club every rich person wants to join but can't.'

People loved what they couldn't easily access, and he knew he'd have no problem with the concept or upping the price of the membership to stratospheric levels.

'But you own multiple clubs, spas and wellness centres. What are you going to do with those buildings?'

He'd given this a lot of thought. 'I'm going to turn them into family-friendly, easily accessible and fun to visit facilities. I'm going to launch a new brand of wellness centres, gyms and spas with new and revamped premises. And I'm going to establish an affordable health line that will appeal to a wider swathe of the population. That feels…'

Calla tipped her head to the side, waiting for him to continue. He rubbed the back of his neck. 'That feels authentic to me, Cal.'

She didn't speak for a beat, maybe two. 'Are you waiting for my input, Judah?'

He nodded. Of course he was, her opinion meant more to him than all his senior management, his board members. She got him, like no one ever had.

'May I ask why?'

It was time to get honest, to call it like it was, to be who he was. Maybe he'd flame out, but all he could do was try. Because if he wasn't living true to his values, what was the point? He was sick of one-night stands, of casual couplings, a dinner here and there, working sixteen-hour days for something he didn't, wholly, believe in, pocketing money he didn't need. He wanted conversations with Calla, deep, light and everything in between, her in his bed, some sort of future, preferably one that resulted in babies, chaos and cohabiting.

'Because when I looked up and took stock of my life and tried to work out when last I felt like myself, I pinpointed it to that weekend I spent with you. And having you back in my life, and in my bed, feels real and right.'

She gripped her bottom lip with her teeth, worry in her eyes. He knew she was about to backpedal. Three, two, one...

'I don't know if I'm there, Judah. I'm not sure if I can give you what you want.' She linked her hands together, and they turned white with pressure. 'I'm not good with trust, Judah, you know this. And you know why.'

He leaned forward, his eyes locked on her. 'I am *not* your ex, Calla.' Her expression turned blank, and a curtain came down in her eyes. Dammit, he didn't want to argue with her. He'd planned on having a romantic evening, some good food, better wine, a walk along the beach before heading home and taking her to bed. They'd moved off Reyes Luxe and somehow skated into a patch of thorns. Should he retreat or should he face this head on? If he backed down, it would only raise its head later on, so he might as well forge forward. But he knew the chances of a romantic walk and a night of hot sex were rapidly dropping.

He raked his hand through his hair. 'Look, I'm not asking you to make a for life commitment here, I'm just telling you that this goes beyond sex for me.'

Calla pushed the tips of her fingers into her forehead. 'Judah, half in and half out, second-guessing everything, and being in limbo doesn't work for me. I need boundaries, boxes, a plan, to be in control. I need a safety net.' She held up her hand. 'And don't tell me you can be that for me!'

She bit down hard on her lip. 'Look, I can't…not *yet*.'

He heard her unspoken words…*maybe not ever*. There was no point pushing her, so he opted to change the subject. 'Shall we eat first and postpone this?'

'No.' Right, her short response wasn't a surprise. 'You obviously have some strong opinions on this, so please carry on.'

He sighed. 'You're hiding away, scared to engage, make a move, be happy, because he was such a dick. You're giving him too much power over you.'

'I'm trying to protect my business,' she stated, her words as pointed as the business end of a fencing sword. 'To regroup and rebuild.'

'I'm not talking about your business or what you do at work, I'm talking about *you*. You're trying to protect yourself. And I hate that you think you have to protect yourself from me, that you have painted us with the same brush.'

'I haven't—'

'You won't take a chance on me, on us, on whatever is

bubbling between us because of him. That's lumping me with him.' And he goddamn hated it.

'That's not fair,' she hissed, her hand gripping the linen serviette and crumpling it into a tight ball. 'I'm also your client and there are six years between us.'

Oh, now she was clutching at straws. His temper started to simmer, but he immediately dialled it down. 'Using our age difference is a B.S. excuse, Calla, and beneath you.'

She flushed, embarrassed, but she still met his eyes. 'You're right, that was beneath me.'

And there it was, one more thing he liked about her. She was quick to apologise and didn't sulk. Nor did she hold grudges. Calla gripped the bridge of her nose with her index finger and thumb and closed her eyes. 'I'm trying, Judah, I *am*.'

He sat back and picked up his glass, draining his beer in one long swallow. 'Are you, Calla? I don't think you are. I think you're pretty comfortable in your emotional suit of armour—you like it there.' Seeing her expression, he curled his fingers around hers, happy she didn't pull away as he expected her to. 'You've got that stubborn look on your face. You feel like I am pushing you.'

She nodded. 'Yes, I do.'

'I am. Someone has to, Calla. And it looks like that somebody is me.'

He'd given her enough to think about, so Judah picked up a menu, wanting to move on and salvage their evening. 'Let's decide what we want to eat and then we'll talk about something else.'

Calla's relief was so obvious he nearly smiled. She liked to skirt emotions, to play it safe. He wasn't prepared to let her do that for much longer. They placed their order— fresh fish for her, kallaloo for him—and Judah topped up her wine glass from the chilly bottle resting in the ice bucket next to their table.

'Talking about business, before we left the house, I signed your electronic contract and paid your deposit.' He watched as his words settled, as excitement turned her chinks pink and put fireworks in her eyes. 'I'd like you to start work renovating my house as soon as possible.'

'*Really?*'

Their disagreement was forgotten, and excitement rolled off her. 'Really.' He lifted a teasing eyebrow, his mouth lifting in a smile he couldn't contain. 'What? You didn't think I brought you to a fantastic restaurant only because I'm crazy about you and want to figure out where we go from here? I have to be able to write this off as a business expense, you know.'

Calla laughed, balled up her linen serviette and threw it at his head. She leaned forward, picked the cloth off his shoulder, and her eyes filled with laughter. 'You liked them, right? My designs?' she asked, vibrating.

That was easy to answer. 'I adore your designs.' *I adore you.*

It was her turn to lift a naughty, suggestive eyebrow. 'Then do you think your expense account will stretch to a bottle of champagne?'

Later that evening, Calla lay facing Judah on his extra-wide, extra-long bed. Through the open window, the moon tossed shadows on his face as it played peekaboo with the clouds. His hand lay heavy on her hip, and she lifted her finger to lightly, softly, trace the arch of his right eyebrow, before sliding it down his cheek and across his stubbled jaw. She was perfectly content lying here looking at him and suspected that she would be happy to pass most of her nights this way. But she couldn't think straight when she lay this close to him, and she desperately needed to make sense of what she was thinking and feeling.

Calla lifted his hand to place it on the empty space next to him. 'Don't go, Cal,' he muttered, in a growly, saturated-with-sleep voice. For tonight or forever? Both were tempting...

Calla slipped out of his bed, pulled on his shirt and picked up the half-empty bottle of champagne on the bed-side table. They'd brought the expensive bottle back to bed with them, but as soon as their clothes started to fly, heads and hearts raced, and the expensive liquor was forgotten. Taking a sip, she carried it out onto the balcony and leaned back against the bedroom wall, feeling like she was hovering somewhere between the sea and the stars. A bit shaky, she slid down the wall and sat down.

Calla took in the sea beyond the tempered glass barrier, a part of her wishing it wasn't such a gorgeous night. Thoughts like hers, complicated and chaotic, deserved thunder and lightning, or fog, something that matched her mood. Not a warm, fragrant night with stars that glittered and gleamed, sparkly celestial fruit hanging low in the sky.

Having you back in my life, and my bed, feels real, and right.

Doubts, hot and hard, rolled through her. While she was so excited about renovating Sol House—and the opportunities it afforded her for bigger and better projects—on a personal level, she was terrified at how fast her and Judah's relationship was moving. She lifted the champagne bottle to her lips, her head whirling. Judah had asked too much of her and pushed too hard. He was being unreasonable. Who made life-changing decisions after just a few weeks? Who changed the way they lived their life, did a complete one-eighty because of some lovely conversations and good sex? He was asking for too much, too soon. Assuming too much…

Seeing too much.

But, dammit, they were great together. They just worked. She had the creative flair, he had a brain for numbers, but they were intellectual equals, and their conversations covered a wide range of subjects. They could discuss politics over breakfast, argue about organised religion over dinner and then fall into bed, completely in sync, giving and taking pleasure.

His comment about her measuring him against Jack had landed like a gut punch—mostly because, deep down, she knew he wasn't wrong. Calla placed her fist into her sternum, trying to will the burn away. Why did it have to hurt? She thought she was over being hurt by anything Jack-related.

She'd believed she'd built enough walls to keep the hurt out. But here she was—reeling from Judah's words, stung by truths she didn't want to face, little burrs she couldn't shake. And damn it, they hurt because they were true. *'Hiding', 'scared', 'you've given up your power'.*

She winced and shoved her hands into her hair, tugging on the strands. She wished she could discount his words, brush them off, but that was impossible. Judah was important to her, had been from the moment they first connected last year. But did she value him enough, care about him—love him?—enough to take a chance, to change?

What was she prepared to give up to be with Judah?

Along with being hypervigilant about her reputation, she'd been determined to control every aspect of her life and had vowed never to give up her independence, to let another man control her again. After what Jack did to her, she was allowed to feel that way, to protect herself.

And yes, maybe she did associate emotional vulnerability with humiliation and powerlessness, and still believed survival, emotional and financial, depended on never relying on anyone again. And for the first time, she admitted it—she was still carrying so much shame. For falling for Jack. For letting him twist her mind and heart. For handing over her heart like a fool and pretending she didn't see the cracks forming, for letting him get away with treating her like trash. And while she was admitting uncomfortable truths...

Judah was right when he said she'd painted him with the same brush, that she was judging him by what her ex-husband did. And that, God...that wasn't fair. Or right. Judah was the antithesis of her ex, someone who'd never once made her feel less than, powerless or unseen. He listened when she spoke, considered her opinions; sometimes agreeing with her, sometimes not. But he respected her right to have them. He valued her work and frequently complimented what she did and how she approached a subject or a problem. And when he disagreed with her, he kept his tone respectful, his attitude open. She wasn't his punching bag, a way to make himself feel better, or there to prop up his ego.

Judah saw her as an equal, an adult. There would never be one set of rules for him, another for her. Their relationship would be a partnership; sometimes he would lead, sometimes she'd step up to the plate. There would be times when she'd pull him through a rough patch, and he'd do the same for her. They'd be a team, and they'd operate on a level playing field. Could she do it?

Calla looked at the dark sea beyond the transparent balcony. The moon peeked out from the clouds, its silvery light turning the sea's surface to the same deep blue as

Judah's eyes. Could she live without his eyes on her? She didn't think so. And if she didn't take this second chance Fate was offering her, would she regret it for the rest of her life? Yes, she thought she would.

But that meant being brave, fighting against her instinct to retreat, to hide behind her suit of emotional armour, as Judah called it. She would have to gather every bit of courage she possessed and go to Judah, suggesting they take the next (baby) steps. What those were, she wasn't sure. Maybe just admitting she was prepared to try was the first step on what she knew might be a long journey.

But she wasn't alone. As Judah said, he'd be there every step of the way. And she believed he meant it.

And that was everything, wasn't it?

CHAPTER TEN

THE NEXT MORNING, Judah looked at the message he received from his head of his PR department, stunned at what he was seeing. On his screen was a photo of him and Calla, taken yesterday outside the restaurant in Christiansted. His hand rested low on her back, his head bent to listen to her, an affectionate smile on his face. Calla's expression was even more revealing; her eyes sparkled, and her smile wide and sexy.

Everyone with a brain in their head could tell their relationship went far beyond the professional.

Judah released a long, desperate curse and scowled at the headline. Calla West, Cougar Designer, Snags Billionaire Heir.

Seriously? *What the actual*...? He ran his hand through his hair and walked from his study onto the wraparound patio of his master suite and looked down. On the entertainment deck below him, Calla sat on the edge of a lounger under the shade of an umbrella, her attention on the tablet resting on her knee and her phone plastered to her ear. She'd been quiet earlier when they parted ways for the day ahead, not sulky but introspective. Judah suspected she was working through their conversation, trying to process what he said about her ex and her emotional armour. He was happy to give her time to think; he wanted

Calla to come to him, warm and willing and optimistic about the future.

But this article would hit her like an emotional napalm strike, and because of who he was, it would go viral—if it hadn't already. That was the world they lived in. Judah rubbed the back of his neck, frustrated. Why hadn't he trusted his instincts when he thought someone was watching them? Why hadn't he kept Calla at home instead of exposing her to someone's photo lens and vitriolic pen? Why hadn't he considered all the consequences of them being seen in public?

And while he was at it, maybe he could try thinking a little more and talking a little less when it came to their relationship? Approach the situation with more caution instead of acting like a bull caught between a matador and an escape route?

What was wrong with him?

Judah rested his forearms on the toughened glass walls, his eyes on Calla's head. The implications in the article were vicious, and the timing, just a day after she announced she'd landed the commission to renovate Sol House on social media, was highly suspect. It wasn't just bad press, it was a character assassination. Against a woman who'd already rebuilt herself from scratch. Judah had no doubt her ex was behind it...

What could he do? How could he crush the cockroach? His PR department back in the UK was already doing what they could to negate the impact of the article. But spin could only go so far and had a limited effect; the internet was a powerful beast and not easily contained or corralled.

Once the shock wore off, how would she take it? What would she do next? He didn't know—and that uncertainty scared the hell out of him. Judah shivered, suddenly cold. Unfortunately, he didn't have much faith she'd be able to shrug it off. As he'd said earlier, her wounds were deep and she'd never allowed them to heal.

This might split them wide open again.

Later that day, Calla knocked on the doorframe to Judah's study. It took a moment for him to raise his head, for his eyes to focus on her leaning against the door-frame. She still wasn't used to seeing him wearing glasses, and she smiled, thinking he rocked the look. Sexy and studious, a killer combination. Judah pulled the black frames off his face and tossed them onto his desk. He leaned back in his chair and gestured for her to come inside.

'Hi. I was just finishing up and I was going to come find you, but you beat me to it.' He pushed back his chair and walked around the desk to stand in front of her. 'Are you okay?'

She reached out to grab his shirt, twisting the cotton fabric between her fingers, before stroking it smooth, leaving her hand on his chest. God, she loved touching him. 'Mm, I'm fine. I've been doing a lot of thinking, and I'm better than I thought I would be.'

She felt some tension leave his body, a little surprised he was still worried about their discussion last night. Did he think she was fragile? He hadn't yelled at her, nor had he been nasty; he'd simply, clearly and calmly, stated his thoughts. Sure, they'd been hard to hear, but that didn't mean he was wrong. She still had things to work through, some old habits to discard, but she'd decided to make some changes, to explore this second shot at something special.

Calla rested her forehead against his chest and gripped his sides, feeling the warmth of his skin beneath the thin cotton of his shirt. 'I thought you would be on either your surf or paddleboard, not sitting in your office.'

'I wanted to stick around, to keep an eye on you, see how you were doing.' He lifted his hand to stroke her hair. 'You're taking this a lot better than I thought. I've been so worried about you.'

It was sweet of him to care so much about a small argument. Jack never worried about her; her feelings never registered with him. In Judah, she'd found a man completely opposite to her waste-of-space ex. He actually cared about her, cared about what she was thinking and feeling. It felt both strange and completely wonderful. She snuggled into him, her arms tightening around his lower back. She didn't know how they were going to make this work, but she wanted to spend the rest of her life in his arms.

'I'd love to explore other restaurants in Christiansted or, well, anywhere with you. Maybe we could skip the minor argument next time?'

Judah's grip tightened, and tension slid into him. Calla frowned and pulled back. She tipped her head back and took in his confused expression. 'Why are you looking so serious?' she asked. 'Did the restaurant burn down or something?'

He stroked her arm and stepped back, resting his butt on his wide desk. 'You're here to talk about our conversation last night?'

She spread her hands. Well, yes. What else was there to talk about? 'I've been thinking about what you said and maybe it's time for me to—'

'Nobody sent you the link?' he asked, abruptly interrupting her.

'What are you talking about, Judah?' she asked, scared by his sombre expression and the hesitation in his eyes.

'I would've thought one of your people would've kept you up-to-date.'

Her people? She employed three designers on an ad-hoc basis, and she was her own secretary, accountant, promoter and scheduler. She was *it*. She hadn't been able to afford permanent staff since she lost her half of Atelier Abernathy.

'I don't have people, Judah. I'm a one-man band,' she explained. 'What link and what are you talking about?'

He pushed his hand through his hair, his lips a thin slash in his face. He dropped an F-bomb and reached back to pick up his phone. 'I thought you were here to talk about this.'

He activated face recognition, then held the phone out for her to take. Calla frowned, her heart thumping against her ribs. She hesitated, instinctively fighting the urge to run. Whatever he wanted her to look at would, she knew, change everything.

It took her a while to look down. It took her even longer to make sense of the headline.

Calla West, Cougar Designer, Snags Billionaire Heir.

She skimmed the article, just enough to catch the gut punches and for the words to form ice crystals in her blood.

In St Croix to renovate his house, she has moved into his bedroom.

Did she use time-tested techniques to secure future projects?

Was once married to celebrity designer Jack Abernathy of Atelier Abernathy.

Her eyes tripped over the words, and she had to, once or twice, go back to read a sentence again. It was clever, in the way poison often was—a sprinkling of truth and just enough innuendo to make people think her and Judah's association was…dirty. There was nothing explicitly false; the truth was hidden behind layers of supposition and just enough to make the article credible. It was clever, but supremely ugly, journalism.

Her brain stalled. Her breath too. She was in a tunnel, wind howling through it—icy, sharp, bitter—carrying her old friend, panic, betrayal and shame.

She couldn't breathe.

The article's photo took up half the screen, high-res and unmistakably her. Her head thrown back, laughing up at Judah, his hand proprietary on her back. That damned dress—she'd loved it up until a few minutes ago. She'd loved how she'd felt in it. Confident, sexy, so feminine. Alive.

They looked like a couple sharing an inside joke, like the kind of couple who didn't have to try too hard. Like she was…*his*. She'd been cold a few seconds ago, but now an intense heat hit her in waves—jagged and rising. Her lungs tightened, and her vision blurred at the edges. She staggered back, bile lacing her throat, her stomach threatening to revolt. She swallowed it down.

Lie after lie, coated in just enough truth. But that wasn't even the worst part. The worst part was how familiar it all felt. How awful it felt to have her work and personal life collide, how helpless she felt to watch everything she'd worked so hard for evaporate. The reputation she'd tried to restore, the long hours, the way she'd hustled meant nothing. Thanks to this article, it had been a complete waste of her time and energy.

It didn't matter that she'd handed Judah an amazing design, that she'd perfectly interpreted—after a few rough starts—what he wanted. That her renderings were flawless, and that he'd signed off on her work with a satisfied grin and a 'damn, you nailed it'.

She'd worked harder than she ever had in her life—because it was Judah. And because her pride demanded that she do her best, give him all she had, because she never wanted anyone, especially him, to think she'd slacked off because of their history and their previous and personal connection. What mattered—what always seemed to matter—was the story. And this article insinuated she'd set out to seduce Judah, that she'd slept with him for this, and future, contracts. Just like Jack always hinted before, during and after their divorce; it was an essential part of his smear campaign. It was always tucked between the insinuations that she was 'emotional', 'unreliable' and 'unbalanced.' It was his way of continuously reminding the world that she was unworthy and not to be trusted.

She knew how this would play out. The Reyes Luxe board would see the article, and she'd be painted as a liability. The people in Judah's PR department would curse her from here to Sunday. Judah would be asked—no, pressured—to distance himself. He'd pay the penalty clause to terminate her contract, because having her out of his life, and house, would be easier. So much cleaner. And it was just like Jack wanted.

As for her...

The calls enquiring whether she'd be interested in design projects would stop coming, the emails would dry up and the whispers and rumours, fed by Jack, would spread. Clients, future and present, would hear of Judah pulling out, and they'd boycott her. *'Check her out, she's the one who couldn't hold onto her marriage or business. And, apparently, Judah Reyes.'*

'That's what happens when you think you can fly close to the sun.'

'It's rumoured she can't manage her emotions.'

'She's unstable.'

Unworthy.

And every woman in the industry who'd clawed her way up without compromising her ethics would view her as the poster girl for sleeping her way into the spotlight. A million fire ants crawled under her skin.

'Calla, say something,' Judah's voice sliced through the silence, sharp with worry.

She blinked, looked at him, then down at his phone. That picture of them, intimate and connected, mocked her.

'What's there to say?' she whispered.

'It's bullshit,' he insisted.

She met his eyes, heart pounding like it was trying to break free of her chest. 'You think that matters?' she asked quietly. 'Do you honestly think truth beats perception? That talent beats gossip?'

Judah looked furious. And—God help her—unsure, like he didn't know what to do or how to help. But all she could feel was fear. A full-body, spine-deep panic.

Judah stepped forward, his hands coming to her arms. She wrenched back. *'Don't.'*

'Calla…'

'This always happens,' she said, her voice cracking. 'I let myself feel safe. With you. And look where it got me.'

He flinched like she'd hit him. 'I didn't do this.'

It should matter, but she couldn't let it. 'I let you in. And now I'm the woman I promised myself I'd never be again.'

'You're just you and the article is garbage,' Judah said again, voice low, intense. 'It doesn't change anything.'

'It changes *everything*.' Her voice rose, sharp with panic. 'Don't you get it? This isn't just PR for me, Judah. This is my *life*. My reputation. My future. You can survive this, I can't.'

'I need to go,' she said, stepping back, heart breaking with every inch of distance. 'I should never have stayed this long. I should've got to work sooner, worked harder and smarter. I knew better than to mix business and pleasure.'

His expression twisted, like he wanted to argue. But she couldn't afford to let him talk, because she ached to believe this was survivable. It wasn't. 'Do you think that walking away fixes this?' he asked, frustrated.

Nothing could fix the pain, the landslide of devastation sliding through her heart. 'No.' Her voice softened. 'But it's what I know how to do.'

Because if she stayed, she'd start leaning on him. And that was a risk she couldn't take. Not again. Judah would tend to her wounds, talk her down and patch her up. He was a protector and a white knight, he lived to make people feel better. But the patches peeled and the painkillers wore off. Eventually, those wounds would open up again, and she'd start bleeding again.

It would be a never-ending cycle of waiting for the pain to return.

So she steeled herself, turned and walked away. It wasn't because she didn't care, but because she cared too much.

And the next time they saw or spoke to each other— she needed to know what he intended to do about her contract to revamp his house—he'd get the version of her with walls so high, no one could scale them. She'd be professional. Cold. Controlled.

Everything she should've been and wasn't.

Calla rested her head against the rim of the plane's window and stared into the clouds below the wing of the aircraft. Her heart already ached to be back in St Croix, to be with Judah, but that wasn't an option.

She was back where she was before…no, she was many steps behind. Calla banged her head, a part of her wishing he'd never contacted her. She could've just kept chugging along in New York City, taking on one project at a time, chipping away at Jack's influence on their industry. But she'd been ambitious, and she'd wanted more.

And because she'd mixed business and pleasure, look where she was now. Her reputation was shredded, more tarnished than it was before, and Judah, she was sure, was regretting bringing her to the island and handing her the commission to revamp Sol House.

Oh, she'd received a few messages from him—she was ignoring his calls—and he talked a good game, saying that he still wanted her as his designer and his lover. But Calla knew that in a few days, when the dust settled and the distance between them widened, his sharp, strategic brain would kick in. When that happened, he'd appreciate her leaving, for removing herself calmly and quietly from his life. He'd realise that being with her meant facing more attacks like this from Jack, and that he'd be caught up in all the nastiness her ex could, and would, generate.

He'd soon realise he'd had a lucky escape.

Jack, dammit, was so clever. She did not doubt that the photograph and its accompanying article were his work. By implying she'd used sex to win Judah's high-profile project was confirmation bias for everyone who'd listened when he disparaged her. It was validation that she relied on manipulation instead of talent and hard work. So many people, ex-clients, current clients, industry heavyweights, would now believe she didn't earn this project—she'd seduced it.

She'd clung to the idea that she could go up against Jack and his family, that through hard work, grit and producing excellent designs, she could rehabilitate her reputation. That, with one high-profile client, she could reclaim her name, brand and reputation. It was stunning to realise that she could still be so naive. But, because she'd been blinded by the urge to get ahead, to take the next step, she'd ignored her instinct to leave St Croix after discovering Judah was her client. And when their attraction flared hot and bright, she convinced herself she could keep their professional and personal lives separate. Hah! What a joke. They'd collided spectacularly.

With Judah, she'd lost the control she'd clung to like a life ring in a stormy sea. She'd allowed her boundaries to be obliterated and her feelings for him—written on her face and captured by that photograph—were out there for the world to see, oh-so visible.

She'd let her walls be washed away by laughter and fantastic sex, by easy conversations and St Croix's summer breeze. Worst of all, she forgot that the best predictor of the future was the past. She'd let someone in and lost everything again.

She'd never allow that to happen again. And this time her words were cast in stone.

She'd walked away. *Again.*

Judah stood next to the infinity pool, his hip against the balustrade, utterly confounded. He'd expected a fight, tears, for them to scrap and scramble their way through this, but she'd just packed her stuff and bolted. What the hell?

No dramatic pause, no glance over her shoulder. She'd just turned and went, oblivious to the fact that she'd cracked his chest open and taken his heart with her. Calla walking away gutted him in ways he didn't expect. He'd let himself believe that instinct might be enough—that maybe he didn't need every answer or a polished plan to be worthy of love, to be the leader of Reyes Luxe, to enjoy the life and wealth he'd inherited. She made him feel like it was okay to like and trust himself again. And now she was gone.

And the old, gnawing fear—that he wasn't enough, not for her, not for the company, not for this life handed to him before he was ready—was back, simmering under the surface. Calla had quieted his doubts for a while, but with her gone, they were back, louder than before.

The sea rolled up on the rocks, liquid and lazy, and the sky blazed blue. The sun still shone, and everyone on the island carried on, but Judah simply stood there, motionless. Numb. Honestly, it would've been so much easier if she'd left because she was a gold-digger, or if he'd caught her with someone else, if she'd been mean and selfish and annoying. But she'd been, dammit, well, not perfect, but for the little time they'd spent together, perfect for him.

He couldn't help but pull out his phone and find the picture he'd saved from that article, staring at it as if he could mentally will her back to St Croix. She looked so radiant, open, and so herself. He looked a little dopey, completely under her spell, like she hung the damn moon.

They looked happy. But someone, her ex, he presumed, took whatever the hell they had—they hadn't even had time to define it properly—and weaponised it. That was unforgivable. He shoved his phone back into his pocket, dragged both hands over his face, and sat down hard on the edge of a lounger.

She thought this couldn't be recovered from. That it was the end. That he'd take the easy way out and allow her to fade from her life. That he'd let her ex have the last word. Well, screw that. And screw his insecurities. He wasn't allowing them a seat at his table.

Calla probably believed he'd cut his losses, minimise the damage and move on. He had no doubt she thought he'd treat her, and what they had, as a mistake. Hadn't she heard him when he told her she was the first real thing in his life since his father died? Okay, maybe he hadn't clearly explained how she brought colour, spark and goddamn soul back into his world.

But that's how he felt.

And he never walked away from something he wanted, never ran away from a fight. God, why hadn't she planted her feet, and stayed, fought instead of fleeing?

They had something—it had been there ten months ago, and was bigger and brighter now. And he *wanted* her. Not because she'd do an amazing job revamping his house, or for the work she did. Or because she was an amazing lover and set his blood on fire.

She was, simply, the best thing, then and now, that ever happened to him. Because she saw him. Because she made him feel whole.

And now she was gone, all because some parasitic rag splattered her insecurities and fears all over the 'net. God, the look on her face when she read the article...like it confirmed every terrible thing she'd ever been told, all that she'd been taught to believe about herself.

And the knife through his soul?

Being away from normal life, caught up in her and the way she made him feel, he'd forgotten he was Judah Reyes. He hadn't seen the article coming and hadn't protected her from it. He was used to media storms. He knew how to play that game—shrug, smile, deny, distract. But this wasn't just another PR flare-up, a passing storm. This was Calla's *life*. Her career. Her name.

Judah pushed the heels of his hands into his eye sockets, wishing that she'd trusted him more with her wounds, with her battered soul. Had he understood, really understood, how deep her cuts were, he would've held her so damn carefully.

But he hadn't, and she'd run. And this time, he didn't think she'd come back. If she did, for the sake of renovating his house, she'd be wrapped up in layers of professionalism and pride. He leaned forward, elbows on his knees, staring at the sleepy sea like it held his answers in its blue depths. His jaw locked, breath struggling up his tight throat, heart low and sore in his chest.

He could go after her; he could easily track her down. He was a guy who could find some words and say something big, sweeping and heartfelt.

But Calla didn't need to be rescued by him. She wanted, *needed*, to rescue herself. Wasn't everything she'd done since leaving her marriage centred around that belief? She simply wanted to stand in her own space, seen for her talent and her incredible work ethic. She wanted truth. Security. Belief.

But he knew, somehow, from a place deep inside him, that right now all he could give her was space. So Judah forced himself to sit there, his house empty and silent behind him, while the day morphed into night and that damned article kept multiplying across the internet.

He'd let her go. But he wouldn't give her up. Not yet. Not ever.

He knew it before, but it made complete sense to him now. If he was ever going to be the man he wanted to be, authentic, real, grounded, it started and ended with her.

CHAPTER ELEVEN

IT HAD BEEN a hell of a week.

Calla was in her Brooklyn shoebox apartment, eating takeaway and trying not to feel sorry for herself. In a pair of men's boxers and a thin, often washed T-shirt over a sports bra, she sat cross-legged on her sofa, her laptop open but untouched. She'd spent the week reaching out to clients, old, new and potential, and she'd had a few emails back—three, no four—all polite, all unencouraging.

'Regretfully.' 'Temporarily.' 'Given the sensitivity of the situation.'

As she'd thought, she was back to square one, maybe even at minus one. If her life was a snakes and ladders game, she'd be off the board. God, she sounded so damn sorry for herself, and she hated that she did, but this was so hard. So demoralizing. And she missed St Croix…

But more than St Croix, she missed Judah. Missed his half-smile, his deep voice, missed the way he listened to her, like what she had to say was important, like she mattered. And while she was independent and able to look after herself, she did miss how safe she felt in his arms, the feeling she had someone in her corner.

But, damn, when it really mattered, she hadn't let him support her. She'd chosen to run instead. But what other choice did she have? Running, bailing, dropping out—

call it what you will—it had been the best thing, the only thing, to do. Nothing else made sense.

Calla's head lifted at the sound of her phone ringing. She frowned and glanced over her shoulder to check the clock on her kitchen wall. It was past ten, too late for a casual or business call.

Annoyed, she stood up and walked over to her desk, looked at her phone and saw the incoming video call from Judah.

She wasn't surprised to hear from him; Judah wasn't someone who'd simply let it end. He wasn't the type to let anything fade away, especially when something mattered to him. And she did.

Her heart bounced off her ribcage as she swiped, and his face filled her screen. Honestly, he looked like hell. His stubble was rougher than usual, his wrinkled shirt open at the collar. Tired, like he hadn't slept properly in days. He also looked—what was the word?—frayed. Calla winced when she caught a glimpse of her face in the small frame in the corner of her phone. Limp hair, white face. Big eyes with blue stripes under them. She looked as rough as he did.

'You shouldn't have called, Judah.' Because how was she supposed to resist him? How could she get used to living without him if he kept showing up?

'Yet I did, and you answered.'

So logical.

Calla sat down on the edge of the couch and waited for him to end the awkward silence, and to explain why he'd called. He just stared at her, hunger in his eyes, and said, 'I needed to check on you.'

That threw her. She gripped her phone tighter. 'Why?'

'Because you matter. Because you're hurting. And I don't want you to do that alone.' Despite the half a second of lag, his concern-filled voice hit her like a wave. Calla swallowed. Her throat ached.

'I'm not some PR mess you can spin. You can't fix me, Judah.'

'I know, and I don't want or need to fix you. You don't *need* fixing.' His voice was quiet, but so sincere. 'I've been doing a lot of thinking, and I think you're a woman who's been dragged through hell by people who thought they had the right to define you. And I'm not going to be another person who does that to you.'

A breath shuddered out of her. How was it that he was always able to see her? To understand? She propped the phone against her laptop screen, too tired to hold it but unable to look away.

'I'm not here about the article, Calla,' he said. 'There are steps I can take… I could issue a statement, push back harder, put my lawyers onto them, and make them hurt. But I'm not going to do that.'

She blinked, trying to make sense of his words.

'And I'm not trying to convince you to stay with me, if you really believe we're better off apart.' His blue eyes didn't waver, his voice was completely calm, and all his focus was on her. 'But I am going to say something I should've said in St Croix.'

She didn't speak. She couldn't; her tongue had lost the ability to form words.

'Firstly, you're a great designer, and I loved your vision for Sol House. I gave you that contract because it's how I want my house to look. It had nothing to do with us.'

She'd learned to read his eyes and knew he spoke the truth. But she'd never doubted his ability to separate work and romance. She'd never doubted him. She was the one with issues.

'That's work. As for how I feel about you as a woman...' His expression remained steady, his eyes didn't leave hers. 'I didn't fall for you because of a one-night stand ten months ago or because we still have the same insane chemistry. I fell for you, back then and now, because you are sharp and stubborn and talented as hell. Because, right from the beginning, I saw you for who you are and what you stand for—I believe you and believe *in* you. You also made me believe in myself and what I was doing and made me understand that I'm allowed to step away from my dad's legacy. You made me want to build something that mattered.'

Calla closed her eyes, her chest still aching.

'I don't care what some trashy headline says,' Judah continued. 'I know who you are. And if the world doesn't see it, then sod them.'

Calla's voice cracked when she finally spoke. 'It's not just the world, Judah. It's me. I see it. That version of me. That woman in the article.' Her mouth twisted. 'And it makes me feel small. Like I've spent too much time dragging myself out of the mud only to fall face-first back in.'

'You didn't fall,' he said, voice like gravel and heat. 'You were pushed. And I get it—you don't want to need anyone. But needing someone isn't weakness, Calla. It's real. It's human.

'I want you,' he continued. 'Not for the project. Not because of our history. Just...you. As you are. Fear and fury and brilliance and all.'

Calla blinked fast, vision blurring. Her armour wavered, then cracked. But it didn't shatter. She wouldn't let it.

Despite the miles between them, his slow, intense smile caressed her. 'I'd love you to see yourself as I see you, as a woman who's strong and bold and courageous. But I can't do that for you—no one can. It's up to you what you do next, Calla. Are you going to believe Jack's version of you, or mine?'

His question ripped through her. She wanted to scream that it wasn't that simple, that people didn't just shed the skin of who they used to be. She'd spent years protecting herself, learning not to need anyone, not to trust. And yet here was Judah, offering something different. Something terrifying. Not a rescue, but complete understanding.

Oh, God, it was too much. 'Judah…'

He shook his head, his eyes warm, full of love. 'That's enough for now, Calla. Just know I'm waiting for you, whenever you're ready. I loved you back then, and I love you now. And I will love you more tomorrow.'

God, it would be so easy to reach for him, to beg him to fly over or to tell him she'd be on the first flight she could find. To run to him, to lose herself in him, in the hope that he could make everything she was wrestling with disappear. But that would be another cop-out. And if she went to him now, without figuring out who she was for once and for all, she'd only lose herself again.

She bit her lip as she held his gaze as he lifted his hand to sign off, her chest tight and her throat raw. When he was gone, she kept staring at the now-blank screen.

He was right.

Before she could be part of them, she needed to know who she was. To stand tall, to not bend, to be a better version of herself.

Not for Judah, but for herself.

Calla had snuck out of enough Abernathy parties over the years to know exactly how to slip into this one. The

Fourth of July bash in the Hamptons was exactly as she remembered: tasteful red, white, and blue decor, the scent of overpriced flowers in the air, and a guest list carefully chosen of the wealthy, influential and powerful. She stood on the terrace for a moment, taking it all in—the champagne flutes, the air-kissed greetings, the casually bored mix of investors, designers and editors. And society journalists whose sole job was to report on how wonderful they all were.

She descended the stone steps and crossed the manicured lawn, surprisingly unbothered by the fact that she hadn't been invited and didn't belong. Her sleeveless forest green jumpsuit wasn't designer, her sandals were flat, her glasses oversized, and her bun loose. She hadn't bothered with make-up—just mascara and gloss—but she didn't care.

She. Didn't. Care. It was wonderful. And freeing.

The Abernathy clan stood in the centre of the garden, East Coast royalty. Jack had a blonde draped on his arm; Candice, his mum, wore natural pearls and snootiness, Jack's father, Edward, was brooding and unreadable. Jack's hand rested on his date's hip, and he held a glass of whiskey in his other hand. It was just gone noon, a bit early for hard liquor, but his drinking, thank God, wasn't her problem anymore.

She approached, sunglasses in hand, tapping them lightly against her thigh. Conversation around them began to slow as people turned and recognised her.

Candice's voice broke through first, pure ice. 'Calla. I don't believe you were invited.'

'I wasn't.' Calla shrugged, grateful she no longer had her as a mother-in-law. 'I gatecrashed. But as always, Candice, it all looks stunning. Elegant and ostentatious.'

Jack broke away from his companion, already bristling.

'If you're here to insult us, you can leave. Now. You're not part of this family anymore.'

'Something I thank God for,' she replied smoothly. 'But you can't blame me for thinking otherwise.'

Jack blinked. 'What's that supposed to mean?' he demanded.

She cocked her head. 'You've been asking me to come back. To return to Atelier Abernathy.'

'You're lying,' he spat, too fast, his eyes flicking nervously. 'I'd rather shove my face into hot coals.'

Calla lifted her phone. 'Really? Because I have messages. Lots of them. I'll read you some... Come back to AA. You know this is where you belong. You can't succeed on your own.' She read the next one slowly: 'I will keep sabotaging you until you return to me.'

Gasps rippled through the crowd.

'Jack's had trouble letting go,' Calla told the crowd, keeping her tone light. Her breathing was easier, her nerves gone. 'It's become...tiresome.'

Candice flushed purple. Jack's mouth opened, but no sound came out.

'And since we're being honest...' Calla continued, 'he was a pretty awful husband. He slept with my friends, our staff and our clients. He stole from our business and habitually humiliated me. I kept quiet out of shame. But not anymore.'

A murmur passed through the crowd—agreement? Disbelief? Their opinion didn't matter.

'He's also, frankly, a mediocre designer,' she added, shrugging as if it didn't hurt her. And it didn't. Jack's actions had no power over her anymore.

'Talking of designers who are subpar, how did you manage to land a commission like Sol House?' Jack demanded.

She tilted her head. 'You're about to accuse me of sleeping with Judah Reyes to get the commission, aren't you?'

His chin lifted, confirming her suspicions.

'I presume you sicced the paparazzi on us, right?' she said, sighing loudly. 'You're boring, Jack. So predictable and oh-so petty.'

'But you're still the slut who slept with her client!'

Knowing he'd lost the power to hurt her, Calla didn't flinch at his accusation. She was over letting him have any say in how she felt and what she did. She stepped in close, jabbing a finger into his chest. 'I am so done with you. With your sabotage, your lies, your tantrums. I want nothing to do with you or this family. Don't test me, Jack.'

He laughed, bitter and brittle. 'And how exactly do you plan to stop me?'

Calla was pretty sure Judah wouldn't mind her borrowing his clout. 'Oh, Jack...' She smiled. 'You seem to have forgotten who my "*client*" is. Judah Reyes, *the* Judah Reyes. If I ask, he'll put the word out and everyone will stop taking your calls.' She looked at Edward, then at Candice. '*All* of your calls.' She lifted an eyebrow. 'And you know that's not a bluff.'

Edward blanched. Candice looked like she might faint. Yeah, they understood the repercussions of going up against Judah.

'You can't come into our house and threaten—' Jack blustered.

'Jack, be quiet,' Candice snapped.

'I'm not going to just stand here—'

'Enough!' his father barked. He looked at Calla and nodded. 'This ends today. It will stop, Calla. You have my word.'

She held his gaze for a long, intense minute. 'Good.'

She turned to the crowd, who were still hanging on every word. This would be a party they remembered for all the wrong-for-the-Abernathys, right-for-her reasons. 'My apologies for the interruption. Enjoy your celebration. I'm Calla West, of Maison West.'

She walked away, shoulders straight, sunglasses back on, the guests buzzing behind her. She wouldn't look back.

She wasn't going in that direction anymore.

The sky was that impossible shade of island gold, a sunset so intense it made everything look like it had been kissed by honey and fire. Far out to sea, purple thunderclouds touched the ocean, the wind from the storm pushing the waves to crash over the rocks below.

Calla waited outside on Judah's vast outdoor area, sunglasses shielding her eyes. She hadn't wanted to knock on the front door like a visitor and didn't think she could walk into the house like it was hers. All she could do was wait. Calla slipped her foot out of her sandal and swished her toes through the pool's warm water. After Judah called her ten days ago, she'd spent the rest of the night thinking, and by morning, she knew what she had to do. Then, after she'd confronted the Abernathys, she'd given herself time for her new reality to settle, for the fears to calm down, to gather her courage.

Two weeks apart wasn't too long, right?

Calla heard the sliding door open, and she sucked in a long breath. But she still didn't run to him, waiting until he stepped out, barefoot, a beer in one hand. She recognised the exhaustion on his face.

He stilled at the sight of her, surprise flashing across his face before he buried it beneath his habitually implacable expression. She spoke before she lost her nerve. 'I'm not here for work or anything to do with work.'

Yet again, Judah's expression stayed neutral, but something flickered in his eyes—hope, maybe. She saw it, felt the pull of it. But she couldn't go there. Not yet.

'I'm here because I've got a few things to say.' She hauled in some air and brushed her fingers across her forehead, brushing a few strands of hair away. 'Will you listen?'

'Always.'

It was one simple word, but it gave her courage to continue. Judah gestured to the couches and waited for her to join him. After she sat down, he took the chair opposite her and rested his ankle on his knee. By not saying anything, he handed the moment over to her, and it was even more scary than she thought it would be.

'From the time I was young, I was Jack's wife, his family's daughter-in-law, the creative force behind their agency. After we divorced, I was the one who walked away, and everyone told me I wouldn't make it without them, and that I needed them to succeed.' She heard his growl of disagreement and appreciated it. 'That's not the case anymore.'

He heard something in her voice and tipped his head to the side. He narrowed his eyes. 'What did you do?' he asked.

It was a source of constant amazement that he, even after so little time, knew her so well.

'Well, the Abernathys always have a massive July Fourth gathering at their place in the Hamptons. It's one of the social events of the year.' Seeing his interest, and a hint of amusement on his face, a little of her tension dissipated. 'I gatecrashed it. And I caused a bit of a scene.'

'How big a scene?' he murmured, folding his arms. Was that a smidge of approval she heard in his voice?

She briefly described her confrontation with Jack and the back and forth between him and her.

Judah sat up straighter, his eyebrows lowering, and she knew he was angry. Calla held up her hand, silently asking him to settle down. 'I stood up for myself, told them, and everyone there, how Jack cheated on me, stole from me and that he's been hassling me to return to Atelier Abernathy.'

'Over my dead body.'

It wasn't, and would never be, an option. 'I also implied that he couldn't design himself out of a cereal box. Oh, and I borrowed you.'

'You did? How?'

'I hinted that the next time they swiped at me publicly, they'd better be prepared to take a financial beating because my lover was far richer and far more influential and would kill their businesses and source of income. Or words to that effect.'

'And he would, if that's what his lover asked him to do.'

Calla shook her head and placed her hand on her stomach, feeling the warmth deep inside her. 'The only thing they are truly scared of is having their good name tarnished and their business blackballed. I threatened both.'

'Good for you,' Judah quietly stated, his intense blue eyes not leaving her face. Calla knew what he was doing, and that he was waiting for her to come to him on her own terms.

And the beauty of it, the acceptance, made her want to cry.

'For ten years,' she said, voice low but steady, 'I tried to prove I belonged in their world, that I was good enough, for him and for them. Afterwards I wanted to prove them wrong, to prove that I wasn't weak. And that I wasn't their version of me, that I didn't need them to give me value.'

Judah's jaw ticked, but he still didn't speak.

Calla took a breath. 'But what I've really been doing is punishing myself. Jack never cared about me, he only cared that I had the balls to walk away from him without his permission, that I stepped away from him and his name. After him, I built a life with determination, steel and grit. But along the way, I forgot that you can't build anything real without softness too. I forgot, or was too scared, to let someone, anyone, in.'

She twisted her hands in her lap, fighting the urge to gnaw on her lip. 'Then I let you in, Judah. And I hated myself for it. Because I thought it made me weak and foolish. And worst of all, vulnerable.' Her chin lifted. 'But what I realised was that it made me brave.'

Judah finally exhaled. A long, slow breath. But he still didn't move. 'Calla...'

She shook her head, cutting him off gently. 'You don't need to say anything. I'm not even sure what comes next. I just—' Her voice broke. 'I just wanted to be the one who ran to you for once, the person who stays. I want to fight for the thing that made me feel alive again. And that's you.'

She made herself look at him, for their eyes to connect. 'But I might be too late. I really hope I'm not.'

'I told you I'd wait for you. I meant that,' he said quietly, his voice hoarser than before. Something fractured in his expression, then softened. 'I'm so glad you're here.'

He stood up, and with a quick shove of his bare foot pushed away the coffee table, and breeched the space between them. He hauled her up and into him. It felt like he'd been waiting to breathe deeply and then exhale, and now he finally could. Or maybe that was her.

Calla pressed her face to his chest, feeling his heartbeat steady and strong against her cheek.

For the first time in days, in weeks, maybe even years, she felt like she was where she belonged. But more than that? She felt whole.

Calla didn't know how long they stood there like that, wrapped around each other while the surf crashed and tumbled far below. Long enough for the heat of him to seep into her bones. Long enough for her pulse to slow and her heart to stop skittering like it was afraid of its own beat.

'I love you, Judah.'

'I love you, Cal. So much.' Judah pulled back just far enough to look at her. With a soft, full-of-wonder expression on his gorgeous face, he cradled her face like she was made of finely spun gold in danger of cracking. Infinitely rare and precious. 'I'm not going to lie, I had some sleepless nights wondering if I'd lost you. It was the longest two weeks of my life,' he said, voice rough with emotion.

'I'm sorry I made you wait,' Calla told him. 'And I'm glad you were still here at Sol House. That being said, I was prepared to go to London or back to New York to track you down. Even to Singapore.'

'I couldn't leave here without you,' he admitted.

Calla's throat tightened. 'Thank you for waiting for me.' Her voice trembled. 'I'm sorry I took so long, but I had to fight the urge to hide, to convince myself that, although I am too messy, too emotional, too much, I had to take a chance on you. On us.' She had to pull back, to loosen her hold. And yes, she was being insecure, but she needed to make sure...

'Can you tell me again? That you love me, that we are good?'

He closed his eyes for a beat and shook his head. 'Calla,' he said quietly, 'nothing has changed. I still love you. I will always love you. You are the only thing in my life that makes complete sense.'

She blinked, her heart stuttering. 'Really?'

'I've spent the best part of a year being who people needed me to be. The good heir. The golden boy son, the face of the brand. And it all felt so damn fake. Then you came back into my life—creative and brilliant and walking around pretending your heart didn't bleed—and you reminded me who I was.'

She shook her head. 'Judah...'

'You think you're the only one with wounds, that you're the one who's messy and messed up. But I've been hiding behind my fancy desk and title, behind the carefully curated social media posts uploaded by an intern in PR. My life looked great online, but until you came along, it felt like I wore a skin of sandpaper.'

His gaze pinned her feet to the floor. 'I needed to make some life changes, and so did you, sweetheart.'

She couldn't argue with that. Her eyes burned. 'It was tough without you, but I needed to do it by myself.'

'I know.' He grimaced. 'Walking away from you two weeks ago was so damn hard, but I didn't want to be one more person pushing you past your breaking point. I knew you had to walk this path alone. I just wasn't sure whether you would come back to me.'

A tear slipped down her cheek, and he caught it with his thumb. 'Can your end of the road be me, Calla? I'm yours if you want me,' he said, his voice fierce. She searched his face. Saw everything she'd been too afraid to believe:

truth, acceptance, longing, desire—and his particular kind of love, deep and steady. Unquenchable.

'I'm scared,' she admitted.

'Me too,' he replied.

'But I don't want to run.'

He stepped closer. 'Then stay. Love me. Let me love you.'

'I do love you, and I am staying.' She rose onto her toes and kissed him. His hands found her waist, and hers curled around the back of his neck, and everything fell away. The fear, the past and the anxiety quieted.

They had no guarantees. No control.

But they had this moment. And more in the future. They were together. And this time, neither of them was letting go.

EPILOGUE

Six years later...

CALLA PUSHED HERSELF UP on the surfboard, wobbled, lost her balance and plummeted sideways, taking in a mouthful of seawater as a wave crashed over her head. Sighing, she used the sea-floor to push herself to the surface and raked her hair back from her face.

Unlike her five-year-old son, Cody, who whizzed past her, expertly riding a wave on his smaller board, she was surfing challenged. She placed her hands on her hips and shook her head, proud of him and frustrated with herself. What was wrong with her? Why couldn't she do this?

'Don't give up your day job as Manhattan's most in-demand designer to become a professional surfer, sweetheart.'

Calla swivelled to look at her bare-chested husband, standing thigh deep in the sea, designer sunglasses on his face and their three-year-old daughter on his hip. Ivy held a conch shell in her hand and was inspecting it like it held all the secrets of the universe.

'You're really bad at surfing, but incredible at everything else,' he told her, his voice filled with love, that sexy smirk on his gorgeous face. Her heart stuttered; she was as much in love with Judah, no, more in love with him, than she'd ever been. Sexy, supportive and an utterly amazing dad, he was her world.

'Could it be that I have a terrible surfing instructor?' she mock demanded, hands on her hips.

'Dad, did you see me?' Cody yelled from the shore, his face alight with excitement. 'I did what you said, and I rode the wave to the shore!'

'You're amazing, bud,' Judah told him, his smile wide. He lifted his eyebrow at Calla, laughing. 'Our son doesn't think I'm so bad.'

Okay, maybe he was a decent instructor, and she was an awful surfer. That made more sense. Calla walked over to him, placed her hand on Ivy's chubby thigh and stood on her tiptoes to kiss the mouth that still made her insides clench and the space between her thighs heat. 'I will get up one day,' she told him, determination in her voice.

He nodded, curled his free arm around her waist, and hauled her closer to him. He kissed her wet head. 'I believe in you.'

It was a simple sentence, but it encapsulated so much about their relationship. Judah absolutely, fundamentally, from his head to the toes on his big feet, believed in her. When she took on her first major project after Sol House, and despite Judah spearheading Reyes Luxe's massive rebranding project, he'd listened to, encouraged and held her as she bombarded him with her thoughts, fears and worries.

When she spent three months suffering from morning sickness at the beginning of both her pregnancies, he fed her ginger crackers and sliced-up green apples, urging her to eat to combat the nausea. When she told him she wasn't strong enough to push their children into the world, that she was too exhausted, he kissed her forehead and reminded her that she was about to meet their son and daughter, and that she was already a marvellous mom. That she was all he needed, all he wanted...

Ivy tumbled from Judah's arms into hers, and they watched Cody lying flat on his board as he paddled over to him. When he reached them, Judah's mini-me sat astride his board and grinned at them. 'This is my favourite place in the world,' he informed them, his eyes sparkling.

In unison, she and Judah lifted their eyes to look at Sol House perched on the cliff high above them. The floor of the great room was covered in dinosaurs and dolls, cars and books. Pool toys littered the surface of their sexy infinity pool, and she was pretty certain Cody'd left a wet towel on a lounger. Earlier, Ivy had smooshed a biscuit into a cushion on the outdoor couch, and there was a good chance their new great dane puppy, Bandit, who'd they'd left to sleep, had chewed a flip-flop. Or two.

Their life, juggling parenthood and businesses, clients and the Reyes Luxe corporation, was full to overflowing, but Calla wouldn't swap it for anything, anywhere. Sol House and St Croix was her favourite home, and Judah, Cody, and Ivy were her everything.

She placed a kiss on Judah's tanned shoulder. 'Thank you for giving me this life,' she told him, her voice husky with emotion.

He covered his mouth with hers, lingering, feeding her his love. 'It is, as always, a joint effort, sweetheart. Thank you for walking out of that bar with me.'

She smiled and placed her hand on his rough-with-stubble cheek. 'Best decision ever.'

'Let's keep making those,' he murmured, pulling her closer, and Calla knew neither of them would ever let go.

* * * * *

*If you enjoyed this story, check out these
other great reads from Joss Wood*

Fast-Track Dating Deception
The Tycoon's Diamond Demand
A Nine-Month Deal with Her Husband
Hired for the Billionaire's Secret Son

All available now!

MILLS & BOON®

Coming next month

OFF GRID AND OFF LIMITS
Jenni Fletcher

'Why don't you come to the race this weekend and see what you think?' Dario suggested. 'I'll go as fast as I can. Just for you.'

He chuckled and held a hand out. 'What do you say, Ms. Thorne? Do we have a deal?'

'Livi.' She seemed to take a deep breath before wrapping her fingers around his. 'And yes, we have a deal.'

'Good.' He stiffened, surprised by a sudden buzz of heat, like electricity shooting up his arm. If he wasn't mistaken, her pupils flared at the same moment, as if she felt it too, before she yanked her hand away again.

'That's settled then.' She spun on her heel, practically running away from him toward the door. 'I'll go and find Camille.'

'Good idea.' He flexed his fingers. He had no idea what had just happened, but now it seemed he had two objectives for the weekend—to win the race and to convince her.

He wasn't sure which was going to be the bigger challenge.

Continue reading

OFF GRID AND OFF LIMITS
Jenni Fletcher

Available next month
millsandboon.co.uk

COMING SOON!

We really hope you enjoyed reading this book.
If you're looking for more romance
be sure to head to the shops when
new books are available on

Thursday 26th March

To see which titles are coming soon, please visit
millsandboon.co.uk/nextmonth

MILLS & BOON

FOUR BRAND NEW BOOKS FROM
MILLS & BOON MODERN

Indulge in desire, drama, and breathtaking romance – where passion knows no bounds!

OUT NOW

LET'S TALK

Romance

For exclusive extracts, competitions and special offers, find us online:

f MillsandBoon

X @MillsandBoon

O @MillsandBoonUK

♪ @MillsandBoonUK

Get in touch on 01413 063 232